COME IN NUMBER ONE,
YOUR TIME IS UP

The last word on how we may live or die
    Rests today with such quiet
Men, working too hard in rooms that are too big,
    Reducing to figures
What is the matter, what is to be done.

W. H. Auden: *The Managers*
(Faber & Faber, London; Random House, New York)

COME IN
NUMBER ONE,
YOUR TIME IS UP

A Business Entertainment

DEREK JEWELL

MACMILLAN

© Derek Jewell 1971

All rights reserved. No part of this publication may be reproduced or transmitted, in any form or by any means, without permission.

SBN Boards: 333 11058 7

First published 1971 by
MACMILLAN LONDON LTD
London and Basingstoke
Associated companies in New York Toronto
Dublin Melbourne Johannesburg & Madras

Printed in Great Britain by
WESTERN PRINTING SERVICES LTD
Bristol

For
Liz, Len, Maud, Mick and Jack
all of whom helped
make this possible

THE CHARACTERS

THE PROSPERO GROUP

The Board

Bernard Grant: Chairman and Managing Director
Michael Grant: Joint Deputy Managing Director (development)
Harold Armfield: Joint Deputy Managing Director (finance)
Barry Prosser: Personnel Director
Lionel Westbrook: Marketing Director

– – – –

Frank Bartram: Director (& Managing Director, Supergear Clothing Co.)
Sir Giles Lymington: Director
Lord Bender: Director (& Chairman, Mondor Insurance Co.)

The Subsidiary Companies

Gerald Fielder: Sales Director, Supergear Clothing Co.
William Oldershaw: Managing Director, Brasserton's Ltd
Tom Colley: General Manager, Brasserton's Ltd

The Rest

Alison Bennett: PR Assistant, Prospero Group
Colin Hardy: Marketing Executive, Prospero Group
Miss Harris: Secretary to Bernard Grant
John Howland: Chief PRO, Prospero Group
Joseph Karian: Assistant to Bernard Grant
Earl Sanger: Assistant to Michael Grant
Arnold Sims: Chief Accountant, Prospero Group
David Travis: Marketing Executive, Prospero Group
Antony Talbot-Brown: Assistant to Harold Armfield

THE AMERICANS

Ed Corsino
Gelson
Kerridge

THE OTHER MEN
Simon Dickson MP
Philip Lovelace

THE OTHER WOMEN
Mary Armfield
Margaret Fielder
Esther Lymington
Frances Prosser
Sheila Travis
Diana Westbrook

All the characters (whether individual, corporate or otherwise) who play any part in the story of this novel are entirely fictitious. They do not depict and are not based, wholly or partly, on any real person, company, firm, etc., to whom no reference or resemblance is intended.

Contents

1 Alliances in prospect   9

2 Power no longer divine   37

3 Excite me with enmity   58

4 Gentlemen and players   83

5 One kind of politician   103

6 Everything a girl should know   123

7 Bed and board   147

8 Nothing man and working wife   174

9 The going price   193

10 Come in number seven   221

11 Virtue wasn't in the contract   248

12 No sinners, only survivors   270

13 Even rattlesnakes are moral   300

14 We have each other, haven't we?   317

1. Alliances in prospect

NINE DAYS into December. Karian ran his finger down the list of names before him, tugging nervously with his other hand at the sprigs of coarse black hair which sprouted from his nose.

Rabble, he said to himself. Upstarts. Freeloaders.

He despised the names themselves – some of the people he did not even know – and he despised them because he feared what they might do to him. If there were a mistake on the list of those who had been invited to the party he would be blamed, his pride scourged by the casual flick of the Chairman's sarcasm.

His apprehension was mingled with melancholy. He hated the black mornings and the scatter of lights through the city beyond his window, twenty floors up beside the dimly seen river. Half-darkness at eleven was almost obscene, the enemy of labour and clear thought, like the clammy blanket of warmth whispering from the slats of the heaters.

He looked irritably at his watch. Where was David Travis? The figures for the Chairman's speech should have been with him ten minutes ago. Travis was all right. Brown wavy hair, tall, rosy-complexioned, never seemed to need a shave; very English, but not aloof. Karian almost liked Travis, yet the boy – Karian thought of all thirty-year-olds as boys – was as unreliable about time, other people's time, as the rest. Karian lived his life by the hands on other people's watches.

When the figures arrived with Travis, two minutes later, Karian regarded them suspiciously.

'Are you sure they're correct?' *Correct* was a word he used a great deal; correctness was never as much in evidence as he believed it should be.

'Don't worry,' said David. 'Hardy checked them. I checked them.'

'Is Hardy in?'

'No,' said David. 'He's away for the rest of the day.

They had tossed a coin to decide who should be lumbered with the duty of attendance at the party, who should be free to go to the University Match at Twickenham. Lucky sod, Hardy. But wasn't Hardy always lucky?

'Yes,' said Karian. 'Thank you, then.' But he still appeared worried. David stood looking down at him, hunched over the desk. Bald dome rising from a scruffy monk's fringe: almost a joke mitteleuropean face as delineated in a thousand movies – large flattish nose, thick flaccid lips and black hair thrusting from nose, ears and every pore of skin, so that no matter how lately he shaved he always seemed to need the razor. God knows why Karian worries so much, David thought, but he would not do a Hardy on him. Hardy would have mocked, gently exacerbating Karian's fears. It wasn't David's style; not yet.

'I'll be in my room if there's anything else you want,' he said. 'See you at the party.'

Karian was already absorbed in the papers on the desk. He prayed, as always, that the figures were right. Production, targets, company by company; on track each one of them. Again, he consulted his watch. Too little time. There never was much time in December for Karian. The meetings, the committees, the occasions cluttered the days. Struggling with pages of names, tickets, hotel bookings and company reports, or working out the hazards of protocol and late cancellations, he thanked God for that unvarying element of ritual which he never had to bother about. This morning, half an hour before noon, he knew exactly how it would be.

Beneath the large chandelier, Bernard Grant, Chairman and Managing Director of the Prospero Group, facing confidently down the room which was his creation. Surprisingly excellent taste for a property tycoon, so an architect, insolent-drunk, had once observed to Karian, not knowing he was Grant's man. The chandelier, Waterford Georgian, improbably saved from the rape of a palace in St Petersburg in 1917; the eight chairs, English Chippendale; a bracket clock in mahogany, inlaid with ebony strings; and three paintings only, Picasso and two English primitives, artfully placed to catch the full light of the dominating windows. Apart from these things there was little ornamentation; just warm wood, richly oiled but unpolished, matt white paint, and plain chocolate carpet, fitted and soft to the feet.

Such sparseness, a luxurious austerity, was right for Grant. It was a large room, but he would fill it with his presence. For a

10

man who had thrashed his way through a hundred heavy deals in search of a fortune, or whatever it was that motivated him, Grant was enviably well preserved; an unbent six feet two, no belly, and a face smooth as a child's, with only a tracery of worry lines at the corners of the eyes – so fine a needle might have scratched them – to witness the years of scrabbling for the big prizes. The shaggy eyebrows beneath the carefully waved grey hair were the only spiky feature of Grant's smoothly pressed outline; even the nose was not more than faintly hooked, an eager nose, forever scenting advantage. Bernard Grant, God's gift to a tailor's window, built rooms as he built his personal image, with expensive lack of emphasis.

Armfield, the senior of Grant's two deputy managing directors, would have done it differently, of course, would restlessly have overcrowded the room with junk. He would be at Grant's side, motionless except for the thumb endlessly teasing the rim of his glass, and the pale eyes, slightly enlarged by gold-rimmed spectacles, flicking around the faces of the guests, judging the impact of the words, seeking out strengths and weaknesses. Goldfish-bowl eyes.

The words which Grant would speak in half an hour's time were the ritual, a liturgy familiar on these occasions. Rising output. Targets achieved or exceeded. Buildings constructed, machines made, food packaged, clothing fashioned, deals done, revenue gathered in. The statistics would change, the place names would be shuffled, but never the form or intention of the final Gloria. All this – the products and the pounds – had been achieved by people, Grant would say; and people could only operate with satisfaction, release their talents and initiative, in an environment of business freedom. Grant complained about bureaucratic constraints upon the orderly conduct of business as regularly as other elderly beings spoke ill of students, lumbago, traffic jams, taxes, pop singers, blocked drains and the asbestos taste of frozen food.

It was a good speech, even Karian, who had heard it so often, had to admit. Grant believed it; that was the impression, wondrously created and sustained, growing more real down the years. Even Karian believed it now. But should it be said so often, with such fervent monotony? And was the record of growth and profitability inside the spectacularly sprawling empire of the Prospero Group always as impeccable as its founder pretended? Karian knew that there were some directors, including Grant's son, who strained already after a new order.

11

Afterwards would come the decorous drinking, the nibbling at nuts and canapés, Grant striding from group to group, welcoming old companions and confidently winning over new ones, expecting Karian to be at his heels, a drum to bounce jokes off. 'Karian – Joseph to us all – has been with me many years. I don't trust these Slavs, but I am one myself. I know in which pocket they hide the knife.' And the great laugh would boom out. The bizarre humour went with Grant's power, was accepted and even enjoyed because of it.

He was big, this little Caesar, no doubt of that. Who but Grant, after all, could have got away with calling his tentacular conglomerate after an emigrant Shakespearean magician? He had wanted originally to name it the Jupiter Organisation – and that was Grant too, not merely casting himself as a deity, but having to be chairman of the gods as well – and had only gone off the idea when several dozen other Jupiter companies were found in the register of companies. So Prospero it was. Grant liked the association of *prospering*, him and his shareholders; he liked the idea of himself as a species of magician, silver into gold; he liked the suggestion that he was oozing with culture, English culture. *We are such stuff as dreams are made on* and the rest. He chose to ignore, or had never realised the existence of, that Epilogue which Prospero speaks in the play.

Did Karian really wish that the chandelier would fall, crushing the man who capered beneath it? That was the image, ludicrously melodramatic, often conjured, born of reading too many bad novels in his youth. Did he wish it? If he were honest with himself, no. The swift anger of humiliation would pass, and Karian would subside again into the cocoon of acceptance. He would persuade himself to forget for another week that almost twenty years ago, when Grant was still combing the Deaths columns in the newspapers looking for leads to widows who might want to sell their houses, he had assumed that the two of them would rise, in partnership, as equals. Grant had long since left Karian trailing, hanging on in the role of glorified personal assistant, never daring to address his employer other than formally even after what felt like a working lifetime together. But at least he *belonged*. So Karian argued to himself. It mattered to belong. It mattered to have employment. There had been favours given as well as humiliations inflicted. He could, though, never shed the temporary allure of violence.

Karian became aware of the secretary at the door. 'Mr Grant is ready for you.' He reached for the single sheet of paper whose

12

figures Grant would memorise in two minutes flat, moving them into their ordained places in the speech. He folded it, very precisely, squinted at the shoulders of his jacket and flicked away a speck or two of dandruff. Then he rose and walked swiftly through the outer office. He must, he remembered, ask the Chairman if his chest were better.

*

Twenty minutes later, Grant began to speak to the fifty men and six women who had been invited to the third pre-Christmas party to eat and drink and be impressed with the good news he had to give them. They were senior managers from various Prospero subsidiaries, with a smattering of outside directors and agency men. David Travis stood close to the continuous strip of glass which banded one side of the room. The view was the best thing about Prospect House, standing sharp as a needle and almost as silvery upstream from the Houses of Parliament, vying with Millbank Tower and the other mini-skyscrapers which inside a few years had re-created the London skyline. The December mist and the haze from the milkchurn quartet of chimneys at Battersea power station laid a soft curtain over the city, killing the colours of stone and grass and the vista which went clear out to Greenwich and beyond, past Parliament's sugar-icing pinnacles and St Paul's Cathedral and Tower Bridge and the spiky cranes of dockland. *Ships, towers, domes, theatres and temples . . . all bright and glittering in the smokeless air.* Poor Wordsworth, he thought. Look at it now. Sooty stone, the green lung of St James's and Hyde Parks, and that enormous garden the Archbishop had at Lambeth Palace, plus bare trees, the enfolding concrete jungle and the toy-train necklace of tracks running into Waterloo Station. Yet one could still see what the old London had been, its squares and edifices like an uncleaned watercolour on which the latter-day junk had been dumped, the whole threaded together by the river, with ugly bare fringes of muddy hard beside the brown water. Through the gloom a firefloat was thrusting against the tide, an ink-blob man skirting its dull red deck.

David tuned in to the words. 'Despite the assistance which a gracious government' – ironic laughs – 'has striven to offer us. . . .' Grant was talking about the property end of the Prospero business, and as usual was at his most eloquent. He might allow other men to play around with the multitude of more recently acquired companies in the group. But the property company, which had been the beginning of empire, he kept to himself, first and last love. Not even Armfield, whose sole gift was an ability to juggle figures, was allowed to dip his fingers very deeply into that. David tuned out again. The ink-blob had reached the stern of the fire-boat as it swept beneath Vauxhall Bridge. He wondered if men ever fell off, and if the cleaner Thames had yet removed the necessity of stomach pumps for those who did.

He realised that Grant had stopped speaking. No one was applauding. The Chairman was rubbing his chest, looking puzzled. He coughed and began to talk again, the voice husky. He pulled the sheet of paper from his right coat pocket, slant-wise-cut, as if uncertain of the next phrase or two, and a spasm of apprehension touched David's stomach. The figures; Karian couldn't have got them down wrong, could he? There would be hell to pay. Karian was looking at the carpet.

Grant paused again, and his right hand moved to grasp his jaw, like a slow-motion pantomime of a man with toothache. There was an awkward silence during which Armfield laid aside his glass and took a pace forward, frowning.

'Ladies and gentlemen, you must excuse me.' Grant stepped back, an arm groping for support. He was suddenly pale as his neat grey suit, speckles of sweat above the tufting brows. Some-one shoved a Chippendale under him, and his head drooped. There was a hesitant shuffle of people towards the chair, drawn by the instinctively morbid curiosity which makes all disasters the most compulsive of spectator sports.

'I'm sorry, forgive **me**,' Grant said softly. 'I cannot go on.'

'What is it, Chairman?' said Armfield.

'I feel rather unwell. A little faint. Too hot in here. I shall be all right in a moment.' He tried to rise, but the effort was plainly too much.

Prosser, the personnel director, was whispering to Karian. 'Joseph. Warn Sister. *Quietly*, for God's sake. The phone in the alcove.'

I know where the phone is, Karian wanted to say, and I have practised discretion in this company for almost twenty years. Aloud, he said, 'It's the heat. These radiators are murderous.'

Armfield was waving people away, thinning the thicket of bodies until only the directors were left around Grant. He leant to allow the Chairman to sip a glass of water and that was the moment when the scene became, in David's mind, a kind of symbolic tableau. Like a miniature board meeting, he thought, with the two competing teams ranged against each other – as if

14

they had deliberately chosen their positions on different sides of Grant's chair.

To the Chairman's right, Armfield and Lymington of the old guard. They looked it too. Armfield believed so ardently in short back and sides, his neck and temples had the appearance of having been freshly scraped each morning. His suit was non-descript blue, trousers bagging behind the knees, and his face was the kind which once seen would never have been remembered but for the careful gold spectacles and the pale eyes behind them. The eyes betrayed him: a fanatic, whose religion was figures, coldly harbouring his status as deputy managing director. At Armfield's elbow, Lymington appeared like the former diplomat he was: stiff white collar, indeterminate club tie, pale-striped shirt, striped pants, black coat. The skin of his face, grey as his slicked hair, was pulled so tight over the bones it could have been a mask. His hand, white-knuckled, was scarcely able to control the glass of gin.

Westbrook, marketing director and David's boss, faced them on the Chairman's left: fortyish, handsome in a Robert Taylor kind of way, but running to fat in face and belly, which his tight-cut jacket and trousers, bronze and raise-stitched, only emphasised. His long hair bushed thickly to his collar and fell across his narrow forehead as he leaned forward. A few feet away – as if he inclined towards Westbrook's camp but hadn't quite yet committed himself – stood Prosser, short and curly black-haired, peering through thick horn-rims like an over-burdened schoolmaster. His rumpled grey flannel suit suggested it would give off chalk-dust if beaten.

There were three directors missing from the line-up, David realised, including the Chairman's son, but the balance of power was accurately represented. New guard against old guard. Westbrook and the advocates of change against Armfield and the ones who wanted their world to stay much as it was. He hoped to God, for the sake of his own job at least, that Westbrook didn't lose. He believed it would also be sad for the organisation, which to him felt flabby and complacent these days, but that was a thought which came second. *Sauve qui peut.*

'Sister,' he heard Karian saying. 'Can you come upstairs, please?'

Grant was sitting very still. Armfield nodded to Westbrook, who broke away from the chair, speaking at once. 'Ladies and gentlemen. I'm sure we should just leave the Chairman quietly for a moment. . . .' He did it well, smooth and controlled, with

15

just the right amount of humanity in his voice. Karian, still holding the telephone, realised that the dialling tone was pouring into the room. He replaced the receiver and focused his mind in time to overhear one of the visitors whisper to a companion. 'Heart, old boy. Do you remember when Peter Abbott bought it?'

Michael Grant, thought Karian. Someone should tell him. Karian didn't want Armfield lording it around the place without a rival for longer than necessary. The younger Grant was needed there to redress the balance, even though Karian distrusted the alliance of the Chairman's son and Westbrook, pushing their American ideas of business, almost as much as he disliked Armfield and despised Lymington. He looked at the clock. In New York it would be just after six. The call could wait until half an hour closer to dawn in America, but no longer.

✻

'We've spent too much time on this bloody thing already and we've still got nowhere. I think we should leave it. We could all do with some lunch.'

Frank Bartram's voice, Manchester-hard, lacked its usual conviction. He knew he would not wrap the thing up now, not with Fielder in such a querulous mood; but Bartram still wanted to stop the man damaging himself more dangerously in the eyes of the others around the table. He had always accepted his sales director's weaknesses, had some sympathy with Fielder's problem. Wives could be hell, and hell was what Gerald Fielder's wife must be to live with.

Everyone, Bartram believed, would feel better if they stopped now. It had been a rough morning for the board of Supergear, which in less trendy days had been called the Belliza Clothing Company. Bartram was sure his end-year projection of profitability was sound, on paper at least. But the pressure from Prospect House was being applied steadily. As a director on the main board of the Prospero Group, as well as chief executive of Supergear, he could have ignored Michael Grant's requests for further explanations of the trading accounts, or even picked a quarrel. Bartram wanted peace, however, and was politician enough to want to know precisely how much information the Chairman's son possessed about the unpublicised affairs of Supergear. For this reason he had all morning tried to cajole his board into going along willingly with London's requests for still more detailed information. He would vet it, but the work had to be done. Papers were scattered untidily across the table. There was too much cigarette smoke; too many empty coffee cups. His head throbbed and he could feel the wetness beneath his armpits.

'The fact remains,' said Fielder, looking crossly around the table, 'that no one's given us a single valid reason for this inquisition. It's unfair to load all this work on us just before Christmas. It won't help sell a single bloody garment.'

'Christ, Gerald, not again. Of course there's a reason. It's group policy,' said Bartram.

'Michael Grant's policy, maybe. Or Westbrook's. I'll bet the rest of the board don't know about it.' Fielder spoke and looked like a sulky child, his forehead exaggeratedly wrinkled, lower lip drooping above a tumbling chin. 'Maybe we have had a rough year, but we're not the only ones. I'd like to know what Bernard Grant thinks.'

'You'll have to make do with what your own managing director thinks,' said Bartram. 'As a subsidiary company, we're in a difficult position here. We had to go to London for money only six months ago; or perhaps you'd forgotten, Gerald. If I want a fight, I'll choose an issue that's worth it. In this case I think we say yes, gracefully.'

The girl had glided in behind Bartram's chair. He smelled her before he saw her. She whispered and passed a note. Fielder stabbed a spoon moodily at the milk scum in his coffee cup while Bartram glanced at the paper and waved the secretary from the room. As the door closed, Fielder burst out again.

'London seem to think we've nothing better to do than fill in reams of bloody paper.'

'Shut up,' said Bartram. The voice was steel, suddenly angry. Then it turned reverently husky. 'I'm afraid the Chairman's been taken ill.' His eyes searched the men around him, wanting them to help him. 'Let's call it a day. I must speak to London.'

＊

Colin Hardy switched off the car radio in the DB6 and stepped out on to the wet grass of the East car park. The ritual Twickenham glass of champagne was stuffed into his hand.

'What's new, then?' said the man who owned the DB6, dressed in black-leather mid-calf topcoat, like an extra trying to play a Nazi in a war movie. He was a kind of friend, whom Hardy saw only once or twice a year, but usually at Twickenham.

'The poor old sod. Who'd have guessed it?'

'Come on. Have your pheasant. What are you on about?'

'Chairman Mao. Bernard Plato Grant, né Granowitz. He's collapsed. I heard it on the Radio One grapevine, just now. Sounds like heart to me.'

The black-leather man shrugged and spoke through a mouthful of meat. 'It happens to them all. Who'll win the war?'

'Our side, of course,' said Hardy. 'Me and a few junior officers like the Chairman's son.'

'Does it matter?'

'It matters to *me*, chum.'

'Oh well. I'll measure you for the chair *after* the match. If Cambridge win as well, we'll really have something to celebrate.'

'They won't win scoring tries, that's for sure. It'll be all goal-kicking as usual.'

'Don't be so morose, Colin. It doesn't suit you.' Black-leather's new girl – they always were new – smiled as she spoke, nuzzling her sheepskin against him. The vibrations were good, but Hardy ignored her. He was thinking about one of the hundred happy anecdotes which the newspaper feature-writers always trotted out when they did their bigger pieces on the business pages: Bernard Grant, back in the crude days of the easy property take-overs, hammering a table so hard that a silver inkstand had leapt from it and thrown its contents in the lap of an unwilling director of the company which Grant was aiming to rape. Somehow he couldn't imagine Grant collapsing.

The girl was still bothering him. Why did his chum always pick up women who wanted to make it with someone else after one week flat? Maybe black-leather, with his father's money, never tried hard enough to keep them. There were always others. Standing in line to lie down, said black-leather, whose sojourn at Stanford some years before – as well as the paternal hand-outs which enabled him to run a DB6, a motor-sailer of luxurious dimensions, and unlimited sexual extravaganzas – had done him no good at all. This one wore high boots and tight white trousers that did more for her than the obvious come-on of a mini-skirt. She shivered in the dank air, still pressing her hot eyes at Hardy. Looking at the blatant outline of her crotch he wanted to tell her to wear woolly drawers and then she wouldn't feel the draught.

'You captains of industry disturb me,' she said. 'So attached to the treadmill. Does your stricken master want you back to hold his hand?'

'He'd break every bone in it,' said Hardy brusquely.

18

'Serve you right, girl.' Black-leather beamed and poured the rest of his champagne on the ground. 'This stuff is piss. Where did you get it?'

She pouted. 'It came with the hamper. *Service complet.* Join me in a brandy then, darling.'

'Women,' said Hardy, 'should touch no spirits before they are forty, and certainly not at this ungodly hour of the afternoon. Cognac is the seducer's friend.'

'You're feeling better, Colin. Wonderful!' said black-leather. 'Let's go.' He flung his arm around the girl, deliberately ruffling her breast, enjoying his ownership. She looked broodily at Hardy, piqued at the points he had scored, allowing herself to be mauled. 'Cognac, darling? If you're interested in my maidenhead, that is.'

Hardy speared a foil-cased piece of Camembert. 'My friend here has always believed in regular refreshment, but he hates having to uncork the bottles. So you must be joking.'

'Hush, children,' said black-leather. 'Let us go see the gladiators.'

They swept up the others and picked their way between the office Rollses and Rovers, the flat caps and tweed skirts and fat legs and shooting-sticks. Hardy was never completely at ease in the thick of this middle-class fiesta. The high-pitched voices, the stuffing of food and wines laid out in car boots and on roofs, the faintly hysterical bonhomie repelled him; and the game was too often a bore. Young men too fit, too dedicated, too immature for the overblown big occasion. It inevitably degenerated into crunch and punch and dropped passes with, occasionally, a spectacularly embarrassing piece of dirty play. But he enjoyed rugby, and like many sporting fantasists believed the next time must be better than the last. His friend always had tickets, took their reunion for granted. One kept in touch.

Behind the East stand, Hardy dived at a trolley and scooped up the last six cushions. As his friend paid the attendant, a plump man, already flushed of face, grew redder, wiped his ginger moustache, and began to splutter. 'You've taken the lot. That's not fair.'

'Sorry, old boy,' said Hardy, and smiled dazzlingly. 'That's showbiz. Try over there.'

The man looked as if he might argue, but Hardy, short and springy, was already moving away. He spoke very loudly to his friend, 'I wonder if his boss knows where he really is this afternoon.'

Black-leather laughed. 'Does yours?'

'If you mean Lionel Westbrook, yes. If you mean our ailing Chairman, then no. I don't think he'd approve of rugby. He'd be baffled by any game where there's no end-product. Money, I mean. He's a round-ball man. All middle Europeans are, except the Romanians, which is quaint.'

'Seriously,' said black-leather. 'Will he live?'

'The radio gave no idea. Too early for a hospital bulletin. Just the flash about him being taken ill. I wonder what the hell John Howland was doing.'

'How who?'

'Howland. Our chief PR genius. It's not like Bernard Grant to want private grief spread around so quickly, even when it's not about profit and loss accounts.'

'Should I sell my shares?' asked black-leather.

'Not yet. Bernie isn't Superman, not any more, though he thinks he is. So if he died it could, frankly, even help Prospero. But if my mob don't win control afterwards, saints preserve us.'

'Keep me posted, then.'

'Naturally.'

'Perhaps,' guessed black-leather, 'it's a diplomatic illness.'

'No reason for it. None that I know. Look, maybe I'd better phone the office. Just to be sure.' He grabbed a ticket from the sheaf his friend held.

'Making your power play? Or just worried in case they want to know why you've gone missing?' said the girl, showing her even white teeth in a clever smile and investing the movement with all the meaning of unzipping her trousers.

'Hide those claws,' said black-leather, 'or I shall put you across my knee.' He sounded as if he would enjoy it, and so did she.

'Yes, please,' she giggled. 'Beat me.'

'The pleasures of the affluent,' sighed Hardy. 'I should have time to be so normal. See you in the stand.'

'Don't get trampled to death,' said black-leather, whose father had made his money out of betting-shops. 'The public school proletariat grows thicker on the ground every year.' He yelled after Hardy who plunged through a crocodile of schoolboys. 'Cambridge by six points for a quid?'

Hardy called back. 'You always were a sucker for punishment.'

❋

Inside the Mondor Insurance building, in a brown old-fashioned room which had never seen a rubber plant nor heard a designer say *bürolandschaft*, Lord Bender pushed aside the remains of the cold beef which he often took at his desk these days.

'It's bad luck on Bernard. He really is very fit. So much for protein diets and no smoking.'

Lord Bender picked a Romeo and Juliet from the box before him and rolled it in his fingers. Like Grant, he believed in meat and eggs and greenery; he didn't drink much either, and women to him were now units of labour or objects of companionship. Cigars were different. It was the one breach in his palisade of asceticism, though he often thought how foolish it was that the aroma of Havanas should be equated by the world with power. He had known too many phoney cigar-toters who assumed that a blanket of blue smoke was the passport to their share of the lavish funds whose investment Lord Bender ultimately controlled.

'I'm sorry about Mr Grant, sir,' said the man who stood opposite him, one of Mondor's investment managers. 'He was among your oldest friends, I know.'

'*Is* among my oldest friends.' Lord Bender's soft smile made the reproof a gentle one. 'I can't imagine he won't pull through. It's his first coronary. People get second chances.'

The serious expression on the face of his companion did not change. Investment managers tended to be a gloomy species in Lord Bender's experience, and he scarcely blamed them for that. If they weren't concerned for the company's holdings, who would be? Lord Bender rose, a small man, drably dressed, with a soft walk and a face like parchment but always capable of kindness. His hand sought the grey stubble at his ears where the baldness began, a sign with him of slightly worried thought. He would have passed for one of the clerks on the lower floors, bent heads at desk lines searching through claims and medical assessments and the stiff, crackling piles of policies; but Lord Bender had the power, if he chose to use it, to depose one chairman a week in the companies to whom he lent the support of Mondor and the various funds which he also manipulated. Important heads had rolled because Lord Bender said they must. A gentle man, but realistic.

'Don't look so damn worried,' he said, sensing the need to encourage the investment man. 'We won't lose any of our money in Prospero, whatever happens. The succession is assured. I made certain of that.'

'But, sir. Michael Grant – pardon my saying so – but he is rather *young*.'

'And good. Very good.'

'Even so.'

'It may not be Michael who will succeed,' said Lord Bender. 'I've an open mind. There are other candidates. Armfield is good too – good at handling money, at least. The new men know their stuff. It'll be all right.'

He looked through the window at the dome of St Paul's Cathedral, to him a kind of talisman that the City still existed and had substance. Then he came back to his desk and flicked the ugly plastic box. 'Get me Charing Cross Hospital, please.'

❊

Michael Grant, in a hotel in mid-Manhattan, sat on the edge of the bed in his pyjamas. The icy orange juice cleansed his mouth and burned it slightly too; like most things American, the concept of coolth could go too far. Outside, even eighteen floors up, he could hear the grumble of New York's nine o'clock traffic as the midtown morning rush hit Sixth Avenue, choking the arteries and veins of the city. He grimaced at the sickness of his unspoken thoughts. The telephone rang.

'Mr Sanger, please. Yes, Mr Earl Sanger.' He dragged the phone across the room and slipped the blind to blot out the unexpected sharpness of the early sunshine, angular as New York light always is.

'Hello, Earl? Listen, if you're still interested in that job, can you lunch?'

'Sure, but what's the hurry?'

'I'll explain later, but I'm serious. Really serious. Could you come to us fast if the price was right?'

'Depends.'

'Think about it. Check it. Whatever you have to do. This morning, Earl. Say one o'clock at The Four Seasons?'

'Fine.'

'I have to catch a plane tonight. Something urgent.'

'Night plane? Do you like travelling rough?'

'There's nothing sooner – not even for me. And I need to talk to you.'

Michael Grant picked up the atmosphere of the place where he happened to be fast, as a magnet snatches at iron filings. His shaving, which he now began, had urgency too; the blade was swept in broad swathes with a taut nervous energy. He retained his enthusiasm even when it came to the annihilation of bristles. He examined a small blemish beside his nose, but did nothing about it. He had inherited everything good from his father –

22

strong black hair, unjowly face, good teeth – but he felt as yet no compulsion of vanity to keep his features that way. Unlike Bernard Grant, he had no need.

Fourteen hours later, the VC10 knifed through fluffy cloud over Kennedy. He was worried but buoyant. The sight of New York, glimpsed below, was part of it. Even at night, it did this to him, uplifting the spirit. The lights seemed more fabulously profuse, brighter than in any other city. It looked as dangerous, ridiculous, exciting as it was. He knew the drawbacks, of course: the new dangers in the streets, the friends who believed themselves lucky if their apartments survived three months without being burgled, the aura of fear which was the patina laid gently on every cocktail party. But to the outsider, untroubled by the anguish of the *New York Times* editorial writers, knowing it was not his mess to clear up, the city could still be magic, a Niagara of brains and money like no one in the world had ever seen, the only place where yearning skyscrapers seemed to sprout the minute you turned your back. The contracts in his briefcase felt good; and Earl Sanger was coming. The news of his father had been better that evening, and the captain of the aircraft had promised to keep him in touch. He took the blanket the stewardess proffered, tipped the seat, and closed his eyes.

He awoke cold, from uneasy sleep. Why did they let the temperature of these planes fall so low at night? Across the aisle, a long-haired girl was talking loudly in Watford cockney to a middle-aged American, grizzled crew-cut, business-journeying on the loose, encouraged by the sight of her thighs. Her talk was of surfing and parties and photographers and groups and the money which magazines had paid her, and everything was fantastic or fabulous or boring or grotty. The American was saying they might share a cab from the airport. He offered her a cigarette and dropped his gold lighter. Bending to reach it, his face touched her thigh.

Michael shivered in embarrassment. He wished all English dollies dead. He was tired of mini-skirts and pop singers and faggy boutique owners and photographers who earned more in a month than a good salesman would get in a year, even more tired of Americans who *still* wanted to hear about swinging London. After all these years? Whoever had lumbered us with that phrase? Swinging on the scaffold, maybe. Why did we lay ourselves so stupidly open to the sarcasm of foreign bankers? He remembered how one of them had recited over dinner in Washington all the great English talents: a national debt of

23

thirty-odd billion or whatever the current deficit stood at, a gift for begging round the finance houses of the world, an unseemly haste to opt out of international commitments, and Twiggy. Strikes, pot, Mick Jagger and endless telecasts of football matches were fine for countries which could afford them, like the Americans. Britain had other fish to fry, and too few cooks in the kitchen.

New York was one thing. He doubted if we would ever catch up with the armies of genius in Wall Street and Park Avenue and Madison. But the other places were different. He knew he could run rings round most of those grey-suited men in Indianapolis and Philadelphia and Atlanta, hiding their hangovers behind black coffee and morning after-shave, liberally applied, treating him with casual charity, as if it was their divine right to know what business was *really* about. They had no such right, he knew, but business schools like Harvard and a thousand others gave them the illusionist's box of tricks, and they wasted no time mounting the stage. Britain had to learn that still, in numbers sufficient to command. Meantime, we might need to employ a few mercenaries, like Earl Sanger.

And then? His company, at least, would show them. All right, his *father's* company. But that would not be for ever. He had believed, even before the news from London, that his father was slipping; living too long and too expansively on the legends of early days. Bernard as rough, tough dealer in the years of the property boom was one proposition. That was the time when a man might unconcernedly hazard the last £100,000 of a disputed site price on the toss of a coin, as Bernard had once done to hasten a purchase he wanted to ensure. Grant had lost, but the pickings were rich enough for it not to matter. The sixties, though, were a new dawn, when any company could fall flat on its nose unless it controlled its costs and learned, through the American-spawned disciplines of operational research, O. and M., venture planning and the rest, to price right and sell to the appropriate markets. His father had little idea, he was convinced, of how to re-order and rule the sprawling empire which the Prospero Group had become. It was no environment for the exercise of idiosyncratic despotism or patronage, which for too long had been the British way. To Michael it was a point of faith that the command structure must change and the dead wood be ruthlessly hacked away: dead wood called Lymington, Bartram and perhaps Armfield – maybe even Bernard Grant too.

What would the doctors say about his father? He would be

ready. He had spent a long time becoming so: years at business schools, years in the ground-floor jobs of the organisation where, so it had sometimes seemed, Bernard wanted him to stay. Doing a small job in a small way, reliant on his father for real money and some scraps of power. He had fought Bernard savagely to get where he was now, close to the top. In his mind he replanned the area on the nineteenth floor where Earl Sanger would have his office. A long way from Armfield's rooms; himself, Sanger, Westbrook in a tight enclave. Maybe Prosser too. But Prosser he wasn't sure about. Prosser was as yet one-third his father's man.

Customs were customarily slow. He liked the pun. Like father like son, he supposed. Sometimes the old adages fitted. The officers moved with insolent lassitude, as if they resented having to look for cameras and cannabis so early in the morning.

The long-haired girl, fresh and very desirable even in the hard artificial light, allowed the American to hold her by the waist for a moment, but squirmed free when his hand tried to make it higher. 'How much do cabs in this town run?' the American inquired. Not good, thought Michael; small-time. The American looked tired, grey and stubbly, and it sounded ludicrously off-key when he asked her about dinner that night. 'Sorry. I've got to see some friends.' She evaded his request for a phone number too. 'You see, I'm not *really* sure where I'll be staying.'

Do you no good if you knew, Michael suspected. She probably shares a flat with three other girls. Swinging London is different, old chum. Bed, yes, but not American-style. In London, for guys like you it is just as likely to be a club hostess or a call girl. Not the New York deal of casual pick-up, college-educated, come-in-for-a-nightcap-and-then. . . . Not unless you fancy late coffee and awkward conversation and doing it in a shared bedroom over-looking the Cromwell Road. Manhattan was something quite else. Its girls might be less eager, unaffected by the frantic sexuality in theatres and the bookshops on 42nd Street, but the life-pattern was more advantageous to middle-aged operators: one girl to one flat, which was among the better implications of an apart-ment society.

'Of course I'll get in touch. I've got your number,' the girl said as the American tailed her quickly towards the exit. Don't ring us, we'll ring you. Michael liked it, and his other prejudices tempered his earlier sourness. Not a bad performance for a dolly. Don't sell yourself short, girl. Not for the price of a cab ride and a dinner. The going rate ought to be higher. Keep him guessing.

The Customs man coughed. Michael offered him a new

25

Japanese miniature tape-recorder which had taken his fancy in Bloomingdale's at Lexington and 59th. 'Nothing else to declare,' he said.

'Business trip, sir?' the man asked, lingering gently on the final word. He knew who was master here. His eyes were revenue man's eyes, seeing through cases, x-raying pockets. Michael felt as embarrassed as he always did, as helpless as any Costa Brava tourist sweating on the extra bottle of Fundador nestling among the soiled shirts.

'Yes. Just business. No cigarettes, no liquor, nothing.'

The eyes looked him over again, amused at the prolongation of the encounter. 'Quite sure, sir?'

Then, as if tired of the game, he quickly chalked the crosses. Michael went in search of the office car. It was good to be back. Despite the scores he had to settle with his father, he would be considerate. Soft and sane. But of what the end result must be he had no doubt.

*

At Victoria, David tried hard to avoid Sims. He couldn't face, not now, the lecture on What In My View Southern Region Should Do. Sims's greatest gift as a conversationalist was the occasional burst of silence. David had fought his way into the narrow, ill-lit compartment, had stood so tight-packed he hadn't been able to open his *Times*, and finally had suffered further as the train waited for ten minutes, two hundred tantalising yards short of the terminus.

Some of the travellers played the usual records, Family Unfavourites – the timetables, late trains, the weather, their gardens, the cost of living, the mysteries of their offspring – and that had been bad enough. But Sims would, of course, have worse horror stories from the Purley line. He always did. He'd even had a letter in the *Telegraph* about late trains, which made him, in his own esteem, an expert.

David was caught on the escalator.

'Morning,' said Sims. 'I hear you were there. What happened exactly?'

David was unprepared. Sims was usually more devious. He stalled. 'Where?'

'You know.' Sims thrust his pointed nose close, conspiratorially. David saw the yellow smudge of cornflake on the teeth, turned slowly away from the early morning sourness of the little man's breath. 'The party. Mr Grant. Did you hear the news on the radio this morning? Not giving away much, are they?'

David still scarcely believed what he had seen yesterday. Men like Bernard Grant simply didn't have heart attacks in the middle of speeches. It was ridiculous to see that towering figure, slim, confident, overpowering, and so wonderfully preserved, reduced in a few minutes to an ashen deflated joke-man, sitting helplessly in a carver which must have cost several hundred pounds.

They had eased most of the visitors out of the room before he vomited, dribbling obscenely down the elegant waistcoat. David and half a dozen other company men watched while the nurse wiped the Chairman's lips. She had been wonderfully cool. David wasn't sure how, in her place, he would have dealt with a multi-millionaire employer who was undiplomatic enough to throw up in public.

'It was all a bit of a shock,' he said.

'I heard he fell down.'

'No. Nothing like that. He was just a bit pale. He sat down, and after a few minutes the doctor came. That's all.'

If you want any more, ask your master, he thought. Armfield had summoned every one of them to his office within minutes. It was a real CO's parade, battle plan to the troops. 'As deputy managing director, I have a duty to speak seriously to you. It is absolutely essential that you maintain total security about what you have seen. The Chairman felt ill – that is all. It would be distressing if the unfortunate details were to be bandied about. So not a word to *anyone*. Refer every inquiry to Mr Howland.'

Howland, nervously fiddling with the thin gold chain which embraced his stomach, without which David always felt he would look naked, had seemed for once as if he relished the task of solitary PR oracle not at all. His Etonian cool disappeared into twitchiness. The directors stood like good junior officers, staring non-committally into the middle distance. Even Westbrook hadn't flashed his usual glance of challenge to Armfield's opinions. David had followed his director's lead and gone home early to avoid the questions.

Sims was still eagerly beside him as they shoved towards the platform and the silver train clattered in. 'He didn't fall down?'

'That's right. Just rested in the chair. It didn't look too serious.' Hardy had wormed the facts out of him on the telephone, last night, late. Sheila told him he was a fool to tell even Hardy. But his wife didn't know how persuasive Hardy could be. That was the only time he'd risk it, though. Sims was virtually Armfield's adjutant; a chief accountant without whose support and information and general obnoxiousness Armfield could not have survived as one of the two deputy managing directors *and* held down his long-time speciality as director in charge of finance. That was typical of Armfield; wanting no competition from another figures man on the board. Sims's eager, scurrying questioning was typical too. Even if Armfield hadn't asked his creature to conduct this particular loyalty test, the news of any leaks would get back as fast as Sims hit the twentieth floor that morning.

'What will happen now, though?' asked Sims as they just beat the closing doors. The train jerked forwards.

'Depends.'

'If he – if it was really bad?'

'The radio says he's comfortable.'

'That's what they always say. Eyewash.'

'He didn't look too bad.'

Sims persisted. 'Come on. You marketing bods are *always* told things before us wage slaves.'

David tried to keep the conversation at this new level. 'If you believe that you'll believe anything. Accounts know the lot. You see all the documents, all the secrets. I know who to go to for the real gen.' He chose the word carefully. He had also heard, too often, Sims's reminiscences of five years in the RAF during the war.

'What I mean is – well, people do *die* of heart attacks. And then the balloon would really go up.'

Not for you, David thought. Not for me. We'll wait on the sidelines while Grant Junior and Armfield, and possibly Westbrook, fight it out. There might also be a dark horse – Lord Bender of Mondor Insurance – but no one else. In the final analysis, the others on the board didn't count. If Prosser or Lymington or Bartram had any hopes of ascending to the top seat, they were wasting their dreams.

He and Hardy had spent many lunch-times working out the strengths and weaknesses of the players. Mondor had five per cent of the shares in Prospero, the holding company which controlled as diverse a conglomeration of enterprises as even the growing fashion in the nation's business provided. Five per cent wasn't large in itself, but Lord Bender was also chairman of the trustees of four industrial pension funds. Their holdings were bigger, so that one way or another Lord Bender could influence thirty-five per cent of Prospero equity, a bigger slice even than Bernard Grant's twenty-five per cent. Equally to the point, Lord Bender was the only major shareholder who from time to time

28

had a truckful of hard cash available instead of pieces of paper and promises; and expansionists like Bernard Grant loved the sight of ready money, sunshine in a wintry business environment of freeze and squeeze. All this made Lord Bender king if he wanted to be, except that as boss of Mondor he probably had more than enough on his plate.

Bender was bound to be king*maker*, though. Insurance companies let no one play around with *their* investments. Nor do pension funds. David wondered what Lord Bender thought of Grant Junior. And did Armfield hold any hidden aces? Hardy seemed to think not, but Armfield had been Bernard Grant's financial backstop from the beginning. Only one thing was for sure. Michael Grant and Armfield might be falling over each other to buy lunch for Lord Bender very soon. Flattering words over the smoked salmon.

Sims was still talking. 'Perhaps there'll be more news at the office.'

'Probably,' said David.

'If we ever get there,' said Sims. 'How late was your train this morning?'

✻

It was 10.10 a.m. when John Howland walked through the entrance of Prospect House; tall, thin-faced, slightly stooping, elegantly but semi-officially dressed, a three-piece-suit man whatever the temperature. Normally he would have looked with pleasure at the small stainless steel plate which bore the name of the building. It had been his first triumph, stabilising his relationship with Bernard Grant.

The Chairman and Managing Director, Hungarian before he became British, liked subdued plays on words, and some not so subdued. Howland always assumed this was because the understanding of verbal nuances flattered the émigré's feeling that he really had conquered the adopted language. He was assimilated.

'Not to use my own name is right. Nor Prospero. That is too obvious. But Prospect, yes, I like your idea,' Grant had told him. 'Close enough to Prospero, yet different. Here is a tall building so that we shall see above the crowd. Many tall buildings, that is our style. . . . A noble prospect. Overtones of Shakespeare? No, that was *aspect*, eh boy? *Then lend the eye a terrible aspect.* Yes? But it has the ring. Prospects for the coming year – good. More overtones. Prospectus. Better and better. Why not, boy? Why not? Let's do it.'

Grant would have made a great actor, Howland thought then,

and still thought. But he *was* an actor, in effect, using the board-room and business banquets and Whitehall corridors as his stage, giving frequent contributions to arts festivals and itinerant painters to show where he wished the world to believe his heart really lay. Grant had worked hard at his image once he had trodden on a multitude of heads to get to the top. His perfor-mance that morning six years ago had lasted a long time. Tearing a passion to tatters, all over those two words: Prospect House. Howland had never looked back.

But this morning he gave it not a glance or a thought. It had been a hard night. The bulletin had gone out through Press Association, the basic source for all newspapers, but its bland words had, predictably, only started the telephones ringing all the harder.

'Look, John,' one of his Fleet Street contacts had pleaded. 'Supposing he does snuff it. . . . All right, I know he isn't, so they say, but just let's say he did. The cuttings don't give us a chance. All finance page gobbledygook, or his charitable works. What makes him tick? What about those war years? How in God's name did a Jew survive five years in Germany and Poland? Help us.'

'I would if I could,' Howland said. 'When have I ever let you down? But I just *don't know.*'

'He was in Sachsenhausen?'

'Don't waste my time, Dennis. You know damn well it's all in the cuttings.'

'But what did he *do*? What does he feel about it now? Does he hate the Germans still?'

'He never talks about it. And frankly, I understand it. Surely you can too. You've seen the pictures of those places.'

'Does he ever mention his wife?'

'Not now. But there was one interview – oh, about six, seven years ago. It should be in your files. *Observer*, I think. He said you only fall in love once. Something like that.'

'Why didn't he come to England with her?'

'It happened all the time, then. You got your wife and kids out first and tried to follow once you'd salvaged what you could. He was unlucky.'

'That was 1939?'

'Yes,' said Howland, hoping that his inquisitor would take pity on the weariness in his voice.

'And he wouldn't have known she'd died?'

'She didn't know *he* was still alive either. I suppose that in 1943 anyone would have assumed the worst.'

30

'Yeah. I've got that here. Margit Granowitz. Died 15 August 1943, natural causes. This idiot's got a quote about her dying of a broken heart.'

'People do. Why not?'

'Would his son take over?'

'I can't speculate on that. You know I can't.'

'Give me a lead, though. Background only. How do they line up? Armfield's been around a long time. Is he as much of a financial genius as they make out?'

'The best finance director in the country.' Howland grimaced, remembering all the speeches he had helped to shape. 'You'll find *that* in a hundred cuttings too. Grant saying it – even Armfield saying that Grant had said it. He doesn't exactly hide his light under a bushel.'

The questions had gone on for another fifteen minutes. Grant's history from the days of the first property deal back in 1951. The lush years of the fifties – the office blocks, the development deals, the friendships with insurance men like Bender, the foundation stones of the empire. Then, when property had finished its big run, the explosion of the sixties: the urge to diversify, the sudden rash of takeovers with Grant's high-value shares used as currency, the resulting chain of subsidiaries. Everything from freezing peas to turning out collectors' art books at twenty guineas a throw.

Howland had played the game with growing irritation. All this was so well known that no reporter needed it confirmed. It would already be there, committed in the dull silver lines of type, the prepared obituary from which the compositors in every newspaper office would have wiped the dust in readiness. The game for the reporter was to go through it all, item by item, in the hope of a slight bonus from him, a fact or two about Grant which the cuttings didn't reveal. Howland had to appear helpful, to submit to this cross-examination to safeguard his lines to the newspapers for the future. He needed them, as they needed him. So let them all ask. He was fireproof. What he didn't know, he couldn't be indiscreet about. Who would want to talk about being forced to bury bodies in quicklime and wondering whether you were going to be in the next consignment? If the old man wished to shut out that nightmare for good, *he* understood it. It was only human.

He found himself toying with a chess piece, his fingers enjoying the smooth cool feel of the crystal. He did not play chess, but he liked old and beautiful things. This set was rock crystal and smoky topaz, silver-gilded, made in Burgundy, fifteenth century. The pieces were ridiculously rare. To Great Aunt Jane, pleased that if he had to be a boy he was at least not a rumbustious specimen, he owed this useful insurance against hard times. But he hoped he would never have to sell them, nor the harpsichord which had come with them. He didn't play that either, but it looked splendid; culture for culture's sake in the precisely ordered apartment of a bachelor who had been to one of the right schools.

Listen to what the man is saying, he told himself. You're not fireproof. Not even with the treasures of Great Aunt Jane. Not without Grant.

'Westbrook and Prosser. Why did he need them? He's always talked about his nice tight little operation: how it worked well that way.'

'That was the fifties. The group's grown so big now we had to have more expertise at the centre, more creative direction. The work load has grown out of all recognition.' These were the lines he had written three years ago, now smooth as beach pebbles from the pounding of repetition. 'Constant re-appraisal of the markets we're in and evaluation of those we might jump into. That's Westbrook's job. Prosser's here to look after the career development of all the people we employ – and to be our expert on the industrial relations front. That's what the press releases said, and we meant it.'

Howland didn't mean it, though. He had a job to do and he did it. But he smiled in his heart at the fashionable growth of business science, the newly discovered hunger for management education – all those heavy tomes going on and bloody on about the perfectly obvious – and the fortunes which some men were making from it. Howland believed in ego massage for all top management, and especially chairmen and managing directors. He did not believe in organisation structures, company consultants, job descriptions, bills with expenses claims, open-plan offices, personnel departments, multiple regression analyses, operational research or computers, which he dismissed as fallible adding-machines creating jobs for mathematicians who were unable to communicate in other than statistical grunts. What Howland did *not* believe in would have filled a book about non-management. But now, as ever, he kept on quoting the party line.

'Armfield didn't much like the new men coming in,' said the reporter. 'That's the suggestion in one of the pieces here.'

'Balls. Pure guesswork. He's always accepted the need to expand the team, to provide a succession for the future.'

'Christ, John, stop sounding like a company report. How does that all fit in with Grant's ideas anyway? There's a paragraph here and a quote: *I find the managers and then I let them get on with it.* How much does Westbrook interfere with the subsidiaries? He's shot his mouth off in public enough to be running the whole shoot. And all your companies haven't got their own marketing departments, which gives Westbrook a great excuse for poking his nose in.'

'We're building up marketing departments in all our companies. But it takes time. Meanwhile, Westbrook doesn't *interfere*. Not like that. The main board decides strategy, very generally. All the other companies get on with the tactics, playing it on their own. They've virtually total freedom.'

'Virtually?'

'Give-and-take, it works. Westbrook and company are there to suggest lines of general policy, either to marketing men in the subsidiaries, or to the managing directors. Any of the subsidiaries can take their own line even if our people in London *don't* agree.'

'But God help them if they happen to be wrong, especially about capital expenditure – is that it?'

'Every company in the group's responsible for its own performance, if that's what you mean. So we have healthy differences of opinion – yes. Tension between the operating companies and the centre. What group doesn't, if it's got any damn life?'

'Michael Grant. How does he get on with Dad?'

'Fine.'

'They live apart.'

'He's a big boy now. Thirty-four. It's not unusual.'

'But Dad doesn't always sound very friendly. There's a quote here, what, four, five years ago, after he'd crashed at Brands in a sports car race. Quote: *If he wants to risk his neck, it's his neck.* Unquote. Not very paterfamilias.'

'He always speaks his mind. Anyway, Michael doesn't race now.'

'Why doesn't that boy get married? At 34 – Christ! Is he queer or something?'

'Perhaps he likes being London's most eligible bachelor.'

'Yeah, but who are his birds? Does he keep them all chained up? He sure as God never takes them to the Ivy. Or Annabel's.'

Howland couldn't resist laughing. It eased the tension. 'You've no imagination, Dennis.'

'Very funny.'

'I'd like to help, honestly. But I can't. He's not about to die, anyway. Go and tell your news editor how bloody useless PROs are. You'll feel better.'

'Thanks for nothing. See you.'

'El Vino's. Friday lunchtime. If I survive.'

None of the other calls had been so long, or so direct, but they kept coming until past midnight. Then, in self-defence, he took the telephone off the hook, after checking with the hospital. He'd nothing to tell the papers that they'd want to change a page for. Let the presses run, and let me get some sleep.

Now, riding the lift upwards, he still felt tired, pleased with his performance last night, but uneasy, for reasons he understood only too well. The medical bulletin that morning had been as totally non-committal as such things often were. Maybe he would ring a chum at the hospital who might do an old friend a favour and find out the real score. Howland badly wanted a re-assurance that Bernard Grant would not die. He liked the pros-pect of neither boy Grant nor Harold Ironsides Armfield in the chair. Everyone makes mistakes, and mine has been to be the old man's golden boy too long.

*

Joseph Karian was worried too. Armfield had already visited him, rudely walking straight past the secretary outside, without even knocking. He found Karian with his head buried in his hands.

'*Mister* Karian.' Like some bad old imitation of Charles Laugh-ton playing Captain Bligh. 'Mister Karian, the Chairman will expect us to keep the ship moving while he's away. He wouldn't thank you for grief, not yet.'

Karian may have been moved to loathe Grant at times, but he knew he was safe there, unlikely now to be fired, and occasion-ally tossed crumbs of useful information, provided the gesture cost the Chairman's personal pocket not a penny. That was Grant: flamboyant with gifts the world would be impressed by, and which probably saved him tax anyway, but sticky with the petty cash. Armfield, however, went further than disdain in his attitude to Karian. He missed no chance to express his incredulity that Grant should continue to employ *that refugee*. Karian had heard Armfield say it once, talking loosely as he walked down a corridor. 'That man *still* has his accent. No drive at all. Is he the image this organisation should present to the world?'

34

This morning, Karian was frightened. Not only for his job. When he had, a week earlier, unwittingly overheard part of an unscrambled telephone call made by Grant to Lord Bender, discussing the idea of taking over Burgham's, he had been delighted. Karian's eavesdropping had been a rare piece of fortune, in the early operational hours of the new equipment which Michael Grant had insisted should be installed in his own and his father's offices. Telephones with scramblers put them one up on most other London companies, but Bernard was as yet unused to remembering to flick the switch. Perhaps he forgot deliberately, scornful of notions as novel as electronic espionage.

Karian needed some luck with Burgham's. His shares in that medium-sized engineering company had been bought a year ago on the strongest tip he had ever been given, since when they had slipped a penny or two a week with dire regularity. Karian had put far more than he could truly afford into them, dreaming of the house in Malta tomorrow, instead of ten years away if his pension was enough. He had summoned up all his courage and spoken to Grant, confessing his fault, but pleading its accidental nature. Grant had frowned, controlled himself, and taken a soft line in his anxiety to preserve the secrecy of his intentions.

'This is quite, but utterly confidential, Joseph. Yes, I may take over Burgham's when I am ready. But not until the shares are much lower, as they will be.'

Karian had felt very grey-faced at that moment. He needed take-over rumours to float for a few days and the shares to rise in sympathy. He told Grant everything, stumbling through panic-stricken sentences, and the Chairman had smiled his superior smile before speaking again.

'My dear Joseph, why do you do these things? Why not ask *my* advice? You must be the worst stock-picker in the world. When we last discussed your portfolio it seemed to me as unhappy a collection of dubious business taste as I had ever seen. Now you seem to have wrecked it completely. If they struck oil in your garden tomorrow, you would be the one man to invest in the only dry well.'

He had had his joke at Karian's expense; now he was, uncharacteristically, apparently ready to be magnanimous even at cost to himself. It was scarcely generosity, since this was a time when he needed to buy Karian's silence.

'Do not worry, Joseph. Since I may have some responsibility for the state of the market in Burgham's I'll see the lawyers and find out if there's any way of taking your shares back at a special price. It won't be easy – you know how tight the rules of take-overs are. The same price for everyone. But if I can, I'll do it. At least what you paid for them – and perhaps a ten per cent premium too. Shall we say that is your Christmas bonus? And *my* gift from you shall be your total, absolute silence about this affair.'

On that day Karian had gratefully accepted the favour, though he was not deceived by Grant's gesture. The words about the difficulties of take-over law were a typical Grant smokescreen, for since the Chairman was not yet actively engaged in bidding for Burgham's he could, in fact, there and then have bought Karian's shares at any price he chose. But it suited Karian's condition to say no more, as he did not dare to tell Grant quite how big a holding he had, and the next morning – confirmed in his complicity by Grant's implicating innuendo – had been used as messenger boy to carry a personal note to a scruffy office in a dreary City alley which he had visited before, the base of a hack practised in spreading tittle-tattle around the Stock Exchange for quite modest fees.

'Burgham business, Joseph,' the Chairman had smiled. 'But don't let your blood pressure suffer. I won't forget my promise.'

Now Karian dementedly prayed that Grant might be spared to do just that. His lips were forming words. Oh God, he said, oh God please let him live.

2. Power no longer divine

BERNARD GRANT did not shout when he was angry. That was one of the first essentials of Englishness he had taught himself. It went along with Cooper's Oxford marmalade for breakfast, Taylor's '27 in his cellar, Rockingham on his table, shirts from Turnbull and Asser, almost everything else from Harrods.

Occasionally he permitted himself a touch of supra-national classical modernity. He did own one rug from Casa Pupo and there was, in his town house in Kensington, a Barcelona chair according to the scriptures of Mies van der Rohe, crossed steel and leather, as well as a cushioned basket which Le Corbusier had named Grand Confort. But such aberrations were strictly controlled. Grant had been anxious to let the world forget he was once a Hungarian, domiciled pre-war in Vienna, who had stumbled into England in 1946 and spent three months searching for a son whose future was then in the hands of an institution for orphans. So he had worked at and mastered the upper-class liturgy of things English, as he had also absorbed – before rejecting them – the prejudices of the bourgeoisie during the years which now seemed like past centuries, when Michael and he had lived in a dark upstairs room in Fulham, blotchy prints of Naomi and Joseph and Ruth frowning biblically in sepia from the muddy-coloured walls, paying 25s a week, clerking by day, sweating to break into the estate agency game by night.

Shouting was for the Welsh and the Americans, and for those émigrés in England who had never truly become integrated. Karian, Grant believed, might shout, away from the office, frustratedly bouncing impotent words from the walls of the neat suburban box where he lay down with his peasant wife. And Prosser, the personnel director, a necessary adjunct in the socially conscious sixties, even for a property-based conglomerate, might shout too, for was he not Welsh and a hysteric beneath the softening veneer of redbrick education?

37

Grant, when he was still Granowitz, had shouted with the pain and loss and the impossibility of starting again in a strange land without Margit, but with a son of twelve who viewed him silently and suspiciously, scarcely remembering him. Then, as the successes had come, he had more gently spun the cocoon of nativeness which England makes easy for those incomers who accept her national gods.

'Why has the appointment been cancelled? By whom? I find it hard to believe.' His voice was pitched low and even, with a hint of childlike wonderment, as if he truly sorrowed for Karian's judgement in allowing so simple a detail to be botched by the finely tuned machinery which a personal assistant's office should be. Karian avoided his eyes.

'It was Mr Michael, sir. He believed you would wish for an uncommitted day on your return. He was trying to act for the best.'

'If I wished to do nothing, I would have not come in at all.' Grant smiled at winning the point, showing his teeth, each perfectly capped. He towered above his assistant, resplendently signalling his return to Prospect House by wearing a white carnation in the buttonhole of his superbly cut English worsted, in dark fawn, minutely checked. His right hand rubbed the raised seam of his trousers, the sole gesture of uncertainty which he ever permitted himself, as if he found reassurance in the fact that the stitching had not gone away. 'Perhaps you would be kind enough to restore the appointment if Lord Bender is still free. Tell him it is important. And ask my son to join us at, say, noon. I have not become an invalid in the last six weeks.'

He felt fine. It had been an easy convalescence, except for the injections. He grew cold even now, remembering the daily ceremony which still frightened him. He had demanded and demanded to know what they were pumping into him from the moment he had reached the private room, blinds drawn, that critical afternoon. Momentarily he had lost control. The fear had been too great, the sense of oppression destructive. His doctor had known the panic must be answered with cool, clinical near-honesty. 'Morphia, Mr Grant. It will kill the pain.' Grant had welcomed it, feeling the weight begin to lift from his chest, the dull ache in his jaw recede. 'You have a splendid physique. It just needs a little help. Heparin. One of the anti-coagulants, as they're called. When you've had some sleep, you'll feel a lot better. You understand?'

Grant understood only too well. No one mentioned the word

thrombosis until the third day. Then the specialist had said that the damage to the heart muscle was not too serious, whatever that might mean. His own doctor had remained not nearly explicit enough ever since. 'We must see how you go before we can know definitely. A little at a time. Slow down your pace. That's essential. A lighter working programme. You must delegate more, Mr Grant. That is the watchword, I'd say. Delegation.' It was his son's watchword too, and in the wake of his thrombosis it had an ominous ring.

He was ashamed of the whole thing now; that it should have happened to him, so that the whole world he cared about should know. The sordidness of his exhibition appalled him. To be ill in public, and then to suffer the indignity of realising that the fresh-faced girls with rustling uniforms and cool hands sensed his fear of the needle. He had dreamed again too, irregularly but vividly; the old nightmares which had all but disappeared in the last ten years. He was fighting and clawing to stay on his feet in a dark railway wagon, suffocating flesh and bone around him, a woman screaming over and over in the blackness, the stench of vomit and human excreta stuffing his nose. And then a man in white, skeleton-faced, would lunge at him with a hypodermic. The needle would miss, but the thrust would be repeatedly made, Granowitz opening his mouth each time, too parched for sounds to come, endlessly crying with no voice.

Tablets controlled the dreams now, contriving for him the oblivion of those hours after he had been given the morphia on the day of the thrombosis. Morphia, Morpheus, god of dreams. The language, the aptness, delighted him as always. Who then was the devil of dreams? He willed himself once more into the old ways of thought. He would need to convince Benjamin Bender first. He was fine, his old self, ready for battle. Everyone, including Michael, could dismiss any notion that he would step down. The only tactic was to shrug off his illness, to behave as if it had never happened.

He sat easily, enjoying the familiar indentations of the leather chair. It was good to be back. The objects around him were full of reassurance. He saw that a tiny corner of the leather on the partner's desk had uncurled, wrinkling the fine gold tooling at the edge. Not encouraging for as theoretically genuine a piece as ever fetched two thousand at auction; 1790 and restored, with even the secret compartment in the top right-hand drawer in working order. They could restore it some more, without cost. He licked his finger and pushed the olive-green material flat, jotted a reminder on his pad, then let his fingers idly play on the strings of the small Hepworth bronze which was the sole ornamentation on the bare expanse of mahogany and leather before him. Less is more, said his designer back in the fifties; another lesson meticulously learned, so that while others who had made it in the glorious free-for-all of the Macmillan years were loading their walls with too many ephemeral paintings, their wives with diamonds, and their green-belt acres with pools and pagodas, freezers and Ferraris, Grant had chosen carefully, wisely, sparsely. A solitary, vast Dufy, lit with a soft radiance of light whose source was not even apparent, dominated his room. It had taken him almost two years to stop Karian calling it the office.

He spent the next half-hour dictating to his senior secretary, Miss Harris. Could he even remember her first name? These letters were the normal minutiae, important but not essential: acceptance of a few invitations to dinner, carefully considered; rejection of many more; a reminder to his publishing company about a young novelist he had encouraged; confirmation for the guests who would join him next week at Covent Garden for the gala performance of *Don Giovanni*; a promise of support for the new arts festival in Kent – if it got off the ground. He was only interested in patronage that paid off in some way.

As he talked, he relaxed, finally rising from the chair to pace slowly around the room. That was normal too, as were his gestures when he paused before the long gilt-framed mirror, pulling the knot of the tie tighter, smoothing away any suggestion of curl in his waistcoat points. He looked not bad – his face slightly suntanned, the eyebrows aggressively bushing, no new lines on the skin – and he believed he felt even better.

Business as usual. Not so. *No* business, as usual; not in his letters.

He liked that, recalling what he had once said to Lord Bender: business is too important to be drowned in a sea of carbon copies. If the City of London had taught anything to the world, it was that the most significant deals were not committed to paper in their infancy. The paperwork was simply a peace treaty, signed when the battles were won, the war in real terms at an end. If he could never overcome his suspicion of the indolent arrogance of certain bankers and brokers, he approved powerfully of the traditionalist attitudes through which words were still the bonds of such men. He was now practised in manipulating the easy network by which arrangements were made, knew that the City was slower to change its ways than the financial writers in the

40

newspapers made out. The economists on the staff, computers in the backroom, stainless steel cutlery in the boardrooms were often only window-dressing, signifying nothing. Grant distrusted Michael's passion for paper records, the array of press-button gadgetry on his son's desk, the eternal use of dictating devices, a new one every month, so it seemed, each smaller than the last, and always Japanese. He was intuitively suspicious of American company science, liking more the traditionally slow pace and comparative dignity of British business, understanding too that this style gave him more chance to apply his flair for smart dealing. He even argued to himself that where Michael communed with *things*, he preferred contact with people, even the non-committal and tightly armoured Miss Harris, who proclaimed her dependability to the world by favouring white and partly transparent blouses through which a bewildering rigging of straps and subsidiary coverings showed how guardedly she locked her employer's secrets to her chaste bosom. He would ask after her mother once every week, and the answer would always be the same, revealing nothing. She would, he supposed, never marry. Could anyone be expected to unravel that rigging?

She reminded him that Lord Bender was almost due, then departed, hoarding her shorthand notebook like a First Folio. Looking down from the window he could see his son's car. He knew little and cared less about the details, but Oldershaw, the scruffy engineer who ran Brasserton's in Staffordshire, one of the Prospero subsidiaries, had told him that the silver body housed a seven-litre engine, which even he understood as powerful. Grant remembered the awe in Oldershaw's voice as he spoke of the car, the longing in his eyes. This, too, he did not understand. Such lust for steel and glass and rubber, a mere mode of movement from place to place, was childish. The sun was glinting off the large area of glass at the back of the car. It reminded him of a greenhouse. Now that Michael had given up racing, had been forced to give it up before Grant would yield him parity with Armfield on the board, he wished his son would also stop fooling around with automobiles which went too fast and split the ears with their clamour, expensive playthings for children. Such pursuits did not accord with the dignity which he felt should belong to a deputy managing director of a concern like the Prospero Group, any more than motor racing had been the kind of skill for which he wished his son might be known to the world.

The urge for a kind of dignity sat heavily upon Grant, a re-action to the lack of it which some of his early dealings in the property market had entailed. There was a newspaper cartoon in 1959, after he had bought a desirable West End site, which showed him, in caricature, looking avariciously at the Houses of Parliament, a man with a theodolite beside him. He hadn't sued – again, part of learning to be English, the ability to take a joke in the yellow Press – but he had turned the screw of restraint harder on Michael. That was the year his son was going to Harvard Business School. By limiting Michael's allowance there strictly, Grant had ensured – as he thought – that his son would scarcely have the means to do other than stick to books and seminars. No beating up the town; no chance of further stories in the newspapers; no threat to dignity. The ploy had almost succeeded.

It was good to see Benjamin Bender in familiar surroundings again, for Grant had been unable to talk about matters of business in the sickroom atmosphere of the past weeks. However, it took him a heavy half-hour to feel that his old friend was fully convinced about the rightness of his judgement on the Burgham affair.

'The shares are as low as they're likely to go without someone else getting interested. We should move now,' Grant insisted.

'It's because they have fallen that I feel diffident. Are they worth having? Burgham's need a big injection of capital for new machinery, and my information is that they've been losing customers for more than a twelvemonth. It will take us years to see any return on our money.'

'They'll be perfect for Oldershaw to take under his wing,' said Grant, who knew that many of the rumours about Burgham's instability had emanated from that office in a City passage to which he had fed the leads. 'He'll lick the company into shape at no great cost.'

'But does he *want* Burgham? Personally, I mean. You're very naughty not to have told him.'

'He'll do as I say,' said Grant. 'He must learn to stop thinking of Brasserton's as a cottage industry. He needs growth if he wants to survive, him or his factory.'

'Local loyalty is part of his strength. The best labour record in the group. That's important. Besides, the board may not like it.' Lord Bender was giving out his signal of unease, rubbing vigorously at the short hair beside his ears. He still could not understand Bernard's enthusiasm for so paltry a prize as the Burgham company. The suspicion in his mind was that Grant needed a symbol to the world that the master was back on the rostrum again; a take-over for the sake of taking over just to show that the fiddles were still in tune after overhaul. Lord Bender had seen other men fall prey to that disease, wheeling and dealing to keep their hand in. Grant smiled at him, placatingly.

'You worry too much, Benjamin. Haven't you seen the stories in the newspapers about Burgham?'

'Encouraged by you, doubtless.'

Grant laughed expansively and lied. 'Of course not. I have no need. Burgham's are rocky – and we can use them.'

'Oldershaw can, you said.'

'Certainly. Even Brasserton's cannot stand still. No business can. Expand or perish. Oldershaw can be convinced. And if you're worried about his workers and *their* desire to stay in the same cosy little nest, then a bonus or two should settle them.'

'I wish I had your sublime faith in the power of the pay packet,' said Lord Bender. 'Men do sometimes work for other motives. And, I repeat, the board may not like it. You know Michael's views. Burgham seems to me exactly the kind of old-fashioned business he doesn't believe we should expand into further.'

Grant's tone was perceptibly harder. 'Michael does not yet fully understand that you sometimes must think in the short term to make money. This is my speciality, not his.'

'Michael,' Lord Bender reminded him gently, 'is your joint deputy managing director.'

'And fortunate to be so. He must be patient until he has learned more.'

'The young are never patient,' said Lord Bender. 'Michael least of all. But he has a fine mind, and he cares for our future, perhaps more than any of us. You must have confidence.'

'In most matters, yes.' Grant was at his most charming again. 'But when we acquire new companies, you have had no cause to doubt my judgement in fifteen years, have you? *Our* judgement, I should say. We have made a good team, you and I. Why should it be different with Burgham? If you are convinced, I am happy. The board will accept it.'

'But you will tell Michael?'

'Only when the ground is totally prepared. And the board will follow. Harold Armfield and Giles Lymington we can count on. Probably Prosser. Michael and Westbrook will fall in, I don't doubt. This is where a managing director must be a leader.'

'You're looking quite remarkably well. Will you be at Guildhall tonight?' Lord Bender's change of line, Grant knew, meant that he had conceded.

'Certainly. I promised.'

'You must be careful, Bernard. Pace yourself.'

'Ha! You sound like Michael. Trying to run my life. I know myself better than anyone.'

'But you have been very ill.'

'I am not a child.' Grant gestured mildly with his hands, holding back the words. Control, control; always control. 'The regimen is simple. *You must watch your weight, Mr Grant*, they tell me. Have I not always done so?' He straightened himself before the mirror and struck his stomach lightly with his fist. 'See, no spare flesh. As it always was. *No smoking, Mr Grant.* Since when have I smoked? As for my work-load, which everyone is so fond of telling me about, you better than anyone know about that.'

Lord Bender knew. He had heard the gospel at a hundred board meetings. Bernard found the finance, chose the men, then let them get on with it; more or less let them get on with it.

'I allow responsibility, I applaud initiative,' Grant continued. 'I do not interfere with any of our companies except in matters of urgent principle.' Fair, thought Lord Bender. There had been the odd cases when he had wondered, but not many. The point stood. 'But in certain matters I must be master. Otherwise I am not a managing director.'

'You must think of the future too,' said Lord Bender, making his point carefully. 'You are sixty-six. One day you will not be a managing director.'

'I am not ready to be just a chairman yet,' Grant was more incisive, as close to anger as he ever allowed himself to come.

'Not yet,' said Lord Bender soothingly. 'I know that. But don't underestimate yourself. A chairman is what you make him. You can be an emperor if you want to be.'

Grant shrugged. 'The world no longer believes in the divine right of kings. You know how things are going. Chairmen are nursemaids, and I am not yet ready to start wiping noses or bottoms. I want to stay on the bridge and guide this ship, not hang about at the captain's table swilling cocktails with favoured passengers.'

Lord Bender lifted his hands in a gesture which both accepted and placated. 'You can mix me that drink now. And since we're also mixing our metaphors, you don't have to worry. I'm not thinking of leading a palace revolution.'

Michael Grant joined them a few minutes later, and when Lord Bender had left, he stood uneasily at the window, waiting for the inevitable words from his father.

'I know that by re-arranging my appointments you did what

44

you imagined to be in my interests, but you must let me decide that. I have lived long enough to know,' said Bernard Grant.

'I want you to go on living.'

'That's melodramatic nonsense and you know it. People have had thromboses before. It's not the end of the world.'

Both men remained in control, for they were aware of the front on which they fought, the battle of attrition which had begun after Christmas. During the holiday it had been all filial piety and sympathy, Grant recalled. A quiet time too. These were the few days of the year when Grant wished his son had given him grandchildren – from the right wife. There had been the Boston lady Michael had met at Harvard, of course. But Grant had opposed that, to the point of threatening disinheritance – an absurdly Victorian procedure, which had surprised even him when it worked. He wanted Michael to marry in England, and to marry English, or so he argued to himself, and at least this was consistent with that instinctive anti-American posture which so many Europeans with cultural pretensions, Grant among them, affect. He would not accept the fact that his displeasure had been aroused because he had had nothing to do with the arranging of the nascent alliance.

Marriage was now a subject they did not discuss much. Grant knew it was no use. Michael would marry when it pleased Michael. To push, cajole, plead, invite sympathy would only delay the process further. Early in the New Year, his son had begun to press the questions. How well did he feel? What did the specialists really think? Perhaps board responsibilities should be re-arranged? Never the direct suggestion that Grant should cease to be managing director, but always the implication. Once, Grant had become explicit.

'*How*, boy, *how*? How can board duties be re-allocated, as you put it, unless I step down. If you're thinking of my health, that's all you *can* mean.'

'You know I would never suggest that, Father. You will stay until you decide it is time to hand over. But we can strengthen your supports. That will help. Lymington is getting past it, surely you can see that. And Armfield's vision is limited.'

'You have been saying that for some years,' said Grant tolerantly. 'I know the limitations of both, but I also appreciate their strengths. Giles Lymington's contacts in Whitehall and Parliament remain valuable.'

'But old-hat. The younger men scarcely know him and those that do are inclined to laugh.'

'Men never laugh at the prospect of favours to come, whoever offers them. Age is irrelevant,' Grant said. 'Besides, he gave me what this country chooses to call respectability at a time when our organisation needed it – when *I* needed it. So I have a debt of loyalty to repay. As for Harold Armfield, well, I do not believe he even regards you as the heir presumptive.'

Grant was at his blandest when he said that, and no conversation between the two had yet returned to the point. The old man had gone to spend a quiet week in Monaco. While he was away, Londoner's Diary in the *Standard* had announced that Earl Sanger was joining the Prospero Group. The story described him as a former class-mate of Michael's at Harvard, winner of a couple of promising-businessman citations since then, and most recently known for being the common factor in three separate teams from a management consultancy firm in whose wake dire carnage had been wrought among the senior vice-presidents of the companies they investigated. The *Standard* put three and one together and came up with Earl Sanger as a hard man, going places.

Grant had decided not to fight his son over that. Michael had mentioned that he might strengthen his personal staff, and Grant had agreed. Sanger seemed suspiciously heavyweight for that role, but with the announcement made, a withdrawal would have made the group look foolish. Howland should have warned him that the story was appearing, but the chief PRO had been away. Michael had put out the announcement through the new girl who had recently come in to assist Howland.

Now, facing his son across the room, the traces of Lord Bender's cigar still hazing the shafts of pale winter sunlight, Grant pulled together all the threads of the past month or so. He must meet Earl Sanger soon, sound out the quality of the man, know whether he was Michael's creature or could be suborned. And the girl in Howland's office; Grant hoped that Michael's use of her had been accidental, that Howland knew what he was doing in taking her on.

'Father, I have a lunch date,' said Michael. 'I'm glad to see you looking so well. And do as you wish with your appointment book. I was only trying to help.'

Grant acceded to the signals of truce. 'I understand. It's good to be back.' As his son walked across the room, back to the light, he felt a pride in the strength of the man's frame, the lean face taut over high cheekbones. He saw himself when young, and even admired the stroke by which Michael had brought Earl

46

Sanger to Prospect House. It was exactly how he might have played the game himself. It would be all right. For the present, he must concentrate on Burgham. He would be happier when that was tied up. Then they would begin to know again who was master.

'Oh father, one small thing.' Michael was at the door, turning. 'If it was Burgham you were so anxious to see Benjamin about, I think I should say I might have to oppose you over that.'

*

David arrived in the pub to meet Hardy, as arranged, at one fifteen. It was a weekly date, established soon after Westbrook had brought him down from the North to join the marketing staff at group headquarters. Hardy was a Westbrook man too, a specialist in operational research, but given far wider responsibilities in the long-range planning exercises which Michael Grant had been gingering in the past year.

'O.R.' Hardy said, after Westbrook had assigned David to his charge in the early months, 'is the art of creating systems suitable only to a perfect world which must be understood by people who don't know what you're talking about and who resent even having to make the effort. It's an intellectual game, lad, suitable only for failed fellows of All Souls.'

David was not fooled for long. The languor remained an armour which even Hardy himself seemed to acknowledge was worn for the hell of it. The brilliance of his work was obvious. There were times when David found himself envying Hardy's ability to produce reports of such insight and power.

He looked across the crowded bar, but Hardy was not there. He extracted a glass of bitter from a sullen, elderly barmaid. The sweat was making her mascara run, and she seemed to blame her breathlessness on everyone who gave an order and hadn't the right money, doubling her journey to the till. The beef in the dining-room at the back might be good, but he decided he really couldn't stand the bar for many more lunchtime meetings.

It was all red leatherette, and pale wood and hunting prints, the predictable result when the art nouveau glass and curlecues he remembered from his younger days in town had been ripped out by the new brewery. Tarted-up pubs got tarted-up people, he suspected. In the evenings there were young executives from the blocks nearby, sharp suits a touch creased after the day's labour, chins shadowed with the growth they would need to remove if their plans for dinner and a fast grope with the assorted secretaries and receptionists they escorted were to mature successfully later on. The evening girls impassively killed vodka martinis. At lunchtime the drinks were bitter beer or gin and tonic, and the crowd was usually older, dominated by lower management figures who now would never make it to departmental head or board, and swarms of salesmen, competing only in their self-importance, the magnitude of their ill-fortune at golf, or, occasionally, their sexual conquests out in the field. The latter subject seemed to be thought bad form, especially by one group, regulars, who wore regimental ties and even a curled moustache or two, handlebar rather than Zapata. They were trying, Hardy and he had long since agreed, to make the pub their mess again, a quarter of a century on. Why did wars leave such counterfeit marks on men for life?

All the seats were filled. He leaned against the wall near the Ladies, sipped his beer and relaxed, letting the gusts of talk slide over him. The regimental mob were winning.

'Of course it's the bloody government. The War Office would pay up if the politicians didn't stop them. But they're so keen to give money these days to lousy long-haired students, they haven't any left for people who were daft enough to get in the way of a bit of Rommel's shrapnel. I get so much stiffness in the joint now I don't know if I'll be able to make the captain's foursomes this year. It wouldn't be fair to lumber old Henry with a cripple.' The speaker swilled down the best part of a pint, patted his ample middle. He was over-fiftyish, tweed-suited, tanned as a Rhodesian tobacco farmer.

'You won it last year, didn't you Johnnie?' said one of his companions, small and dumpy, about the same age.

'On the last green, squire,' said tweed-suit. 'The old knee was giving me hell. It was only my late lamented father's remedy that got me through, God rest his soul.'

'What's that, sir?' This time the inquirer was rather younger, eager, very neat-suited. One of nature's second lieutenants.

'Horse liniment and cognac. Rub in one, drink the other, last thing at night, with hot lemon. And don't mix 'em up!' Tweed-suit bellowed appreciation for his quip. 'Cure any muscle trouble. Kept the old man going till he was eighty-four. He used to join the same party in Scotland for the grouse every September till he was nearly eighty. Household Regiment crowd. Two of them were Bisley men. But he bagged more than any of them. Left me his guns. Lovely things. Not my style though. Sold them to a man

48

from Bradford of all places. Four foot nothing, in textiles. That's the only sort who can afford them these days.'

None of his companions looked as if disbelief was possible. David, who thought it was, knew that this was part of the game. Each man accepted the rules, knowing that his own hyperboles would pass unchallenged when the time came. In this atmosphere they opened up like hothouse orchids. At night they went back to querulous women in Purley, or small hotels in Fulham and Bayswater. They were often gardeners and made considerable sacrifices to play golf.

'Hello,' said Hardy. 'Stop propping up the Ladies and buy a girl a drink.' He had stolen up on David. Extending his hand in mock introduction, he drew forward the girl at his side. 'Do you know Alison Bennett? She's come to help Howland the Press keep us out of the papers.'

David liked what he saw. High boots, shiny black, reaching to the fur-trimmed edge of her coat. Beneath, as it swung open, a long stretch of thigh. Her face, very pretty, lips curling with humour, seemed neckless in the wispy fur that piled up to meet her red hair.

'I heard you were here,' he said. 'Glad to have you aboard, or don't you like war movies?'

'Do you always talk so intellectually at lunchtime?' she said. 'You boys from the think-tank are enough to put a good girl down.'

'Take no notice of him, love,' said Hardy. 'He compensates for missing his Purple Heart in the last lot by watching John Wayne in Okinawa once a week on the box. Actually he's very virile, despite his fantasy life.'

'I'm parched,' she said, as David jingled coins in his pocket. 'Thanks for the offer. Scotch?'

'Beer,' said Hardy. 'We can't all be expensive.'

David looked back at her as he waited to be served. She was delicious, even by the high standards of Prospect House. She stood beautifully, a touch arrogantly, with one knee bent and hand on hip, dipping her head to light a cigarette from Hardy's match. Hardy looked up, saw him watching, and smiled knowingly, nose reaching further down towards upturned chin, like Punch. David felt the same stirrings he felt most days as he passed the self-assured girls who swayed down the corridors in their apologetic wisps of skirts. He never did anything about it. It wasn't a case of never on your own doorstep, but rather of not rushing in until one really knew the lie of the land and where

49

the quicksands were. That, at least, was how he had rational-ised it to himself for the past year. He even knew that a year was a suspiciously long time if he really meant what he thought.

'Alison has this morning been getting her first lesson in explain-ing our master's speeches to the follow-up men of the evening papers,' announced Hardy as David returned with the drinks. 'Last night he spoke hotly on the subject of import controls.'

'It seemed,' she said, 'that Lionel Westbrook was saying quite the opposite of what he said a year ago. The newspapers were puzzled.'

'Our marketing director is one of the crosses John Howland has to bear – and now you must bear it too,' said Hardy. 'But business is like that, and at least Westbrook is original. Surprise is a quality not much in evidence in the corridors of power, or among those who aspire to tread them.'

Hardy cocked his head towards a group of young men in very dark suits and very floral ties. He put a finger to his lips, in-viting David and the girl to listen. They were arguing hotly about discounted cash flow and an exercise they had been set on critical path analysis during a recent training course. The air was sticky with jargon.

'Charming children, are they not?' said Hardy. 'Seven years ago they were just as serious about midnight feasts in the dorm. Five years ago they would have settled for bowler hats and a Guards tie. Now, stuffed full of theory, they see themselves as incipient generals directing the strategy of a holy business war. Modern war, of course. So their ties are gay and their sideburns long, and I guarantee the incense of their after-shave will knock you down. Can England survive?'

'I shan't if I don't eat soon,' said Alison. 'I still have some work to do with Lionel Westbrook.'

'God go with you,' said Hardy.

She excused herself halfway through coffee to make a phone call. David had enjoyed her and, feeling idiotically formal about it, told Hardy so.

'*Would* like to enjoy her, rather,' said Hardy, grinning. 'Perhaps you will.'

'Balls,' said David.

'As you wish,' said Hardy. 'I have the feeling she could be in search of the highest bidder, so even as delectable a stallion as yourself may have to wait his turn.'

'After you?' said David.

50

'Not at all, dear boy,' said Hardy. 'Don't misunderstand my intentions. Strictly business.'

'You were bloody rude about Lionel Westbrook. What's the idea?'

'Now that our Chairman and Managing Director has returned to the bridge, things are going to warm up again. We must know the dispositions of the enemy. Is Alison for us or against us? The easiest way to find out is to hint that one might oneself be a fifth columnist in the Westbrook brigade. If she is a loyalist, and tells him, he will understand, being a man of the world. If she is not, to invite a proposition from her on behalf of, say, Armfield – or even Bernie Grant himself – will show swiftly the way things are.'

'Too devious,' said David. 'You'll choke yourself on your double-bluffs one of these days. Where has she come from?'

'A year in New York advertising, then some London gloss. Television was the latest, until she got tired of selling poncy directors and poncier pop shows. She thought she needed the redder meat of business. Jungle red in tooth and claw, and particularly Clore, as Earl Attlee once told the House of Lords. I never really believed that little man could be so witty.'

'Have you heard about Armfield's recruit?' said David.

'If you mean his new Captain Marvel, yes. Name of Talbot-Brown, in case you didn't know. Brought in as a counterweight to Grant junior's Master Sanger. Very predictable and very boring. The continuing story of Prospect Place needs a new scriptwriter at the moment.'

'Is he any good?'

'Antony Talbot-Brown is smooth and very practised for a boy of such tender years. Armfield's idea of the new hard young man. But frankly not in Sanger's class as a brain. Sims, by the way, is furious. He sees it as disloyalty by Armfield, a poor reward for his faithful boot-licking all these years. He's been heard complaining that Talbot-Brown's office has got wall-to-wall carpeting *and* a leather swivel chair. Sims has had to make do with a tattered pseudo-Persian square and a fabric-covered seat for five years. Could he be a defector to the armies of righteousness?'

David laughed. 'Don't be daft. You should have heard Sims when Earl Sanger got in a designer for *his* office. I believe he sticks pins in wax figures of the whole damn lot of us.'

Alison was back. David realised for the first time what had been reminding him uneasily of his wife Sheila all through lunch. It was her blue-green eyes. He was mildly amused. He rarely

51

spent much time looking at women's eyes, and Alison's shape had done nothing to make him change his habits. As they parted, he looked a touch longer and harder than he needed into those eyes, and spent odd minutes throughout the afternoon trying to decide whether his signal had been returned.

*

Grant was insistent in his questioning. Karian found his employer's behaviour intolerable, but despite his anger heard himself answering meekly, as he always did.

'But Mr Grant, I gave my word. Besides, I have been depending on your offer to help me with the shares I own. What could I hope to gain by revealing our intentions?'

'Indiscretion, Joseph. An accidental word at the wrong moment. How else could my son have heard about my interest in taking over Burgham's? Only you knew of that.' Grant paused, as if daring Karian to interrupt. 'You can become as hysterical as a child if you believe you're in danger. Did you think I would die and leave you stranded? Did you?'

'That is quite unfair, Mr Grant. In all the years we have worked together. . . .'

'All right, all right,' snapped Grant. 'Don't give me your loyalty oath *again*. I accept what you say. And for God's sake brush the dandruff off your collar. It's revolting.'

It wasn't that Grant had not believed him, but that his Chairman should even have suspected him which affronted Karian. His behavioural patterns were not complicated, and he lacked real vindictiveness or a desire to become more deeply involved in the political game. What, Karian asked himself, would Michael Grant have thought of me if I *had* leaked the news? Surely the Chairman could see that much?

*

Earl Sanger played with the spring-loaded button at the end of his ballpoint, then tapped his teeth with it. Good teeth, white and even as a shark's, set in a pale face with chin blunt and predatory, fair hair startlingly *en brosse*. He observed with distaste through his thin horn-rims that Westbrook was lighting another cigarette. The glass ashtray on the table, heavy, green-tinted, expensive, was already piled high with half-smoked butts. It must be the eighth the man had lit in the last hour or so. Sanger screwed up his eyes and spoke across the table to Michael Grant.

'Apart from Bartram, there's this guy Gerald Fielder. Jesus!'

52

'I know what you mean,' said Michael.

'And it was your *father*'s idea that Fielder took over the selling side at Supergear?' Sanger sounded incredulous.

'Yes,' said Michael. 'He created the job for Fielder.'

'It makes no goddam sense,' said Sanger with the calculated offensiveness that passes in some circles for plain speaking. 'Your old man didn't build a fortune making mistakes like that.'

'Fielder was an embarrassment in London. He didn't fit in. Besides, he has wife trouble.'

'Why didn't you get rid of him altogether?'

'It's not an unknown manoeuvre,' said Westbrook. 'If you don't make it down here, you get shipped off to Bradford or somewhere.'

'But he's a disaster,' said Sanger. 'Him and Bartram both.'

'The profit on turnover wasn't bad last year.'

'Before tax, it should have doubled at least,' said Sanger dismissively. 'And the turnover's been sliding down and down for three years – ever since Fielder went there. Bartram's record before that was bad enough. Why keep people like these in the organisation at all?'

'Sending people to work their passage with a smaller company in the group has been the making of several of our managers,' said Westbrook stiffly. 'They feel the challenge. Good men don't grow on trees.'

Westbrook did not dispute the judgement on Gerald Fielder. The man *was* increasingly less useful. But he didn't like the way Sanger barged in, as if to any Harvard School of Business graduate it was child's play to put his finger on the reason why a company started to slide. Inside a few weeks Westbrook had learned how quick to despise Sanger could be. The American was a man who sat at high speed whenever a balance sheet was placed before him, flicking out critiques like razors. Sanger suddenly got up, hitching his trousers in nervous displeasure, a gesture already familiar to his companions.

Michael Grant played peacemaker. 'I think you take Lionel's point, Earl. But we're all agreed, I suppose, that we'll need to re-shuffle?'

'Does that mean Fielder goes?' asked Sanger sarcastically.

'Probably,' said Michael.

'We'll need to tread carefully,' said Westbrook. 'Your father, Michael – forgive my asking, but it's unavoidable – can you predict his attitude?'

'Difficult, I suspect.'

'What the hell for?' asked Sanger.

'The bad old days,' said Michael, 'when we were still in nappies, as he likes to tell us. Fielder did a job for him, one of the first big property deals. He needed a single piece of the jigsaw completed on a city site. One old man was holding out. Fielder did the persuasion.'

Sanger stopped pacing. 'I don't believe it. Chicago-style, you mean?'

Michael's laughter came expansively and naturally, and Westbrook felt the tension momentarily leave him. Laughter was good. It hadn't been much in evidence that afternoon.

'Sorry to disappoint you, Earl,' said Michael. 'It's not really the English way. No, Fielder was subtler. Rather conveniently for us, he fell for the daughter. Bedded her, hooked her, and ended up damn well marrying her. She pushed her old man into it.'

'And promptly turned into a lush,' said Westbrook. 'That's Fielder's problem.'

Michael objected to the over-simplification with a grunt, but said nothing immediately.

'So?' said Sanger.

'So my father has always had a soft spot for him. Brought him to London, and when he didn't make it, fixed the Supergear job for him.'

'So he has a meal ticket for life?' Sanger really did sound incredulous. 'Just like a Tammany ward captain? There must be some way to shift him.'

'There will be – if the figures are persuasive enough,' said Michael. 'Lionel, you'd better send someone up to have a look at the operation on the spot. Get the facts – and the evidence. Maybe the board there needs a new director.'

'Yes,' said Westbrook.

'And make it fast,' said Sanger. 'What the hell have that guy's salesmen been doing? Sitting on their cans?'

'We'll do it as fast as we can,' said Westbrook. 'Fast enough.'

'If the intelligence report on his competitors is right, fast enough may be too slow,' said Sanger. 'We need to grab the pickings while there are pickings to be had. To me it smells.'

Westbrook wished Sanger wouldn't be quite so enthusiastic. He understood all about that side of the game himself, for he had spent fifteen years getting to know it the hard way: selling and marketing everything from roller skates to hair tonic, with seven different companies, using brainpower and push, picking up the tricks, building the whizzkid halo even before the word was the over-used currency of business-page features. He had never sold refrigerators to Eskimos, but he had learned how to assess salesmen by glancing at the speedos on their cars and checking the readings against the dates when they'd taken delivery. That told you how avidly a man covered his territory. Small things like that. Westbrook knew the lot, or thought he did – but why, he resentfully asked himself, did Sanger make such a bloody big production out of everything, turning business into a sort of lousy amateur dramatics?

He tugged at his collar. The migraine was today only on one side of his head, mildly throbbing, not causing the nausea which he felt when the pain was violent and shifting as it could be on the occasional bad days. He was too hot for comfort, and would have removed his jacket except that by now he would appear to be aping the shirt-sleeved American, whose neat grey coat hung on a chair nearby. Westbrook felt constricted in his high-buttoned suit and regretted allowing his tailor to talk him into a new, tight, tube line – or, alternatively, that he hadn't had the will-power to eat less at the twenty-five high-calorie lunches he had attended in the last six weeks. The toughest part at the top is the eating, Hardy, was it, who'd said that? He shifted uneasily in his chair and imagined he could still taste the moussaka he had enjoyed at the White Tower two hours before. He rose and walked across the room to pour himself some water from the carafe on the low plate-glass table which gleamed beside the black leather settee running along one wall. He noticed that there was a slight film of dust in the neck of the carafe, but knew how foolish he would feel if he stopped now. Grimacing, he poured the water.

'We're all set on today's deliberate mistake, Lionel?' Michael asked him. 'I want every business editor in London to hear this particular leak.'

Westbrook sipped his water. He always felt good when he had anticipated a question, was well briefed. Even more so because this time he could advise Michael to amend tactics, and could demonstrate his command in front of Sanger, who would be a brilliant ally, but needed watching. Delusions of grandeur happened so easily.

'It's all arranged,' he said, 'through friends other than Howland's, of course. But not *blanket* coverage. That way it will look too much like pre-meditated misinformation. It'll be in the right places, never fear. It may even make a few page ones. And that will really send the price sky-high.'

*

Three days later, Benjamin Bender, Baron Bender of Kingsway, telephoned Bernard Grant on his private line, equipped with a scrambler device, like his friend's.

'Bernard, I'm sorry I can't make our date. Life is hell today. You know why I've called, of course.'

'I can guess.'

'We cannot do it, not now. The shares were marked up another five this morning.'

'Do you take me for a fool, Benjamin?' said Grant. 'I know we cannot do it. Where did the newspapers get wind of it? That's the only thing that concerns me now.'

Across the desk lay the early afternoon edition of the *Standard*, folded open at Page Four. PROSPERO STILL SILENT ON BURGHAM BID said the headline, a strong single column.

'Have you seen the *Standard*?' said Grant. 'They're suggesting we should have to offer the equivalent of forty shillings a share. Ridiculous. We could have had them three days ago for one third the price. I'll tell Howland to put them out of their misery. Who leaked, Benjamin? Who?'

'To tell you the truth, I'm a bit relieved,' said Lord Bender. 'I was never quite sure.'

'I'm glad someone's pleased,' said Grant.

Lord Bender chuckled. 'Don't tell me there's no silver lining.'

'What do you mean?'

'If you haven't been buying shares yourself – very discreetly of course – then you're losing your touch.'

Grant ignored the words. 'By God,' he said, 'someone's going to lose a packet when we pull out of the game.' He sounded almost pleased, despite his disappointment.

＊

In the early evening, sitting in his study, a room dark and broodingly quiet, Lord Bender made another call. It was answered in a spacious modern flat, high over Chelsea, looking towards the river and the stream of lights pricking along the Embankment as the late commuter crush headed through a light sleeting for Putney and points south-west.

'Good evening, Michael,' said Lord Bender. 'All right, boy, I'll admit it was a neat stroke. Technically well executed.'

'I don't understand.'

'Come now, I'm talking about the way you've dealt with Burgham. Spreading the word that your father was going to make a bid.' He spoke through the beginning of Michael's next sentence. 'Don't bother to confirm or deny, dear boy. I just want you to know that I'm not as impressed as all that. Number one, you run the risk of being too transparent. Your father must have guessed. Number two, I agree it's a poor company, but it wasn't an issue big enough for you to go out of your way to arouse your father's hostility further. You must learn to sort out your priorities. Number three, to play a spoiling game is not difficult. I'll need more positive proof than this of what you can do before you stand a chance of changing my mind about Bernard continuing in office.'

'No comment,' said Michael.

'Understandably,' said Lord Bender calmly. 'I just thought I'd let you know. Sell now if you've bought any, by the way. When we say No at lunchtime tomorrow, the market will collapse again. Goodnight, Michael.'

3. Excite me with enmity

DAVID rolled over and stretched out an arm. Each day the softness became tauter, or so it seemed. The gentle tumescence attracted his hands, was pleasing to the touch. Was that usual? He also wondered about the sense of satisfaction in his mind at these moments, and what caused it. Boring old proof of virility? Paternal feelings unsuspected? That was a laugh. Or was it just a symbol to the world that one had a squaw, so look at me, big man?

In the end he did not mind much. The best joke really was the inexplicable simplicity of the reassurance he felt and supposed that other men with pregnant wives did too. Corsairs of industry, as they liked to imagine themselves, reduced at the end of the day to finding this hiding-place. Sheltered, untouchable, within sheets and darkness, the same necessities for all kinds of men. What did Sims do in bed, or frightened little Karian, or dead-fish Armfield? Single beds for Armfield, he would take odds on that. He tried to picture Armfield's wife, who never turned up at office occasions. It had been quite a day.

'What do you think, David?'

He had lost the drift of her talk. 'The blue dress? Yes, I like that.'

'I've just been explaining. It's too tight. I'm getting to be a big girl now.'

'Then let's tell the world and stop worrying. Hardy knows. Why shouldn't Westbrook?'

'You're not much help. I don't want to start living in tents quite yet, thanks. It's something in-between I need.'

'So buy it.'

'The bank statement, darling, looks bloody.'

'Sod the statement, I don't get made a director every day. Treat yourself. I want you to look good.'

'What's her name, the Westbrook woman. . . .'

58

'Diana.'

'She'll be trying hard as usual?'

'Don't know. Maybe at home she relaxes.'

'She's lucky.'

'How?'

'She's so slim it hurts. She must be all of forty. Years, not pounds.'

'It's running round after all those pouffs she gets her fifteen per cent from. Keeps her young.'

Old-young, rather, he thought. She had been at one of the Christmas presentation parties. Dressed tightly in black jump-suit; almost a boy's figure, with a diamond bracelet the sole ornamentation upon her. Diamonds according to Hardy, that was. With the crocodile handbag that meant a likely couple of thousand on her back. It was the third time he had seen her, and she had always worn trousers. Did she have bad legs, then, with perhaps a hint of varicose tracery betraying her age? Her face, even in December, was nut-brown beneath the cropped helmet of black hair, like someone who communed for hours with a sun lamp. It was a face unlined, yet tough: a city face, with the dark eyes nervously moving, restlessly appraising the price of everything and everyone in the room.

They had danced at the party, not the childlike all-purpose Shake or Idiot Dancing or whatever it was currently called, but 1940s close, and her body was as taut as her face, except for the soft swelling around the hips which David's right hand finally found. During a slow George Shearing piece on the speakers, she eased her lemon breasts against him; then, just as he began to fancy her, she seemed to think better of it. Directors' wives will please refrain, he sang inwardly to the old locker-room tune.

But she had not been unfriendly, asking him with a hint of subdued amusement about his job, where he'd worked before, even about his accent. She seemed intrigued when he identified its faint overtones as Cornish, but then people usually did. 'Let me guess. Your father was a schoolmaster in Falmouth – or a tin miner, maybe hotelier. No, a fisherman – he owned a boat?'

He laughed with her. 'The nearest I've been to owning a boat was helping out at the local kids' lake during the summer holidays. I *felt* like an owner, anyway. Owner of a fleet of paddle-boats. Big deal. Fifteen bob for the weekend – my first wages, aged twelve.'

She smiled back. 'A younger capitalist than Lionel, yet. I hated people like you. The ones who bawled down the megaphone to end the fun. *Come in number seven, your time is up.* I used to turn scarlet when they called my number. Still, it's a living.'

David liked the ease of her talk, her unselfconsciousness. Above all he remembered her scent. It was like nothing within his sparse vocabulary of such things, the detritus of Christmas and wedding anniversary hustles. Not Arpège or Miss Dior or Je Reviens, even he would swear. Again, Hardy had helped. Neither civet, nor ambergris, he had ventured. Nothing animal. Probably Vivara, by Emilio Pucci. He reckoned even Diana Westbrook didn't yet rate the jasmine elusiveness of Joy, 'By Patou, lad. The most expensive scent in the world.' Hardy sometimes sounded too good to be true. How the hell did *he* know?

'Thanks, love,' said Sheila. 'I'll get something then, if that's what you'd like. We can use that extra five hundred.'

'And the profits bonus,' he said. 'If there are any profits.'

'What's happened then?' she said. 'Isn't that company any good since you were up there? Is that why they've made you a director?'

'Not exactly.' He patted her. 'I'm only a trainee tycoon, remember. Supergear makes money – but not enough, according to Lionel Westbrook. It's changed a lot in three years. They've jumped right out of the old dears' market. No more tents for matrons in solid Harris tweed. Now it's trendy gear for trendy mums – topcoats with bits of fur and buckles. The only snag is they always seem to be one trend too late. Do you remember Gerald Fielder?'

'Will I ever forget him,' Sheila huffed. 'His wife spilled coffee all over that white Dior copy I bought soon after we'd moved into the first flat.'

'Really?'

'Don't you remember?'

He didn't, but he murmured vague recollection and accepted Sheila's word for it. Women, as Hardy was always saying, remember everything they have worn on every important occasion of their lives, and frequently the unimportant ones. Right down to the last shoe buckle.

'What about Gerald Fielder, then?'

'He's the problem, so they think. Not much use. Hence me. I'm supposed to keep an eye on things, or maybe stir them.'

'Will you have to go up north very often?'

'Couple of times a month, maybe. It's difficult to tell yet.'

'You'll like that. Seeing your darling Liver Building again.' There was an edge to her voice, the heritage of the subdued bickering of a couple of years back, when she had urged him to push for a move south. She was the daughter of her father in that at least. With him, she shared an incurable distaste for the North. Not that it had done her father any good at all. Three times he had turned down the certainty of chairs north of the Trent, preferring to take his chance of academic grandeur in the Oxford he knew. He lost the game, outwitted in college and university elections both, which left her half-pitying and half-despising him, hating the polite quicksands of university politics and the effete sterility of the closed college world which made her childhood so stifled and unnatural.

But on the subject of the North she went along with her father. Merseyside had not been for her. She was repelled by the defeated whine of its accent. She loathed the wind that scythed through the streets every month of the year. She disliked the men, treating their women with bullying patronage, like something out of the *Barretts of Wimpole Street*. The last English bastion of industrial feudalism, she had snapped at David once.

He was still too excited about what the day had brought to feed her incipient irritation. 'It's just a visiting job,' he said, 'It could be Timbuctu for all I care. We're based in London for keeps – I hope.'

He eased a thigh tight against her, and his hand moved from her stomach to her left breast. He began gently to caress the nipple, tracing the rough aureole around it first, then with thumb and two fingers stimulating it. As always it swelled and stiffened.

Sheila knew what was coming, tried to rationalise her rejection. 'Please, love. Not now. I'm sorry. I'm worn out. We both need some sleep.'

David thought it was the last thing he needed right now. He squeezed the nipple deliberately hard.

'All right, bloody Tarzan,' she said. 'I did say I was sorry.'

'What's up? I thought you liked it.'

Sheila dug him gently with an elbow. 'Go to sleep, lover. Your company needs you.'

'Stuff the company,' he said.

He lay for a time recalling with satisfaction the scene with Westbrook, imprinting the words and gestures on his mind. He supposed he might want to savour it again one day. So he stored away the details. Westbrook had talked about the decline of Supergear, running through the names of the managers, many of them new since the few months David had spent with the company when it was called Belliza Clothing, as part of his traineeship in the Prospero Group. The reports which West-brook threw across the table had all the mustiness of bad news even before he'd started reading them.

'Will anything happen to Fielder?' asked Sheila.

'God knows,' he said. 'It doesn't look too good, though. He may have to be paid off.'

Sheila was silent for a moment. 'Wasn't he pretty nice to you when you started?'

'Don't be simple-minded, girl. If he's buggering things up, what do you expect us to do?'

'All right. I know.'

'I don't like it particularly either.'

'I understand.'

'One man can ruin the jobs of several hundred others. It's them you have to think of. You can't be sentimental about it.'

'Lionel Westbrook would be proud of you.'

'No, seriously.'

'Yes,' she said. She had been a copywriter in an advertising agency before she married David, and for a year afterwards, until they moved north. She had heard the argument over and over, when copywriters or account executives were eased out. Its logic was flawless, this she knew. That was business, the only way. You can't make an omelette without breaking eggs, her copy chief used to say. He also had a notice pinned over his desk, an old American jingle much favoured by the first Lord Leverhulme.

> *If you whisper down a well*
> *About the goods you have to sell*
> *You will not make as many dollars*
> *As the man who climbs a tree and hollers.*

'You see that, don't you?' said David.

'Of course,' she said. 'Don't take it to heart.'

Hardy had come into David's room late that afternoon, using much the same words, congratulating David on the directorship. 'For most men, a seat on the Supergear board would be a case of getting sent to Siberia,' he said. 'But you, lad, you're the visiting commissar, come to call the deviationists and revisionists to book! Poor Fielder. You know him, don't you?'

'A bit. Yes.'

'People call it being ruthless. It isn't that at all. If you don't cut out the dead wood, the whole tree dies.'

'Isn't that prejudging the issue?' said David.

'Fair point,' said Hardy. 'They'll just ask you for a recom-

62

mendation.' He smiled crookedly. 'You'll be free to make up your own mind.'

As he left, he had turned and said. 'Not to worry. You'll find the second job's easier after you've done the first. And the third's a piece of cake.'

*

The chauffeur drove Armfield sedately westwards after his lunch in the City. The Bentley T purred and murmured, smooth gears meshing, as if disdainful of red lights and the glutinous traffic in the narrow canyons around the Bank of England. Armfield sat clenched in thought, hand trailing loosely on the pulldown leather roof-grip. A girl detached herself from a herd of women padding along Threadneedle Street and darted across the road. The chauffeur braked sharply, and Armfield rode the reaction at some strain to his right wrist.

'Silly young bitch,' he said.

'Yes sir?' said the chauffeur, turning his head slightly.

Armfield gave no answer. He did not encourage conversation with chauffeurs. That was the trouble with the City nowadays. Those monstrous regiments of women who had flooded in since the war, scurrying like ants round files and typewriters and adding-machines, leaving their tissues and red-stained cigarette butts and smell in every corner of every office. In the days when he had slogged his way through accountancy exams, before they had whisked him away to join Auchinleck's army on the umpteenth retreat down the coast road from Benghazi, the City had really been a place to which a young grammar school swot might aspire to belong. A man's world, quiet and decorous. The City is a village, his father, who was a clerk within it, had told him. Now it was increasingly like any suburban jungle; same chromium eating-houses, same tarty girls, same standardised slabs of buildings overpowering the pieces of history.

The car passed St Paul's Cathedral, drove faster into Holborn. He looked sourly at the *Mirror* building and its poster-paint modernity. A small crowd was gathered round its show window, and he glimpsed the vast blow-up photographs they were looking at and the word HUNGER eight feet high in black lettering. He turned with expected relief to let his eyes slide over the warm red façade of the Prudential headquarters opposite. That *was* a building, with the feel of history in its towering pinnacles and rows of pointed windows. A Gothic castle raised to the glory of life insurance. More like a college, like Keble in Oxford where he had once attended a summer school. Dignified, built to last.

Something to shout about, those millions of Prudential policies; guarantees against mischance – solid, dependable, firmly based, like the Victorian roots from which this remarkable institution had grown. He did not like it when people called it the Pru.

Armfield could even stomach the busy girls inside the castle. He had noticed, on two visits there, that the shining pillars and stained-glass windows and funereal lettering seemed to tame everyone who entered into a kind of reverence. He wished Bernard Grant had built Prospect House like this, though he had never mentioned it, not even when Westbrook once quietly baited him after luncheon in the directors' suite.

'Why, Harold?' Westbrook said. 'Why do you like the Betjemanesque in business architecture so much? They're fantasies. Monuments of romance and fantasy. Do you know the *Tribune* tower in Chicago? Like a Gothic temple at the bottom, then two hundred or something floors of pure slabcake skyscraper, then a bloody great explosion of Gothic again miles up in the air at the top. A sort of Castle of Otranto stuck on as an afterthought. *And* a set of bells playing the latest pop, with hymns at Christmas. That's what business is if you're not careful, Harold. Men trying to stamp their image on the landscape for ever – all in fantasy form. Building mausoleums to their dominion the way we did when we had an empire. Have you been to India? There are lizards sleeping up there in the roof of the Taj Mahal, for crying out loud.'

'What's that got to do with anything?' Armfield had snapped, offended by the slick Americanese as much as anything.

'Nothing, Harold, nothing,' said Westbrook. 'I just remembered it. Funny. But the Taj, that's the point. Your Pru building's like the Taj in a way. It's just the gods and emperors that are different.'

'Nonsense.' It had been the best Armfield could do.

'Not at all,' said Westbrook. 'Offices can be like cathedrals. In Japan they sing each day before they start work. Hymns to the glory of the company. An act of worship. How do you fancy that?'

The infinitely clever Mr Westbrook. He had drunk too much that lunchtime, Armfield was sure. He would not have said all that had Bernard Grant been there. Too near the bone. Westbrook was a man given to excess, Armfield believed. In speech, in gesture, in food and drink; in women too, so he had heard. One day Westbrook would get his cumuppance; but not today, not if Westbrook's gang proved their point about Supergear. They were scoring too freely of late, the whole damned lot of them: Westbrook and Michael Grant and Sanger. *Earl* Sanger. What kind of name was that? Damned Americans. Getting their greedy paws on to everything, not understanding the way business was conducted in London. And why hadn't Sims picked up the weaknesses in Supergear's performance before young Grant got on to them? Armfield told himself that he couldn't be expected to have his finger on *every* detail of the dozens of operating companies. Knowing that Supergear was a special case, what with Bartram and Fielder there by royal command, he hadn't bothered too much with the company anyway. Sims was to blame. Sims could be getting past it. Talbot-Brown had better begin earning his bread, and quickly. Armfield said not one word to the chauffeur as he hurried into Prospect House.

✢

Talbot-Brown arrived to the minute, as ordered, half an hour later.

'Well?' said Armfield.

The young man before him adjusted the knees of his trousers with careful slowness as he sat down, uninvited. Armfield wanted to say something about the bold gesture and the bold stripe in the over-bright suiting. It could almost be called mauve. He was as yet not at all sure about Talbot-Brown, who cultivated a latter-day public-school voice, pink public-school cheeks and a lank Etonian hair style, but had in hard actuality only just made it into an Essex grammar school in the red-brick desert country of outer North-East London. For the present, however, Armfield simply said, 'I'm waiting.'

'Sorry, sir,' Talbot-Brown could even make that, in Armfield's ears, sound like an insult. 'But it's worth savouring.'

'Yes?'

'It's confirmed. My source is certain. It could be worth around five million, spread over three years.'

'Client?' asked Armfield, who rarely used the word 'customer'.

'Government agents. Part of the power-station programme. The contract would be exactly right for Brasserton's.'

'Will Oldershaw know it's in the wind?'

'No one at the plant can possibly know. You will be able to appear as the founder of the feast.'

Talbot-Brown's tone had, in Armfield's view, the edge of insolence.

'Don't be dramatic with me, boy. It will be put out to tender. Bound to be.'

'That can be looked after, I think.' Talbot-Brown began counting his fingers. 'Number one, speed of delivery. Brasserton's has the spare capacity. Two, proven performance by Oldershaw and his team. Three, we should have enough experience by now to judge what might be the right price to quote.' Talbot-Brown smiled knowingly.

'Not you. Not this time,' said Armfield.

'I'm sorry, sir. I don't follow.'

'Not your field,' said Armfield. 'I shall work out the tactics. And Sir Giles Lymington will do what else has to be done.'

'But Mr Armfield, my contacts are good.'

'Sir Giles will look after it. You must not try to run before you can walk.' The sententious clichés flowed like heavy water from his lips. 'You are my intelligence in this affair and I am grateful to have your information. But you must not expect to decide the master plan or to fight the battle. Lymington is invaluable in such engagements.'

Oh Christ, thought Talbot-Brown; another correspondence-course field marshal. He hoped Lymington wouldn't cock it up. Talbot-Brown believed no more in clapped-out diplomats than, so he had heard, did Michael Grant.

'Very well, sir.' he said. 'I see your point.'

'Thank you,' said Armfield. A contract worth several millions fixed by him for Oldershaw and the Brasserton's plant would make whatever Westbrook and company did to revitalise Super-gear seem small beer. It would more than pay for Oldershaw's computer too. Armfield felt almost happy.

*

David pointed the Cortina GT down the Edgware Road and raced a Cooper S with smoked windows across three lights in succession as the yellow flipped to red. Then, fluffing a gear change, he let the Cooper sprint away with a derisive puff of blue exhaust, just making it through the fourth light. David had to brake against the blank red. He tightened his lips.

'Okay, Stirling Moss. You've proved your point,' said Sheila.

'It's the release syndrome,' he said. 'Getting the office out of my system. Part of the deal.'

'Remember junior,' she said. 'And stop dreaming you're in Michael Grant's Jensen.'

'Roll on the day,' he said. 'But I won't use it as a sex substitute. Cars *and* women, that's for me. He could have any bird in town, but he gets his orgasms pressing the accelerator. Funny. I've never quite got the sex in cars bit. If the car is the woman, how come it has all the aggression? It's a male phallic symbol, isn't it?'

66

Sheila shrugged her shoulders. He leaned over and kissed her. 'You look great.' Her face was slim and fine-boned, the hair dark brown. She held her long body tense in the seat, hands across the slightly swollen stomach. Without the bulge and the resigned gesture she would have looked almost Australian-athletic; a tennis girl, but without a tennis mind.

'Thank you, breadwinner,' she said. 'It's your overdraft.' She thrust out her bosom, well-shaped but not abundant. 'Enough?'

'Your best feature,' he said. 'Well, two of your best.'

'Forty quid for this little number, and it's not even in fashion. Officially breasts still do not exist.'

'Bugger fashion and all those titless wonders in *Vogue*,' he said. 'Fashion is created by fags and displayed by flat-chested lesbians, oozing with envy about what nature left them without. How would they know what men want? You stay with the fuller figure, girl. Men don't want limbs like willow wands.'

'McDiarmid,' she said. 'Hugh McDiarmid. You're still not attributing your quotes.'

They laughed. This was what made it for them; the need for no explanations, the intimacy of books remembered, thoughts bounced between them down the years. Six years ago they had met, Sheila in her first big agency job, David wandering around in the disappointment of having been rejected as a starter on *The Times*. Then he had gone into business, refusing the advice of an ageing sub-editor that he should try a provincial paper. Both he and Sheila had read English, David at Cambridge, along with Economics, she at Oxford, wallowing through the morass of Anglo-Saxon. It seemed a world away from their life now. Irrelevant. That was one of the many words in the fashionable vocabulary of student revolt of which she approved. David, less committed, thrashed the young at one moment, questioned the rationale of his business career the next. Ambivalence was fashionable too.

'And I've got all dolled up to spend an evening watching the box?' she said.

'Lionel Westbrook apologised,' said David, 'but we only knew today. Bernard Grant's never done it before. No one quite knows why he's decided to expose himself.'

'Indecently?' she said.

'Anything is possible with him. Hardy suggests that after his thrombosis he has intimations of mortality. Thinks he should leave his last will and telly testament. It'll only be half an hour, and we eat first.'

They were silent as he turned right into the wide terraces of St John's Wood, switching on the headlights to search for the street names. A car flashed its lights at them persistently.

'Get stuffed,' said David.

'I'd still like to live a bit closer to town one day,' she said.

'Yes?' David laughed. 'Hardy said I was becoming a prime example of Suburban Man today.'

'He would. Will he be there?'

'No. Just us. He'll be putting the kids to bed. The Prossers are coming like I said. It's my celebration. Nothing to do with Hardy.'

'He allows that you've graduated, then?'

'*Cum laude*,' said David. 'One of his prize pupils. Don't worry about Hardy. His cynicism hides a heart of gold.'

'A sheep in wolf's clothing you'll be telling me next.'

'No. Just a useful teacher.'

'As long as that's all.'

'That's all.'

'What do I call him? Westbrook, I mean. What do *you* call him?'

'Depends. Try Mr Westbrook to start with.'

The house was standard St John's Wood Victorian. Lionel Westbrook had not yet made it to the Regency league, but had ambitions. His residence was three-storeyed, with basement garage, bright in yellow and white. Sugar-cake. On a gate pillar the number was written in lower-case italics of wrought iron: *forty four*. Disappointing, she thought. The front door was fluted, misted glass, reinforced by more wrought iron. A swarthy woman, around fifty, answered the bell, standing mutely till Westbrook appeared behind her.

'Thank you, Lucrezia. Good to see you, David. Come in, Mrs Travis.' He was ebullient, wearing a close-fitting suit, coloured light stone, double-breasted, wide-lapelled. It flared extravagantly from the waist; gave him the look of an overweight ballet dancer, she thought. He opened the suit as he sat down with them. His tie, broad blue and yellow stripes, was five inches wide at the bottom.

'Sorry,' he said. 'Diana's been delayed. A deal with *Paris Match* that's so hot it can't wait. She runs photographers, and other bits of tat. Did you know? But Lucrezia will look after us.'

He spoke confidently in what David took to be Spanish or Portuguese. One up, if not two, thought David. Martinis appeared. Westbrook had a lot going for him, even outside the office.

'Sheila, isn't it? Well, here's to the new director. And many more directorships.' Westbrook raised his glass. 'I'm very glad to have him with me. A brave lieutenant, my dear. You might say a commando.'

'Raiding Merseyside, Mr Westbrook?' said Sheila.

'Good, yes, that's more or less it,' he said. He rose and moved towards a record-player beneath a vast bright painting, Mediterranean, blues and burnt-brown and yellows sloshed around. The player had a transparent acrylic lid, curved at the front, the ends square-cut. He lifted it carefully as if he relished its silky feel.

'I hope you like Segovia.'

Sheila wasn't sure. 'Of course,' she said.

The notes splashed around the room like light rain. Perhaps that's why the guitar belongs to rainless countries, David speculated. Reminds them of fountains tinkling.

'Do you smoke?' said Westbrook to Sheila. He offered her an inlaid mother-of-pearl box. She declined. He shook himself one from a crumpled packet marked with a deep-brown disc. 'Excuse me. Negritas. A private perversion. The result of too many holidays in the Algarve. Do you know it?' He lit the almost black stem of the cigarette and flopped into a deep swivel armchair, mounted on a stainless steel base.

'No,' she said. 'Spain, yes. You know – the usual package tour. We've been twice. Good value, but you can't be choosey. Chips with everything. *And* rice.'

David wasn't sure if he liked her honesty or whether he'd sooner she wasn't so brash about their comparative ordinariness. But Westbrook showed no signs of having listened. 'We have a place near Albufeira,' he said. 'The pop singer's Blackpool. That's where we found Lucrezia.'

'The Algarve is still okay?' said David.

'They're throwing up villas like molehills,' said Westbrook. 'And the would-be jet-setters have settled in. But there's a lot of space. You should see that coastline. Beaches you can't get at except from the sea. Cliffs and caves that remind you of the moon, coloured purple and pitted and cratered like they've been there since pre-history. Rocks like giant toads crouching or pterodactyls with lumbago. Ridiculous. It will take a really monstrous holiday camp king to spoil that lot. And the water's splendid. Warm as the Med but a bit more restless, which is nice. And the Atlantic winds temper the sun. It doesn't shrivel you up like Spain.'

He was an enthusiast, whatever else, Sheila thought. His talk roared along like fire with the wind whipping it. He glanced at his watch. 'Where are they all? We want to be on the coffee by 9.30.'

He turned to Sheila. 'Yes, we have a job on with Supergear.' She suddenly thought how stupid the name sounded. 'David will look after it though. But you mustn't let him waste too much energy on it. It's a side-issue.'

'I see,' said Sheila. She must have sounded disappointed, for Westbrook laughed. Then he switched off the flipness and was serious. For the first time she warmed to him. He seemed so anxious to make her believe that *he* believed in David.

'Don't misunderstand me, Sheila. I didn't mean it's a non-job. It's important. Very. But it's only part of the game to prove a point to the accountant side of our business. If we win this, we'll have our hands much more free for the future. I expect David's told you all about it.'

'Well, not *all*,' she said.

Westbrook leaned forward. 'Sometimes they tell me I get too worked up about what we can do, but what the hell. The world's our oyster. So many new things we can develop. The trouble with this organisation is old thinking. The money was made in property, but that's finished now. The finance brains don't always see it, though. Harold Armfield – I expect you've heard of him.' He chose his words carefully, trying to brake his tongue. 'A nice man. Solid. But he hasn't got the vision. Stonewalls *too* much. He's typical of accountants. They think because we've diversified a bit, that's enough. But what we've done is too automatic, a kind of business noughts and crosses. You've got the cash to spare, so you pick up companies here and there. Going concerns that run like clockwork, more or less. Very boring. We're at the stage now where we should be pulling things together. Chopping off the dull stuff, knitting the rest of the companies together into a coherent whole, so that they relate to each other – do you see?'

'I think so,' she said.

'Companies doing similar things,' he said.

'You've got a boat company, so buy a sailmaker's to go with it?' said Sheila. She remembered the campaign her agency had run for a small marine company five years back. The firm had gone bankrupt.

'Something like that,' said Westbrook. 'The Prospero Group is all over the place just now. Sound, of course, but not as well positioned for the future as it could be. Like a lot of British companies. There's this sort of inbred inertia, as if they've a

70

pathological fear of doing anything differently from how they did it last year. You know what I mean?'

She was prudent enough to do no more than nod.

'Here's a case in point. We have this firm making sporty car gear up in the Midlands. Steering-wheels, gloves, accessories, that kind of thing. But it's difficult for them to grab a decent market share in competition with the older-established suppliers. Say we had a car company, though – small, specialist, sporty. Good enough to win some races or rallies. Feed the accessories in with that, and you might have a snowball. That's the way we've got to think. Armfield just wants to go on building office blocks and doing little deals, because that's the business he feels *comfortable* with. He's like a man in business corsets.'

Westbrook glowed as he talked, his hands shaping suns and satellites in the air, the sentences tumbling. 'It's fantastically exciting if only we can persuade our Chairman. And God help us if we don't. With an organisation like ours you have to keep the momentum going, otherwise it falls apart from the effort to stand still. The Chairman's son needs no persuading, praise be. A lot of fun, but simple logic really. We've got to fit things together. David knows the philosophy. The Unilever idea – once you've spent a fortune getting into the housewife's kitchen to find out why she buys sausages, you might as well find out why she buys everything else. Wouldn't you say that was simple? But it takes a lot to convince these damned accountants. Businessmen listen to them too much. Just because they know about the mysteries of the tax game, it's given them a licence to infect everyone with creeping paralysis. Caution, I mean. That's something else taxation has done for this long-suffering country. Made the accountants into high priests, if not gods. We need a whiff of straight old Yankee grab-or-bust.' He took breath and smiled. 'Sorry, Sheila. Am I boring you?'

'I'm fascinated,' she said. She hoped she sounded as if she meant it, because she did. Westbrook came alive when he spoke like this. She glanced at David as their host rose to answer the bell. David lifted his eyebrows and nodded, pleased.

It was the Prossers. Barry Prosser, as he introduced himself, looked uneasy, peering through spectacles a touch too large. Whenever they slipped, he pushed them nervously back on to the bridge of his pug nose. He tried hard to be light-hearted. It smelt like that kind of evening, where you'd really have to pump to stop it going down; a slow-puncture evening.

'I didn't pick him myself,' he told Sheila, nodding towards

71

David. 'Before my time. But he seems to be making it without benefit of clergy.'

Sheila acted puzzled till David jogged her memory. 'Mr Prosser is our personnel director.'

She wanted to hear Westbrook talk some more, but Prosser's wife, Frances, twin-setted and pearled, swiftly steered the conversation the way she wanted it to go. She nudged words, hauled them, fussed them, like a tugboat at work. Her accent was faintly Midlands, but overlaid with Virginia Water, which was where they lived. Addressing herself almost solely to Sheila she laid out her life as shopkeepers lay out vegetables. She rode twice a week. She ran a Herald Convertible and coffee mornings for several charities. She felt that the general enthusiasm to shop at Marks and Spencer for *everything* that didn't show had gone a *teeny* bit too far. Her son was at Rugby and sometimes she thought she knew him not at all.

'We don't make a *thing* out of it,' she said, repeating one of her favourite words again, 'but Roger doesn't seem to show much appreciation for what we've done for him. He's *quite* a nice boy, but a bit disappointing. Do you know what I mean?'

'It's a different world,' said Sheila. 'It takes some understanding.'

'Have you children, Mr Westbrook?' said Mrs Prosser, sidestepping the tackle.

'Two,' said Westbrook. 'Boy and girl. Mine's the boy. From our first marriages.' Sheila could tell he liked saying it, in that way at this moment to this woman.

'Oh,' said Mrs Prosser. She floated a smile towards Sheila with the care of a boy launching a model boat he'd fashioned himself, then lowered her gaze to navel-height. 'Your first?'

'Well, yes,' said Sheila, angry at feeling the heat in her face.

'Your troubles,' said Frances Prosser, 'are only just beginning.' She patted her tight-curled hair, 1939-style, as if that was the definitive word on the subject.

'Don't frighten the girl,' said her husband, very Welsh. 'What would life be without kids?'

'Very dull,' said Westbrook. 'Congratulations in advance. He'll be just in time to lead the final revolt against beastly adults. The organisation's almost ready. Mine was distributing pamphlets for something called the Schools Reform Union last holidays. They want to vote on whether teachers can stay on the staff or not. He's just thirteen.'

'You're not castigating that son of yours again, are you?' said

Diana Westbrook. She walked quietly through the open archway from the hall beyond. 'He'll be lobby fodder like the rest of the teenybop revolutionaries by the time he's twenty. Just give them enough cake and they'll choke themselves.'

'Or maybe just be sick all over us,' said Westbrook.

David admitted he'd been wrong about her legs. She wore a simple shirt-waister, very short. She was as sleek from mid-thigh down as she was above it. Her hair was longer than when he'd last seen her, streaming darkly over her shoulders. Too young, thought Sheila, wondering whether it was a wig; thirty's the limit for the groupie look.

Westbrook had risen, seemingly not too pleased. 'Glad you called,' he said. 'I've made your apologies.' He rattled off the introductions. 'We'd better eat if we're to catch up with the evening. I hope it was worth it.'

'I got his fee up, if that's what you mean,' said his wife. 'And a couple of jobs with *Elle* for good measure.'

'They like the way his lens bores in on the pelvis,' said Westbrook. 'Sex without action. Like photographing sea shells. Very clinical. Do you see *Elle*, Frances?'

'Sometimes,' said the Prosser woman, meaning that she didn't know what the hell he was on about. 'I've heard about your work, Mrs Westbrook. It sounds very interesting. I don't know how you find the time.' The simple words marched in column, brandishing implications of house-neglect, husband-neglect, child-neglect. Frances Prosser had got the reasons for Diana Westbrook's divorce wrapped up right there.

'With the children away at school, I need something to keep me occupied,' Diana Westbrook said sweetly. 'It's a sort of pact between us. Lionel has his fun, I have mine. The Prospero Group doesn't leave him much time for thinking about what wallpaper he'd like to hang in the spare room next weekend.'

Frances Prosser fell upon that cue like a dog who hasn't seen a decent bone in six months. The hours that Barry Prosser worked, the long telephone calls which ravaged their weekends, the sudden journeys to Birmingham and Manchester and points north, not to mention the conferences in Basle and Bordeaux and Boston to which wives were not invited. It was virtually a monologue, lasting through the Parma ham and melon, and continuing deep into the *coq au vin*, all of which they ate in an alcove screened by a dangly bamboo curtain, around a rosewood table laid with heavy Georgian silver.

'We weren't very happy with the Coal Board either,' said

73

Prosser at last, carefully using the plural pronoun, 'and that was strictly ten till six.'

'That was different,' said his wife. 'What they paid you was ridiculous.'

'You came from the Coal Board,' said Diana Westbrook. 'Wasn't that a bit restricted? Or what?'

'Not really,' he said, 'I liked it. I come from the valleys, see. Tonypandy. I felt I had a bit to repay.' He smiled awkwardly. 'Social conscience. The dreams of youth. All that. I don't regret it, and once Alf Robens became boss it livened up a lot. I wasn't sure I wanted to leave, but you know how it is. Bernard Grant's offer was one I couldn't turn down.'

Westbrook was up-beat again, insisting on ladling more food on to Frances Prosser's plate. She had a healthy appetite, as it is sometimes miscalled, and she often spoke through what satisfied it. Her fork never left her hand, food balanced on it waiting to be delivered, as if she were in fear it would go away. 'Barry,' said Westbrook, 'is good for us. Our non-conformist conscience. He prevents us becoming vainglorious in the way we decorate our rooms or what we allow ourselves to eat at board lunches. We need him and know the strain it must have been when he came. The eternal conflict between service and profit.'

'Come on, Lionel,' said Prosser. 'Not in front of the young.'

They all laughed. David had never heard Prosser in this flipper vein. The personnel director must also have realised that Westbrook was leading him on too fast.

'Frankly,' he said, all evangelical, 'it wasn't really the money. It's a bit like divorce, I suppose. I no longer believed. Once I did, but not now. Nationalised industries, well, they kill the spirit. No competition, no joy, nothing to stretch the muscles. Like divorce, as I was saying. The love affair had already gone sour. I would have quit anyway. Bernard's offer was just like a surprise in the shape of bloody good alimony.'

'Lucky for us you still carry the marks,' said Westbrook. 'It does us good to be reminded of the dark-brown paint and the chipped teacups of government service. I mean it, Barry.'

Prosser said simply: 'We have to think of the people we employ. We can't be Roman emperors any more. I just believe I can do more to change things from the base I have now. I've no regrets about that either.'

'Nor has Frances, I'm sure,' said Diana Westbrook, 'except that we never see our husbands. They moan about not getting home, but secretly I think they enjoy it.'

74

Frances Prosser seemed to be adding up the Herald, the eight-bedroomed house, the daily woman daily, the gardener, the two horses, the large life insurance, the top-hat pension, the school fees and the month spent every year in Ibiza before she agreed.

'We're forgetting the cause of the party,' Diana said sharply, as if apprehensive that the panorama of lovely downtown Virginia Water might again be unfurled. 'Here's to both of you.' She took David's arm, and with her other hand lifted the claret glass in Sheila's direction. 'And to the hours you'll spend wondering when the hell he's coming home.'

'I can take it,' said Sheila. 'He doesn't exactly sit at the fireside in his woolly slippers at the moment.'

'When did you last need a pair, Lionel?' asked Diana.

'No, squire,' he said, doing his rustic imitation. 'She sits on 'er soid of the foir and oi sits on moin and we 'ates the bloody sight of each other.' They laughed.

'Charming,' said his wife.

'No chance of domestic bliss with the snap-happy boys around,' said Westbrook. 'They keep you at it. Ever since they acquired agents, photographers have got above themselves. Straight out of art school, one up from an Instamatic, and they want two hundred quid a spread.'

The exchange suddenly had a sharpness in it.

'You pay for talent, that's all,' said his wife. 'The market sets the price. I don't make the market. It's the people trying to sell your damned products.'

'It's all a conspiracy,' said Westbrook, 'and you're one of the witches with your talons in the pot.'

Unexpectedly the conversation died as conversations do when two experienced in-fighters run out of steam or the desire to trade punches.

'Show-time,' said Westbrook, rising. 'I hope you don't mind, but we ought to watch. And,' he said, smiling warmly on Sheila, 'the gentlemen do not expect to be left with their port.'

Diana Westbrook plainly hadn't known of the plan to watch Bernard Grant on the screen. She was a touch sulky as they arranged themselves round the bulky colour set. Sheila flipped a glance at David, but missed him. The talk had been freer than she had expected: senior directors trying to prove they were human. Westbrook was in a huddle with Prosser.

'You should know about this,' he called to David. 'It's the computer for Brasserton's.'

75

Prosser was uneasy at the invitation to widen their talk. 'It's going all right, I think.'

Westbrook put his arm round the personnel director. 'David's discreet,' he said. 'And he may get involved.'

Prosser smiled thinly. 'Yes, I suppose so. Your men get involved in most things. The umbrella man, that's you Lionel. There'll be some redundancy. And we'll need to do some re-training. We must try to get Michael not to push too hard. It's important we take it in easy stages.'

David said: 'But it could mean more jobs one day. I've read the market study. It looks good ultimately.'

'Ultimately is not a word the unions like,' said Prosser. 'Jobs today, not jam tomorrow.'

'Of course,' said David.

'If it goes well this time, it could be a prototype deal for the whole group,' Prosser said.

'It must go well,' said Westbrook. 'We need that computer.'

'Some hard bargaining,' said Prosser.

'You must persuade them, Barry.'

'I know.'

'That's your speciality,' said Westbrook. 'You talk the language.'

Very few chairmen would not have envied Bernard Grant's television performance. He was perfect, a natural. Grave but not miserable, a likeable elder statesman, the sense of purpose shot through with humanity and wit. No script from the Institute of Directors could have put the case for private enterprise, for incentives, for enlightened self-interest better.

'But can't conglomerate enterprises be a danger – too much control in too few hands?' asked the interviewer.

'Big businesses, if they are well run, are in the public interest,' said Grant.

'Why?'

'First, they mean cheaper prices. We have the size to produce goods in bulk, which means more cheaply. Companies which have good ideas but not the capital to develop, we can help, supporting them with our more immediately profitable enterprises.'

'You make large profits, though?'

'And the public purse has benefited as a result,' smiled Grant at his most honest. 'The more we make, the more tax we pay. People forget that. This is the joy of the British system. No secrets. No graft. Everyone knows what we earn. Our books are open. We are answerable – to those who own us, to the Government, to an army of inquirers. And everyone has the chance to do the same as I have done if they apply themselves.'

'But surely they must also have your gift, your secret?'

'I have no secret,' said Grant.

'Surely . . .' said the interviewer.

'No secret,' Grant repeated. 'Only hard work and attention to detail. That, I think, is the most important of all. Attention to detail.'

'Could you explain that further?'

'Yes. One watches what is happening in society all the time. In the 1950s, when I was still only in the property business, I went to America. In California I saw how the young people had begun to do things with their motor cars. Strange shapes and designs, emblems of all kinds. They called it customising, and there was a bizarre new vocabulary with words like chopping and channelling, which meant lowering and raising the body, I believe. I do not understand much about automobiles, you see.'

'Despite your son?' said the interviewer.

'Despite Michael, yes,' said Grant, smiling graciously but unwilling to be deflected. 'This cult in California even I could scarcely miss. When we began to diversify, I was very happy to approve my son's suggestion that we should take over a small car firm which specialised in modifications to standard models.' He smiled more broadly. 'I am not sure why people desire such changes, but if they do, then I am happy to meet their needs.'

'You have taken over many companies, Mr Grant. Can you tell us what you see as the advantages of take-overs?'

'There are so many. The companies that are taken over may need capital, or they may find that their raw material sources or perhaps their sales outlets are improved by going in with another group. From the point of view of a dynamic organisation, as mine has been, to take over someone is often a quick way of expanding without having to wait for new plant and factories to be built. Is that enough?'

'Your base in property was useful, I understand, once you began diversifying your group?'

'True. I was able to raise money by selling off freehold sites I owned – to people like insurance companies. That way I could always finance my bids impressively. People knew I meant business.'

'And then you'd keep an interest in the sites by taking them back on long-term leases?'

Grant smiled. 'That was sometimes the arrangement.'

'Has there been any – well – pattern governing the take-overs you make? Or do you just look for what might be called best buys?'

'I began with the necessities. Property, then food and electrical and engineering companies – oh, and clothing, the Supergear company. Then, as the 1960s developed, I saw that there were other opportunities. Once people have eaten, given themselves a roof over their heads, I thought they would wish to better themselves, to enjoy their new leisure. That is why I am in the hire-purchase business, in boats, in automobile accessories. What I have done has been to anticipate and meet the needs of ordinary people.'

David looked up, trying to catch Sheila's eye, but she was intent on the screen. Instead, he found himself looking at Diana Westbrook. She sat with an amused half-smile on her lips. She raised her brows and rolled her eyes to follow them, inviting him to take it as unseriously as she did. Not knowing exactly how to respond, he simply smiled. Then, seeing Westbrook turn, he looked again at Grant's head, handsome as a Roman elder in profile, grey hair immaculate, nose proud and prominent.

'No,' Grant was saying. 'Politics has no attraction for me. It is too much a matter of unfinished buildings, if you understand me. You never know who will change the plan, destroy what you have created. Business, on the other hand, is like painting. You can complete the canvas, see the finished masterpiece. Say I lay out some millions, construct a factory, give jobs to several thousand people and earn perhaps fifteen per cent on my investment. That is that. I can sleep happily and any politician who wants can shout his head off about it. He cannot destroy my work because it exists, it *is*. Next day I shall begin to paint again. There is nothing like it.'

This time Sheila was looking. She nodded approval to David and Westbrook leaned across to squeeze her arm. Even Diana Westbrook stuck up a thumb to her husband.

'I appreciate,' said Grant, 'that the English do not like success. But that is perhaps a reflection of the days when privilege was rampant, when there was no equality of opportunity. That someone such as myself, who began with nothing, and – this I must say – after great suffering, can be successful is the most striking demonstration of the equality and justice and goodness of this society. Those who believe that Britain is finished must be joking, yes?' David thought it was the only middle-Europeanism yet.

78

'You talk of suffering, Mr Grant. What do you feel now about your wartime experiences?'

'Some sadness, I suppose. Sorrow too. Sorrow that men could be so deluded as to do what they did. Apart from that, nothing. One does not wish to relive such things.'

Grant looked stricken when he said that. The interviewer tried to push him further, but Grant turned on him almost angrily. It harmed him not at all. Telepundits who overstep the bounds of propriety can expect no mercy from their audience, who are not averse to seeing an interviewer savaged if he deserves it. Like the Romans, they can give the thumbs down without pity. You could hear the clucks of sympathy with Grant rising in every mortgaged town house from Altrincham to Weybridge.

'Good,' said Westbrook. 'Very good.'

'Lest we forget,' said Prosser.

'Would you do business with a German now, Mr Grant?' said the interviewer. It was a nice move; getting the audience back on his side by playing on their latent feelings of jingoism.

'I have not sought such business,' said Grant, 'but if it happened so, then yes. I do not believe that the sins of the fathers should be visited upon the generations that follow. Not in life, not in business.' Now Grant's footwork was good: no krautlover, but forgiving. Clever.

'These are high standards, Mr Grant,' said the interviewer. 'Do you believe that such standards prevail in business generally?'

'That is a difficult question.'

The interviewer scented advantage. 'Youth today do not seem to believe that these standards exist. There is disenchantment.'

'Young people are searching,' said Grant. 'I believe they will find.'

'Find what exactly?'

'They are misunderstood,' said Grant. 'Not in the way *they* mean. This generation has not tasted success, that is part of the trouble. Oh, they have affluence, but what is affluence without power? Once it was simple. If you reached a certain level, a certain position, you felt you controlled the world. Now, it should be utopia, but it is not. They have lost their certainties. They want the success of power, and they grow sulky when they fail to grasp it. They are alive and, I believe, loving, the young. They will understand, and when they do, we shall forget they once were paper tigers.'

'America has power. No country has more,' said the interviewer. 'Yet the young people there. . . .'

'If their country had won in Vietnam after one year, it would have been quite different. They do not like defeats. It is a new experience for them. They see that the Castros and the Mao Tse-tungs appear to be winners, so they shout for them. It will change.'

'To take up the point about ethics of business again,' said the interviewer.

Grant spread his hands. 'There are some rogues in business, as there have been some crooked politicians, fallen priests and murderous saints. We make mistakes. I make them. Who does not? We are not supermen. Just men. No one people or profession has a monopoly of virtue. Businessmen work for reward, true. But the reward is not always to be measured in terms of money. Satisfaction in what they do is even more important. You may think me sentimental, but I honestly believe that the sense of service, the sense of community, the sense of perfection – all these are important to most businessmen, even if they do not articulate those feelings. That is certainly true of my colleagues as I have observed them. From Harold Armfield, who is my oldest colleague, right through to men like Sir Giles Lymington, who joined me later. His tradition of service once found its outlet in caring for this nation's interests abroad. Now, he makes his contribution to industry. We are fortunate to have men of such calibre within our organisation.'

It was neat, honest, convincing. Straight stuff, no messing. Grant could not have been so great had he not been speaking the truth, his truth. He believed every word of it, and no amount of television expertise or camera coaching could have shielded him had he not. The television critics would be dialling now, trying to prise a hundred or two more words out of their night editors. It was that good.

*

David drove home slowly, rather drowsy from the food and wine. 'Your Chairman is quite a man,' said Sheila. 'The Bayswater birds might even call him a sweetie. His public image scarcely does him justice.'

'And Lionel Westbrook?'

'I quite liked him in the end. He's a bit of a laugh in some ways, but okay. I think he means to see you all right.'

'Diana's a bit weird.'

80

'She likes you.'

'Oh yeah.'

Flogging the Jag hard down the A30, Prosser was also tuned in to his wife; but there were few natural breaks. 'I give those two a couple of years at most,' she said. 'Did you see the way she was looking at that Travis boy? Man-eater. And Lionel Westbrook wants to act his age. He couldn't stop touching the girl.'

Prosser wanted to ask her if she was jealous, but did not. 'That suit,' she said. 'Ridiculous. Is he any good at his job?'

'Very,' said Prosser.

Diana Westbrook stretched full-length on the floor, shoes off, rubbing her cheek against a bear-skin, holding a Scotch up to the light. 'What a terrible cow,' she said. 'Sorry to repeat myself.'

'Never again,' said Westbrook. 'We've done our duty. I've promised, so don't keep on about it. You still like the Travis kids?'

'Nice,' said Diana. She rolled over and looked seriously at her husband. 'Lionel, don't eat him. Let him breathe, be himself.'

'For God's sake,' he said. 'Not again. Every time you see some kid you fancy, you cast me as Frankenstein or something.'

'Sometimes you act that way.'

'If you were so bloody worried, you might have turned up on time for a change,' said Westbrook. 'Where did tonight's deal get consummated? On your back?'

'You are sometimes a total bastard,' she said.

'I've had cause,' he said.

'Haven't we all,' she said. 'But please – leave it. We agreed, remember? I'm going to bed.'

Westbrook put Bacharach on the record-player, the man himself, at piano, with brass and strings and no words, filled his glass and spent an hour in his study shuffling through papers, underlining sentences, ticking paragraphs, scribbling notes. When he went to their bedroom his wife was, as often, asleep. He slipped into his bed quietly, lay wondering what increased market share they might reasonably expect to achieve with the Supergear company – and, equally important, what Earl Sanger might regard as reasonable.

For some reason, he found himself thinking of Chris, who now lived in Bristol. His first wife had been very calm the night she told him she was leaving.

'I know you're in great shape, Lionel,' she said, 'but I'm not. I've seen the way that business wives curl up and age faster than their men. Well, that's not going to be me. I just don't aim to exhaust myself with the struggle to keep up with you, that's all. I appreciate that *you* can't do anything about getting off the escalator. I'm not taking the ride, I'm afraid.'

He had asked her, feeling like a bad actor with a B movie script, whether they would still be friends.

'You wouldn't enjoy that, dear boy,' she said. 'You need rivals, not friends. You need to be excited with enmity, not soothed with friendship or love. That's the way you'll make it, darling. That's the way all of them bloody do.'

4. Gentlemen and players

SIR GILES LYMINGTON, KBE, MC, sat in his unlit drawing-room within the City of Westminster and said he couldn't. Not only that, of course, but adding all the circumstances of why, not excluding a hint of hard-luck story. And for that he scorned himself as much as he disliked the measured voice in his ear.

'We have waited a long time,' said the man on the telephone. 'Very patiently.'

'Yes. I appreciate that,' said Lymington, 'you have been very reasonable.' Normally he might have said decent, but not now.

Normally, too, his voice had the baying certainty of the commanding classes, enriched to a fine mellowness in a dozen capitals around the world, thick with the confidence of Her Britannic Majesty's authority. Its peremptory tone had not been diminished even when Lymington sensed years ago that he might have to learn to be the representative of a second-class power. Diplomatic voices nurtured on Victorian memories and a tradition which overcame reality were still the mark of his Foreign Office generation, for immediately after the war Britain had stood as a victor, and in the final years of his service during the late 1950s, arriving affluence had seemed a mirage that would last for ever. Now he spoke little above a whisper, praying that his wife Esther would stay out of the room.

'There are problems, Sir Giles,' said the man. 'Is it fair to us?'

'You said three months, and there is still some time to go.'

'Four days, to be precise.'

'I asked you not to ring me here.'

He wanted to end the conversation, was appalled at how freely the man spoke. Who might not be listening? He distrusted the telephone, a reflex nurtured both in Whitehall and in uncertain embassies abroad. But he was in no position to slam down the receiver, and he felt any confidence that he might deflect his caller's purpose drain away. He watched the cigarette

83

ash lengthen in the tray before him, saw the spines of his meticulously aligned first editions shimmer in the splashing light of the fire, and was afraid. The fish in the soft-lit tank a few feet away peered at him non-committally.

'There is some urgency,' said the voice lazily. 'Else we would not have called. If you had kept to the arrangement it would not have been necessary.'

'But I specifically asked,' said Lymington dully, driven to repetition. It was as if he had not spoken. The voice flowed on.

'We do not want our relationship marred by such things, naturally. No unfortunate consequences. It would be a pity.'

Six months' hard in the claustrophobic forests of Burma, feeling the destruction of self, rotting, degrading, blinded with monsoon rain, always in terror of the cobra. He was too old for that. Why hadn't they chosen a younger man? The MC when he blasted seventeen Nips out of a well-hidden command post. Malaria, which still afflicted him. Fifteen years of diplomacy afterwards to add to the years pre-war, when the world was falling apart and Munich had shamed them all. Fifteen years, never putting a foot wrong, despite the temptations. The grind of the ladder of secretaryships, the years as counsellor before the embassy of his own. Fifteen years of maintaining the façade, through endless boring cocktail parties and dinners, always with the same faces floating before him, wherever it was, South America or Europe, Middle East or Asia, in capitals where the women were hot-eyed and the casinos just around the corner, in others where you spoke the truth only in the streets, lying stiffly to the tiny microphones hidden behind pots and pictures. Sometimes, if one were going on a simple errand, one forgot to lie; and when you went into the street, a taxi would, coincidentally, happen to be cruising by to pick you up. Fifteen years of keeping his nose clean, building his contacts, waiting for the day, named in the end by Bernard Grant, though it might have been any company chairman of half a dozen others. It was a noble retirement, fairly rewarded, balanced, civilised. He did a job, gave counsel. The flaw which the telephone call was probing was so stupid, so unnecessary; held in check for years. Why had he not stopped earlier, cut his losses, even told Esther and ridden it out?

'Are you there, Lymington?' said the man.

'Yes,' he said.

'It can't be *so* difficult. The money is immaterial. Other things can help. Information about your organisation.'

'No,' said Lymington.

84

'But last time, things worked out excellently. Half your debt wiped out. And who suffered? No one, except a few who were too greedy. Surely there must be *something*?'

'I know nothing,' said Lymington. 'Nothing to help you.'

'Hard to believe,' said the man.

'Nothing. You must believe me,' Lymington told the telephone. 'Besides, in my position – there is the question of trust. . . .'

'Honour, I believe you said last time,' said the voice. 'A luxury, Lymington.'

'A month,' he said. 'You have my word.'

'Tomorrow,' said the man. 'I can understand you need time to think it over. Your word on that, Sir Giles. I shall be in touch. Good night.'

Lymington sat for perhaps a minute, listening without moving to the snarl of the telephone, pushing at the thin grey hair which lay flatly on his scalp. Then he slowly put the white receiver back on its rest, looked at the manicured fingers lying defeated on the desk, rose and walked to the tank. As he sipped his drink, two of the tiger barbs began to fight, nipping viciously at the glowing flesh, black and orange, ducking and weaving in the pale green water.

✻

'Perfect,' said Hardy. He tossed his *Times* across the table, folded at one of the inside pages. 'Bottom of column one. Motoring Correspondent. Small enough to miss. You know what it means?'

'It means,' said David, 'that they may, only *may*, have to give up racing.'

'It means,' said Hardy, 'that the noble Lovelace Motor Company might say yes to the last waltz, happy to be seen home by us.'

'Possible.'

'More than that. Probable.'

'Six months ago you said they'd never consider giving up their independence, not if they were down to their last hub-cap. So?'

'Times change,' said Hardy. 'They still thought they could live on tick. No one believed the squeeze would really squeeze. Now the bankers are in the nutcracker themselves, and they're passing on that crunchy feeling to the customers. You know it, everyone knows it. Or haven't you got an overdraft?'

'Don't tell me,' said David. 'I'm only testing your argument. Doing you a favour.'

'No problem,' said Hardy. 'The document's as good as written. If Lovelace's don't race, they don't sell cars – not their kind of cars, anyway. They must try to show they're that bit hairier than Porsche or Lotus. Even their independence isn't inviolate. They may act like virgins, but you can always lift up their skirts.'

'Go on, surprise me,' prompted David. He had grown rather used to fuelling the Hardy engine when it was going well.

'All here, boy,' said Hardy, tapping the green folder before him. 'What would we do without father–son situations – in Lovelace's, in Prospero, everywhere? And what would all those telly-script writers do? It's touching. Dad built it. Wants to keep his hands in the sump and his legs in overalls. Son wants to expand, build more, even try a dose of automation. Blocked by Dad. But now the cash flow situation is so bloody that even the one-horse operation is in danger. Enter the Prospero Group bearing gifts. It isn't only the racing. They could probably do without it in hard economic terms. They've a good name and it will last. But their racing tradition goes back beyond the days when Nuvolari was laying down rubber. To end *that* will strike at their pride. These automaniacs are emotional deep down. It all helps.'

'May I?' said David.

'Be my guest.' Hardy pushed the folder towards him. 'The hard stuff is on the first two pages.'

'Where else?'

'I'll need to update it a bit, but the slaves did a good job, I think.' Hardy savoured the way he might express what came next. 'Digging out stuff on these private companies is blue bloody murder. Takes the best Bonds in the business. No, not Bond. Too hammy. There are no birds or karate chops about *this*. Just talking to salesmen in boring pubs week after week. Bits and pieces that add up.'

'Let me concentrate,' said David. He took in the facts quickly; it was easy to do that with a Hardy document.

'Sales down ten per cent last year. Is that a reliable estimate?'

'Give or take the odd point,' said Hardy. 'Have faith. It isn't the only argument.'

David saw the estimate of how much money it might take. 'Christ,' he said. 'I don't give it less than six to four against if all I hear about Bernard Grant's views on fast cars is right. He hates them.'

'I thought you said you *listened* to that programme as well as swooning at his profile,' said Hardy. 'Did you have the sound turned down as a mark of respect? Bernie may not like cars, but he was daft enough to talk about his California dreaming and being a good businessman and letting Michael have his way with the surgery for fantasy motors etcetera *ad nauseam*. He'll come the sardonic bit about playing with toys, but once he's got his laughs he may not be immovable.'

'There are other directors,' said David.

'Like Armfield,' said Hardy, 'who will no doubt do his nut. He wants to go on peddling office blocks, and he's concerned about cash flow. So, isn't he always? Sir Galahad of Lymington will say sod all. Bartram will do as he's told. Lord Generalissimo Bender and Prosser will be open-minded. Michael and Lionel Westbrook will say yes. I'd reckon fifty-fifty, unless Bernie has been rubbed up the wrong way by his sole heir lately.'

'Which we all think he has.'

'All right. Six to four, like you say. But worth a try. And whether it comes off or not is not our problem. We've given our masters the ammunition. We are splendid chaps. If they can't shoot straight, well. . . .'

'*You* are a splendid chap,' said David. 'It's your paper – and good luck to all who sail in her.'

'It's not whether one is right or not,' said Hardy, 'but the moment when you strike. A bad idea at the right moment is worth ten of something bloody good launched on a dying market. Remember your first principles of management. Timing is all. And who told me about Westbrook instructing whose wife in why we need a stake in cars? That's what comes of dining with top board directors. You're bound to make it.'

'I need a beer,' said David.

'That old report might have gone on gathering dust but for your graphic account of a night with the ever-loving Westbrooks.' He swept up the file and pushed it into the top drawer of his desk, carefully locking it. 'With luck the gnomes won't be going through our personal files this lunch-hour.' He rose, dusted off his jacket, and slung it on. As they rode down in the lift he asked: 'Are you going on that course at Ashridge?'

'Not on your life,' said David. 'Take two weeks off just now? Prosser must be out of his mind.'

'One should see personnel men a great deal or never,' said Hardy. 'If they suddenly spot you after long absence and someone tells them you're bright, they get this irresistible urge to send you on a course. If they see you all the time, though, they imagine you're indispensable.'

'Maybe Prosser doesn't know about the Supergear business,' said David. 'I mean, why I was put on the board. I was tempted to go on that course though. They've got two MIT guys coming over. Marketing the hard way.'

'Sensible decision, nevertheless,' said Hardy. 'Men who go on long courses are, in the nature of things, those who can be spared without things coming to a dead halt. An immutable law of business. It's all in Drucker.'

'Too pat, Colin. Those who never go are the ones who are frightened of finding someone else in their jobs when they return. It's like growing a beard in business. If you do, you're either a failure and grown resigned to it – or a huge success, able to get away with being hirsute even.'

'That,' groaned Hardy, 'is the trouble with this game. Armies of arguments on both sides of every question. You can make anything sound good sense.'

They went to the new pub, quieter than their usual, more of a cocktail lounge after the Madison Avenue fashion: softly upholstered alcoves, stools with cushioned backs at the bar, a waiter in white who could mix a martini without being instructed, and gentle Erroll Garner dripping from unseen speakers. It was earlyish, and the price of the drinks kept the crowd thin. In a nook tucked away, but visible, Alison Bennett sat with Talbot-Brown.

'Our duty to intervene,' said Hardy. 'Can't you hear the trumpets sounding?'

'Of course,' said David. He had seen her three times since they had talked in the old pub. Corridor meetings, her eyes provocatively friendly, hand pushing at the copper hair, a gesture which raised her breasts in a way that made him want to prolong their talk. Twice he had suggested that they should have a drink together one evening, or even dinner, and she had been modestly compliant. 'Try me,' she said. 'But don't expect me to telephone you' – which left him still undecided how probable bed might be, if that was what he wanted. He was still working out whether he did want it. Of course he did, in theory. Who wouldn't, with Miss Bennett? But would it be worth the decision, the doubts, the risk, the trouble, the living with?

'That bloody man Talbot-sodding-Brown,' he said to Hardy. The same old textbook stuff, he realised. You can take a bird or leave her until someone you don't like starts chasing. Then you feel you have to join the hunt. Even when it's someone you *do* like who starts playing hound dog. So Talbot-Brown at her side made the girl seem twice as sexy. Ridiculous. Being a human male was very trying at times.

'Bloody but natural,' said Hardy. 'He's only doing what we did. Testing the ground. A bit later than us, naturally.'

They carried their drinks and sandwiches towards the alcove, acted surprised when Alison smiled out at them. Whether her look was an invitation or only a reflex was uncertain. They sat down just the same. Talbot-Brown, surprisingly, seemed not notably put out. They talked, predictably, about Grant on the box; also of the decline of Bob Dylan since he went country-and-western sentimental, of the prospects for the England–Wales match at Twickenham, about which the girl seemed surprisingly knowledgeable, of the death of unisex and the price of suits from Blades. Talbot-Brown, smoothing his many pockets, believed one could tell a *really* good tailor by whether or not he made every button buttonable. They talked about everything except what might in hard fact be on the mind of any one of the four of them.

Alison looked great, David thought. Each time she recrossed her legs, he became very interested in the colour of the beer on the low table before them. It was really too obvious, but he gave not a damn.

'Miss Bennett's desirable thighs will be your undoing,' said Hardy as they left, alone. 'Personally I regret the coming of tights. No delicious flashes of flesh above the stocking-top these days. And so unfair to seducers. Getting your hand into position with any subtlety is quite impossible, they tell me. It's like getting caught up in one of those nets the Roman gladiators used. Tights are a virgin's best friend.'

'You were looking in that direction too, no doubt,' said David with satisfaction.

'Certainly not,' said Hardy. 'I was merely observing *you*.'

'Voyeur,' said David.

'As you wish,' said Hardy. 'More importantly, Master Talbot-Brown seems so pleased with himself, it's painful to see.'

'You know why, naturally,' said David, acidly.

'He bears watching,' said Hardy, unperturbed. 'A coup from Harold Armfield is much overdue.'

❃

Earl Sanger was adamant. He waved his hand at the spread of files before him, then pulled a tissue from the box in the open drawer to wipe the dust from his fingers. Sanger disliked dirt. He spent more time going to the men's room to wash his hands than anyone else on the nineteenth or twentieth floors, where those regarded as the management cream clotted sourly together.

'How in hell is one expected to make sense of that deal? There are too many pieces of paper missing. Letters apparently unanswered on both sides. It's hard to give an opinion. Lymington was in it a lot. Your father only occasionally.'

'He's not good at writing that sort of letter,' said Michael.

'Some of them had to have an answer,' said Sanger. 'In writing.'

'They're probably in Lymington's personal files,' said Michael. Westbrook said nothing. He didn't particularly like the fact that they were sitting in Sanger's office. Two directors visiting a man technically subordinate. Sanger's flat statement on the phone that the files were spread all round his room if anyone wanted to see them had sounded more like a challenge than a plea. Apart from the files, there was nothing, the desk clear of paper; no baskets of documents and letters in or out. It was a clinical room; steel and glass and two paintings. The migraine was strong this afternoon. Psychosomatic, he wondered?

'So what do we do?' asked Sanger, using sarcasm again with the subtlety of a flail. 'Just walk in and start opening up the old guy's cabinets?'

Michael ignored him. 'What do you think we do, Lionel?'

'If Earl believes it's critical to know all this' – Westbrook was playing for time, thinking – 'I see no reason why we can't just *ask* Lymington. But is it worth making a big issue out of it?'

Sanger shrugged. 'No disrespect, but it's not my money, and it's a while back. A few millions shakily invested in an ex-colony. Water under the bridge. All I can tell you is that documents are missing. And it's not clear who made the mistake or why. You tell me if it's important. I'm just playing jigsaws.'

'Let it go,' said Michael, 'for the time being. But it gives me that shivery feeling.'

'Me too,' said Sanger. 'Do you know how I got these files? Just walked in, smiled at some kid there and opened the drawers. They weren't even locked.'

'I've talked about security for months,' said Westbrook, anxious to get back in play. 'The others nod and smile as if they're humouring me and Lionel, dear boy, you shouldn't watch all those old spy films late at night. Armfield was supposed to look into it. But nothing happens.'

90

'The shredder in Room 204 has been out of action for a week,' said Sanger, whose memo on the subject was already rustling its way on to a dozen desks, 'but I haven't seen any of the managers eating their confidential wastepaper. A girl scout could find out most anything she wanted inside a week walking this building. What the professionals could do, God knows.'

Even Michael didn't appreciate Sanger's easy attitude of superiority. 'Don't spoil your case, Earl. I suppose *you* check your room for bugs every day.'

'I leave no place for them to be hidden,' he said simply, ignoring Michael's irony. 'And if I *did* suspect anything, I know the rules. From oscilloscopes that check out any strange pulses on electrical circuits to long-wave lamps that pick up new paint.'

'New paint?' said Westbrook, and Sanger answered with an air of infinite patience.

'Where you get an area of new paint on a wall, a bug may have been built in.'

'We'd never do any work at all if we believed everything in those magazine articles,' said Michael.

'*Jesus!*' said Sanger. He leapt from his seat, pulling at the waistband of his trousers. 'I'm not playing games. Do you know that in Japan there are something like ten thousand industrial spies trained every year? It *happens*. I went to a business school out West where they *teach* the stuff – allegedly for defence against industrial espionage, though God knows what the guys who attend that place get up to afterwards.' He smiled carefully. 'They never did have any students from England.'

'All right, Earl,' said Michael. 'I'll buy it.'

'And buy this,' said Sanger. 'There is a management decision room in Dallas, Texas, twenty-two floors up, which is sheeted with copper so that it can't be bugged. It has sliding steel doors, a foot thick, three sets of them. And only six people have the key that will open or close them. It has videotape machines, TV relay, pressbutton controls for instant data retrieval on every one of twenty armchairs. You name it, they have it. And the checks run on the boys who work the electronics in that room would make the CIA look like nuns on a school picnic in the boondocks. It cost half a million dollars, and those guys think it's worth it. I don't make the rules. I just play them.'

'They're more worried than I've ever seen them in the agencies,' said Westbrook, still conscious that his thunder of six months ago was being stolen. 'I lunched with Hamish the other day. They're going over their art and copy teams with a fine toothcomb since someone leaked a campaign. They put up a notice in the loo. Careless Talk Costs Accounts.'

'Message understood,' said Michael. 'Take a look around, Earl. See what you think we need to do as a start. Put it on paper.'

'Naturally,' said Sanger drily. 'Nothing sacred?'

'Nothing,' said Michael. 'But no copies of your report. Just one for me. Handwritten.'

'Good security breaks many backs,' said Sanger.

'We'll see,' said Michael. 'And as for these. . . .' Brusquely he indicated the scattered files. 'If we can think of a course of action, well. . . .'

'We will think,' said Sanger, 'while breaking bones.'

Michael smiled and shook his head. 'At times, Earl, I think you are a touch too peachy-keen.'

'Depends on your point of view,' said the American. He raised his shoulders. 'If you believe that the better a company performs, the better it is for those who work inside it. . . .'

Michael nodded, accepting the point. There was nothing wrong with Sanger's rationale, but the man's enjoyment of the game gave logic another dimension. For Sanger, business was persuasive poetry, a thesaurus of philosophy, and the bigger the organisation the more his yearning would match it. The words of management's modern dictionary were quicksilver on his tongue: appraisals and structures and deficit costings and markets. The prospectus of a course in business education could stir him as pages of Dylan Thomas or a Beethoven score or the sayings of Mao might move other men.

'Peachy or not,' said Michael, 'you're just sharper at the game than most of the others.'

'In my situation,' said Sanger, 'I have to be.'

'I've got an idea or two,' said Westbrook. He wasn't sure he had at that moment, but he managed to switch the drift of talk. If only the pain in his head would go away. 'Anything else?' he asked.

'Nothing,' said Michael. The cable in his pocket was not for discussion with Westbrook yet, nor even with Sanger. It had been sent from a city in New Jersey, and said simply: COMING AS ARRANGED.

＊

They were due to meet out of town, unwilling to break their habit of using the luncheon board as a negotiation table, but satisfied that no one who knew them would be likely to observe their meal together. Lymington's taxi headed east towards

Canning Town. As the East India Dock Road began, so did the jumble of quite passable Chinese restaurants. Inside one, Charles was waiting. They had used it before.

Lymington allowed his overcoat to be taken from him, feeling the usual conflict of mood. The adolescent excitement, the tension which meant the ball was in play again, this he almost enjoyed; but there was also the general unease which always afflicted him when he lunched in places like this. He would have preferred the club: obsequious service, known faces, worn leather, the slow tick of the clock in the reading-room. Marble staircases and busts of Palmerston and Disraeli were part of the world which still made him tread with confidence.

Today his unease was more deep-rooted. Like most professional diplomats, he acutely disliked having to take decisions. His whole background screamed for the comforting altar of memoranda which argued around cases; those exquisite rationalisations of conflicting policies which delayed, sometimes for ever, the need for action. To have to make decisions which were hasty was even more loathsome, and the telephone call two evenings ago had forced a decision that was very hurried indeed. Except that in effect the choice had been made for him, since he had no options open. He wished Armfield had not chosen this week of all weeks to make him perform one of the particular tasks by which he earned his keep.

'Good to see you again, Giles,' said Charles. 'How is Esther?'

'As well as can be expected,' said Lymington. 'She cares little for England in February.'

'Are you going away?'

'You forget,' said Lymington. 'Business. We keep at it.'

They ordered Peking duck. It was the only Chinese food which Lymington truly enjoyed. He was appalled at the rash of restaurants serving Cantonese slush which now covered the country. Chop suey and chips. Peasant food. He grimaced.

For a time, while pale tea was poured into delicate cups, handleless, they fenced. Empty words about empty people; the trivia of acquaintances, rumoured ministerial iniquities, dinner parties attended or ignored. The leavings of the meal had been removed before the questions which mattered were finally put.

'Two years to go, then,' said Lymington.

'Yes.'

'Looking forward to it?'

'Mixed feelings,' said Charles. 'I shall miss it, I expect, but things aren't what they were.'

They had talked about it often. Like Lymington, he would not be averse to leaving the service of Government. Once, Whitehall had been different. They had understood the protocol, the careful manoeuvring, the deference, the network, the whole catalogue of rules. They even liked the passages of the old palaces and houses where the servants of Government conducted their business, decorous honeycombs in whose dark angles files might for ever gather dust in disregarded cabinets whilst aged men walked reverently around them guiding trolleys piled with still more tape-tied bundles headed for uncertain destinations. Now there were too many northern grammar-school boys in a hurry, shoving and sweating, shouting at the world to judge them on merit, openly scornful of salary scales, demanding to know what lay beyond.

'I know what you mean,' said Lymington.

'I shall enjoy getting my teeth into something new,' said Charles.

There was no need for them to discuss the remark or its implications. Charles trusted him and he knew that with Bernard Grant's help, he could deliver the goods. As an adviser in certain spheres, his friend would be invaluable to the organisation. Charles had talent and contacts. A couple of statutory years after retirement, a directorship or two would blossom. It was satisfactory, sensible, for the benefit of business and the nation. Meantime the machinery must be kept ticking over. There was nothing in the rules which said Charles could not own shares in companies with whose contracts he was not involved. Charles now owned many shares. There was no conflict of interest.

'Good,' said Lymington. 'We need chaps like you. All-rounders. There are too many specialists. Can't see the wood for the trees.' Michael Grant could think as he damn well pleased, prattling on like a child about organisation structures and all that American pseudo-science. Some men were leaders, born to it. You had the trick or you hadn't, and that was that. Bernard Grant understood it well. A good man for a foreigner, Bernard: not crude, doing the right things, appreciating the country of his adoption and its ways. Many meetings, many lunches with his chairman had cemented their partnership. A strange man, nevertheless, Grant. Mercurial, was that the word? *My dear Giles, your value we know. Your people are our people.* Then, the glitter from beneath the overbearing brows. *Besides, old chap, you are trustworthy, and trust in these days is rare in business. You won't tell things to the newspapers, eh?* The laughter, ricocheting wildly, would follow. A strange man, undoubtedly, with strange friends; old artists and silent young writers with burning eyes and too much hair.

'You're right,' said Charles. 'The schools don't make leaders nowadays. Pity. A generation of swots or layabouts.'

'Yes,' said Lymington. 'Now, about Brasserton's.'

'No problem, if I'm any judge,' said Charles. 'Your line of country. Your track record is good. Your prices have been fair in the past. You deliver on time. A powerful case.'

'This one is very important,' said Lymington. 'I don't mean only the money.'

'I understand,' said Charles. 'It will be in the public interest, no doubt of that. The chairman of the committee listens to me. . . .'

'The competition?' asked Lymington.

'Not likely to be successful. I'll keep an eye on things. Rely on me.'

'I'll drink to that,' said Lymington, raising his cognac.

The strong adrenalin of relief and reassurance engulfed him, but his head ached, and the worry of the last day or so, the other matters, would not leave him. He looked at the shining face of his friend, the tears of sweat below the bald dome. Nothing was ever finished in this damned game. Another thought, not new, returned to nag him. Men like his friend, who knew where the line between helpfulness and corruption should be drawn, were rare in Whitehall. Who would there be when Charles had gone?

*

Michael Grant lay back low in his seat, arms straight before him, slightly bent at the elbow. Once a race-driver, always a race-driver. Second nature. He felt secure: padded on all sides; a vertical column of dials to his left which gave him the feel of an aircraft cockpit; six point three litres, vee eight, to shift him.

Despite the February drizzle and the crunch of incipient ice on the surface he took even the roundabouts fast, enjoying the hug of four-wheel drive on the ground, jabbing hard at the accelerator as the FF hit the short straight stretches of the A4 again. As he thrust his foot, the automatic transmission jumped gears and fed fat power to the wheels. He had given up the boy-racer yen for gear levers long ago, as he had also chosen a smooth Jensen to drive rather than something as hairy as a Ferrari. In present-day London, too much hairiness in a car was pointlessly romantic and foolishly frustrating. His commonsense constrained his fantasies. He remembered Jim Clark, before his death,

95

arriving among the baleful forests of the Nurburgring in an automatic Galaxie, and one of the flat-topped hangers-on with a Knightsbridge voice affecting surprise. 'Only idiots wear their wrists out when they don't have to,' Clark had said in his low, careful tones.

There was little traffic around in the dead mid-afternoon of Saturday winter. The weekend drivers were spread before TV sets and firesides or had long ago ploughed through the murk to stand and curse on the chipped terraces of football grounds, gladdening the mad hour with a filed coin or two cast at visiting goalkeepers, groaning in orgasms of despair or exhaling fast dirty chants for light relief.

He was always exhilarated inside the car. The power was one thing. Jensen, Porsche, Aston or Maserati, just a few particular marques, they placed you beyond ordinary men and automobiles. There was no need even to try and carve the other cars. You drove alone, totally isolated, passing the pack without effort. Sometimes, when he was preoccupied, a souped-up admass saloon would bang past him, exhaust clamouring in a pretence of power. Then he might respond, slicing through on the inside of a tight bend, going close to the other car, gaining simple satisfaction at the failure of the flash driver's nerve. Weekend cowboys. Yobs in tin cans. He knew their smirks as they frightened timid clerks out on Sunday excursions with the kids. He felt almost a crusader when he could make them sweat some too.

The stereo tape-player, eight-track, emitted the 1812 softly. He turned up the volume. The melodrama of brass and percussion suited the way he felt. It had been a good week. Hardy's paper made sense. It would be great to be mixed up with a racing team again, even though it was unlikely he would dare to drive himself. To win his father over to acquiring the company would be difficult enough; and Lord Bender would need guarantees. No point in complicating the issue, yet. He knew what they would say, of course: playboy Grant wanting to pick up a new plaything. Crap, he told himself. Didn't they know he'd taken his first ride on an American racetrack – a drag strip before he'd graduated to sports cars – to earn money, the dollars which his father had pettishly denied him?

He hoped Corsino's plane would be on time, not caught in the stacking which at Heathrow as at Kennedy nowadays made every journey a gamble of timing. He wanted no nonsenses on this deal. It could be the justification of many things: his

American journeys, his training, his methods. To organise companies according to modern precepts of management – and who the hell cared if they came from America or Mars? – need not mean the demise of flair. Even long-term strategies paid off in short-term results sometimes. His father and the old thinkers around the table needed this demonstration.

Sometimes he sang in the car, insulated, private, shouting his head off. Sometimes he talked. It was like a room in a house, or a whole house in itself. The release was tremendous. 'Bloody amateur,' he said now, aloud. That was for Lymington, who still called him 'boy' from time to time. Men like Lymington offended his sense of justice: the boneless wonders of the old-chap networks, smugly inferring their knowledge of the world, an army of one-time generals, diplomats, minor aristocrats and spent politicians placed on boards for outmoded reasons of status, justified in theory by the all-round view they were supposed to offer. All-round nothing. Their well-fed bellies and inflated notions of their own importance merely obscured the view for the professionals, the managers who knew what it was all about.

His father was too far into the game to abandon the traditions now. An entrepreneur of genius, maybe, but with delusions of grandeur rampant; not what an organisation like the Prospero Group needed in the next ten years. He didn't dislike the old man. He smiled apologetically. Cruel to be kind. But truly the time for flamboyant personal gestures in business was finished. Now you had to think about people not in the old-time way of patting them on the head once a year and giving them hand-outs for good behaviour, but in creating structures within which they could find fulfilment and satisfaction, perhaps in ideas like joint consultation or employee share-holdings; industrial justice which could be seen to be just. No jobs for creeps like Lymington; no jobs for the boys like Fielder. Jobs for those who merited them. Without all this, Michael believed that the Prospero Group would disintegrate and die, as he believed all such companies would. To him, the grand-scale entrepreneurs from the past – his father included – were the dinosaurs of the day.

That was only half-true, though; of course it was. There was something else. Michael Grant had come to understand it in himself, even to control it, but never to forget. Why had the old man not come with them to England all those years ago? Why had his father been so unforgivably inefficient as to get trapped – two days too late to get out of Vienna? The years of happiness with his mother, tinged with the growing realisation that without

Bernard she was only half a woman, were sharply remembered still. She would have lived, he knew, if his father had been there.

Then there were the years in the institution when wartime England had imagined him to be an orphan: the grim dormitories and ill-fitting uniforms, the smell of carbolic and the aura of unforgiving godliness, the unchanging weekly rota of meals compounded from Spam, margarine-smeared bread, dried eggs, dried potatoes and unthinkable parts of animals' insides. There were rules, and punishments, for everything. If he did not eat a course at one meal, which frequently he did not, he would get nothing at the next until he finished off what he had refused – after standing with it in his hand in a bleak corridor during the hours between. He remembered too the indignity of the three-weekly inspection for lice. Twice they found nits in his hair and his scalp was smothered in blue ointment which smelled foul enough to make him retch. When his father had finally tracked him down, in 1946, his feelings were mixed, poised between relief at his escape and indignation that the strange man who took him away was in part the author of his misfortunes. Michael still had this ambivalence of emotion, though at times he admitted to himself his own unfairness.

It was futile to grow angry again with it. He slid smoothly through the last roundabout before the airport, drove fast for another minute or so, then turned right at traffic lights, past the Ariel Hotel, and added his car to the dozen parked near the Bowl.

To his surprise, Corsino was already inside, sipping coffee, black briefcase on the seat next to him, watching the players pushing their bowls down the lanes. The briefcase jarred slightly, but Corsino had had the sense to dress informally. His sports jacket was rust, faintly checked, the trousers a pale shade of grey. He rose as Michael approached, smiling, his olive face creased as though it had often been slept in.

'You look in great shape, Ed,' Michael said. 'Have you been waiting long?'

'Fifteen minutes. Don't give it a thought. The plane was early.'

'Miracles never cease,' said Michael. 'Thanks for coming. The trip's on me. And I'm sorry about this.' He waved a hand round the bowl. A jukebox brayed. A girl bent to tie her bowling shoes, breasts hanging, hair falling, lower backside like an apple.

'Hell, I like it! The view is great.' The American threw back

98

his head and laughed. 'What are you apologising for, Michael? I love leaving the kids at weekends and flying three thousand miles just to go bowling with you. I do it all the time.'

Michael checked himself. The crucial questions could wait. 'It'll be worth it,' he said.

'Sure. But why here?'

'Assuming we can't do this on the phone, and I don't think we can, there was no sense in your coming into town,' said Michael. 'Besides, we might be seen. I wouldn't want that till we're certain.'

'Why not the airport?'

Michael had considered that too. He remembered a business soap opera on TV. There was a scene in which the joke tycoon interviewed a brain-drain researcher who could give him important information. The chosen rendezvous was a restaurant at Kennedy. The idea was secrecy and speed. Superficially sensible, but not if you thought about it. Major airports were like business clubs these days, the waiting-rooms of the world. Too dangerous, except for the purposes of television scriptwriters, stuffing their sketchy plots between the ads.

'I've scarcely yet been through London Airport or Kennedy or, for that matter, Orly without bumping into someone I know. Not secure, in my view. How about you?'

'You play games nicely,' said Corsino.

'And no self-respecting English businessman would be seen dead in a bowling-alley on a Saturday afternoon,' said Michael.

'In America, not so certain,' said Corsino. 'Don't try it in New Jersey.'

'I'll remember that.'

'But here, it's fine, if you say so. I like it. The damnedest board-room I've ever seen.'

Michael walked to the counter, picked up two cups of coffee, and came back. Corsino carefully shook a sweetener into the black liquid. Michael added nothing. Corsino stirred the fizzing spot in the centre of his cup before he spoke.

'By the way,' he said. 'You have a deal. Provided we can agree on one or two general principles. I've brought the draft papers.'

'Fine,' said Michael. He had sensed the man's eagerness once Ed had offered to fly to him. This was what he had played Corsino for over the past year. He knew he had pitched the price right, knew Brasserton's had the capacity to get the order through in time, though the installation of the computer could make things sticky. With Corsino, time was important. Delivery schedules would have to be kept. God help Oldershaw if he fell down on this one. Casually he said: 'How's Marjorie?'

'Great,' said Corsino. 'Just great. Damn it, do you know she sold four of her pictures last week? Seven hundred and fifty bucks for things she knocked off in a couple of weekends. I've told her I'll let her keep me soon.'

'I'm glad,' said Michael. 'You're a lucky man. Beauty *and* talent.'

Corsino reached for the briefcase. 'Take a look at the papers. You can see where your company fits in with the whole scheme. Date schedule, specifications, the lot.'

'Not my line,' said Michael. 'Not as a specialist, you understand.'

'I know,' said Corsino. 'But you can check out the main plot. If that's clear, then okay. Your Chancellor will be proud of you.'

Michael flicked a crumb from the table and grinned. 'Yeah. Another Export plaque to hang on the wall. I'm pitching for a K.'

'Uh?' said Corsino.

'Sorry, Ed. Private English joke. It means they get to call you Sir something. Reward for noble fellows, arse-licking politicians and diplomats who are past it.'

'Are you kidding?' Corsino slapped his back. 'If you get to be *Sir* Michael, let me know. We'll make you a vice-president of our organisation.'

'I'll keep you to that,' said Michael.

For fifteen minutes they shuffled through papers which the American produced, talking easily. When they had finished, in agreement, Corsino leaned back on his chair and glanced at his watch.

'What do you plan to do, Ed?'

'Three hours to plane time. Too early to eat yet.' He jerked a thumb towards the lanes. 'Feel like a game?'

'You're joking.'

'Nope. Come on. The kids drag me to an alley sometimes. I like it.'

'If you really want to, Ed. How can I say no when you've come all this way just for the game?'

Corsino laughed easily. 'You wouldn't want to hear about how I'm shooting at golf, I suppose?'

'No,' said Michael. This was a standing joke between them. 'I just can't bear seeing a grown man cry.'

'Great,' said Corsino. 'You bloody charming Englishmen. You'd con your own grandmothers.'

Michael paid for the bowling-shoes at the counter and they went to their lane. He had bowled very occasionally when he was in America, seven or eight years ago. Week-night college stuff, when a gang of them had roared off in relief from their books. He hadn't been able to do much of that, not on the small allowance to which Bernard had limited him. No big nights out with the boys. No happy weekends in motels with girls. He had made it twice with the Bostonian called Nancy, sweating on a cheap bed, no air-conditioning and no swimming-pool outside, on steamy summer evenings. At the time it had seemed satisfactory, but lacking the glamour that such illicit consummation should have possessed. He supposed they might have become happily married if his father hadn't stopped him. He had heard not one syllable from Nancy in six years.

Corsino was good, smooth as ice where Michael felt awkward handling the heavy bowls again. As they rolled their way through half an hour, Corsino scored strike after strike. Each time the ten pins went down he shouted 'Pow!' like a schoolboy. Not much different from the English, Michael thought. Even the Stock Exchange could seem at times like an old men's kindergarten. Once he had watched a broker spend ten minutes flicking bread pellets with meticulous marksmanship at his colleagues around the hall, feigning absorption with papers as each missile found its target. Michael's bowl landed several times in the gully at the side of the lane and he felt very foolish.

'Hey! Like this,' said Corsino. He took Michael's shoulders in his hands, placed him square on to the pins, then made him walk through the movement, balancing the bowl correctly. 'That's better. Nice and easy. Get the rhythm. Let the ball do the work. Don't push it.' He was like one of those peppy and dedicated American football coaches, thought Michael. 'Say,' said the American, 'do you know these lanes cost at least fifteen or twenty thousand dollars each? Twenty-four of them here. Around half a million dollars in the lanes alone. Do they make money in this country?'

Michael didn't really know. He had seen something recently about bowling-alleys closing down. So he shrugged and stalled. He was too concerned with getting his game right, since he was not a good loser, and if he had to lose, wanted to do so with some style. Towards the end of their time, he was knocking down seven or eight pins at the first attempt.

101

'You've got it,' said Corsino. 'Let's see a strike on the last frame.'

'Some hope,' said Michael, but he cooled every muscle as he prepared to take his four-pace approach. It was the old trick he had perfected when racing. The still pool of total calmness, total control, before the start. Carefully balanced, he flowed into his stride. The heavy ball skidded down the shining yellow wood and the clatter of pins sounded.

'Plumb left of centre,' shouted Corsino. 'That's it.'

He was wrong. Nine pins tumbled, flashing under the lights. The tenth rocked, hesitated, but did not fall.

5. One kind of politician

ARMFIELD did not like parties, neither those staged in pursuit of business, nor those which were primarily social. The latter he avoided, since the avoidance was usually within his control. He attended the first kind because sometimes he had to, though he saw no reason why they were necessary and regretted the latter-day convention which encouraged them. That they were customarily dignified with the title of 'receptions' did nothing to mitigate his distaste. Deals should be hazarded and bargains, if necessary, struck around tables, in the cool clear light of day, with or without food, not in the evening half-haze induced by too many drinks and indigestive canapés. His legs ached when he had to stand too long, clutching his ritual glass, and this made him uncertain of temper.

By such tomfoolery, he believed, was business demeaned. He had noticed a trend at occasions arranged by a minority of the newer, brasher companies for there to be present a few girls who had no apparent place in the executive or staff structure. It would be an exaggeration to say that anyone who could not be slotted into an organisation chart did not, in Armfield's eyes, exist. But his passion for orderliness was extreme, and girls of this kind, in an office context, offended it. These girls spoke little, just hovered; sometimes they served drinks. It was half-jestingly suggested on one occasion that two of them were the mistresses of senior directors.

'That's what they like one to think, anyway,' an acquaintance told him. 'The directors, I mean. I think they're both past it, frankly. They're too interested in money to have time for *that*. A new kind of status symbol, Harold, that's all these girls are. You ought to get one for Christmas.'

Armfield was not amused. Women of self-assurance, confident in the currency of their brains or their breasts, made him uneasy. He did not believe in talking to them seriously, and he floundered

103

when the conversation was frothy. He could not credit, as the heavy Sundays were always suggesting, that a determined storm-troop division of women, possessed both of business sense and sexuality, would one day force their way into the boardroom. But he was glad that he would have left the battlefield for his house near Dartmouth in Devonshire if ever the conquest happened.

This evening's party put him at maximum disadvantage, since it fitted exactly neither of the categories which he recognised. It was one of the occasional affairs which Bernard Grant held to, as he put it, keep in touch with his executives and their families – which could only mean their wives, since children had not yet been invited. Bolted on to the family party this time was the attendance of a considerable flock belonging to what might loosely be called the Cultural Establishment. Grant had just made a generous gift to a prize fund for novelists. That was Bernard's business, of course, but the ensuing influx of ageing publishers, agents, literary parasites and socialising dons, grey hair flowing freely at the neck, eyes prickly with wit or malice, only compounded Armfield's uncertainty. He felt, or imagined he felt, that the university teachers exuded a contrived yet controlled assumption of superiority: men who behaved as if they were intellectually a cut above nuts-and-bolts business, neighing endlessly about Vietnam or black Africa or the lost Kennedys, clucking long words as they assessed Grant's Picassos. He wanted to tell them that they would need to go short of their colleges, their festivals, their sponsored voyages to Greek islands and lost cities of the Middle East were it not for men like himself who really created wealth. He wanted to tell them to quantify what they had to say.

Instead, he found himself cornered by a dumpy woman with frizzy grey hair. Howland, the elegant PRO, introduced her as a novelist, though Armfield suspected she was much more: a general busybody maybe. He vaguely recognised the face, from television perhaps. That was what it looked like; a television discussion face, a *Panorama* face, a face through which to parade the conscience in ten million hot-chocolate-drinking homes. She opened fire at once, spraying Armfield with machine-gun bursts of words.

'I regard it as a good thing, parties like this. A meeting of the two sides,' she said, confident that Armfield would be much improved by her opinions. 'The brains and the men of action brought together. Useful. What do you do, Mr Armfield?'

'I'm deputy managing director.' Armfield never said he was *one* of the deputy managing directors.

'Ah, but what do you *do*? What does to deputy manage and deputy direct *mean*? A title can signify anything you want it to. I've no great faith in handles myself.' She peered at him closely, a believer in spade-calling, proclaiming to the world that she was no respecter of persons until they showed themselves worthy of respect.

'I'm mainly concerned with the financial dealings of our organisation. And I play my part in board decisions generally. The exercise of judgement.'

'Decisions,' she said. 'Yes. You're all great men for decisions, I understand. Twenty decisions a day. What's your score of right ones?'

'I don't think I keep count,' said Armfield. 'As good or bad as most I expect.' Howland found himself silently cheering for his superior, which was a rare feeling. This gorgon brought out the best in Armfield. Funny.

'The ethics, that's what interests me,' she said. 'Who do you think of? Your shareholders, your workers? There's the rub. Not always reconcilable, I fancy. Do you believe in employee participation, Mr Armfield? It will have to come, I suppose. Are you in the vanguard?'

'Our operating companies make their own policies, very much so. We have good schemes. Pensions, recreation, the usual thing.'

Armfield didn't know much about such matters and didn't want to know. As the assault continued, he looked darkly at Howland. He believed that PROs should protect their employers from encounters like this. Howland played with his watch-chain, very cool. He might not have been there so far as the woman was concerned. She burned away at Armfield, and without open rudeness neither man could turn the attack.

Hardy, bent with pleasure, drew the attention of Sheila Travis to the encounter. 'She'll eat him alive,' he said. 'I recognise the type. Writes a letter to *The Times* every week and one to the *New Statesman* on high days and holidays. For bread she turns out novels plump with platonic girls whose profiles are noble and whose eyes are dark, grave and unsmiling, what else?'

'Poor devil,' she said. 'Armfield, that is.'

'No need for pity. It's good for his soul.'

'Who's the redhead?' she asked.

'Alison Bennett. A new PRO.'

'I thought so. David's told me about her.'

'Has he?' said Hardy. The inflection of the question was carefully balanced, and Hardy knew that it was so, even if he was unsure whether he wanted to go through with the ploy. He seemed to be inviting further questions, but implying that he would be uneasy about answering them. Standard wife-bait.

'He keeps me in touch,' said Sheila, a suggestion of offence in her voice. 'Why shouldn't he?'

Hardy smiled, spread his hands. 'Okay, young lovers. No reason. I insinuate nothing.'

'I assume they haven't slipped between sheets yet,' she said.

At that moment, on this level of direct verbal sparring, Hardy could have killed suspicion stone-dead. Half of his mind even wanted to do so, but he went right on riding the rollers. He enjoyed the nervous thrill of mental surfing.

'Not so far as I know,' he said, 'and most things around this place I know.' The *most* was gently emphasised; the bait still bobbed.

'I feel better for that,' said Sheila ironically. Hardy plunged on regardless.

'Good,' he said. 'The time for you to start worrying is when David isn't moved by an inviting thigh. I'd say he was a thigh man, myself. Aren't we all, these days? Business is no friend of sex, though. Too much business dries up the juices.'

'I wouldn't say that was any problem yet for David,' said Sheila. 'He has all the natural appetites.'

'No,' said Hardy. 'I hope I didn't imply he hadn't. He is not what I would call under-sexed.'

The conversation had come full-circle. From appearing to defend his friend from accusations of unfaithfulness, Hardy had moved easily to a position where he could assert David's virility. It was all accomplished in a minute or so. Had he been narcissistic, Hardy would have paused to admire his handiwork. Instead, he drove in the hook.

'Take no notice of me,' he said seriously. 'I play games all the time. But wives should never take husbands for granted, nor husbands their wives. Hardy's marriage guidance bureau. We never closed.'

Sheila both wanted to know more and not to. She knew Hardy for what he was: a stirrer who enjoyed being chef. She looked across the room and saw David talking to the Westbrooks. She had no wish that Hardy should imagine he had her panting on further information.

'How is Teresa?' she asked. 'I thought she'd be here.' Hardy's

106

wife she had met only once, a quiet girl, Dublin-toned, who was a nurse until her marriage.

'Not her scene at all,' said Hardy, 'but she comes when she can. We live a bit too far out, though, and then there are the kids.' He grinned. 'How are *you* doing?'

Sheila looked down. 'This shindig,' she said, 'is positively my last appearance this season. On the office front, certainly.'

'The home front,' said Hardy, also looking down, 'seems to be doing fine.'

Westbrook caught sight of one of the business journalists he lunched with from time to time. He wasn't sure precisely what he would say to the man, only that he might need a friendly ear in the next few weeks. The Lovelace business, the need to get Supergear off the floor again, these things would call for skilful handling, and he knew he might not be able to use Howland's contacts in either affair.

'Excuse me a moment, Diana,' he said.

David made as if to follow him, but Diana Westbrook put out a hand. 'Don't leave me to the mercy of the intellectuals,' she said.

Westbrook had already darted away. 'He might need me,' said David.

She signalled a waiter to stop, lifted a glass from the tray, and carefully sipped gin. The pause diminished the tension in his muscles, but did nothing for the question in his stomach. 'Lionel needs very little,' she said.

Then she turned, inviting him to walk with her. 'Let's look the town over. I've been wanting a talk with you.'

He followed, ill at ease, and they looked out through the glass wall. The solitary building nearby, lower down, was mostly in darkness. A late office light or two burned. Inside one window a man in braces stood up, screwed a piece of paper in his hand, then flopped back again into a chair. As he leaned back his head disappeared, cut off by the angle, and all they could see were the hands placed together, straight out on the desk, as if in prayer. On a higher floor, a woman in a flowered overall lifted a small box from a table and groped round it with a duster. In the arc northwards there were sprays of radiance in places – Trafalgar Square, Piccadilly, Oxford Street – and gobs of blackness between. Below them were streaks of light on the wet Embankment. London ought to look better from above, he thought.

'Not much of a view, is it?' she said.

'Snap,' said David. 'Just what I was thinking.'

107

'New York does it better.

'I don't know it,' he said to encourage her, wondering what the hell she really wanted to say. He understood the score with the Westbrooks better now, but was uncertain what he should do if invited to climb into the ring, either as referee or combatant.

'In London we switch off more than we switch on when it gets dark,' said Diana. 'In New York they make it look like Disneyland, even the places where they'll mug you for a few dollars in daylight.'

'So I hear.'

'Early evening's the best time. Maybe you drive back from Long Island, and if it's a red sky you see all Manhattan spread out in front of you, from Wall Street at one end, way up towards Central Park at the other. The skyscrapers get flattened against the sky, very black. They don't look real, more of a preposterous cut-out backcloth in a musical. Then you get nearer, the sun finally goes, and it's like someone has thrown a master-switch. The lights in the buildings come on together and – I don't know quite how to put it – but all those squashed buildings suddenly leap out at you and they're foursquare, slim or plump. Great cones of green and red and golden light carving out their shapes. All that effort and money. It's like an aspiration, do you see? Meantime the garbage men are probably on strike and a few hundred people are getting a knife in their gut in Harlem, and maybe the fuzz is tossing CS gas at Columbia. That's the bit you don't always see.'

He didn't know what to say, but the way she looked demanded a response. 'You should have been a reporter,' he said. 'You've got me hooked. Perhaps your husband will send me.'

'No doubt of it, one day,' she said. He gripped his glass a little tighter. He sensed the small talk was over.

She looked at him carefully, thin eyebrows lifting towards the unnaturally unwrinkled forehead. 'You're beginning the ride.'

'How?' he said.

'I think Lionel means that you should take off. I'm sure you will, with or without him. Decide the speed you want to fly at and stick to it.'

He was embarrassed, not sure he wanted to submit even to this kind of ego massage. 'If God had meant us to fly, he would have given us airline tickets,' he said, trying an old and somewhat desperate joke.

'It doesn't go with your eyes,' she said. 'One hipster is enough on the Westbrook team. Leave the humour to Hardy.'

108

This woman was too damned sharp. 'Sorry,' he said, 'but I didn't quite know *what* to say.' He was wondering: Why am I doing this honesty bit?

She smiled, trying to dispel his unease, the light glancing off her underlip. She honest to God is pretty good, he thought, and she remembers every lesson Mummy taught her. Make yourself attractive to the nice gentleman, dear. Run your tongue over your lips, then speak.

'I understand,' she said. 'I'm not being very fair. I just feel like saying it.'

He shrugged, feeling in control once more, now oddly wanting to drive her on. 'I'm just not used to pep-talks from directors' wives.'

'I am not a director's wife,' Diana said calmly. 'I am *me*. And I am not trying to seduce you either, though I gather that's mandatory for the director's wife in the usual evolution of this particular scenario. I'm just saying, in my old-fashioned way, that you mustn't let them drain you. They'll try, because that's the game. Unhappy marriages mean men work harder for the organisation. They don't want to go home. It's a common enough theory.'

'I've read the book.'

'You're a big boy, David, so listen. It can be a good life without going the whole hog. You dictate the pace, not them.'

He gave in, nodded seriously. 'I take the point. I'll watch it. And thanks.'

She turned away from the window and said. 'People will say we're in love. Let's find your wife.'

'Yes,' he said. 'And don't laugh at my jokes too much.'

'Good,' said Diana. 'I'm glad you know the words.'

'Of course. Thanks again.'

She looked at him with the slightly crooked smile he now recognised. 'If Sheila weren't so nice, I might easily have felt like making you.'

What have I got to lose, he thought. 'I would have liked that,' he said. Then, to cover up fast if necessary. 'About the other – I mean I *will* watch it. But I'm not devious. I'm Lionel's man, you know, if that helps.'

'Just so long as you're not his boy,' she said.

A wall of bodies surrounded Bernard Grant. He was playing a fast rally with a professor from one of the newer universities whose income from television punditry, magazines and innumerable advisory posts made the stipend received from his academic station seem like beer money.

'But why not television?' said the don. 'Chancy at the time, I give you, but a good risk for men of judgement.'

'Not so,' said Grant. 'A few lush years, and then the squeeze. They're so busy fighting off restrictions, levies and government bear-hugs these days that running a television company must long ago have ceased to be fun.'

The don smiled, knowing he had not lost the point. 'But in the early days, socialistic legislation could not have been foreseen. So why weren't you in on it?'

'Too boring,' said Grant. He was in good form, long since used to the irony that it was in this room he had shrivelled from the coronary a few months ago. 'I would have wanted real control, not merely one way to a quick hundred thousand or so. At that time I had not the money to ensure control. I enjoyed buying a small publishing house more. Room to be creative, and no huckstering. That would surely meet with your approval, as a man of letters?' Grant twisted the tail of the sentence into light sarcasm.

'Your shareholders might not agree with you,' said the don.

'Shareholders? They must allow *me* to be fulfilled also. Else, would I feel like making money for them?'

'It's their investments you use,' said the don.

Grant spread his hands in a parody of gentle rejection. 'It is the money of a few large shareholders that counts. Like Benjamin here.' He motioned towards Lord Bender. 'That is the true dynamic of business. The small men – well, they are important, but they are encouraged sometimes to believe they are *too* important. Gadflies at annual meetings, that is all.'

'Hush,' said the don. 'Is that what you would have me tell my students?'

'You new men of the business schools are plotters more avid than anyone in this building.' Grant laughed, enjoying himself hugely. 'The intrigue of a university, which is the most poisonous of all, mixed in with the usual conspiracies of company men. How do you survive?'

'We buy Lord Bender's personal accident policies,' the don said. 'In vast quantities. We favour in particular those premiums which give cover against accidents caused by sharp instruments wielded from behind. Then we can enjoy luxurious convalescences.'

'I like it,' said Grant, acknowledging his opponent's skills. 'We must keep Benjamin's funds topped up. For all our sakes.'

'You may have ignored commercial television,' said the don,

110

anxious for a final thrust, which was totally amiable in the context of this conversation, 'but I hear you have taken out options in the radio field.'

'Ah,' said Grant, mischievously, 'I understand from your Vice-Chancellor that you wanted to be a disc jockey. And I like to look after my friends.'

There was laughter all round. That was the thing about a Grant party. It was almost as good as nuts and port in the Senior Common Room after a high table feast at Oxford; provided you could take a few barbed jokes, provided you let Grant make most of them.

At the edge of the circle, Gerald Fielder laughed too. Then he resumed his efforts to infiltrate. An MP, who had miraculously stayed silent as Grant and the don wrestled, looked haughtily at him. Fielder turned away. It was the third group around which he had hovered without a word being addressed to him. Well, not quite. He had plunged at the second knot of people he'd approached, desperately foreseeing how disastrous the evening would be, yet unable to control his desire to be welcomed in. 'Good evening. I'm Gerald Fielder. Part of the organisation.' A thin man, dressed as stiffly as a Guards officer, had murmured 'Oh yes?' before resuming his conversation with a girl in yellow trouser-suit and a cleric who acted suspiciously South Bank radical.

Fielder stood still, wondering why he had bothered. Perhaps it would have been better had he not come. He dipped a finger in his sweet vermouth to fish out the cherry and looked hopefully for friends.

'The pathos of rejection,' Hardy told David. 'See him stand and ponder the future. Don't look so bloody sorry for him. He's coming over.'

'I don't mind,' said David. 'Why is he here?'

'Just happened to be in town and smelled the liquor,' said Hardy. 'He'll try special pleading. Beware.'

'Give the poor sod a chance,' said David quietly, then: 'Hello Gerald.'

'A strange do, this,' said Fielder. 'Who *are* all these people?'

'The drones of the metropolis,' said Hardy. 'You've heard of them up in your territory, surely.'

'We're not still in woad,' said Fielder irritably. 'I don't like freeloaders, that's all. Especially when they act like they own the place.'

'Tell it to Harold Armfield,' said Hardy. 'He'll love you for it.'

111

'They keep the Chairman happy,' said David. 'Good for business.'

'Please yourself,' said Fielder. 'When are you coming up to see us?'

'In a week or two.'

Fielder looked crossly at Hardy, wishing him away. 'You won't find much wrong. We're just as swinging as when you left – though we miss you.'

'I'm not a *Gauleiter*, Gerald. I'm supposed to help, not just sniff round for fiddles in the books.'

'I believe you,' said Fielder. 'Thousands wouldn't. Look, just let me know when. I really would like the chance for a *proper* chat. There's a lot you ought to know. Perhaps we could have a meal or something?'

'Surely,' said David. 'I'd like that.'

'Isn't that your wife?' Fielder asked. Sheila was talking to Diana Westbrook. David nodded. 'I must say hello.'

'What did I tell you?' said Hardy, as Fielder moved on. 'You'll get the whole sob-story. And if he reckons he can't win you, he'll start hinting at the size of the handshake he'd like.'

Karian found himself face to face with Lady Lymington. Life was like that. She was bony, breastless and very tall. He wished he were somewhere far away. The business of the Burgham shares sat like a raven on his shoulder.

'I hope you are enjoying the party, Mr Karian,' she said, smiling. Her face folded into a parcel of lines when she did that, the sort of lines which had grown from social smiles, produced with effort, at a lifetime of receptions round the world.

'Oh yes,' he said.

'It is distinctly my kind of party. Quite like old times.' That, Karian imagined, meant she was pleased to have the straight dose of business sweetened with the sugar-water of the intelligentsia. She never seemed to like her husband's business associates very much, smiling coolly through Grant's receptions, a glacial memsahib used to command, always poised to clap her hands and summon the native labour. 'They talk my language, you see,' she said, towering over Karian. 'I have never really gained an understanding of the usual conversation at these affairs. What *is* an open item system of invoicing, Mr Karian?'

He stumbled into an explanation, but she appeared not to be listening, her gaze swinging around the room like a lighthouse beam. She cut in halfway through his speech to tell him about a novelist she had met. She spoke with the confident dexterity

112

that her background had given her, a voice that was used to being listened to, patiently and unstoppably going its way. In this fashion she had, through a million dinner parties, ensured that silences were filled, embarrassments diluted and made un-poisonous.

He wished she would shut up, though he had no desire to talk himself. Why wouldn't Grant even mention the Burgham business? Karian had dropped hints as profusely as a man shaking salt, but the Chairman had never returned to the promise that he would do something about redeeming Karian's holding. The market in the shares was worse than ever since Grant had flatly denied any intention of a take-over, and now Karian was afraid to mention the subject directly. The size of his holding would shake even Grant. The gesture needed to come from his employer. If Grant did not move soon, Karian saw the savings of ten years evaporating. He was paying his bills very slowly at present.

'The surprise may be a very pleasant one,' Armfield told Lord Bender secretively, away from the loud chatter, in a corner of the room. 'A seven-figure surprise.'

He had winkled Bender out of Grant's group and for the first time this evening found he was almost enjoying himself.

'Good,' said Lord Bender. 'Need any help?'

'No thanks,' said Armfield. 'I have it under control. It was just an idea I had, and it's worked out.' If he didn't suggest to Bender how useful he was, no one would. He believed in pushing his goods, credit where credit was due, even when the credit was his own. Especially when the credit was his own.

'Tell me more, Harold.'

'Sorry, Benjamin, but it's not quite the time. You'll be the first to know when it's set.' Armfield would honour that promise too. Lord Bender was a man to be cajoled, to have on your side. Meantime, Armfield would keep Brasserton's contract to himself. That Lymington and Talbot-Brown also knew about it was un-settling enough. Armfield approved of secret diplomacy.

'I'll be looking for your support,' he told Lord Bender.

'You'll have it, if the project's a good one.' That was the trouble with Bender. Never committing himself totally, sensi-tively suggesting that he was nobody's man. But this time Arm-field felt confident. None of the board would say no to five million going into the Brasserton coffers.

There was a sudden scattering of people at one end of the room. Sir Giles Lymington appeared to have knocked over a tray of drinks. He's getting worse, thought Michael Grant; and

113

looking dreadful too. Skin yellowly pale, and the smooth grey hair like a ghostly halo. A waxwork man.

Alison Bennett came up to the Chairman's son and they shot a quick smile at each other. Michael had avoided her all evening. It seemed the wisest course. One early-morning meeting in his office, briefing her to be ready with material for a quick release about Ed Corsino and the consortium, had been dangerous enough. Her usefulness would be diminished if their contact was obvious. Now, under cover of waiters clearing spilled glass, dabbing at the carpet, she paused and spoke.

'It was difficult to reach you earlier, but I've got some news.'

'Can't it wait?' he said.

'I think not. Tonight or tomorrow morning at the latest.'

'Tonight.'

'Where?'

'Up to you.'

'London's a village. Do you want it really safe?'

'Yes.'

'My flat. Do you know it?'

'No. But I can find out.'

'It's on the office list. Eleven o'clock?'

'Can't it be earlier?'

'I've got a dinner date. Eleven will be pushing it.'

'Fine, then.'

'And don't leave your car outside.'

He liked it. Bold and straight. Almost like propositioning the Chairman's son. He would need to watch that. Miss Bennett was too desirable for his or anyone else's good. She drifted away, looking just as if she'd been telling him about a story she'd found a good home for in the *Financial Times*. He was glad he'd taken the advice of the source who told him she was exactly the girl to fill the vacancy Howland had created. Howland had jumped at her, without a word from him. She was going places, and he pitied anyone who got in her way. He judged her to be that rarity, a woman who valued her brains above her body. Maybe she could afford to, though. Her body would be good for twenty years at least; she wouldn't have to worry about that, not if the overhauls were regular and meticulous.

Half an hour later the party was over. Husbands and wives went home together or to Soho for dinner. Armfield was driven towards Weybridge and the house with black Tudor beams, weathered and good-looking but still mock, where Mary would have little to say beyond a spiteful inquiry or two about the

114

wives she rarely saw. He neither liked nor disliked her. He had married because that was what people did; now, in his thinking and life-pattern, she was irrelevant. One or two aged literati carried off in triumph the young girls they had managed to pick up, belching softly and determined not to worry about the heartburn which cocktail party pastry usually gave them. Most other of those males who were unattached and scholarly and lecherous departed alone and disappointed. They went to many parties like this, full of expectation, were tempted by flesh and made amorous by wine. Then at the end of the evening, in excited glow, nothing. Parties could be the cruellest thing once your hair and your belly went.

Michael and his father were left almost alone. Michael was puzzled that his father's face was so unsmiling.

'I can't stop now,' said Bernard Grant. 'I am host at a dinner. But we must talk tomorrow morning. Harold will join us. Things are happening which I do not understand.'

'What things?'

'Leave it until our meeting. Ten tomorrow in my room.'

✻

Michael was still wondering what had happened to change the old man's mood so drastically as he pressed the glowing bell-button outside a block of flats off Holland Park Avenue. Alison Bennett's voice, distorted over the radio link, told him to come up. The door leading into the hallway buzzed and clicked open. He did not use the lift.

The flat was small and functional, precisely laid out. There was a lot of steel and glass in the furniture. PVC too. Two glaring red chairs which looked like giant blow-up balloons. A chaise longue which might even have been genuine. Piles of *Elle* and *Harper's* and *Vogue* in one corner. The inevitable record-player, with sleeves of Aznavour and Piaf and Mabel Mercer visible near it. That looked odd to Michael. The paraphernalia of a sentimental girl? It seemed not to fit.

'Will you have a drink?' she asked.

'Thanks. Scotch if you have it.'

'I'll join you.'

She didn't look as if she'd rushed through dinner and spent the last few minutes or so plumping up cushions and removing hair pins and stray stockings from odd corners of the room. Her hair was shining and slightly disarranged in the fashion it takes ten minutes' hard labour with brush and fingers to achieve.

115

Beneath a loose man's-sweater her breasts moved gently as she walked to fetch the drinks. She wasn't usually without support in that region, whatever the fashion writers of the moment might be saying. He wondered that she, of all people, should be so obvious. With everything else that was going for her, she had no need of the tit bit. Puns again, he grimaced. Bernard seemed to sit on his shoulder in too many ways.

'What is it, then?' he said. 'What couldn't wait? I feel like Rasputin coming to visit Mata Hari.' He took off the lightly tinted glasses he had almost forgotten he was wearing. Miss Bennett looked even better now, sitting down opposite him and crossing her long legs so that the calf muscles bunched powerfully against the knee.

'Well, it's. . . .' She hesitated, then laughed nervously.

'What is it?' he asked.

'It's so absurd. I don't know what to call you.'

'How do you mean?'

'Do I say "sir"? I feel I should. I've never called you anything else.'

'Call me what you like – only give, girl. The suspense is killing me.'

'Someone else is interested in Brasserton's,' she said. 'And I take it that your deal with the New Jersey man is still on?'

'Corsino? Of course. What about Brasserton's?'

'It looks like the plant could be needed for another job.'

'What job?'

'A Government contract.'

'The hell with that. There's been no mention of it at board level. Are you sure?'

'A reliable source.'

'Who?'

'Talbot-Brown.'

'He wouldn't know. Dammit, how would *he* know?'

'You haven't been keeping your eyes open lately, sir – oh hell, *Michael*.' She grinned, and he held up his glass to signify he accepted the gesture. He had to admit she had done that bit well. As she leaned forward to pour another Scotch, he carefully turned his eyes from her breasts, moving heavily inside the wool. 'What haven't I been noticing?' he said slowly.

'How pleased Harold Armfield is with himself.'

'And Talbot-Brown's likely to tell *you* his master's business,' he said ironically.

'Come on, Michael. No man keeps his mouth shut all the time.

116

Those who are married have their wives to boast about their cleverness to. Those who aren't, well....' She shrugged. 'They have girls like me.'

'You've been to bed with him?' The question sounded to Michael as if he were asking it in an empty bathroom, tiled, unnaturally echoing. She took it without a flicker.

'As it happens, no. Antony Talbot-Brown doesn't really want sex. He just wants to flash me around like a diamond-studded wristwatch. An extra possession, three points more in the league table. All he needs is someone to bounce his ego against. A boy with a ball. He talked a bit about the deal. Enough to whet my appetite and make him appear The Boy Most Likely To Succeed. Then he went all Strictly Private and Confidential.'

'He could've been having you on.'

'There was something else. The clincher. He's furious he's not being allowed to negotiate the deal. He simply *had* to tell someone how clever he is before Armfield and Sir Giles Lymington steal the show. Every man has his weakness. That's Talbot-Brown's. He wants the world to know what a little genius he is. He gets no kick unless he hears that old applause.'

'Lymington? Why Lymington?'

'He's talking with someone in Whitehall about the deal. It would be a couple of years' work for Brasserton's. And that's about as much as I know.'

Michael leaned back thoughtfully. He wondered if his father knew about Armfield's negotiations. He also hoped that Alison Bennett never changed sides. She was devastating. What might she not say about him one day, stripping him slowly like a pathologist at a post-mortem? He flicked through the options open to him on Brasserton's, playing the game as he had been trained to; a Harvard-like exercise, nearly academic. As he lay there thinking, the girl rose and quietly put on a record, soft harpsichord and susurrant voices.

'Good girl,' he said at last. 'Find out anything else you can, but don't push it. Nothing obvious.'

'Please,' she said. 'You're about to insult my *modus operandi*.'

He looked at his watch. 'It's been a long day.'

The girl was leaning back against the table, stretching like a cat, skirt lifting. In most other women it would have been tarty. She came towards him and sat down again. 'I assume you don't want to stay.'

She said it naturally, signalling her availability without making an issue of it.

'Don't underestimate yourself, Alison,' he said apologetically, inwardly hugging the thought that this was a modesty she was never likely to indulge in. 'Want to stay, yes. Can stay, no.'

'I suppose that's right,' she said.

'To share your bed once isn't on, is it? Not if you think about it.'

She looked hard at him. 'Smash and grab isn't exactly what I had in mind.'

'Be your age, Alison. A permanent arrangement is even less possible. Starting up something like this is too easy. How do you end it? Until I've done what I have to do, I've no time. Nothing personal, you understand. I've just no hours for mistresses. Or wives.' With Nancy from Boston he might have had time, but that was another age. There had been girls at the race circuits too; that also was finished – for the present.

'A pity,' she said. 'But I understand.'

He rose and put down his glass. 'I think you're as delicious a girl as I've ever met, if that's what you're worried about.' Even she, he imagined, would not be averse to hearing that. Women, he had found, were rarely tired of repeated compliments, enjoying treading an endless carpet of admiration, even when reason told them the words of the weave were meaningless. 'It's just that I'm trying to give it up for a while. So let's not excite ourselves wondering whether we ought to make public relations private.'

'I'm not worried about it, no,' she said, ignoring the joke, which he looked a touch too pleased about. 'I've become rather used to playing second fiddle to the work that men do, even at my tender age. We haven't got a chance really, have we? What have we to offer except tea and sympathy between battles? The wars you fight are far more fulfilling than the relieving of a slight irritation in the loins. You lust for abstract success rather than bed.'

'You may be right.'

'But thanks for the explanation. It helps.'

He leant and kissed her cheek. 'Meantime,' he said, 'I've asked you to join the battle too. Maybe one day we can take our ease in our tents.'

'No one would believe we hadn't already done so,' she said as she opened the door for him.

❋

'I wanted to strike him,' said Bernard Grant. 'He was so full of this – this overweening confidence. Making a mockery of *me*, at my own party. As if it mattered not at all that I should know.'

118

Grant was talking about Barstow, a guest at the previous night's party and chairman of QFN, a group rather smaller than the Prospero Group. An arm of QFN was a close competitor in the convenience foods field. Armfield looked gravely across the desk at his chairman. He had rarely seen Bernard so angry. And physical violence was not Grant's line at all.

'He knew everything. The campaign, the new product, the test market area. He's going to step up his own promotion there at the same time so we'll never know what our results might have been under normal conditions.'

'A classic spoiling operation,' said Michael. 'Case histories by the mile.'

'Don't quote your business-school lectures at me, Michael.' Grant was virtually sneering, humiliating his son in the way he sometimes had when things were going wrong and Michael hazarded an opinion. 'Barstow seemed totally scornful of our efforts. Insufferable.'

'Shall we still go ahead?' asked Armfield.

'Well, Michael? You're the *expert* in these ultra-scientific test-market operations.' Each word which Grant spoke was leisurely, squirming with sarcasm. Michael made the effort to keep his voice down.

'We have no choice, Father. The campaign is poised to run. It's far too late to cancel television time, I imagine, so we'd lose the money anyway. We shall simply work at half-steam, that's all.'

'This is the third time in six months I've heard about a leak of this kind,' his father said. 'Who, Michael? The advertising agency?'

'Possible,' said Michael, 'but unlikely.'

'We must do something,' said Armfield unhelpfully.

'I believe you were asked to do just that, Harold. Wasn't it around six months ago?' Michael pushed hard.

'I have made all kinds of new arrangements around the building,' said Armfield. 'The security staff at night is stronger. All departments have had instructions. But this kind of thing is different.'

'Stop squabbling,' said Grant. 'The point is what we do *now*.'

'Let Harold and I look at it together.'

'If you think that's necessary,' said Armfield stiffly.

'Please, Harold,' said Michael. 'Let's think about the company, not private empire-building.' It was a nice speech, shrewdly turned to his father's ear. For Armfield, there was no wriggling out of the corner. Reluctantly he agreed. He had another card, of far higher face-value, to play. He waited until Michael had gone before explaining to Bernard, for the first time, about the prospect for Brasserton's.

'Thank you, Harold. Thank you very much,' said Grant. 'I needed some good news this morning.'

'It will be a good contract,' said Armfield. 'Brasserton's at full capacity for two years. And very satisfactory margins if they compare with what we've had before.'

'Oldershaw will be pleased,' said Grant. 'Does he know?'

'Not yet. I want it tied up first.'

'Which will take how long?'

'Two months. Maybe less. We'll have some idea before that point, though.'

'What could go wrong?'

Even Armfield, who believed that money was nothing to laugh about, could not resist a half-smile, which emerged as condescension. 'Nothing, if Giles's information is correct. He knows the ropes there. We shall be hot favourites.'

'I'm glad for you, Harold. Glad for *us*. But,' said Grant, not a little proud of knowing the idiom, 'don't count your chickens.'

✻

Simon Dickson, politician, had not yet made the uppermost echelon of his party. But he had high hopes. He had been called 'promising' for a long time and worried sometimes that it might have been too long. Backwoodsmen occasionally muttered, as they had done of others, that he was too clever by half; but that was when all-night sittings and bad Commons coffee and the feel of stubble on their cheeks made them particularly irritable. Dickson didn't mind. He went to the right parties, was taken gently by the arm and led aside by the right veterans, yet had never been told 'Enough is enough'. His wife was radiant, ten years younger, and popular. He was a bright young middle-aged politician still in with a chance and knew it.

His voice helped. It was flat and classless, the success voice of the age, used by TV intellectuals gone pop and pop stars gone intellectual and fashion models created to Frankenstein formulae by their public-school agents. It had helped him to win a constituency where they weighed his party's votes rather than counted them, and he knew how to change its tones to suit working-class hustings or Surrey selection committees bristling with flowery hats and fancy spectacles. He could have belonged to any party, and in a sense he did; a smooth man for all seasons and all swings of public sentiment, one kind of politician and every

120

kind. He had natural-born timing too, even when he was eating. He played meals that mattered with the finesse of a Hamlet handling Yorick's skull.

Michael Grant watched him carefully peel the skin from the flesh of his duckling, cut a forkful, and speak with the food poised half-way to his mouth.

'This unnamed company you are talking about. It could arrange credit facilities which would make the export deal a certainty?'

'Credit is probably not necessary,' said Michael. 'But if it were, there should be no problem. The contracts could be signed tomorrow.'

'And this company cannot, definitely, cope with both orders simultaneously?'

'No.'

Michael's companion chewed sagely, as if trying to imitate Gladstone's sixty mastications per mouthful, then sipped slowly at his burgundy. It was a good move, slowing down the pace of conversation. It gave him time to think and it haloed his plump face with *gravitas*, an aura which he believed suited his image. Silences hurt no one. When he spoke, his judgement was final.

'Then I see no argument. There are several companies who could do the power station work you have described.' He flashed a clever smile at Michael. 'Including at least one of your own. But export orders of the size involved in the other deal do not grow on trees. It is obviously more important. Any minister, whatever his politics, would see it this way. So?'

'The company in question should not get a certain contract.'

'An outcome which would be in the national interest,' Dickson pronounced.

'Precisely.'

'Chapter and verse of the American contract could be provided, for my eyes only?'

'Certainly,' said Michael. 'As soon as you wish.'

For ten minutes more they talked tactics. Dickson suggested that the legal department of a Ministry might be approached. He had friends at that particular court. So many contracts had come the way of the unnamed company, if he understood Michael correctly, that it almost looked like restraint of trade, did it not? He believed the legal department would be able to mount a strong case. It was not unknown, he explained, for even the Minister himself to have his advice to industry confounded once legal brains in Whitehall got to work. If the worst happened, there could always be a question or two in Parliament about the

121

circumstances in which certain contracts seemed consistently to flow in one direction. But he did not himself think such crude manoeuvring would be necessary. He put his knife and fork together in the centre of his plate with mathematical finality. Perhaps Michael had some other problems?

Michael had none, only the thought that he would like to have been able to tell his father about the encounter. Maybe one day, far distant, he would. Bernard Grant had discoursed too often on the futility of cultivating politicians, announcing his belief that in present circumstances the best route to official assistance was the direct line to Whitehall, rather than via the palace of Westminster. Did he not realise, Michael wondered, that politicians might know civil servants at least as influential as Lymington's friends?

They had finished coffee. Dickson suggested a turn on the terrace. At times his phraseology could be deliciously stuffy; old-fashioned sixth-form debating society. A March sun, defiant against the bruise-bellied clouds, set even the brown Thames on fire. They were dazzled by the needlepoints of reflected light as they strolled and looked up-river towards Vauxhall.

'It's time you came down for the weekend,' said Dickson. He was working hard on his weekend parties, a high-cost investment on making Minister of State when the time came. 'We have a lot more to talk about. I'm fascinated by what you tell me about the sports car company. I might like to be in on that.'

'I'll give you a ring,' said Michael. 'I'd enjoy Sussex now that spring's on the brink.'

'That's a promise, then. Look, I must dash now. By the way, it *is* one of your companies we've been talking about, I suppose?'

'Of course,' said Michael. 'You'd better know the name.'

'Who are you crossing, and why?' asked his companion. 'You're growing very devious.'

'Devious? Come. You said yourself it is clear where the national interest lies.'

'Patriotism,' said Dickson, preening himself for a final thrust, debating as earnestly as when he became President of the Union at Oxford an age ago, 'is the last refuge of the scoundrel.'

'One of the few nuggets of wisdom that Johnson ever dropped,' said Michael. 'I prefer Nurse Cavell.'

'Ah yes,' said Dickson, hanging out the words to catch the wind. 'Patriotism . . .?'

'. . . is not enough,' said Michael.

'Hallelujah,' said the politician, walking swiftly towards the lobby.

122

6. Everything a girl should know

THERE was no direct mention of the Prospero Group in the story; nor did the name of Burgham appear. But one of the examples given, with no names, fitted what had been happening to the Burgham shares a few weeks ago too snugly for comfort. And Howland knew enough of Bernard Grant's games there, though not all, to be apprehensive. He held the cutting gingerly, a potential bomb. It was a feature from the *Financial Times*, combing through the kind of Stock Exchange phenomena which might be a cause of concern to the City Panel on Takeovers and Mergers. Only *might*, of course; but the qualification was pointedly placed. The argument particularly mentioned shares whose price fluctuated uneasily under rumours of on–off takeover bids.

Grant was inclined to discount its significance. It was, again, one of his carnation days. The blood-red flower stained the pearl-grey of his suit as he leaned back behind the desk. Yet Howland felt the old man was not as relaxed as usual.

'You are over-concerned, John,' said Grant, who wanted no further digging by Howland. The PR man could become huffy if he suspected any deal smelt *too* much. Howland was strange that way; a kernel of integrity beneath a shell of cynical insouciance. 'We do ourselves damage by being too subtle. Creating trouble where none existed until we stirred the broth.'

Howland shrugged. 'There is nothing I can do specifically, sir. It's too vague. I simply wanted us to be forearmed. Make some discreet soundings.'

'You are very good at that, John.' Grant smiled at the wisdom of his judgement in having so good a PRO. 'But leave it, please. If you go asking, even with discretion, people will wonder why we imagine the cap fits us. The Burgham business is dead. Just a ripple on the pond when the breeze passed by. They will not revive it now.'

Howland wished he could be so sure. He tucked the cutting

into a waistcoat pocket for his Maybe file. Grant said: 'If your detective's nose could find out anything about the colander through which information from this building apparently pours, I would be more grateful than for your unwittingly encouraging talk about Burgham's.'

'Of course,' said Howland. 'How serious is it?'

'So far, only a minor irritation, John. But personally, very upsetting. You understand?'

Howland had no problem in understanding. Grant had already spoken to him about the incident with Barstow at the reception, which might never have happened had Armfield refrained from making such heavy-breathing weather of that bloody woman. It had kept Howland too long from Bernard's side; had he been there he could have steered Barstow away. Howland was more interested in keeping Bernard Grant happy than in thinking it a good thing for his Chairman to be forewarned of hostile action by a rival company. That was the way his mind worked. A vulgar little man, Barstow; a jumped-up grocer who probably, in Howland's view, actually ate the frozen slush foods one of his companies produced. Ugh. Howland's slim frame, nurtured on rice puddings and roast beef, shuddered. So his Chairman was a touch vain about such things as sarcasms that went against him; very vain, if it came to the point. There were worse sins than vanity in Howland's book. The old man was entitled to *that*. He had something to be vain about.

'Never mind that now.' Grant, typically, was switching the flow of his thought. 'There is a more specific reason for our talk. I want you to do a job for me.'

'Sir?'

'Go up to Brasserton's and have a chat with Oldershaw. Something which needs careful handling.'

The thought of the excursion, the brute walls of the factory and the aura of grease, warmth and overalls did Howland no good at all. He had been there once; a place where men sweated at lathes and looked at him with curious, hostile eyes as he walked through the noisy workshops to reach Oldershaw's office. His shoes, light suède, were scuffed with oil by the time he got back to his hotel. He listened patiently while Grant explained the background to the government contract for Brasserton's.

'But it's not agreed yet?'

'The contract will be ours, I have no doubt,' said Grant. 'I want Oldershaw to know in good time.'

'Am I the right man, really?' Howland was not only thinking

124

of the greyness of a day and maybe night in Staffordshire. He genuinely doubted the Chairman's judgement. Engineers like Oldershaw made him feel uneasy, essentially a parasite on the hard shoulders of the men who made machines he did not understand and who talked an arcane scientific Chinese of their own. Oldershaw's factory, created from nothing in thirty short years before the need for capital had driven it into Bernard's empire, was conspiratorial. The man who had made it knew all its inmates, called them by their Christian names, jealously guarding its specialness. Howland, who needed to be surrounded by people from his own world so that he could measure his talents against them or discover some tangible relationship of reassurance, felt an intruder on Oldershaw's shop-floor.

Grant allowed himself a chuckle. 'I know he is not your kind of person, John. But the circumstances are special. I cannot go myself. Harold, who is the only other appropriate person, will do it too heavy-handedly. I'm anxious to keep Oldershaw feeling happy. What my son might describe as positively motivated. If I call him to London, it will be too much like the headmaster summoning a promising pupil to his study. I think of such things, John. They are important.'

Howland still looked doubtful. 'I understand, sir. Even so. . . .'

'I seem to remember hearing you talk quite cheerfully about cars with Oldershaw on one occasion, do I not? It will not be too bad.'

Howland had to admit that there was a period of perhaps ten minutes when Oldershaw and he had hit it off. They had ticked through the merits of Jensen, Aston, Ferrari, Lamborghini. About the Monteverdi, whose 7.2 litre engine had made Oldershaw suck his breath in wonder, they agreed it was too early to make a judgement, especially with that five-figure price-tag. Howland could still not be sure, however, that the new encounter proposed by Grant would not be a disaster.

'Oldershaw will be flattered that someone has come from London to put him in the picture. And I see no reason why he should not be delighted at the order which is coming his way.'

'He may think he's being spoon-fed, may he not, sir?' Howland was not sure whether he should have spoken the sentence, but Grant had relaxed him and now took the point easily.

'Perhaps. In my judgement he is likelier to be glad for the assurance of profitability it will give him over a year or two. He is not a man yet used to moving in the bigger pool we have built for him. Besides, he'll need to expand if he's to make best use of the computer we propose to give him. You will handle it well, I know.'

'I'll do my best.'

'Naturally,' said Grant. 'And secrecy at this stage is, of course, essential.'

Half an hour later, Grant was thinking of leaving for the lunch at which he planned to let Lord Bender know about the Brasserton contract when Karian asked if he might see him.

'Forgive me for raising this, Mr Grant. But you may remember what you said some months ago about my holding in Burgham.'

It had taken Karian weeks of rehearsing his opening lines to reach this point; weeks during which his resolution had stiffened as he went to sleep each night, and regularly had crumbled once he walked through the entrance of Prospect House in the lightening mornings. He had excused himself by repeating that the right moment had never arrived, but knew this was not true. Now, before Grant, he had by heart what he must say.

Grant laughed at him. 'You didn't sell your shares at the top of the market, before our announcement?'

'No.'

'Joseph, you're a fool. What do you expect me to do now? My offer of help was conditional upon our taking over Burgham. Surely you understood that?'

Karian spoke dispiritedly. 'I wasn't sure.'

'You are not *that* worried, are you? If I know you, your holding will be a modest one. And things will improve. Keep your nerve, Joseph. I would do you no service at all if I wet-nursed you over this.'

Karian realised quite clearly that this was the moment above all when he must push. Grant must learn how huge a stake, by his standards, he had in Burgham. He must throw himself on Grant's generosity, plead or wheedle, even try to hold the Chairman to the promise given – anything, so long as he kept the conversation going, the door open. He looked down at his shoes, noticed a spatter of mud spots on the shiny black leather, and listened to himself agreeing with Grant.

That's the trouble with you, Karian, he told himself. No guts, no resolve, no cheek even. In the hopeless clarity of self-understanding he thanked the Chairman, turned, and walked through the door. What in God's name, Karian wondered, am I thanking him for?

❈

Lymington was an autumn man. He had soaked in his fill of sunshine from the years abroad. He liked London best in the bitter-sweet of October, when the leaves crunched and rotted and burned like incense, and a thin mist softened the buildings. At that time he felt he walked through the ghost city of his past, the classic capital of the days before glowing windows in Piccadilly were allowed to poke fun at Lord Kitchener and long-haired hooligans to vomit in packs beneath the streaming fountains of Eros or squat in their excrement on other people's property.

So the blinding sun-green of Hyde Park and the late March prickle of leaves did nothing to elate him as he was driven towards Prospect House. Not that any natural phenomenon could have undermined his obsessive melancholy at this moment. True, his decision to ride out the pressure from the club appeared to be working; he had managed to raise some money and pay off a fraction more of the debt. But every day he feared the persecution might begin again. He kept remembering the remark Soames had made somewhere in *The Forsyte Saga* about British credit being the wonder of the world, but how long could you live on wonder. Once he had thought it immensely funny.

Now, after a joyless night without sleep, listening to Esther smack her lips and suck her breath and mutter as she slept, he had to face Armfield. He had spent four days anxiously telephoning Charles or meeting him in ridiculous places. Once they had created a neurotic rendezvous in St James's Park, standing together as if they were strangers, exchanging words but pretending not to talk, like bad actors playing at men from MI5. Last night, he had never seen Charles so close to tears.

Armfield neither blenched nor reddened when Lymington told him, except in the flush at the back of his shaven neck. Slowly his face grew more clenched, the gold spectacles shifting minutely on the nose, until his expression was that contortion between slyness and anger which his form-master in the indifferent suburban grammar school would have remembered from the days when Armfield, Harold J., regularly just failed to achieve the best mark in mathematics.

'How can you ask me to believe this? What have you been doing?' When Lymington had arrived, Armfield had called him Giles, smilingly. Now he gave him no name.

'There is no doubt,' said Lymington. He felt humiliated, yet had a powerful urge to strike the face of the man opposite him. What was Armfield but a nobody, a common grammar-school snob who had been fortunate enough to be in front of the crowd when a bandwagon passed by? 'Charles has done nothing for the past seven days but try to change the way things are going, to discover the cause of it all. There are objections on many grounds. Brasserton's have had too large a share of the cake already, that is the main reason given. The contract will go elsewhere. It will be announced any day.'

'What in God's name do you think you are on this board *for*, Lymington?' The name, when it came, was heavily emphasised, Armfield in his Dr Arnold mood.

'Perhaps you should ask the Chairman that question,' Lymington said crisply. 'Meantime, shut up. I am a fellow director, not your creature.' He surprised himself with his spirit, the reserves of spurious dignity.

'You are here to do a job,' said Armfield evenly. 'And you have made a nonsense of it.'

'Even you cannot expect always to make the governors of this country think your way,' said Lymington. 'They are my people, and I understand that sometimes there are skirmishes to be lost.'

'This is a disaster, not a skirmish,' said Armfield. He stood up, picked up a metal ruler and bent it savagely. 'Bernard knows.'

'Dear Christ,' Lymington felt the water begin to slide from his stomach. 'Who told him?'

'I did, of course. Who else could have?'

'But why? Before it was certain?'

Armfield looked scornfully at the grey man before him. '*You* said it was certain. Besides, it was necessary. I had good reasons.'

'You vain bloody fool,' said Lymington. Armfield wondered for a long time afterwards why he did not reply. There were times when he almost believed it was because at that moment he felt too ashamed.

✸

The wind hammered so hard on David's ears that the siren of the tatty coaster beating along the channel between the sandbanks only faintly reached him. He could see the single funnel and masts of the ship, but not the deck. It passed like a toy through a valley of sand, as if it moved across dry land.

He wished the tide had been up, bursting against the sea wall. Instead, tiny particles of sand, dragged from the beach, stung his cheeks. Sheila would have hated it, but he minded not at all. This was the way he had planned it. To come north a night early, to walk on the white-elephant promenade facing the Irish Sea, where the grass was scrubby and the soft gardens and solid hotels dreamt of in the thirties had never grown. It cleared his mind wondrously, but that was only part of it. Why the hell should he be ashamed of nostalgia? This was where he had started. He was coming back. Corny, but maybe he *was* corny. The docks across the Mersey stuck rude crane fingers at the sky, scraping the low clouds. He glanced at his watch. It was time to go and meet Bartram.

There was nothing super about the administrative offices of the Supergear clothing company. They had been tacked on to the long, low, oblong factory like an afterthought, the brick walls streaked with soot, and windows so small that at a distance they were invisible except when the sun caught them. Since David was last there the entrance hall had been tarted up: desk in light wood, low chairs in black leather and steel, rubber plants. Instead of the asthmatic commissionaire who had guarded the approach in his day, there was a girl with too vacuous a smile on too white a face. She sized up his rank with native insolence before she decided to lift the phone and contact Bartram's office.

While he waited, he walked across and pushed open the swing doors which led into the factory. It was much as he remembered it: the zum-zum of the machines as they sewed the pieces of cloth together, puffs of steam from the pressing-machines, women and a few men putting in linings, marking hemlines in chalk, sewing on buttons and collars and cuffs, all absorbed and rather silent. If he put out a hand he could touch the smooth plastic of a sizing-model, hipped and breasted but gruesomely featureless: no eyes, no nose, no navel, no nipples, no excrescences of any kind. He looked more intently at the lines of machines and tables and presses. It was like old times. Only the faces had changed.

The managing director of Supergear looked tired, David thought. But he appeared friendly, which in the circumstances was modestly surprising.

'All right, David,' said Bartram, almost before his visitor had sat down. 'I know why you're here. Would you like some coffee? It's not exactly French, but the sugar kills the worst of the taste.'

He pressed a buzzer, spoke to the secretary. Then he picked up a stapled sheaf of paper, flicked through it and pushed it across his desk.

'Analysis of the last three years, lad.' He smiled wryly. 'We've done your work for you. No point in trying to con anyone. Maybe you can help us.'

David didn't know what to say. He unzipped his document case and started to pull out some papers.

'What do you think?' asked Bartram.

'I don't really know.'

Bartram rubbed his jaw. 'I'm glad you've been made a director, David. I knew you had it in you, even when you were here. Start acting like one.' His smile, which crinkled the deep lines in his forehead, took all offensiveness out of the remark.

'I'll try,' said David. 'If I can help, I will.'

'Good.' The door opened and Bartram lit a cigarette as the girl placed pale blue cups upon a side table, pushing aside some copies of *Management Today*, mint-fresh, unopened status symbols. As she left, he pointed to the document before him.

'I'm not ducking my share of the responsibility. No escaping it. I've seen it happen in other companies. A little over-certainty. Some complacency. It's nothing new.'

'Do you want to say all this?'

'No,' said Bartram. 'But I *have* to say it. I know I'm a member of the main board and you're a new boy. But I'm not in the scapegoat business. I'll talk to Bernard in due course. It would be better if we had a few more answers before I meet him, that's all.'

'What's the problem exactly?'

'Two problems, really.'

'Yes?'

'The first in a way is me – *was* me, rather. You remember what it was like when you spent your three months here? A good steady business. Hadn't changed in years. Topcoats for matrons. Nothing fancy. Just good solid protective clothing.'

David nodded.

'It all seemed to happen without much thinking about it. I suppose I thought it was too easy. When Bernard made me managing director here, six years ago, I always reckoned it was a bit of a sinecure. Putting a good old horse out to lush pasture after years of service. I did well by Bernard in the early days, even though I say it myself.'

'The best property man in the north. Everyone knows.'

'I never wanted to go to London.' He motioned to a coloured photograph that stood on a bookcase near his desk. A beefy, laughing woman sat on a white ranch fence with four kids, two dogs and a horse encamped around her. 'Happy enough up here.' Bartram banged the desk in mock anger. 'I'm sorry, that's not the point. The thing is I suppose I took a time to learn the business – and after two years we began to slip.'

'You were slipping a bit when I was here.'

'Sure. So we had the marketing whizz-kids in' – the words were tight and scornful – 'and we decided we had to change. Instead of aiming for the old dears, it was to be the young mums – twenty-five to forty. Really *designed* coats, with all the trimmings.'

'It sounds all right.'

'Except it hasn't come off. Our sales have gone down and down. It doesn't seem to matter what cloth we buy, what designers we get. God knows I've tried. It's like musical chairs here with designers going in and out. I've cut every bit of superfluous costs I can, but the line on the graph still goes down.'

'What does your sales director say? Hasn't he been worried or angry or *something*?'

'Fielder? I wondered when you'd get round to him. He has the world's greatest fund of hard-luck stories. That fund took a long time to run out. Now he's blaming the salesmen, the agents, the product – anything he can lay his hands on.'

'Is he any good, honestly?' David chanced the blunt question, led on by Bartram.

'Honestly – not much. I took him because that's what Bernard wanted. Hell, I'm not making excuses. It was my judgement, my responsibility. That's the trouble with our kind of set-up, I suppose. You're always looking over your shoulder at what London wants. Occasionally they want you to do something you wouldn't normally do. Business is no place for sentiment.'

'You're being. . . .' David was still struggling to keep his feet on bottom as Bartram kept the true confessions flooding. 'You're very frank.' Too late he realised the pun, but the other man ignored it.

'No point in being otherwise,' said Bartram. 'It's no time for doing the double-shuffle. I owe that much to Bernard.'

David sensed an inconsistency in the words, and Bartram knew it.

'And that's not sentiment, lad. It's duty. There is a difference.'

'What was the other problem you were talking about?'

'Partly Gerald Fielder. He's not the man to run a sales force. I know that now. The men think he's wet. The agents get tired of him going on at them. They've grown resentful and complacent. Bad morale. But to be fair, they've not had much to sell. The designers have slipped too. I've spent a fortune sending them to Paris, paying for patterns and models from *good* houses. They don't seem to have the flair to do the right variations on what the top couturiers are turning out, and they're too bloody slow giving us the stuff to get into production. The competition's been running rings round us.'

David sat back. There were brown-paper coat-patterns hanging in the office, strange shapes and bits and pieces clipped together, the raw material from which cloth would be cut before the machining and pressing and tailoring began. In a corner lay two putters and a golf ball, shiny and new, contrasting with the dusty, grubby surface of the patterns.

'Yes,' said Bartram, seeing David looking at the patterns. 'And not one seller among them.'

'What's happening now?'

'I think I've caught it in time. But we need help. From you first, then from outside. The market's tricky. The past three months I've virtually been running the sales side myself. The figures are better.'

'And Gerald?'

'Limping around like a demented hen. But you make up your own mind, lad. I've said more than enough already. If London wants to know – and that's why you're here – then you tell them. Straight. I won't stop you.'

'But if Gerald had to go?'

'Maybe I'll have to go too. I'm not worried. I've had a good innings. I could do with the rest.'

'I'm not that daft, sir.'

'And don't call me bloody sir.'

Bartram got up and walked around the room. He picked up a biscuit and nibbled it, then sat down on the edge of the desk. 'Look, David, I'm not worried about my pride. I've seen too much stupidity of that sort in my time. And I'm not worried about Gerald Fielder's pride either. If that gets hurt, it's part of the business. Just so long as you don't kick him in the balls for the hell of it – or in the pocket. If he has to go – if *you* think he has to go – then make it easy for him.'

'That's not fair. I'm just a very new director up here. And in London, well, smaller fry still.'

Bartram laughed curtly and ran a hand over his hair. 'They'll listen to you, David. I know how the game is lining up down there. I don't want Gerald crucified. Pay him off generously. He's earned it years back.'

He picked up the documents and handed them to David. 'A good morning's homework for you. Have you seen Gerald yet?'

'I'm having dinner with him tonight.'

'Good luck,' said Bartram. 'I've fixed up an office for you this morning. As soon as you're ready, I'll talk over those papers with you. Then you can look round the factory.'

David began awkwardly to push the papers into his case, and Bartram walked across the room. He picked up a putter and crouched to play a make-believe eight-yarder, last hole of the Open, fantasy Royal and Ancient stuff.

'You're not a shit, are you, lad?' It was more of a statement than a question. 'People like you don't change in a couple of years.'

David looked up, and the answer came without thought. 'I don't know,' he said. 'I'm still trying to find out.'

*

At the club Fielder was the big man. The barman knew him by name. So did the head-waiter. A woman alone at the bar, girdled rump tight on a high stool and one silver shoe wagging with gin-drinker's ennui, smiled at him, inquiring after his wife like a good-time girl of ancient stock, one of those who knew her place. She wore a white dress, one size too small, breasts spilling over the top in a shelf of pinched flesh. Her brown arms said paint-on suntan too obviously. David understood quite well why he had been brought here. He might have done something similar in these circumstances, though his choice of venue would have been different.

Fielder had driven the Rover 2000 many miles east to reach it, across Wirral and the plump pastures where Liverpool's gentlemen had built their solid houses once the city's suburbs turned unfashionably into colonies of bed-sitters and immigrant staging-posts, distancing themselves from docks and strangers behind a moat of Mersey, wind-bent trees and golf courses. Fielder was plunging into the wealthy Manchester hinterland, much the same except for the absence of sea and gale, before the club appeared.

'I felt it was best. A bit away from it all. No interruptions. They watch who joins in this place, keep out the roughnecks. Modern without being too much, if you understand me. They look after me well. I often bring Margaret.'

He hadn't played much more than enigma variations on that theme throughout the drive. David had pleaded a headache and sometimes dozed.

It turned out to be standard Mark Two lush-life in the out-of-town money belt. Striped wallpaper, Regency; wrought iron breaking the restaurant into sections; stalagmite candles embedded drippily in sad Chianti bottles; vast artificial roses in pink-lit alcoves. Too good to be true, except these places always were. Even the lavatories had no names. Just a boss with a top-hat symbol on one door, handbag on the other. His and Hers with knobs on. This Tuesday night, with the crowd thin, the organ-led quartet played the soft stuff, *Days of Wine and Roses* and *Moonglow*, saving the hard rock for weekends when the kids of the ten-thousand-a-year men came to play games in their Spitfires and MGBs; drive-in amorists to a man, and girl, as Hardy once observed.

'London hasn't got all of it,' Fielder said after a few minutes.

David was thinking it was a long way to come just for a poxy dinner. But that was before he tasted the food. It was fine. Tournedos that surrendered as the knife dipped, melting apart. The head waiter talked strawberries at them: strawberries in March, sir, special for you, the old routine. David gave in out of fatigue, and surprisingly even the fruit tasted as if it hadn't come from California, deep-frozen out of its wits. Now they sipped coffee, bitter against the gentle burn of the cognac.

'Everyone knows it,' said Fielder. 'It's been a tough year or two. No one's found it easy. There's simply not been the money about, especially up here. Have you seen the unemployment figures for this region?'

It was both climax and reprise, emphasising all that had gone before. Fielder went through the book. First, the defence – loyal and vigorous – of his company's change of strategy to a younger market. David liked him for that. Later came the qualifications. If they hadn't done better, what could anyone expect? Bartram kept a tight hand on the purse-strings. They didn't pay enough to get the right calibre of salesmen. The agents were squeezed on commission. They had indifferent designers too, bits of art-school kids, some of them, wanting the earth in wages, acting like they knew it all. Bartram was more interested in what went on at main board level up in London than in his own staff. London used them as guinea-pigs for fancy consultants in this and that to play around with. London didn't understand the market conditions. London didn't understand anything much, unlike the men on the ground. Bloody London. It was an up-and-down game, rough years with smooth. You couldn't be blue-chip *every* year.

There was a lot in what Fielder said; David knew it. He had done his homework before coming north, apart from the three hours he had spent with Bartram's documents that morning and four more after lunch looking, sensing, questioning. But there was something missing in Fielder's monologue, the element which might have given hope. Fielder was muffled in that total defensive

134

acceptance of adversity which indicated the classic nullity-state of management textbooks. He had lost battles for so long, he seemed to have forgotten how to win them, whatever weapons were handed to him.

'Do you manage to get around much, then?' asked David. He said it lightly, though his intention was more serious. He hadn't found much evidence that Fielder went out on the territory with agents or salesmen to see the customers.

'What do you think?' Fielder sounded indignant. 'Desk-bloody-bound, that's us today. So much paperwork we're tied to the office. That's your bloody consultants and their systems.'

'It can't be *that* bad.'

'I'm telling you. Fat lot of use it would be anyway with some of the people we've got working for us. No interest. The buyers from the stores aren't much better. They don't like our prices or our designs. Don't think I haven't tried.'

The band was playing happy birthday dear Betty, or it could have been Hetty, to a thin woman with fancy wings on her glasses at a table across the dance-floor. David watched a waitress, long-legged and tilt-breasted, carry over the cake on which perched a single candle. Fielder had drunk enough, the words loosening and beginning occasionally to splinter, but his sulkiness lifted momentarily.

'I'll tell Sheila,' he said. 'You naughty lusting lad.'

'Not bad,' said David.

'She's a scrubber, boy. I'll have to keep you out of mischief. Or do you want an introduction?'

'No time,' said David.

Fielder had relaxed, the intense red lines of temper on his forehead falling away, the subject a relief to him. 'I'll bet you've found time on occasions. What about that little redhead at the party? Very bedworthy. You've laid her for sure. Own up.'

David was caught between the pleasure of being suspected as a womaniser, even in minor key, and the embarrassment of Fielder's obviousness. He felt pity for the man at the same time as he questioned his right to have any such emotion. Did all men who passed others on the climb up come to be like this, snapping out mental judgements to order like school reports? Must try harder. Needs to develop his concentration. Too easily distracted from the task in hand. It was bloody ridiculous. He looked across at Fielder, mouth half-open, waiting to seize on whatever reply David made.

'She's rather a dish,' he said non-committally.

'I thought so,' said Fielder, believing what he wanted to believe. 'You can still *tell* me, even if you are on the board.'

David wanted to turn the questioning. 'You should know. You've been a director longer than me. What's sex like in the stratosphere?'

'You're like all the flaming rest,' said Fielder, and it was a few moments before David realised that the older man's mood had changed. He was serious and indignant again. And drunker.

'What is it?'

'Christ, *you* know.' Fielder was angry.

'Don't be silly.'

'I know what they say behind my back. Fielder the great lover. Screwed a girl in the service of the company. Bernard Grant gets the piece of land he wanted from her dad. Gerald gets his pay-off. Big deal.'

'What are you talking about?'

Fielder hadn't heard him. He looked at the pale gold of the brandy glass. 'Wish it were bloody true. Hell, I don't even mind your knowing. Margaret was the one. Couldn't get enough of it. Her old man died soon afterwards. She'd persuaded him to sell up. He'd got the money, but without his business he'd nothing to live for. So then she blames me and hits the bottle. Fourteen sodding years of it. Correction. Sodden years. Joke. Sometimes I'm sorry for her. Sometimes I want to strangle her.'

He picked up a fork that still lay unused on the table and began to draw tramlines, digging them into the linen. 'If you want to know it, I'm not much good at the bed bit anyway. That's a laugh.'

His face asked for a reply. When David said nothing he added: 'Well?'

'What do you want me to say, Gerald?'

'Don't be one of those undertakers, David. Not one of the London men. I'm just telling you, that's all. It's not easy, having a lush for a wife. Lumbered. Story of my life.'

David looked down. 'I'm sorry.' Then he heard himself saying: 'We'll get things sorted out, if it's at all possible.'

'You're learning to qualify your generosity already,' said Fielder in a sullen monotone.

David looked at his watch. 'I think perhaps we should get back. It's been a long day.'

Fielder had slowed down completely, pondering what he had said, counting the cuts, self-inflicted. 'You wouldn't shop me, not knowing it all, would you David?'

'I won't shop anybody,' said David. 'I'll just do the job. Fairly.

What the hell else do you expect me to do? It won't be my decision.' It was a pompous string of nothing.

'For an absentee landlord, you're the best we can expect, I suppose. You're a bastard like all of them, but not a bad bastard.' Fielder leaned across. 'To tell you the truth I don't like salesmen much. Those ghastly pubs at lunchtime. Always pretending it's going well. Moaning about the pricks in head office. Belching bitter and pork pie behind the wheel in the afternoon, worrying about the breathalyser and the cops. I was glad to get that off my back. Selling isn't my game. You get conned yourself half the time, like Margaret conned me. Perhaps I need a change of job.'

Then he drained his glass, scribbled on the bill which had appeared on the table, and got up. The woman on the bar-stool was still there. One of her shoes lay on the floor.

'Good night, Enrico,' said Fielder.

'Give my regards to Mrs Fielder,' said the waiter.

'Of course. Yes. Thank you.' He churned the change in his pocket, searching for the car keys. '*Ciao*,' he said. '*Ciao*, Enrico,' like any man after his first holiday in Rimini. As they walked into the open air he spoke to David. 'And don't tell me I can't bloody drive.'

*

Michael Grant timed his moment meticulously. His father had all but exhausted the fund of quickfire good news. Lord Bender was leaning back happily, sipping the obligatory glass of water after his pills, a cigar smoking in the ashtray before him. Secure in the knowledge of three phone calls from Dickson in the past four days, as well as the gloomy cast of Armfield's face that morning, Michael spoke.

'I may have something useful.'

'What is it, Michael?' asked his father. The tone was tetchy, not liking his son taking charge.

'You remember Ed Corsino? The New Jersey man. He's been on to me.'

'I don't know him,' said Lord Bender.

'A sort of fixer,' Michael explained. 'Strictly legitimate, I mean. You might call him an engineering broker. He puts consortia together for major projects. Dams, industrial plant, highways – that kind of thing. Specialises in Africa and South America. The usual developing countries routine – well, who else wants dams? He's a genius at lining up world funds for his projects.'

'So?' said his father.

'He's almost completed a package for Ecuador. To build a petro-chemical plant there. Now the country's oil is really beginning to flow, they want one. It's a nice size of deal. A hundred and fifty million – dollars, that is. He wants us to come in.'

'Us?' said Lord Bender. 'In what way?'

'Specifically through Brasserton's. Two years' work for the factory and seven or eight million sterling in the kitty. Maybe ten. There could be a lot more to follow too.'

'And what's the catch?' asked Bernard Grant.

Michael flicked a glance at Lord Bender; here I am doing my damnedest for the company and this is what happens, it said. Then he looked coolly at his father. 'I don't see your point.'

'There is not exactly a dearth in America of engineering companies who make servo-mechanisms and control gear as Brasserton's do. Why should they give us a handout?'

'Salesmanship,' said his son. 'Give me some credit, father. What do you think I do with my time when I go to the States? It wasn't too difficult. I showed Oldershaw's designs to Corsino. He liked them, or his boffins did. We've got a bloody good product, haven't we? Reliable, keenly priced. Besides we're willing to have a go at something different. It's amazing what can be sold over there if only people get off their arses and try. They hadn't seen anyone from a British company in five months when I called.'

Bernard Grant ignored the sales talk and homed right in on the sentence which mattered. 'What do you mean, Michael, about having a go? What's so new about all this?'

'It isn't only servo-mechanisms. Corsino wants us to provide the process control complete. We'd buy in a computer from, say, Ferranti or Honeywell and couple up all our equipment with it – control valves, switch gear, servo-mechanisms, everything.'

'Interesting,' said Lord Bender. 'Can Brasserton's handle all that? I mean, I'm not a technician. . . .'

'No reason why not.'

'Unfortunately,' said Bernard Grant, 'whatever our experts say about feasibility, there's a snag.'

'What snag, father?'

'Brasserton's won't have the time or the space. Their capacity's going to be fully booked.'

Lord Bender sipped his water, sensing trouble.

'How can that be?' said Michael. 'I checked only last week. They're not fully booked.'

'Sorry, Michael, but if they aren't now, they soon will be.'

138

'The thing you mentioned when we lunched?' asked Lord Bender.

'Yes. A government contract, Michael. Equipment for power stations. It's certain, I understand.'

Michael revelled in simulating subdued indignation now as much as Bernard Grant had enjoyed the last minute or so of imagining he knew more than his son about Brasserton's. 'Why haven't I heard about that? I would have thought that as deputy managing director. . . .'

'Oldershaw is *supposed* to be autonomous,' said Bernard Grant softly. 'Besides, the board have not exactly been privy to your own negotiations have they?'

'That's different,' said Michael. 'I'm opening up new business, not dealing in routine government contracts. Don't you realise this is a chance for Brasserton's to move into the big international league at long last? Corsino had to fend off the lobbyists on Capitol Hill. If this flops after everything, I shall look a complete fool.'

Lord Bender intervened diplomatically. 'Let's not count our chickens, any of us. From your description, Michael, I take it this job might carry some risks?'

'What job that's worth doing doesn't? Yes, it has risks, but we can't just dump it.'

'We may have to,' said his father. 'The other business has gone too far.'

'We've got to talk it out,' said Michael.

'Of course,' said Lord Bender. He smiled encouragingly, doubting Michael's judgement on the score of over-commitment and over-enthusiasm, and Bernard's for so cockily blocking his son. He recalled particularly Bernard's words when they were talking about the abortive Burgham take-over. *Even Brasserton's cannot stand still. No business can. Expand or perish. Oldershaw can be convinced.* None of this matched up with Grant's attitude now. Lord Bender was rubbing his temple as he continued. 'Come on, Michael. You've done an excellent job. And so have Harold and Giles.' He knew he was waving a red rag; and he waited for the reaction like an examiner.

'The power station job – that's their deal?' asked Michael. 'Not Oldershaw's?'

'Apparently,' said Lord Bender. 'It *is* certain, Bernard?'

'Cast-iron, Harold says.' He felt he could afford magnanimity now. 'Look, Michael, we'll do our best to help you with Corsino. I'll see Harold this afternoon.' Abruptly he changed the subject.

'What about Lovelace's?' He had no intention of allowing Michael to have his way over the sports car company. Armfield had been talking to him about cash flow problems and investment priorities. That alone could clinch the argument whether at this stage they should dive in after a shaky outfit like Lovelace's. But it would be instructive as well as amusing to hear the debate. It could do no harm to let Michael talk about it. He threw what he imagined to be a crumb of comfort almost negligently towards his son.

'The case is ready,' said Michael. 'I'd like it on the agenda for the next board meeting.'

'Agreed,' said his father. Inwardly, Michael felt good. Point one scored almost too easily. If his father had not been glowing so much over the Brasserton's business, he might have battled for a long time to win it. He moved in carefully for point number two.

'Perhaps you'd like to see a paper I've had prepared on Lovelace's,' he said to Lord Bender. 'If you've no objection, father?'

Bernard Grant still felt secure and generous. 'By all means.'

'I'd value your opinion.' Michael added flattery to the mix, then the note of decent caution, the semblance of level-headedness. 'It looks an attractive proposition to me, but I'm not *that* committed to my view. It's essentially a board decision.'

Lord Bender sensed that Michael was keeping his cards tight to his chest, but the situation remained innocuous on the surface. 'I'll be delighted,' he said.

'About Corsino,' said Michael, rising to leave. 'I'll be bitterly disappointed if that's ballsed up, but I reckon I can handle him if necessary. I'm glad Oldershaw's got so much going for him. Give Harold my congratulations.'

He departed with the aura of the good loser who could still keep his defences well marshalled to protect the organisation's name and reputation. Bernard beamed shrewdly at Lord Bender, who wondered why the old man was accepting Michael's performance so completely at its face value.

*

Bernard Grant's words, later that day, both enraged Armfield and touched his stomach with the prickles of nervous uncertainty.

'You're losing your touch, Harold,' said Grant coldly after Armfield had explained the imminent collapse of the power

140

station contract for Brasserton's. 'And you've placed me in a position where Benjamin will think I'm losing mine. Howland has been up to talk with Oldershaw too. It's a mess.'

It was an uncomfortable interview, and Armfield took instinctive counter-action. Arnold Sims, bearing news from an accountant contact at Supergear of the papers which had been prepared on the company's situation by Bartram, received none of the expected kudos. Instead of climbing back a little into favour, he was ground into the office floor. With razored sarcasm, Armfield again expounded his assistant's failure to detect the troubles at Supergear before Earl Sanger did. 'Another lapse like this,' he said, 'and we may have to reconsider your future.' Sims, fifty and fearful, glowered at Talbot-Brown who was waiting in the outer office. He hoped the young pretender was due for punishment too.

He would not have been disappointed. Armfield easily laid responsibility for the Brasserton's fiasco on Talbot-Brown. Who was it, after all, who had first raised the possibility of the power-station contract? Talbot-Brown, unabashed, began to pour poison on Lymington until Armfield stormed him down. He still sat, though, with the infinitely superior expression that said I told you so. Armfield would like to have fired this smartyboots there and then, but he needed the man's talents. It annoyed him to be so dependent.

'You have little time to persuade me you are worth keeping. I want to know all about Corsino. Every deal he has made. No one can do business in Africa without committing some indiscretions. Sniff them out. And find out quickly what problems could arise in the kind of deal which the Chairman's son is now suggesting. As for Lovelace's, Michael Grant has done a report. In an excess of generosity, our Chairman has agreed to let it be discussed at the next board meeting. I want a reasoned rebuttal of his arguments.' It was the Lovelace's business which genuinely infuriated Armfield. Did the Chairman's son think that money for toys grew on trees?

'The report. Have you got a copy?' asked Talbot-Brown.

Armfield relished his chance. 'Don't bother me with detail, man. How you get hold of the document is your problem.'

Talbot-Brown smiled and picked up the file at his feet. 'I only wondered,' he said. 'Perhaps you'd care to look at it tonight.' He rose, placed a copy of Hardy's report on the desk, and walked out.

*

The car swept David along the upper heights of the city, past the two great cathedrals and the sad houses where only chipped pillars and wide windows reminded those who knew the history of the place that traders of great substance and slavemasters had once lived there.

He had come the long way round deliberately, unwilling to destroy the mood of easy evocation which somehow, he argued within himself, made the problem of making a judgement on Supergear easier. The light was going. The sky over the river was crisscrossed with a dirty tracery of smoke lines and there was a stormy orange glow over the warehouses, black as coffins waiting to be dropped into the empty granite graves of the docks.

To chop Gerald Fielder was too easy. Fielder was part of the trouble for sure, but only because as sales director he was in the most exposed position. If the stuff didn't sell, no revenue. Simple. Change the man who looks after the selling.

But there was so much else that was wrong. There was a sloppiness about the whole operation. All the directors tended to blame each other, or the market, or no money. Anything but themselves or their departments. One of them, recently uplifted, had moaned about a designer wanting a raise from £1,500 to £2,000. 'Cheeky young bitch,' said the director. 'I only get four and a half myself.' David reckoned that fifteen hundred a year didn't buy much designing these days.

Then there was Bartram. For all his attempts at bluff openness, Bartram talked too much and too indiscriminately. He said he was willing to accept *part* of the responsibility, but David wondered whether he shouldered too little of it. He introduced David to one of the younger sales executives – described, inevitably, as bright – who then had shown the visitor around. Afterwards Bartram praised the man's work to the skies. The implication was plain: a contrast with Fielder's fumbling and an attempt to demonstrate that the sales director had nothing to grumble about in his subordinates. It was an old ploy.

A lot of other evidence was lying around quite plainly. Two of the principals were still there from the old days: the chief cloth-buyer, aged maybe fifty-five, boasting about the marvellous quality stuff he still got from Yorkshire, and the chief designer, a woman in her late forties, who he had been told three years ago was a great craftswoman but believed that a topcoat should be built to last. When the fashion changed every few months, what the hell did the market they were now in want with coats that never wore out?

142

Midway through one afternoon, David had lost a button on his jacket. He was almost forcibly dragged to a girl in the factory by Bartram. Seven people stopped work to watch her sew it back on. They couldn't do much else, since the flow of garments halted anyway with her withdrawal from the line. She liked it here, she said. Nobody pushed her. When David apologised for holding her up she assured him he needn't worry. Didn't Mr Bartram often ask her to do a job for him?

In the end it came back to Bartram. He should have provided the leadership, have cracked the whip when necessary, have spent much more time than he apparently did on the job. 'Hello, Frank,' the chief accountant said when Bartram took David to him. 'Long time no see.' It was typical.

David wondered whether he could avoid doing a written report on his week's visit. He would much sooner talk about it, drop verbal hints, let Westbrook and the others follow them up and come to their own conclusions. To put down what he really believed was going to be difficult.

Bartram's appointment had been the mistake. It was a perfect illustration of that fashionable doctrine from the doctor in California. . . . In a hierarchy every employee tends to rise to the level of his incompetence. . . . The gospel according to St Laurence J. Peter. The Peter Principle. A load of fun, maybe. A nice joke which only Americans could take seriously. But for Bartram, perfect. That was Bartram, the perfect deputy. Okay so long as someone like Bernard Grant was around to direct him. But give him the reins, and you got trouble. Bartram was a chief of staff, not a commander. And it was Grant's mistake, or whoever's, down at Prospect House, which had over-promoted him. That was the trouble with big organisations. Their momentum disguised the bits of the machine that were going wrong until suddenly the whole thing stalled.

How can David Anthony Travis point the finger at Bartram and, by implication, at the men who had given him the running of Supergear, which had once been the Belliza Clothing Company? Yet if Bartram stayed, the company could get no better, with or without Fielder and the other small fry who might get the push. In the long run that could rebound on D. A. Travis, could it not? The specialist who made the diagnosis and then ordered the amputation of the wrong limb?

It was going to be tricky. Westbrook would have to help him with the politics. Perhaps he could suggest that consultants should go in with a new brief. Not decisive enough, David

143

judged. What did bloody consultants know about the rag trade? You could have the best systems in the world, but if you didn't have the flair – or make sure you bought it – you stood not a chance. 'You're only as good as last season's collection,' the long-service designer had told him, with an air of having solved the riddle of the Dead Sea Scrolls. Dusty clichés from the bumper book of fashion fun hints weren't much help. He would talk to Hardy when he got back. We can work it out. He pushed nervously at his hair and let the song of the Beatle four run madly round his skull as the car dived down towards the soot-soaked canyons and twisting new concrete curves of the commercial centre.

Back at the hotel – dark brown corridors and signs to the Gents shaped like pointing hands, with lovingly painted fingernails and shirt-cuffs – he rang his home. Sheila sounded cheerful. She had been to the clinic that morning. Everything seemed fine. Six weeks to go and no sign of difficulties.

'I'm trying to make it back tomorrow night, but it's doubtful,' he said. 'More like Friday morning.' He knew exactly what he planned to do next. He was keeping his options open.

'Don't kill yourself to catch a train,' said his wife. 'Marion's asked me to a meal tomorrow night if I want to go.'

The idea had pressured David as he worked out the timetable of what remained to be done the next day. He knew it had been there the whole week past. Although he told himself in one corner of his mind he was a bastard, he also argued that he deserved something after the uneasy, unpleasant days he had just been spending. There was nothing worse than working in bland hotel rooms in the evenings. It gave the soul the taste of cardboard cornflakes.

When Alison answered the phone he didn't know whether he was pleased or not. He had half-hoped she would be out. Then he wouldn't have needed to put his resolution to the test.

'Liverpool? Poor boy,' she said. 'How could I say no to dinner tomorrow night when you tell me that hard-luck story?'

'Good. I was beginning to think we'd never make it.'

'Perhaps we won't.'

'No jokes. I'm not in the mood.'

'Been having a tough time?'

'Very. By the way, about tomorrow. . . .'

'You don't want me to do a Press release on our date?'

'Something like that.'

'I'm a big girl, David.'

144

'All right. I only meant. . . .'

'You only meant you don't wish to be taken in sin – gluttony or whatever. *Please*, David. What do you think I am?'

'I've been waiting a long time to find out.'

'Goodnight.'

'Where shall we meet?'

'Pick me up at the flat if you like. Do you know where I live?'

'Yes.'

She laughed. 'A planner, God help us. I'll have to watch you.'

'See you later, then.'

'Have fun.'

He was exhilarated, no conflict in his mind now. Only nervous fear in his stomach. But he realised that the enjoyment sprang as much from the fantasy of the telephone conversation as from the prospect of the meeting itself. Better to travel hopefully etcetera. Talking to her on the phone had been like slowly undressing her. It was just as they said it was. Apprehension pleasurable. A schoolboy entering the orchard for apples, looking out for the watchman, wondering if he wouldn't rather enjoy the chase. He hadn't had the feeling for years.

Alison Bennett had a fantasy of her own.

'Listen, Michael,' she was saying on the telephone, 'I've got this sweet young boy here, cocksure as hell. What do you want to know about him – specifically I mean? Loyalty test? Views on Westbrook, or Sanger, or *you*? Do I switch on the bedside tape-recorder, the one disguised as a Gideon Bible?'

Even as a dream-sequence it was lousy; an insult to her intelligence, and to Michael's idea of her, to think that she needed a briefing, fantasy-style or for real – provided, of course, that she was interested in a briefing at all. But modern business did that to a girl, didn't it? All those magazine pieces about industrial spying and loveless venues in over-furnished bedrooms. How could anyone still believe that a girl in an office could be a stenographer dreaming of the last dance with the boss's son at the Christmas party and going home instead to egg and chips with Mum in Finchley? It was confusing.

Michael's idea of her? She was more concerned just now with her idea of herself. She sat on the bed and considered again what the idea might be. A girl of twenty-eight. Father dead, one-time civil servant; mother living, seldom visited. The easy guide for employers would call her a career girl, meaning that she had red hair, a ripe body and a nice face, so what could she be doing with that inventory and still single, unless she were whore or

145

gold-hunter or dyke or wanting to prove she could make it in a man's world? Men liked to put women into compartments – good housekeeper; easy lay; nice but has halitosis; chum but not for marrying; talks too damn much; perfect secretary – only in her case there weren't enough compartments. For a woman so intelligent her absence of clear objectives was surprising. She kept her options so open that in the end she possessed only the power of short-term decision, and that was often a matter of impulse.

Now, therefore, she was helping Michael Grant as much because she liked him and was flattered by the notion of his protection in business as because she believed that what he aimed ultimately to achieve was right. She liked David Travis too, which couldn't be bad. In the world of Prospect House, David would make a good winner, and that likewise was a pleasing thought. All this wasn't enough, though. It still didn't tell her which way in life she thought she was headed. Nor did it indicate, at this moment, whether or not she should take young Lochinvar to bed.

7. Bed and board

'LYMINGTON, Karian, Sims,' said Earl Sanger. 'If anyone is responsible, they would be the men.' He was at his crispest, roll-calling the names like a casualty list.

'How can you be sure?' It was Westbrook who asked the question, but Michael Grant would have framed it had he not wanted to stay out of an argument. He was uncertain whether he liked the game which was beginning. Again, and separately, the peace he kept in face of Sanger's frequent arrogance was uneasy.

'I don't mind explaining,' said Sanger. He spoke with conscious forbearance, innocently inferring that minds of like stature would have accepted his judgement without the need to waste time on detailed case-history. Sanger was like that about time. He hoarded it, jealous as a miser. Time equalled work, and for those who did not share his obsession with labour Sanger reserved an imperious scorn. He was a one-man crusade against indolence.

'Lymington,' he went on, 'is up to his grey hairs in debt.' He wanted no compliments, only to get the job done, then flagellate himself with new tasks.

'How do you know?' said Michael.

'It's not difficult. I had a credit check run on him – on all of them, in fact. The usual computer agency. They're learning a lot from America.'

Michael said nothing, but when he pursed his lips, Sanger took it as a cue.

'It cleared Arnold Sims. A small-time man living a small-time life.'

'Then why suspect him?'

'He's frustrated. Since Talbot-Brown arrived, he's no longer Armfield's blue-eyed boy. He's been bawled out a couple of times. He thinks he should be moving onwards and upwards. No one else shares that opinion. Accountants have these fantasies about running companies. They can be dangerous.'

'Right,' said Westbrook. 'He's at his ceiling and doesn't want to be.'

'What could he have to sell, though?' asked Michael.

'There's not much he wouldn't know accounts-wise,' said Sanger. 'He doesn't see all the confidential papers, but he could put two and two together any time from the sums he's been asked to do.'

'All right,' said Michael. He might not like the end-result of the game, nor even the way it was played, but there were sometimes too few alternatives. 'And Lymington?'

'He hasn't paid a bill of any size in a long time. He's on his third different liquor store account in six months. A lot of guys are chasing him to get their money.'

Michael was genuinely perplexed. 'Why? He may be stupid, but he shouldn't be in trouble. He's made a packet out of my father.'

Westbrook burst in. Something he remembered from two years ago; a clue which would get him back in the middle. 'He took me to a gambling club one night. Baccarat. He likes it.'

'Check,' said Sanger, patting a promising pupil on the head. 'I've heard that rumour too.'

'But you don't know?' said Michael.

Sanger shrugged. 'If you want it taken further, there's no problem.'

'Nothing melodramatic,' said Michael.

'We could tap his phone,' said Sanger coolly. 'Watch what he's up to.'

Michael had no time to answer before Westbrook spoke. 'Wouldn't that be – well, risky?'

'A telephone junction box on the roof and one simple wire?' Sanger sounded genuinely incredulous. 'Or a replacement mouthpiece that takes thirty seconds to fix if you can get inside the house? No danger at all if we choose the right man. Prosecution unlikely. The people I know are very discreet.'

'I'd prefer not,' said Michael.

Sanger stared. 'Do you want to stop this organisation being fucked up or don't you?'

'Of course,' Michael snapped – he paused, consciously making what he understood clearly was an evasion, and not liking himself at all – 'I leave it to your judgement, then.'

Sanger looked at him like a man used to encountering indecision when his superiors wanted to keep their coats out of the mud. 'I'll look after it.'

'Karian,' said Michael. 'What about Karian?'

'Another gambler. But he fancies stocks. He's very over-committed.'

'Karian wouldn't sell out this company, surely,' said West-brook. 'He's a nice little man. What they used to call a loyal employee.'

'I would have said the same,' said Michael. 'He's been with my father since the beginning.'

'Your father treats him like dirt, sometimes,' said Sanger. 'Or maybe you've lived around the situation too long to notice. Karian's loyalty is a standing joke. Maybe he's lost his taste for jokes.'

'He knows very little,' said Michael.

Sanger shook his head. 'I must tell you about your father, Michael. I've no alternative, even if you think I'm stepping out of line. He is a man who enjoys his triumphs, and often unwisely savours the anticipation of them. He talks. And Karian listens. You *know* it's like that.'

'Even so. . . .'

'So even pet-dogs like Karian grow desperate when they are hungry. And Karian is starved of money. He sees twenty years' savings going up in smoke. He's been in and out of all the junk that's ever been foisted on gullible investors down the years. Then he really went on a flier. Put almost everything he'd got into Burgham's. . . .'

'Oh no,' said Michael.

'With him, predictable. He bought high. Today he's wondering when they're going to hit bottom.'

'And?' said Michael.

'I think he blames your father.'

'There's no one else?' asked Westbrook.

'You, dear chap,' said Sanger, smiling for the first time and caressing his use of the English idiom, 'are in the clear. Like the rest of us.'

*

William Oldershaw was still trying to be reasonable with the man who sat belligerently across the table in his office. He had known Colley for almost thirty years, since the early days when there were only six of them: himself, old man Brasserton, Colley, and three machine men. They'd converted the abandoned garage into a workshop for tool-making, doing sub-contracting work for bigger firms, a cottage industry in a slumland of weeds and mean houses under a roof of rusting corrugated iron.

Those were the hungry days, when they worked deep into the night, though the money had come soon enough. More, they were the tired days, with every damned local bureaucrat pushing them for more output, more output. Win the war, win the peace, drop dead, make it. Christ, yes, those had been the days. Now Brasserton was dead, the other founder-members gone years ago, broken by the pace. Only he and Colley remained; Oldershaw boss of the plant, Colley boss of the men. How could he get mad at Colley?

'We've a bloody right to know,' said Colley. His vowels were thick Staffordshire, thick as the black in his nails and the muscles of his bulky frame. Oldershaw, smaller and more wiry, with a tight brown face and clipped moustache, understood Colley and the way his mind operated. If anyone had a right to know it was Colley, he thought: a works manager who knew the union rules backwards, who had worked his arse off for Brasserton's right from the start.

'I don't know myself,' said Oldershaw. '*We* don't know. It's still being worked out.'

'We've had this round our necks for six months now. And not a word. Don't you *know* what they're saying in the works?'

'Of course I know. Deciding a change like this takes time.'

'While you're taking time, we're losing men. Three more went last week.'

Oldershaw stubbed out a cigarette angrily on the ashtray, a block of dully shining brass, intricately profiled, machined and polished by himself a few years back, just to show he still could do it. Precisely – to one-thousandth of an inch. 'I know that too. I still can't do anything about it.'

'Why in God's name do we need a computer? No one's told us.'

'Don't be a bloody Luddite,' said Oldershaw.

Colley was annoyed by the crack. 'That's not fair, Bill, and you know it. If we *need* it, if the firm needs it, I'll go along with you, whatever. But you can't even tell us what we'd use it for. Somewhere in bloody production – that's all we've had since those boys came down from London nearly six months ago. For all I know we want it just to add up the sodding wages. It's time everyone made up their minds.'

Oldershaw pushed the rail voucher across the desk. 'I expect that's what *this* is all about. Tomorrow's meeting.'

'His master's voice,' said Colley sourly. 'There was a time you didn't have to go to the bloody smoke to get your orders.'

If voices could go white with anger, that's how Oldershaw sounded when he spoke. 'Men get bloody fired for cracks like that.'

'It's true. That's why you're so damned riled,' said Colley, and Oldershaw knew it was so. He clenched his mouth on the angry words which would do no good. He questioned nothing that had happened in the past. Six years ago Brasserton's had looked like coming to a full stop, trapped in the no-man's land between small-ness and real size. They had needed Bernard Grant's capital to expand. They had needed his deviousness to get rid of old man Brasserton's lifeless son who was slowly suffocating the company. Oldershaw had plotted then with Grant and been glad to do so. Brasserton's had doubled in size and trebled in turnover since then, and everyone had taken their share of the cake. He had been right to turn to Grant, and the world knew it. But he still didn't like looking over his shoulder to London for orders.

'We've been through all that before,' Oldershaw told Colley. 'And we agreed. Going in with Grant was the only way.'

'I'm not arguing, Bill. But they said no strings, or almost no strings. And that means not toss-arsing about waiting to know whether they want us to have a computer or not. It's only an-other bloody status symbol for Grant to write into his annual report.'

'Tom,' said Oldershaw, 'don't push me.'

'Okay,' said Colley, pushing back the chair and rising. 'But don't say I didn't warn you. Once the rot sets in it's difficult to stop. At every works meeting they're talking nothing but redun-dancy. I can't hold the shop stewards much longer. I'm just not. . . .'

'Credible?' said Oldershaw. His face cracked suddenly into a smile, and his ears, large and intimately attached to the facial muscles, rose half an inch. 'All right, you've made your point. But *help* me. For God's sake kill that talk about redundancy.'

'How can I?'

'Because you know as well as I do that there probably won't be any. If we use the computer right, we just make ourselves more efficient. Better management information, better control, the capacity to grow still bigger. I've never yet known a computer that's meant fewer staff. Any gash lads we'll redeploy, give them some new training.'

'You sound like you've swallowed a dozen management text-books.'

'What I say just happens to be the truth.'

'Even if it is, try telling it to the boys. They want to be operators, you know, with something in their minds and their fingers – a skill, something that's theirs. They're frightened they'll just be minders, standing about like spare pricks.'

Oldershaw stood and followed Colley to the glass door. When it opened the soundproofing was broken and he could hear the music of the machines in the works. To him, it was as good as the Hallé Orchestra. His own *Messiah*. The lathes, high-pitched as they machined the metals, were violins and piccolos and sopranos; the planing machines, slow and growling, thudded like drums and tubas and double-basses.

He knew the instruments and what the changes of tempo and tune signified. He could tell when a tea-break was coming a quarter-mile away, from the slight fall in pitch and volume. He even sensed discontent in the works from the sounds which indicated abuse of the mechanism or chances being taken. There were times when he raced on to the shop-floor to tell an operator that something was about to break before the man at the machine knew it himself. To listen to his orchestra was a reassurance he liked to have many times each day.

'Help me, Tom. I'll push those bastards tomorrow.'

'I'll do what I can,' said Colley. 'But for God's sake, Bill, help yourself.'

Oldershaw went back and sat at his desk, feeling at ease again in the blankly functional office. He had resisted the pressure to tart it up. The desk was metal, and there were steel filing cabinets in the corner. The chairs were old, and everything in the room said Brasserton's: the drawings of machines and the evolving servo-mechanism designs, the faded picture of the original workshop, with Brasserton and his Old Bill moustache, the posters about industrial safety and first-aid procedures.

He considered his tactics for London next day. Grant liked a couple of his managing directors from the subsidiaries to come up for main board meetings every so often. It kept him in touch, so he said. But the visits could sometimes turn into inquisitions. It was dicey. Tomorrow, though, was special. He hadn't much cared for that puffball Howland bearing the good news of the power station contract. But the news was more important than the man who brought it. If he'd been summoned to town to get the full story about *that*, it would shut Colley up for a long time.

That really *was* a contract. That was where being in with the big battalions really paid off.

All right, so he wasn't always his own boss. Did any small engineering company stand much chance these days? Even when Grant and the Prospero Group had come along six years back they had been easy meat. No second-line management to speak of, and too little working capital. Now it's still easier, he thought, with private firms forced to file their accounts, so that anyone can go to Companies House in the City Road, hand over a single silver coin, and sneak a look at the life-blood figures of any enterprise in the land.

Oldershaw had been there once, checking on the Prospero Group, and remembering it well because he was so scornful of what the scene represented. Legmen and legwomen for stock-brokers and merchant bankers and accountants and entrepreneurs in general, sitting by the yard at numbered tables in a large room with cream, brown and blue walls. Women in blue overalls pushing the precious files to them on trolleys. Four hundred thousand files in that place, the big companies running to several volumes. Occasionally an ancient hack inside that dreary room might push aside a file and learnedly consult the *Financial Times*, dreaming on pink paper that he too might be a take-over king. That was a gag, a brief signal of forgotten pride. The big operators stayed away from Companies House, paying other people to gut the files of information – maybe a quid a time to have a legman fill in a pre-printed form recording capitalisation, share ownership, profits and the rest. That was the way the expansionists spotted the winners early. And then, the pressure. Sell out, friends, or we'll squeeze you out.

Oldershaw also remembered Bernard Grant smiling when, finally, he had kicked out young Brasserton and confirmed that he would name Oldershaw as managing director.

'You've won, William. *We've* won.'

'I suppose so,' Oldershaw had said.

'You have to win, you see,' said Bernard. 'All or nothing. There are no second prizes in business.'

That was right, except that Oldershaw sometimes still felt like a runner-up. Conglomerates, that was the word they'd brought in from the States. Monster companies; inevitable. He knew he couldn't buck the pattern of business history. Not even when he also knew there were good conglomerates and bad, and that the bad ones were run by men who cared nothing for *what* their companies made or did, knew nothing of *why* men worked at

153

their particular trade. Diversification was fashionable, but it often meant simply spending spare cash, getting a finger in so many different pies that bets were hedged. Something *had* to come off, hadn't it? If the steam goes out of detergents, then let's take our profits from hire purchase. It was a game he understood but had no appetite for.

Why the hell did engineers rate so low in Britain? They were the men who created so much of the wealth, not the city gentle-men who moved capital from square to square like pieces in a chess game. On the Continent it was different. In Switzerland and Germany, Herr Doktor this and that, and everyone looking at them like gods. In Spain, *Ingéniero*. In France, too, *Monsieur l'Ingénieur*, and Légion d'Honneur ribbons spread among them like confetti. *Ingénieur*. It was a nice word; a hint of cleverness, subtlety, brainpower about it.

Give me that computer. Of course he wanted it. Colley still didn't understand what it could do. Oldershaw devoured every report of every application. Computers that monitored a machine's performance once a second on average, working through the night, pushing out a report which the production manager would find on his desk at 8.30 in the morning. That was the future, something like that. Control that kind of operation and a man might really become an *ingénieur*.

He lifted the telephone and asked his secretary to call the car. The London train would leave in half an hour. Tomorrow he would insist on an answer. He had a right to know as well as Colley.

Then he walked out on to the gallery above the large workshop, down the metal stairs towards the rows of lathes. A few heads lifted from the machines as he approached. His eyes were flicking around him, unable to avoid the checking routine. He stopped.

'Christ, Hannah!' he shouted. 'I've told you before. You don't run with the guard off the bloody thing.' The man bending over the whining lathe, poking at something, did not look up. 'Han-nah!' he bellowed, and as the man's head jerked up there came the scream, a taut sound of unbearable agony.

It was Oldershaw himself who switched off the power. Hannah was still standing, his hand trapped. When they eased him away from the lathe his lower right arm was smashed, flesh and blood and bone and shirt sleeve mingled together. They laid him on the floor, sacking beneath and over him. They raised his legs and the St John's man started putting on a tourniquet high up the arm. Hannah was pale, sweating and silent, looking surprised at the activity around him and moaning softly as if he had a hunger for air. Oldershaw stood feeling helpless until the ambulance came, wondering whether it would have happened had he not shouted, and unable to understand why Hannah had stopped screaming.

*

David only began to feel safe once they left the restaurant. It was an unlikely place for anyone he knew to see them together; a bistro in Notting Hill Gate, built to cater for the new lords of creation in Holland Park at Soho-plus prices. He had been nervous nevertheless, hardly tasting the food, his eyes seeking an excuse to slide slowly away from looking at Alison to inspect newcomers each time the door from the street opened.

He realised that she knew the cause of his unease, which made for choppy conversation. The taxi was a black shelter, welcome and relieving. As they waited for it she had leaned easily on his arm. She lay against him now on the seat and suddenly turned to kiss him quickly on the cheek.

'Relax, lover,' she said. 'The worst is over.'

'I'm being stupid. Sorry.'

She smiled, her teeth white and inviting in the half-dark. He had never particularly thought of teeth as sexy before.

'That's all right. It's nice, kind of.'

'Why nice?'

'I judge you don't make a habit of this. And that's flattering. You don't, do you?'

'Not really,' he said.

'That's why you over-tipped.'

'What's that got to do with it?'

'Two pounds on an eight-pound bill is too much.'

'A quid was less than fifteen per cent. I hadn't any change. I wanted to get out, not have to ask them to split a note. It would have made people look at us.'

'Sorry. I thought you did it to impress me.'

Sharp, he thought. All right: if she thinks I need leading, I'll be led.

'Perhaps that was part of it,' he said. A lot of reasons jumbled up. 'Who wouldn't want to impress you?'

'I wouldn't be here if I weren't impressed.'

It was going well. He put a hand on her thigh, experimentally. Obvious, perhaps, but that's what he wanted to do, and how else could he gauge the prospect of the next hour or so? She wore loose satin trousers. It felt good. Warm.

'I never did like hands up my skirt in taxis,' she said.

He didn't know how to take it. He thought, Keep your hand where it is and use your mouth.

'You shouldn't let it all hang out,' he said.

'Don't sound so bloody plastic,' she said. 'There's no need to say *anything*. I feel the same as you.'

This time she kissed him firmly but briefly on the lips. It took the edge out of the words, almost. Was she a teaser or what? Flipness still seemed the only answer. 'I never knew you cared.'

'Why not? Rule number one. Any man who fancies *me* has a lot going for him in return. Rule number two. I've found that when I feel I want to go to bed with someone they've usually had the same idea. I rarely get stirred up when there's nothing doing.'

The brandy they had drunk gave him a ridiculously warm confidence. The taxi stopped under a street light. He was glad he had a raincoat on. To stand around paying fares in his present state would have been embarrassing.

Inside the entrance hall of the flats they waited for the lift.

'I'm glad I came,' he said.

She laughed. 'Darling boy, there's no need to whisper. It's a free country.' He hadn't realised how low his voice was.

'You read me too well.'

'I'm sorry,' she said.

She closed the flat door, turned, and stood awaiting his move.

'Look,' he said. 'I know how obvious this all is, but. . . .'

'Sshh,' she said, 'but take that damned great coat off first.'

He removed it, and she looked down. 'You poor darling. How did you manage to walk?'

'It was worth it.'

'But don't blow up, please. We've all the time in the world.'

Then she put her arms around his neck, ruffling the nape gently, and kissed him, her tongue savage. He caressed her shoulders and back, surprised at how tough and tensed it felt. She thrust against him, arching her body, and he moved his feet quickly to steady himself. Almost violently she broke away.

'Not on the carpet,' she said laughing. 'Sorry, but sit down. I need to recover.'

He felt uncertain, annoyed, embarrassed. She took his hand and dumped him on a red PVC object which he supposed was meant to be accepted as a chair. He felt like he was sitting on a balloon. He looked at her red hair streaming as she switched on the record-player and poured a drink. She was slim, wonderfully

156

lithe at the hips. Sheila was thick and heavy now. He wished he could get the picture of his wife out of his mind. The music began, an American woman he didn't know, the voice bleak and the music quirky, like old-fashioned Bacharach. She handed him a glass.

'Don't look so glum, David. It's *on*, you know. I didn't know whether it would be, but it is. I just want it to be *right*. I'm too old for rape.'

Then she went through a door, and there were only the words in the air and the room. *All in all, it was worth it, that's what I'll say....* The woman sounded old. Yankee Piaf. It was a strange record to choose for love games, but he was learning that Alison Bennett was a strange girl. It made a change from hot-chocolate strings or tinkling bossa nova. There was a creamy fluffy carpet on which stood single chairs, all shapes, and a chaise longue with a straight back where it had a back at all. It curved and flowed in a sort of sideways S. Not a room for the amorist. Ridiculously, he found himself thinking back to all those heavy rexine three-piece suites of his teens in Cornwall: sofas which were fashioned to defeat the act of front-parlour love. One always seemed to be hitting a knee or an elbow on an arm of the damn things, or half-breaking the girl's neck as, with her head supported, her body was pushed lower and lower. You pulled muscles that way, trying to ease hands around in cramped positions to unhook vital straps. Love-groping became messy and destructive of itself. They knew what they were doing, those careful parents who lumbered their living-rooms with lumpish suites. HP furniture, the enemy of love.

He stood up and looked around. Where the hell could you make the preliminary gestures in this room? Only on the floor, rumbling across that tufty carpet, which looked spiteful enough to cover you with sticky wool like a blizzard of dandruff. He put down the glass and saw his case standing in the corner.

'Darling,' said Alison from the doorway, 'are you going to hang around with your clothes on for the rest of the night?'

All she had on was the light, a basketwork globe set low at the head of the bed. As he began to take off his clothes he could see her in the mirror, lying unconcernedly on the bed, arms and legs stretching out like one of those damned girdle ads on the Underground. It was so many years since he had seen any woman except Sheila in this kind of easy, unworried nakedness that he looked at her almost curiously. He wanted to stop thinking about Sheila, but he couldn't. Sheila's breasts were modestly sized and

157

firm, the brown nipple embedded in the aureole so tightly that the outline was virtually unbroken, like a blunt spearhead. Alison's were fuller, even with her arms stretched above her head, and the nipple was pink, clearly separate from the breast, as a piece of angelica might top off a cake. He undid the knot of his tie. It was a body, like any other. A good body, of course, and he wanted it; but now he was taking it easy, knowing he was home, could afford whatever dignity he could muster with his trousers down. He was even a touch disappointed that Alison's flesh didn't glow or shimmer or dazzle him or something. Pornography, Soho-bookshop style, was a lie, wasn't it just? The curtains were open, he noticed, and instinctively he moved to draw them.

'Don't, David. No one can see you. Not eight floors up.'

Their love-making was very like the fantasy he had built of it for himself. She kept the pace slow, kissing him everywhere, brushing her heavy breasts across his chest and stomach, stimulating every part of him from face to knee. He wanted to put the light out, but she said almost savagely 'No. I want to *see* us.' It was a calculated assault upon him, brilliantly done. He felt he stood outside himself, enjoying it, yet observing what was happening, uninvolved. He even thought how stupid he sounded when, breathing heavily, he said 'Don't make me, I can't hold it, I . . .' and she moved her body away, moaning indignantly 'No, please, not yet.' Is that what happened in blue movies, which he had never seen in his life? Again, he thought, predictable – bloody predictable. They had to reach the final rhythm sometime. Gentlemen kneel – the old joke. What's the matter with you Travis, he was thinking. He was into *her*, but he couldn't get into *it*. The outsider, notebook in hand. She was moaning again, 'Darling, darling, yes, oh yes,' and he was thinking that *darling* used to be a special word, and in his mind was a picture of Gerald Fielder. Did he call that girl at the club darling? Maybe Fielder got too drunk these days for sex, illicit or otherwise. Would he get booze or sex if they sacked him? And then David was on the edge and she was ripping her fingers across his back and he thought that *hurts*, it hurts and I don't much like it, and he suddenly bent his head and bit her breast almost as an act of revenge, and all she did was scream a bit and thrash and say 'Hurt me, do it, don't stop, oh darling *please*,' and then he was through and she was whimpering deep in her throat as if she was choking, and when he opened his eyes her face was screwed up and beautiful with the ugliness of her passion.

He moved his legs and let his weight sink on to her. She

158

sounded fine. But he wanted to be sure. He was a textbook lover. She opened her eyes, and he stroked the sweat beaded across her forehead and said, 'Was that – you know. . . .'

Now she smiled and he liked her again. 'You'll kill yourself with worry, darling. It was great.' She pulled his head down and kissed him very gently. 'We'll get better. It takes time. You of all people should know it does. I think I like you very much.' They rolled apart and she said, 'What are you, David? An all-night raver, like they all infer they are until they try it, or just a one-off man?'

'Give me time,' he said, since it seemed the only thing to say.

'This can get morbid,' she said. 'We work it out too much.'

This was true, he thought. Her breasts were soft and tired. It was the act she enjoyed, wrapping herself in it as if it were a mink coat. That was the way *he* wanted it to be too, but he knew it hadn't been on this occasion. Perhaps that would come. He stroked her body and began to enjoy the softness of her skin. Her stomach was flat, and he felt he had almost forgotten what an unripened stomach was like to the touch. Was he a bastard to Sheila or did this kind of reaction happen all the time?

'Please don't start worrying again, David.' Her perception was unnerving. 'We aren't about to fall in love. Not *that* kind of love, anyway.'

'I'm on edge tonight,' he said.

'I even like that too. You must make a very good husband. Want some coffee?'

He nodded, realising that he had smelt the coffee smell for the last few minutes. She put on a housecoat, dead plain and blue. She looked wonderful, the cleft of her breasts visible. When she came back with coffee, in brown pottery mugs, she sat at the foot of the bed and looked at him with an expression that was close to earnestness.

'It can be good, very good,' she said, 'if only we don't get too serious.'

'It's not serious,' said David. 'I just enjoy being with you.'

Her smile was kindly. 'You're a serious man, darling. And divorce isn't funny. It simply upsets your kids and lines the bank balances of lawyers.'

'And you're a strange girl,' he said. He was beginning to enjoy himself now. Sitting around and talking, it was just like being home. He didn't even mind his nakedness any more. Alison had a gift of naturalness which made everything fine.

'There's nothing strange about being realistic,' she said. 'When you start this kind of thing, you need to state your terms from the outset, that's all. Already I'm a bit late about it. I'm breaking the rules.'

'What rules?'

'My rules.'

'Meaning?'

'Just that I shouldn't be going to bed with you.'

'Why not?'

'A private joke.'

'Tell me. Be *fair*.'

She laughed. 'The careful girl's handbook. Choose your men wisely. Executives are okay, but not the ones like *you*. Not the ones who are very close to the top. They're too involved with clawing their way up to give a girl much of a ride.'

'Not necessarily.'

'It makes sense, what I'm saying. On the other hand, be very careful of the men *at* the top as well. They're too damned busy making sure they stay there.'

'You sound like an advice column by Auntie Marjorie.'

She drained her mug, took his from him, and lay down beside him, covering them with the bedclothes, nuzzling her hair against his face. Then she switched off the light.

'A girl,' she said, 'has to have something to live by. You laugh if you want to, but we have to try.'

'I'm not laughing. But rules should be flexible. Every man is himself.'

'They're different round the edges. The package gets tied up with all kinds of ribbons. But inside, it's much the same. I know better than to think I can compete with either a man's work or the convenience which his family gives him.'

'The divorce rate would prove you wrong.'

'The non-divorce rate would prove me right. The habit of marriage is like a drug. Men get addicted. The ones who get divorced I wouldn't on the whole be interested in. They're fantasy people who believe that marriage is one long honeymoon. Like those old Hollywood movies where you knew it was *real* love simply because someone started to play the *Moonlight Sonata* in the background. You *want* me, but you wouldn't want to marry me, would you?'

'That's not fair,' said David. 'Would you want to marry *me*?'

'How the hell do I answer *that*? I scarcely know you.' She raised herself on one elbow and looked down on him. 'We've made love, beautiful love, but I expect you were probably

160

thinking about – oh, I don't know – how you're going to sort out that bloody Supergear company.'

'All right,' he said, and he heard himself going on talking when all he was thinking was that the beautiful love she was speaking of was all tied up with sex and had nothing to do with love. 'So the human mind is a wonderful thing. Several levels of consciousness working at the same time. Actually I wasn't thinking about Supergear, but I might have been. I still don't see how that makes men only half-lovers *all* the time. Isn't there a risk in what's happened tonight? To *me*, not you?'

'Minimal,' she said. 'I love you for doing it, all the same. But you'd think of some plausible story if you *were* found out. Else you're not the kind of man I'd be interested in.'

She has this way of turning insult into compliment, he thought. He wanted to hear her talk some more. He was learning a lot, giving away little.

'Scott Fitzgerald had this remark about men – men who were worth a damn – not being interested in the happiness or the enjoyment which life contains, but only in the struggle. That's the thing. I think that's true.' Her words had an air of utter finality. 'So all the men who attract me are committed. They want power or position or whatever, and they don't deviate. Their work is like sex. They lust after it. It's their drug, their release, their orgasm. What chance do I stand of getting what the women's magazines would call *their all*?'

He slid his hand inside the housecoat. Her breasts were soft and taut at once, and he felt he had been sleeping with her for years. The clock beside the bed said 12.30. Sheila would be asleep. He felt no guilt now.

'Okay,' he said easily, 'I won't argue. But just now I'm more interested in *you* than in sorting out the power game at Supergear.'

'What *are* you going to do about that mess?'

He told her, as she knew he would: about Fielder and Bartram and the difficulties of diplomacy with the report he must make. After sex, men talked, their defences lowered. It was always the same, except with those who just went off to sleep. His talk spilled over into what he thought about Westbrook. He liked his boss, but he shrewdly analysed the man's strengths and weaknesses. The trouble with Lionel Westbrook was that he had this tendency to hysteria, a deviation towards making over-hasty judgements.

David, she judged, was loyal without being obsessive about

161

loyalty, clear-sighted but humane. The name of Hardy clicked often into place. He would enlarge David's education within the next year from the sound of it. Did she like Hardy? Not certain. Their conversation moved on, through Sanger, Armfield, Michael Grant. If David had a fault it was that his admiration for the Chairman's son might become idolatrous. And all the time that her mind recorded the words, she could not be certain why she was doing it. She was growing sleepy and she wished not to sleep yet. She began to stroke the inside of his thighs.

'Am I staying, then?' he said.

'Don't be childish. Of course you're staying.'

One of his old jokes came spinning out of nowhere and he laughed, consciously, wanting her to ask him.

'What is it, David?'

'Something I read once. Guests are like fish – after three days they stink.'

Her hands were busy with him and he responded, despite his tiredness. 'But you'll never be here for three days, darling,' she said, and moved her body on to his, guiding him without formality, as if weary of the big production love-scene. This time they made love quietly, almost passionlessly, in the dark.

❋

The board meeting was already beginning to disintegrate in a way which Bernard Grant did not like. It was Oldershaw's fault. Grant couldn't see any reason for Oldershaw omitting to travel down the evening before just because of an accident at the works. Why did the man get so involved in detail? He should get his priorities right.

When Oldershaw did not arrive, they had started without him, briskly going through the monthly figures, and now, unable to discuss the Brasserton's contract, were involved in Michael's paper on Lovelace's. This issue Bernard Grant had intended to squeeze in on the brink of lunch, hurriedly. But by this stage the thing was becoming a wrangle about realities instead of an academic exercise rushed out of the way after the hard decisions on Brasserton's had been taken. To make matters worse, Oldershaw would come cold into the changed situation on the Brasserton's contract. No cosy private discussion beforehand, leading Oldershaw into the paths of righteous thought, calming him down over the change in plans. Grant did not like the world much today.

'Michael,' Armfield was saying, 'this is wishful thinking and

162

you know it. The cost of anything to do with motor racing has been escalating for years.'

'Our budgetary methods could control costs,' said Michael. 'Look at Lotus. How they grew from nothing in a few years. If you have flair *and* control – and make some of the right deals – it can still be done.'

Westbrook spoke: 'Our estimates of the market are, if anything, pessimistic. And it still looks good. In a world of mass production, more and more people will want something special, something distinctive.' The enthusiastic voice, supporting and encouraging young Grant, riled Armfield. He bit out his next words.

'Not all of us appear to have been favoured with a sight of the documents.'

Michael was all sweet reason. 'I'm sorry about that, Harold. I didn't think we'd dig so deep this time. All I wanted was a decision to take the study further.'

Lord Bender intervened. 'The argument so far seems sound. I'd like to see us make a deeper investigation.' Armfield delayed his response, uncertain of his ground. The trouble with Bender was he was too damned pragmatic. You never knew which way he would jump.

'Nevertheless,' said Bernard Grant, 'it's a matter of investment priorities. And there we have problems.'

Armfield felt better. Trust Bernard to get it right. 'Look, Michael, have you seen what's been happening to Lovelace's American sales lately? The Japanese are murdering them. Undercutting their prices all the way round.'

Oh you fool, you bloody fool, Michael Grant was thinking. Here is my father giving you the let-out, raising the spectre of investment priorities, which is your main hope, and there you go rushing off into the marsh where I can fight you and beat you.

'We know that,' he said quietly, 'but that's because the company don't know how to handle the assets they have.'

'Which are what exactly, Michael?' asked Prosser. It was, he thought, time to speak. These were the periods of board meetings when his mind wandered. Money decisions were not his forte. He preferred to consider the quirks of the human psyche and what made men work. Others who sat round tables like these, their minds occasionally straying, might think about their mistresses, their last game of golf, or have visions of impossible commercial adventures. Prosser was thinking about the figures for staff turnover at Brasserton's which had landed on his desk the day before. What the hell was going on up there? Oldershaw, he'd always been told, was good at labour relations, whatever else the man might lack. For a moment, though, he tuned in to the argument about Lovelace's. He had to show he was awake.

'The special thing about their cars is the mystique,' said Michael. 'They race, they rally, they perform. And sometimes, they still win, if not often enough. Anyone who buys a Lovelace can have this Jackie Stewart fantasy, wind himself up like he was going round Brands Hatch or Indianapolis. We can even provide him with the right gloves, the whole range of bolt-on goodies through our car accessory company. Not that a Lovelace car needs many of them. But the name will help sales of the accessories and vice-versa. It's a two-way thing. As for declining American sales, well, the answer to that is to race and race again over there – and to make as damn sure as you can that you win. Americans are suckers for winning. They'll pay a big price for a premium automobile. That's their snobbery: the snobbery of success. Why do you think Ford's put all that money into racing?'

'The Japanese are still doing well,' said Armfield flatly.

'Because Lovelace's have become so unaggressive. They think they have some divine right to existence. Instead of pushing their race programme, they're trying to economise on it. Cost-cutting where it will hurt them most. Now there's talk they may pull out altogether.'

'Perhaps,' said Lord Bender, 'they simply haven't the funds.'

'That's where we could help,' said Michael. 'That's the point, really.'

'I'm not convinced,' said Armfield. 'It's highly speculative.'

'If the campaign were sharp enough, we could make race-track success even more important,' said Westbrook.

'How do you mean?' Bernard Grant's tone was almost sharp. He knew that if he didn't pin Westbrook down from the start, the man assumed that everyone could follow the track of his unspoken logic. Sometimes Westbrook's more ambitious visions created bizarre misunderstandings around the table. A useful man, Westbrook, but to be kept on a tight rein.

'Run a campaign which virtually challenges the Japs to beat you on the race-track. Do you know the American expression *chicken*? Meaning *afraid*, with overtones of *cowardice*? That would be the way. Imply, cleverly, that if the Japanese ignored the challenge, it was because they were *chicken*. Appeal to the hairy-chested frontier bit of the American psyche.'

164

'It wouldn't work.' Armfield's scepticism of the use of behavioural science in marketing was obvious.'

'Why, Harold?' said Michael.

Armfield tried to make it sound as logical as he could, speaking as Westbrook might speak. 'There's no data for that kind of campaign, I'm sure. And isn't safety the thing these days? Attitudes about cars are changing.'

'Safety,' said Westbrook, 'is a dead duck. It never sold a motor car.'

'There's no precedent for what you suggest,' said Armfield, doggedly sticking to his line. 'We aren't playing with Dinky Toys here, nor with Monopoly money.'

In her office, Miss Harris was dealing with one of those situations she both disliked and enjoyed. She could do nothing when Oldershaw barged in and asked her to look after his suitcase. It was brown, old, battered, and seemed to have the smell of oil and dirty overalls about it. It was not a case for a managing director, nor for the office of a managing director's personal assistant, which was the title she preferred to be known by.

But if all this, and the sight of Oldershaw's uncared-for hands, offended her, then at least she wallowed in her disapproval, gained satisfaction from it. Face crocheted with distaste, mouth stitched in a black thin line, she noted with pleasure that even Oldershaw had got the message. That was her creed: don't let them tread all over you. Her professional skills gave her a secure feeling whenever she stood up for her rights and her special dignities. It wasn't the only job in town, she seemed to say.

'How long have they been going on, then?'

'The meeting,' she said, 'commenced at ten. You're almost an hour late.'

'I know I'm bloody late,' said Oldershaw, slamming through the doorway. That was the only way to treat these old bags. Who the hell did she think she was?

When he entered the boardroom he noticed at once the new table: circular, like the old one, but now in plate glass and steel. That must have cost a few quid. What did they want it for? To see who was playing kneesy with whom?

'Good morning, William,' said Bernard Grant. 'I hope everything's all right now?'

'My apologies for being late, sir. The man's as well as can be expected. He'll lose part of his right arm.'

'I'm sorry,' said Grant, 'very sorry. I trust we're covered. The Factories Acts, I mean. No negligence on our part?'

The question was predictable, thought Oldershaw, but at least he'd said he was sorry.

'No,' he told Grant. 'The damn fool took off the guard on one of the machines, started it up, then fiddled with the belt. You can't stop them.'

Oldershaw looked at the men sitting round the table. Armfield sulky, Michael Grant and Westbrook excited, Lord Bender like a judge, the one with the real power. He had the feeling he'd walked in on something.

'Well,' said Bernard Grant. 'Are we going to waste any more time on Lovelace's?' The question hung in the air, waiting to be savaged.

'Against my better judgement if we worry any further,' said Armfield.

'Benjamin?' asked Grant, still hoping that his old colleague might indicate caution.

'What have we got to lose by digging a bit deeper?' observed Lord Bender, and that was that.

Oldershaw heard the Chairman announce the next item on the agenda. He was astonished as he listened to Grant blandly explaining that the power-station contract for Brasserton's would probably not, after all, come their way. Oldershaw wanted to ask questions, but Grant waved him down, his voice boring on relentlessly. Lymington was picking at his fingers, head lowered. God, thought Oldershaw, the old devil looks like death warmed up. Michael Grant was asked to speak. Oldershaw thought, Why don't they let me have a word about my own factory?

'There's another possible project, though, Bill,' said the Chairman's son. 'It could mean a major leap forward for your company. And you're probably going to need that computer.'

The word hit the button in Oldershaw's mind. The accident yesterday was part of it. When the report came through from the hospital, one of the shop stewards had looked over at Oldershaw insolently. 'Well,' he said, 'I hope he doesn't lose his arm. But we won't need to use our bloody hands in this place much longer if all I hear is true.' Oldershaw had shouted at the man despite the warning in Colley's eyes.

'*What* computer?' he asked Michael acidly, and much too loudly. 'Not one word in three months. If there's a decision to put the thing in, why haven't I been consulted? This government by remote control is becoming a joke.'

Bernard Grant was sharp. 'William. This meeting will not become a shouting match.'

'Forgive me, sir, but I have to say this. The main board just can't sit in London making decisions and expecting us to jump to it like a load of zombies. Morale has gone to pieces with all this uncertainty. We've lost good men, and the unions are hammering on Colley's door wanting to know what's happening. I'm sorry, but what I'm saying needs to be said, Mr Grant. Headquarters can't step in and stir up the muck, then just leave us to get on with it.'

Michael knew what he wanted to say. He wanted to tell them that the long delay over the computer was the inevitable result of having a top board carrying men like Lymington and Bartram, who wasn't even present today, when what they needed was a technical man, an engineer, to overlook the whole group. The consultants who were advising him on the development of Brasserton's had been too slow coming up with their answers. He wanted his own man, a company man, one who would work through nights when the necessity for speed was there. He said nothing of this, however, when his father asked him to speak again.

'If there's any blame, it's mine. I'm sorry, Bill. Just remember that this is a *group*. There are priorities. Naturally to you your company is the most important. And – all right – perhaps there was more urgency than I realised.'

That cheered up Armfield. He had offered no objection to the concept of computerisation at Brasserton's. He even approved it. But he was encouraged to see Michael discomfited. He wondered how many minus points Lord Bender was putting down on the pad he called a mind.

'Right,' said Oldershaw, still growling. 'We've been kept hanging about long enough.'

'Not any more,' said Michael. 'And I apologise.' Lord Bender was thinking, Nice, lad, but don't overdo it; get back in the driving-seat.

'I suppose you've made up our minds for us?' Oldershaw still wasn't giving any sweetness away for free. He didn't approve of chairmen's sons, not even those he sometimes quietly liked. And he was still thinking about Hannah and the way the flesh shredded from the man's mangled arm.

'No,' said Michael. 'We simply have a proposal for you. It's up to you to say yes or no. But let's not get bogged down in that. What I really want to talk about doesn't necessarily depend on whether you have a computer on line or not. Now that the power station thing has fallen through, there's this other proposition that may interest you.'

As Oldershaw listened to Michael expounding the arrangement which Ed Corsino had suggested, his mind was already visualising what might happen at the factory. It was one hell of a gamble. And if he thought so, what would Colley say? Blow his top, if Oldershaw knew anything. But God, what a chance if the Grants would back him with real money. It would mean goodbye to all those small stock jobs they did on the side. This could tie them up for a year, two years. A bit like the war: just flogging away to meet deadlines. That didn't frighten him. But maybe the thought of attempting it without a computerised production line did.

He could see, he thought, how Michael Grant's mind worked. Proposal for a computer? That was eyewash, in his view. If Brasserton's took this job on, whatever Michael Grant had in mind for the production line would *have* to be. No question about it. The boy is clever. Gives me delusions of grandeur – and then he can quietly have his way about how my factory shapes up for the future. Christ, he knows me, knows my vanities. Am I that obvious? Colley was right. Put in a computer for production, and you change what the factory is about. What you need is brain-power, nursemaids with a sense of responsibility and the right certificates, not men with skills in their hands that have been nurtured and passed down over half a century.

Armfield, he noticed, was looking sour again. Lymington had the bland stare of a man whose mind was elsewhere. Lord Bender was alert, Bernard Grant misleadingly acting like a judge undecided whether to don the black cap or not, fooling himself, since Bender was the only one there who had the true ability to adjudicate.

Michael Grant looked at him, eyes steady, expressionless. 'Well, Bill, what do you think?'

'I think it sounds – let's say *possible*,' said Oldershaw. 'But come on, Michael' – he felt warm enough to use the forename – 'let's talk about *my* computer again. Not just the one you want us to slot into the control unit for Ecuador. I reckon we need a computer to tackle a job like this. And that will take time to install and get running right. How *much* time depends on how you use it. What have you got in mind?'

Michael looked at his father. 'Would you like me to explain?'

Lord Bender was already nodding his head. Prosser had woken up too. Bernard Grant waved his hand in a gesture of assent. In any other circumstances, he thought, I would be proud to hear my son speaking with such authority. I have backed computerisation too, but not as a platform for Michael to make himself the centre of decisions on this board.

'If we're going to automate we really want to do a worthwhile job,' said Michael. 'You should have the chance to jump ahead of your competitors. So the idea is not to use the computer simply for production planning and control. We want – well, it's suggested we put it on line, that it controls the machines, the lot. . . .'

'Machining centres?' queried Oldershaw. 'The tape idea?'

'More than that,' said Michael.

Bernard Grant fidgeted. Here he was losing touch with reality, his reality. He always felt this way when technologists began to speak their jargon. He understood figures and the instinctive smell of a deal. The touch and the talents of the entrepreneur in the market-place were his. How, he thought, can I begin to judge this issue? But he wanted not to appear in ignorance. He was glad when Lord Bender spoke the words for him.

'Michael, can you explain that? In layman's language, please?'

'Yes,' said Michael. 'We *could* control Bill's machine tools by programming a computer for certain repetitive jobs. The computer produces punched tape which is fed into the tools, and this governs what they do – drilling, boring or whatever. Each group of satellite tools that gets its ration of punched tape from the computer is called a machining centre.'

'Understood,' said Lord Bender. 'But you want to do more?'

'That's right. We don't want the computer *off*-line, handing out tape to separate machining centres, which are just like a lot of mini-computers. That method's expensive and limited. We want to put the computer *on*-line, so that it's part of the production process all the time – talking to the tools through wires rather than tape, if you like. This way you get constant communication rather than intermittent communication, and you save money. If your programme's flexible enough, the computer can tell the machines to do different jobs instantaneously according to the needs of each batch of work that comes along. You control the whole production line at one go.'

'That's a big jump,' said Oldershaw. 'Really pushing it.'

'Can it be done?' asked Lord Bender.

'Our advice – and it's the best – is yes.' Michael looked around the table. This was the moment when the fighting would really begin. His father fingered the seams of his trousers, and Lord Bender noticed the gesture. Armfield spoke first.

'Assuming – a very big assumption – that all this could work, it still sounds a very expensive miracle. Starting with the computer for Brasserton's. One quarter of a million for that, shall we say?'

It couldn't be a better question, thought Michael. It will get my eye in for the trickier balls. He could afford to be magnanimous. 'That needn't worry you, Harold. We'd rent the computer. Perhaps seventy thousand a year in costs. Not bad.'

Armfield, sniffing around for an ally, turned to the managing director of Brasserton's. 'What do you say, Mr Oldershaw?' He was damned if he was going to go all matey with an engineer.

'It's a very forward-looking scheme. I'd like to try it, of course. But development costs could be high.'

Oldershaw saw Michael frown momentarily. He thought, Frown away, son. This is what I want, deep in my guts. Moving forward, bigness. This is my future. But Brasserton's can't foot the bill. If we're going to go into it, then everyone had better know the costs from the start. I'm not going to be hammered in a year's time for bursting through my budgets. He had attended Bernard's post-mortems on over-spending before. No thanks. It's not worth the candle if the money isn't there. And the Prospero Group must provide it.

Lord Bender probed deeper. 'Apart from the provision of a computer for the Brasserton's plant, which is one issue, there is also a computer involved in the product your American contact wants us to turn out for him?'

'Correct. Normally we would simply supply a whole list of specified control mechanisms to the customer as sub-contractors, then let him assemble whatever he had in mind. Ed Corsino wants us to do the assembly at Brasserton's. Buy in whatever we need, including a computer, and put the whole damn shoot together, including the bits we make. The package we shipped out to South America would, in effect, be the whole process control for the petro-chemical plant.'

Lord Bender was rubbing the side of his head vigorously, flaking off a spot or two of dandruff. Now it was Bernard Grant's turn to register in his mind a colleague's concern. The deal sounded good: neat, progressive, logical. But how could one judge profit margins in an equation like this?'

'I quite like the sound of it,' said Lord Bender, 'but it has the feel of a gamble to me. The Americans are asking you to do something rather unusual, is that right?'

'Yes.' Michael knew that this was the crunch point.

'And they're expecting us to put up the risk capital?'

170

Armfield crowded in heavily. 'That's the snag. And a damned dangerous one.'

Lord Bender serenely continued his line. 'If the thing doesn't work out, they lose nothing. They might even slap us down for failing to meet delivery dates.'

'No,' said Michael. 'Ed Corsino knows there are risks, and so do I. If we're willing to bear the development costs, he won't insist on rigorous penalty clauses on the time-schedule. It's tricky for him too, remember. He has a customer to satisfy. He has to find finance. It's a fair deal.'

'It still means tying up more money than we have to spare,' said Armfield. 'You've seen my paper on our cash-flow problems. I simply don't think we have the capital at present for any high-risk ventures. We're hard up against our borrowing limit, and any money we spend now ought to have a quick return. I doubt if we'll see a penny back on the project you're suggesting for two years or more. That's the trouble with these big capital equipment deals. No one pays till we deliver the goods.'

'That's a major objection, Michael,' said his father. Bernard Grant felt happier. These were terms he understood. Armfield had argued powerfully to him that the capital requests of some of the other subsidiaries should take precedence at present. The company which made frozen foods for one: you began to see your profit every time a housewife in Bolton lifted a packet of peas out of the freezer. That really was business.

'They'll probably be using American funds,' explained Michael. Then, reluctantly, 'If we agreed to go ahead, I *could* try to arrange for substantial forward payments. First, a good down-payment, then instalments dependent on our progress with the work. There's no guarantee, but I think I could swing it.'

In his heart he was far from certain that he could. This was the risk he had now to take. He watched Oldershaw.

'I'd be very willing to have a go,' said the man from Brasserton's. 'It could revolutionise our prospects.'

'That's the real point.' Michael poised himself for the final thrust. 'Either we accept the fact that Brasserton's will paddle on as it is, with the danger of being overtaken by its competitors. Or we take our chances now to put it into the big league. Ecuador is beginning to boom, just like Venezuela fifteen years ago. Oil will make them rich. This chemical plant isn't the end of it. We could learn a lot for the benefit of several other of our companies. If this comes off, Brasserton's alone could win a reputation big enough to give them ten times the turnover in a few years.

There are risks, and they're obvious to all of us. I think we can minimise them. Then we ought to push on.'

Prosser stopped drawing endless series of interlocking rings on the pad before him and spoke. 'One problem we haven't mentioned. What you've been saying could turn Brasserton's upside down. It would become a different company, needing new skills and maybe a lot of new men. We could have big union trouble. And it could take time to find the new people.'

Michael regarded him coolly, but without hostility. 'That would be your baby, Barry. I'm sure we have every confidence that you and Bill could handle it.'

There was an uneasy silence. In the air, illumined by the shafts of sunshine that came through the blinds, the dust danced. Outside, a long way below, an ambulance siren cawed like a rook enraged. Bernard Grant was thinking that his son knew what it was all about: business was risk, no matter how safe the deal looked. You grabbed your chances, took what precautions you could, and prayed. There was the item of natural talent, of course. Some men were born with insight or with luck. Like Bernard Grant. He applauded Michael for sounding as he himself might have sounded in the early difficult years almost two decades ago, yet was jealous of the way his son increasingly these days took initiatives which diminished his control. Grant had always wanted his son in the business, of course; but on his terms, doing things his way. The world of the organisation was changing, and despite his efforts since he had returned after the thrombosis, Grant constantly felt his inability to make decisions work for him as they used to, even on many occasions to make decisions at all. He hadn't even yet had the talk he'd promised himself with Earl Sanger, had he? Nor run a check on that lascivious-looking girl who worked for Howland. What he had been experiencing was like a numbing of the will to act.

The minds of the men around the table with him went on joylessly working. Armfield, genuinely concerned about his responsibility for the group's finances, loathing excessive risks by nature, and sensing that politically he must win this round, wondered whether Talbot-Brown was digging the dirt in New York yet. Lymington contemplated the future bleakly and felt the solid steel chair beneath him melting away. Prosser, believing that Michael Grant thought too little about convincing human beings of the virtues of change, visualised the list of union officials he might need soon to invite to informal lunches. Westbrook, trying to decide whether he should attempt to make love to

172

Diana again after a month's hiatus, but sharply keeping abreast of the board meeting, reckoned it was sixty-forty against Michael at this moment. It depended, as so often, on Lord Bender. Everyone was waiting for the major manipulator of the organisation's shares to speak.

'If,' said Lord Bender, 'you can arrange some kind of part-payment by the customer in advance, I think we might try it.'

Words flowed for another hour, but the crisis had arrived, had passed, and the men around the table mouthed only formalities. Oldershaw exulted inwardly and outwardly spoke technologist's gobbledy-gook. Armfield underlined his reservations, Prosser the size of the task of persuasion with the men, Michael the lustrous future for both Brasserton's and Ecuador. Out of crude oil, he explained, you got naphtha. And once you fed naphtha into the kind of petrochemical plant Corsino's consortium planned for Ecuador, you became a modern magician. The plant was called a steam cracker, and that's just what it was: a bloody big nut-cracker to break up carbon molecules in the naphtha and to get out – well, chiefly a gas named ethylene, but also acrylonitrile, cyclohexane, caprolactam, polypropylene.... You name it, he knew it. When he added polyvinylchloride to the list, someone else muttered PVC, and Michael laid off his primitive-Greek lexicological bit to say what he really meant. Depending how many extra units you built around the basic ethylene cracker plant, you could make fertilisers or textiles, plastic pipes or adhesives or paints. Given oil and crackers, men could eat, dress, build, decorate. Anything. Around *their* crackers, the Japanese were erecting whole industrial cities. Ecuador might do that, too. Maybe the boffins could even bring banana oil into the equation. And Ecuador had a hell of a lot of bananas. Michael sounded like an exam paper on organic chemistry, ecology, South American economics, and the power of positive thinking. His father only half-heard him. Worrying whether Lord Bender viewed what had happened as a defeat for Armfield alone or for the Chairman too, Grant felt a slight pain at his throat but shrugged it away.

As they moved from the room towards lunch, Lord Bender put his hand on Michael's arm and said quietly, 'Well done, boy. And good luck with Corsino.'

Translating the message swiftly, Michael smiled a careful smile. He knew what Lord Bender was saying: the ride is easy, boy, and who is making it so? But fall down on this, and you could quite possibly be a dead man.

173

8. Nothing man and working wife

HARDY had it all wrapped up.

Fielder should go – morally because he deserved to, and politically because he would provide a scapegoat satisfactory to all sides, even old man Grant. David should also report that Bartram, having been concentrating on the sales side himself, was getting some results and was in effect operating a one-man profit-improvement programme.

'They'll like the scientific sound of that. They always do,' he said. 'And it will provide a lever for Westbrook and the young master to suggest, in all innocence, that the programme is formalised so that London can give some help on it if necessary. Once Bartram has to get it down on paper he'll either be shown up for a bloody old fraud or, more likely, he'll have to commit himself to tough targets. In the latter case, that piece of paper can be used to thwack him hard from time to time if he's failing to hit budget.'

'But Bernard Grant won't want to get rid of Bartram. It'll reflect too much on his own judgement for appointing the man in the first place.'

Hardy shrugged. 'Not nearly so much as hanging on to him if month after month the awful truth, spelled out loud and clear, is thrust under the noses of the board. Lord Ben might have something to say about that.'

Sipping his drink, David pondered. Hardy's solution was neat. Too neat. Like an exercise during a management course, a case history. Except that this time it was real money, real bones to be broken. He wished Hardy had not pronounced sentence on Fielder with such relish.

'Besides,' said Hardy, 'you can't be expected to save the company on your own. You can only do your best – and keep your nose clean. Obviously it's not politically possible to recommend that Bartram's fired. Even Michael Grant wouldn't thank you for

174

that, let alone Lionel Westbrook. You'd be failed on diplomatic grounds, lad. So you appear to be helpful – but set the snare. No one can blame *you* if the old man proves obstinate despite everything. God knows, you might even force Bartram into being a real live manager.'

'I rather like him. Bartram, I mean. However good or bad he is as a manager, he seems straight.'

'So you've been saying all through lunch. Don't be fooled by that blunt northerner gag. These boys use their accents like a badge, and everyone south of Watford imagines that a maimed Yorkshire vowel or two equals unimpeachable integrity. It's a myth our less civilised countrymen spend their lives encouraging. Like that crap about fish and chips tasting better in the North. It's psychological warfare, that's all.'

David had been ill at ease that morning, walking alone out of Alison's flat, feeling conspicuous with his suitcase. She had left earlier, understanding how he wanted to get to the office late to maintain the fiction that he had ridden from the North on the early morning train. It was obvious, clumsy, easy. He sat and smoked in the flat, and when he grew tired of looking at the disarray around him washed up the dishes and even smoothed out the bed. It was ridiculously domestic. He felt like a cross between a daily woman and a kept man.

Westbrook, luckily, was out when he got in. Hardy had wanted to work through lunch, but David bribed him with the offer of a French meal and, in an uncharacteristic burst of nervous pressure, champagne with it. He badly wanted to hear Hardy's views before he faced Westbrook.

'Champagne means you've found a way to become MD yourself, or, more boringly, that you're nicely in hand on your expenses,' Hardy had said. 'Still, you know the importance of the business lunch. The art of managing it and holding your liquor is an asset more valuable than two years at Harvard. Who's going to give a contract to a man who falls over as he's leaving the Savoy Grill? Did you know we import more champagne than any other nation in the world? Fifty million glasses sunk annually. There's a true sense of values for you.'

So they had eaten well. David had got the answers he wanted. All in all, it was worth it. He remembered the words unexpectedly, part of a song that woman had been singing last night as he was undressing, before the record clicked off. He'd looked at the sleeve in the morning. Mabel Mercer she was called. Alison had been good, yes, but how good is good? He had been wondering what happened now. In the morning the usual rejection symptoms had set in, a vague regret that he had chanced it and a feeling of resentment that he would need to play out a charade, even for only a few sentences, with Sheila. He hated that part of it. Though he could be a good liar, it would demean their relationship in his eyes. He even imagined he didn't fancy Alison much any more.

'Will Gerald Fielder take it like a man?' Hardy was asking. Don't keep on about it, David thought, and said: 'I suppose so.'

'No regrets,' said Hardy. 'How many more times do I have to tell you? There are a hundred others dependent on your old chum. The greater good of the greater number.'

'He was still a chum,' David insisted.

'A chum, not a friend. I don't take the view that it's a mortal sin to shed your business chums once you make it to a rung of the ladder where they don't belong. Business is business, not to be confused with friendship.'

'But they *are* confused.'

'Sometimes I despair of you. Putting you on that board may have been a mistake. They should have chosen me. Why didn't they, I ask myself?'

David looked curiously at Hardy. Sometimes the acid came into Hardy's voice so sharply you couldn't tell whether he was joking or not. For the first time it occurred to him that Hardy might be envious of his directorship. It was possible, why not? Because Hardy chose the armour of cynicism, that need not preclude ambition. Hardy was human, not an automated joke machine.

'You're welcome,' said David. 'Do you want me to resign?'

Hardy laughed. 'Don't be so po-faced. But there are times when I wish you'd get your standards straight. Business is neither an army of St Georges charging about slaying dragons called inefficiency and excess costs, nor an economic Mafia. Your job is survival and, like I said, the greatest good of the greatest number. That's all. So why weep over Gerald?'

'He's given good value in his time, whatever he is now. And he's been loyal.'

'Loyalty is what's written in the contract, nothing more. I'll give value for money, so long as I get money for value.'

Hardy leaned back as if that were the end of the lesson for the present. 'Doing anything for Easter?' he asked.

'Not really. Not with Sheila like she is.'

'She's blooming?'

'When I see her I'll let you know.'

'Don't let her eat too much stodge. That's the trouble. We select our steaks and salads on expenses or in subsidised restaurants. They make do with shepherd's pie and sandwiches.'

'She's all right.'

'Never take that for granted. The suburbs are slow death to the spirit – and the body if you're not careful.' Hardy smiled with deliberate sweetness. 'Even Miss Bennett will be a *hausfrau* one day. Have you made her yet?'

'I wish I had the time.'

'You wouldn't tell me even if you found the time, I suppose.'

'What do you think?'

'Ah, well. The course of true lust never did run smooth.'

Hardy looked at his watch. 'Look, I'll have to rush. I've only got a few days to clear up a pile of papers, plus four meetings.'

'Why the panic?'

'Teresa and I are going to sunny Tunisia. We've dumped the kids on an army of relatives, like billeting out the military. We take off on Good Friday. Our first holiday alone in six years.'

'Great,' said David, reflecting that Hardy must have got a raise if he could manage Tunisia in the spring *and* bring up a tribe of kids.

*

It had taken Talbot-Brown almost a week to find the man. He might have been wasting his time even then. That was business, he thought: fifty per cent slog, forty-nine per cent good luck, and one per cent bloody good luck. But you had to stick to the rules to make the most of your luck. And one of the rules for discovering the truth about any company was to track down ex-employees of some stature, preferably ex-employees who had been fired.

Gelson, who had tried to be too greedy in acquiring personal stock during one of Ed Corsino's take-overs, sipped his whisky sour. 'Corsino never did like too much competition from his own stable.' He had long pale fingers, yellow hair, and a face in which slyness and prettiness contended. When he spoke, his slack lips slid and glistened. Talbot-Brown felt ill at ease with the man; he kept thinking of Dorian Gray.

'Tell me everything about Hong Kong.'

'Not everything,' said Gelson. 'Not yet. I'll run you a trailer of the movie. You see if you want the whole show.'

'He has a stake in this company?'

'Nothing so crude. He just shipped the nickel to it. Then, as it

177

happens, the nickel was re-exported from Hong Kong to Romania. A little nickel goes a long way when you're making high-tensile steel. The State Department wouldn't like that.'

'He knew it was going to Romania?'

'Who cares? The fact is that it did. Draw your own conclusions.'

'If he *didn't* know, I don't see how he could be blamed.' Talbot-Brown, believing that he might have discovered enough already to fix Corsino, was trying to keep the price down. 'Maybe what you have to tell me isn't worth *too* much.'

'Don't be naïve, sir.' Gelson had this old-fashioned Southern courtesy about him in his speech patterns. It went with his drawl and his insolence. Manners used to score points. 'Spread something like this around Washington and Corsino would be last in the queue when it came to getting funds from any of the government agencies. If anything slays them on Capitol Hill it's the suspicion that a gentleman has been trading with a black-list country. That's all you need. The suspicion. I know what it's worth.'

Talbot-Brown was not surprised that Gelson knew. One of New York's best-known finance columnists – fifth man in the line of contacts which had led him to Gelson – had told him. 'He's greedy, Antony. And he loathes Corsino for knowing he's greedy, as well as for kicking him out a year ago. Maybe that'll help you, though. Men don't always demand money when they're motivated by revenge. Sometimes they do it for love.'

'What about Corsino's other deals abroad?' he asked Gelson.

'Nothing out of the ordinary, so far as I know.'

'No bribes, nothing like that?'

Gelson hissed a laugh. 'Who have you been doing business with, sir? In overseas selling no one's going to worry much over a few thousand dollars on a deal.'

'Corruption is corruption,' said Talbot-Brown, eyes gleaming with insincerity. 'In Tokyo they call it the black mist.' He was still trying to draw Gelson.

'Wrong, sir. All things are relative. If corruption is a custom, it is no longer corruption, since everyone starts equal. It becomes merely a national trait which you must learn about, like learning the local language or not to drink the water. In South America or Africa, a bribe is part of the overheads put into the selling-price. It is no more immoral than the payments with which your British businessmen bribe unions to forget about restrictive practices.'

178

Talbot-Brown snapped his eyes as if offended. 'When countries are poor they shouldn't have to pay outrageous prices for goods and services so that politicians can stack up bank balances.'

'*Please*,' said Gelson. 'How can such places do without their politicians? Men of education and skill are rare. Yet usually, because these nations are poor, their top men are miserably underpaid. Such men would not give the benefit of their talents to government if they had no expectation of using office to make money. No one loses, except the rich nations who can well afford it, and only certain Africans are *too* notorious. In South America they don't really like the straight deposit of funds in Switzerland. They prefer to be able to channel business through companies in which their relatives have an interest. In such Catholic countries, family ties are strong.'

'I'd still call it bribery.'

'They would call it a benefaction, an act of thanksgiving,' said Gelson. 'And because you British – and some Americans – do not understand this, you too often end up with no contracts.'

'You were in on some of Corsino's package deals abroad?' asked Talbot-Brown, tiring of being a grandmother told how to suck eggs.

'Of course.'

'I'd still like to know about them.'

Gelson stroked the side of his glass in a gesture almost lascivious. 'I took the precaution of removing one or two files when I left.'

An hour later, Talbot-Brown lay on his bed. A neon light flicked on and off across the street outside his windows although it was scarcely dark. The chasms of New York were the enemies of daylight. Very little that Gelson had told him was either surprising or shocking. He would have preferred the Hong Kong business to be more watertight. The usual thing was for goods to be bought through a 'paper' company and then sold to the blacklisted country. That way, if you could prove the involvement of the producer or seller of the goods in the 'paper' company, the case was open and shut.

He liked the metaphor, knowing that Americans sometimes called them 'suitcase' companies. Liechtenstein and Luxemburg were full of them, housed in buildings which looked suffocated with the garlands of brass nameplates outside, but inside whose prim portals you were lucky to find more than two or three guys in pinstripe pants, local attorneys with suitcases full of papers that recorded nothing more than the facts that the companies these men nurtured were simply vehicles for money to pass through – bridges between buyers and sellers who had their own reasons for not wishing to trade directly. Okay, so Corsino was clean on that score, but there was enough about him to start smoke. He was not himself certain what good all this would do Armfield. Would his master really use the information to try and screw up Michael Grant's deal? That was carrying company politics a bit far, even in Talbot-Brown's eyes. Or did Armfield have something else in mind? Perhaps he even believed he was working for the good of the organisation as well as settling personal scores.

The radio burbled low beside his bed: the longshoremen were giving trouble again. He had heard the same story pumped out on radio for three days now, had read it in the papers, seen it on TV. They told you things so often, so relentlessly through the American media these days that news lost reality, was processed into a low-pitched buzz, like verbal Muzak. Knowledge without wisdom, facts without understanding. He switched off and thought of the girl from the advertising agency with whom he would dine that evening. What was the question he thought they still asked on the visa form? 'Do you intend visiting the USA for any immoral sexual purposes?' It seemed a quaint inquiry to put to a tripper from London. Who needed to cross the Atlantic for *that*? He often wondered if anyone had ever answered 'Yes', or even 'I live in hope'.

He had met her in a singles bar on Second Avenue, the kind of low-lit place for the lonely full of girls feeling rather faint and looking for somewhere to lie down for maybe an hour, as some musical show he'd seen had put it. And someone to lie down with, inevitably. It was not his usual practice, the pick-up. But two of his friends were out of town. One would be back in two days' time. Though his work was done, he would stay over for a few days. Armfield need not know he had done so well, so fast.

The telephone rang. It was the call he had been expecting. He began to talk guardedly to Harold Armfield.

✽

Prosser did a lot of thinking in his car. Everyone he knew who drove up to town each day said they did the same, though he suspected it wasn't true. Their minds would be like wet blotting paper as they listened to the droning pap of pop on the radio or the inconsequential snippets of non-news and ghastly matey humour which passed for early-morning magazine programmes.

180

None of these things gave Prosser any pleasure, especially the music. The classical music wave-band was too heavy, the pop too discordant. He was a Glenn Miller man, whose taste had been cemented unalterably in the war years when he was a very young staff sergeant. *Moonlight Serenade* was what love and music for loving by was about. Love began with romance, a hundred violins playing at Carnegie Hall while Deanna Durbin looked softly out at you through misty eyes. Romance might die slowly with marriage, but lawful union was a useful discipline, giving stability to society, and both partners had a duty to keep the germ of romance alive through the medium of anniversaries celebrated, good times remembered, and the rest.

He anticipated, too, that men and women might sometimes seek diversions outside their marriages, but that was an experience which should retain the sense of specialness and sin and, according to the laws of Hollywood, circa 1945, could result in the delicious warmth of happy reconciliation between the married offenders. Promiscuity as a doctrine, openly acknowledged, was repugnant to him, chiefly because it offended his sense of order. Indiscriminate personal relationships, with responsibility for the results abandoned, would be as disastrous as lack of order on the factory floor, with small pressure groups breaking away to wreck the control of official union leaders and structures. Accordingly he hated long-haired advocates of sexual anarchy, and the songs which implied the new philosophy, as much as he loathed unofficial strikers and the malicious cells of militants who stirred up trouble in factories in defiance of agreements reached between management and unions. The contract between man and wife should be as basic as agreements in industry; both might occasionally be broken, but they were crucial bulwarks against social collapse.

So Prosser listened to no early-morning pop in the car, though in the evening there were sometimes nostalgic revivals of his kind of music. He sat in silence, cocooned against people and the telephone, and he thought. This morning he had plenty to think about.

The meeting in an hour or so with Michael Grant and the consultants about the precise shape of the reorganisation at Brasserton's was one worry. He reflected that it was strange how so many people, including most of his fellow directors, misunderstood the problem of computers. They thought it was a question of settling new staff levels with the unions, of redundancy and re-training, and it was true that those negotiations took time and trouble. But

181

Prosser could handle all this, else why had Bernard Grant given him the job in the first place? Much more fundamental was the problem of what you had left once computerisation of production had happened in a factory. Men skilled with their hands at shaping metal or wood could have the ambition to improve their skills and climb higher; and those skills induced pride in one's work as well as stirrings of loyalty. Once men became passive tenders of machinery, watchers and checkers instead of makers, ambition and involvement went out of the window. The concern for quality disappeared, and when work became a push-button exercise the only ambition a man might pursue was to have fewer buttons to push than the next man, and to get more money for pushing them.

It was all very well to talk of the age of leisure and of computers freeing men to do more exciting tasks. Supposing they didn't know how to fill the empty hours, except with sleep or bingo and the box, or were unsuited to the only tasks which now remained to be done? Brasserton's, with its reputation for skills, the tight family atmosphere which Oldershaw had nurtured down the years, would be the trickiest kind of place in which to institute the new industrial order of things. Prosser wanted to know exactly what Michael Grant and his experts had in mind, and he hoped they could be persuaded that investment in educational and recreational and employee-counselling facilities was an essential corollary of the reorganisation brought about by the computer. Brasserton's was going to become an entirely different place, and maybe even Oldershaw didn't yet realise all the implications.

He was pushing his way through the last of the Embankment traffic before Prospect House. 'What a bitch you sometimes are,' he said, enjoying the release of speaking aloud. He meant Frances. His wife had drunk too much the night before at dinner with friends, sliding into her most infuriating habit of showing disdain for the work he did.

As marriages went, it was tolerable, and he understood why. She was romantic too, shaped in the same period, except that with her the disease produced symptoms of pure fantasy. For Frances, home life in the Home Counties went on as if in a vacuum. The man departed for the office and an existence apart from the wife's social preoccupations. When they were together, their world should be the home, their local friends, local gossip, with occasional references to the husband's status in the world outside. Only good news from the office was, in her view, a fit topic for evenings at home or for weekends. The problems of her husband's job bored when they did not actually offend her. She wanted to know nothing of the nuts and bolts of industry, its necessary toil and dirt and odours. Her life she wished to be a permanent stage-set from a Noël Coward comedy, and her affaires a succession of Brief Encounters. *Flirting* was an oddly outdated word she used a lot; it went with her primly permed hair.

Prosser had learned to live with the eternal irritations of her pretensions, to swallow the injustice that she accepted the money he earned as some kind of divine right, entailing no duty of involvement in how he earned it. Once, some years ago, he had hit her very hard when his usually reined Welsh temper had burst free, provoked by her scorn at his concern for what she called *those bloody layabouts* in some pit where he was dealing with a strike. Her nose bled, her face was bruised for a fortnight. She valued the perks of her marriage too strongly to leave him. She simply stepped up the pressure for more privileges, to which he yielded, guiltily impelled to make atonement. All this he understood too, aware that she despised him for his weakness. He sensed that one day he might strike her again.

The meeting turned out to be as sticky as Prosser suspected it would be. Westbrook was there with Michael Grant, and so was Earl Sanger. Prosser disliked the habit the Chairman's son had developed of bringing his assistant to conferences without warning. Not that the presence of Sanger, and any of the others around the table, led to disagreement over the consequences of the computer. Their disputes, which at times grew sharp, were over the order of priorities of those consequences.

Westbrook was especially vehement and, Prosser privately admitted, bloody good. Again and again the marketing director urged the absolute priority of working out in detail the implications of computerisation for the kind of business which Brasserton's would now be getting into. He had prepared a tight, logical and typical paper as he often needed to, lacking at this stage enough marketing back-up in the subsidiary companies. He wanted time. He wanted funds. And he seemed to ignore, in Prosser's eyes, some of the more fundamental human problems.

'We'd better,' said Westbrook, rephrasing some of the things already spoken, 'concern ourselves first with what kind of business Brasserton's will be in. It sure as God *won't* be only the making of servo-mechanisms. It's going to be the creation of much bigger industrial packages, a sort of mini-Ed Corsino operation, else where's the return on all the investment we're making? And Oldershaw's outfit just isn't geared to that. Not yet.' He turned to Prosser. 'You can push your staff problems all you like, Barry, but if we aren't sure where we'll sell and what we'll be selling we may not have a business for the people at Brasserton's to work in at all.'

The consultants nodded wisely, which they had been doing all morning. Like Tweedledum and Tweedledee. Westbrook felt good, and he knew he was winning. He had only to keep up the pressure and, occasionally, to let Michael pick up a germ of an idea he had planted and take it over. Michael, despite his flair, was no different from other top men. Westbrook had found that Michael liked to treat any good ideas he found lying around as his own. Even Sanger hadn't been able to seize control of the discussion this time, and Westbrook knew he needed to underline that situation too. Sanger had been doing too much of the marketing thinking lately. A renaissance for Lionel Westbrook was overdue.

Michael Grant, observing all this, and pleased that today the balance of power between Prosser, Sanger and Westbrook was working out much more as he felt it always should, with no one of the three ever gaining a clear-cut ascendancy, was not pleased when the door opened. Westbrook's secretary appeared, looking apprehensive, but still determined. She mumbled apologies as the talking stopped, shoved a sheet of paper under Westbrook's nose, and stood uncertainly, cheeks highly coloured. Westbrook read the note, looked startled, then annoyed. He half-rose, hesitated, sat down again.

'Sorry for the interruption,' he said, 'but it *is* important.'

Then he scribbled quickly on the paper and shooed the girl from the room.

Often, as the arguments continued, he would look at his watch, and everyone in the room sensed his impatience for the thing to be wound up. Sanger was now coming more into the discussion, and to Westbrook the American's relentless logic, teasing and testing every proposition put forward, seemed like pure bloodymindedness, a succession of verbal stratagems sent especially to bitch him. He thought this all the more since Sanger was supposed to be on his side, and the long dissections did not in fact upset the main structure of his marketing arguments. Westbrook went on winning, but Sanger spoiled the taste of victory.

✱

Two hours later, as the meeting was ending, David Travis sat opposite Diana Westbrook in her sitting-room, clutching a glass of whisky, wondering what he should do next. Apart from the strip of plaster on her forehead, she looked fine, which was not exactly what he had expected when he left Prospect House for the hospital.

What the hell was Westbrook playing at, sending him to hold her hand? The secretary said the car had turned over. One of the two passengers was seriously injured. That, Diana said, when he found her in the casualty ward, sitting on the edge of a bed, was a hospital horror story. The car had skidded and struck a bollard. The photographer who was driving her *might* have a broken wrist. She had banged her head, not too hard, hence the cut. Once David appeared she insisted on going home. 'I haven't got concussion, I'm sure. And I know the symptoms to watch for. I'm not staying in this place.' David sympathised with her. The other occupants of the ward would have depressed anyone not too ill to notice.

'It was nice of you to come,' she said in the car as he headed for St John's Wood.

'That's all right.'

'What was this meeting that Lionel couldn't leave?'

'Something to do with a computer for one of our companies. Brasserton's. An engineering firm. I think we talked about it that night of your dinner party.'

'Fascinating,' she said, leaning back and closing her eyes.

'Are you sure you're all right?'

'It doesn't seem to matter very much, does it? Not when there are decisions to be taken about bloody computers.'

He was uncertain what to say. In the end it came out muffled. 'That's not fair.'

'Don't be so bloody loyal, David. I've told you before.' Her hand touched him, and if it was meant as a maternal gesture that wasn't how it felt. 'I appreciate your coming, but for God's sake don't try to excuse Lionel. He's a louse.'

He said: 'Would you like some music?'

'Very low,' she said.

Westbrook's note had been brusque enough. *David. Please look after this. Held up in meeting.* Nine words scrawled below the secretary's message that Mrs Westbrook had been injured in a road accident and was in hospital. What did he expect me to do in the circumstances except rush off to see her? David had tried telephoning, but got no sense out of the switchboard other than that he should come at once. He wondered what use Westbrook believed his presence would have been if the woman was really hurt. He felt resentful and uncomfortable. Yesterday, after lunch, he had spent an hour with Westbrook talking about Supergear. He had not explained particularly well what he intended his report to say. Finally, as he left, Westbrook said quite coolly, 'Get it right, David, please. Else how could I defend you – or myself?'

At the house, Diana insisted that he stay for a drink and something to eat. His morning and his lunch-hour had been ravaged. It was almost two o'clock. From the hospital he had telephoned to tell Westbrook that she was leaving for home, more or less unhurt. He hadn't been able to reach her husband, only the secretary. Now, Diana was having no better luck. She slammed down the phone.

'He'll be on his way,' said David.

'Not on your life,' she said. 'He's at a boardroom lunch.'

'He'll have got my message you're okay.'

'I'd still like to see him, even if I'm not at death's door.'

The Portuguese woman called Lucrezia brought in a tray of cold meats and salad. David sat and forked food on to his plate though he had little appetite. After the woman had gone, Diana looked at him and said: 'Remember the party? Nothing has changed about what I said to you. At the moment I feel very much like taking you to bed. It must be the delayed effects of this morning.'

David said nothing. Apart from everything else, sex in the afternoon with the walking wounded was not quite the way he wanted to play it. She laughed.

'Wishful thinking, dear boy. There's Lucrezia for one thing. She might be suspicious if I suddenly gave her the afternoon off, and the Portuguese are very moral. Or maybe you don't fancy me. Too busy with that PR girl – what's her name – Alison?'

'No,' he said. 'I fancy you. It's just not on, is it? And you're still being bloody unfair.'

'In this game, David, there's no such thing as unfairness. You just play it for yourself. That's what Lionel is doing now. That's what he usually does.'

She stood up and walked across the room to pour herself another whisky. 'I feel like something to warm me up,' she explained. 'Wine isn't for the shell-shocked.' Then she seemed to make a decision. 'Let me tell you something, David, and if it's indiscreet, well, put it down to my condition. It's like I told you before, it's because of Sheila that I don't, not because of Lionel. He and I understand each other. Occasionally, very occasionally, since he rarely has the time, he's had women. The word comes back, and I shrug and know it won't last long. Even his paramours he plays short – on time, on concern, on performance. Do you know that Nina Simone song – *The Other Woman*?'

David was looking down at the floor. He knew the song. What had that got to do with anything? Sentiment for the Surbiton jet-set.

'He's a pretty poor performer, you know. Short and sharp and detached and very greedy, like a little boy stuffing himself with cake. He doesn't care much what the people he sleeps with want. He's never satisfied me or even hurt me in bed, and frankly I think it's not occurred to him I might *want* to be hurt as well as pleasured. He takes what he thinks he needs, breathes very heavily – that's the forty fags a day – and goes to sleep very quickly. Do I shock you?'

'No,' he said. 'Embarrass me, yes. And, if I'm honest, I feel flattered too. Gossip in high places, all that. Why do you take such chances?'

'I don't believe you're a tattler.' She whisked her hand, as if dismissing some other words she might have spoken. 'I'm almost past caring.'

'Why, if it's not a rude question, don't you leave him, then?'

She laughed tartly. 'No – don't get offended. Partly, I suppose, because I'm not entirely blameless.' She was thinking back to an argument in the bedroom, Lionel standing ridiculously in striped underpants and socks, flailing the air with his arms. *Christ, darling, don't you know that working wives are the death of love?* And she, shouting back *Why do you think I work? You're a nothing man, my sweet. All business, all preoccupation. Our love, if that's the word you want to use, was finished long before I found something else to do except sit and worry when you were coming home.* Should she have kept herself together longer, worked harder at their marriage? Who could know.

David was waiting for her to go on. 'And partly it's because I can't really visualise life without him, and I'm sure he wouldn't know what to do without *me*. We're like a rotten house. Leave it alone and it stands. Pull out one timber and the whole damn thing collapses. We're frightened of that, both of us. We need the convenience and the reassurance of what we have.'

He put down his plate. 'I'd better be getting back.'

'It's not unusual, this kind of marriage.'

187

'No,' he said, standing.

'So take it easy. Give Sheila *room* to love you. Build what you want to build together. To hell with the rest.'

She came over to him, picked up a napkin and brushed a crumb from his cheek. Then she kissed him, with skill and enjoyment, nestling. When she disengaged herself, he said: 'It's not that I don't want to. . . .'

'That, I'm glad to say, is obvious. Do you want a cold shower?'

They both laughed, easily, almost for the first time. Then she took his hand and led him to the front door.

'Thank you so much for coming to look after me. It meant a lot.' As he nodded, she said. 'And maybe one day – well, I think we'll both know when that is. Meantime, I'm glad I'm still in competition with Alison, even if she did get to you first.'

He walked quickly to the car, wondering exactly how much she knew.

✿

Even on the telephone, fuzzy from New Jersey, Ed Corsino sounded very angry indeed. Michael had never heard him this way before.

'Listen, Ed. If it's true, I know nothing about it. What do you take me for?'

'My information is reliable. I pay enough for it. Is this goddam phone secure?'

'Yes,' said Michael. It was his private line, totally protected and constantly checked since Earl Sanger had begun his operations.

'Well, this guy of yours has been over here for a week. Poking around all over New York and Washington.'

'Have you got a name?'

'Yeah. Talbot-Brown. Antony Talbot-Brown, for Christ's sake. Do you know him?'

'Yes. He's one of ours. . . .'

'Like I said, then, what gives?'

Why hadn't Sanger or Westbrook or someone got on to this? Michael beat a slow tattoo on the desk with a single finger. 'I don't know, Ed, but I'll damn soon find out. You've got to understand. He doesn't work for *me*. He's not my man.'

'You sound worried, Michael.' Corsino was beginning to thaw, sharing the sense of alarm with someone else. He might even laugh soon.

'Not worried. Curious. What exactly has he been doing?'

'Just asking questions. But I don't like some of the people he's been talking to.'

188

'Who, for instance?'

'At least one guy who knows too damn much about the organisation and hates my guts.'

Michael was beginning to understand, but he still didn't see Armfield's motives altogether clearly. 'Whatever it is,' he said, 'leave it to me. I'll ring as soon as I can. What about the other thing?'

'They're talking in Washington now. The idea would be for a check to be made on your work every month or two. You'd be paid on a strict progress basis. We may have to twist a few arms.'

'Yes?'

'I still have one or two cards to play. Like a scholarship I've been thinking of endowing for a certain college.' Corsino laughed.

'You sound pleased. Am I expected to ask why?'

'The guy we're talking to – one of the guys, anyway – is on the board of trustees. It helps.'

'I see. You're taking a lot of trouble, Ed. I'm grateful, but why all this for us?'

'I love your big blue eyes, of course.'

'Sure.'

'And you're taking a chance, aren't you? Not every company would. Not even over here. If you fall down, I'm not sure I'll be able to help you.'

Corsino's voice was calm and friendly still, like a man warning a friend of a banana skin on the sidewalk. That was what Michael liked about Americans in business. They told it to you straight. No bluff, no dramatics. If you played the game, you were assumed to know the rules, including the price of failure.

'I take your point,' said Michael. 'I've already told the man who'll be in charge that he's on to a fixed share of the profits provided he keeps the thing up to schedule.'

'Will that be in his contract?'

'Yes.'

'Be careful, then. Limit the period for which his profit cut lasts. I knew a guy on an open-ended deal like that who did so well he wound up richer than the president of the company.'

'I'll watch it. Listen, Ed. Tell me about the man Talbot-Brown's been talking to.'

When the call was finished, Michael sat for several minutes thinking. His hands played with a silver model of a car on the desk: a memento from Le Mans. He had had one good year there; no chance of winning against the massively deployed forces of

189

Ferrari and the big manufacturers, but he'd driven hard enough in the rain and dark to be well placed in the Grand Touring class. It had been dangerous, yes, but a kind of pleasure to nurse his car through the uncertain night. That was one of the years before the big American bangers, the Chevvys and Fords, arrived to plod stolidly around the track for twenty-four hours and beat everyone else by sheer persistence and power. Christ, he thought, if anything goes wrong with this Brasserton's deal I can say goodbye to ever putting Lovelace's in the net. Goodbye to a lot of things, including shifting the balance of power away from my father. Maybe not. Can't Lord Bender see how uncertain Bernard's grip is now? The thrombosis has hit him harder than he's telling any of us. Even if one believes that flair is the essence, can't they all see that the flair is dying in Bernard? He put down the car decisively, flicked a switch among the chromium array before him and asked Sanger to come in.

The American's interpretation of Talbot-Brown's visit was precise and fast. You fed facts into Earl Sanger and the data came out with computerised certainty.

'Of course Armfield would bitch up the deal if he could. First, he undermines you. Second, he really believes we should be using our time and money in other directions. He thinks we're overcommitted. Third, he is frightened. He is a traditionalist, bound to traditional ways of making money. He knows that if this organisation develops further it will be beyond his comprehension. He will no longer be able to control it or to believe that one day he might sit at the head of it.'

It was obvious, really, Michael thought. He had, though, never believed that Armfield would go to such lengths. As a politician, the man should have been constrained by his limited imagination in the same way as he was in his business decisions. To send Talbot-Brown across the Atlantic as some kind of freelance saboteur was a new departure. Talbot-Brown must have suggested *that*. He almost admired the counter-ploy with which Armfield had answered the arrival of Sanger. Talbot-Brown was dangerous.

'If we accept that,' he said, 'what should we do now?'

Sanger paused before he answered. 'I think I should go to Geneva.'

'Geneva?'

'That's where we'll *say* I'm going.' Sanger smiled. 'The office machinery will give out that message, right down to the issue of an air ticket. Just in case Armfield has his radar working. In fact,

190

I'll drop in on New York. I don't know this Gelson guy, but a few days' reconnaissance might pay off.'

'Corsino said not to bother.'

'We look after our own interests. I don't believe in leaving it to other people. Do you?'

Michael considered the man opposite him. At first glance one might say that Sangers were a dime a dozen on Madison Avenue or Wall Street, one drop in the cataract of products turned out by the business schools of America. Almost a button-down parody, his pale chunky face framed by short-cut hair, the thin horn-rims gleaming, a whisper of beard shadow on the chin. The exterior hid the razor mind, the ruthlessness, the unswerving commitment to objectives. Michael knew he was taking risks in running Sanger in the race, was always weighing the balance which Sanger held between initiative and insubordination, support and self-seeking.

'You're right,' he said. Sanger glanced at his watch, which was his way of saying he wanted to leave. It was a curiously unspecial gesture for such a man. 'Tell me, Earl, what the hell are you doing working for me?'

'Uh?'

'Why did you bother? You could have made a packet anywhere in the States.'

Sanger gazed down, slowly smiled, and said: 'Here the competition's less fierce. More room for a guy like me to make it fast; on to the board of a major company, for instance.' Michael did not necessarily accept the rationale. He sometimes questioned whether Sanger might not be in Britain to create a beach-head for some sudden American take-over. 'And I know,' Sanger went on, 'that you'll arrange that small thing for me, don't I?'

Michael had been anticipating the question from the time that Sanger had arrived at Prospect House. His answer was almost too pat. 'Could very well be, Earl. Give me time.'

Sanger rose, forefinger pushing his spectacles firmly on to the bridge of his nose, his eyes opening wide as he did so. Then he tugged at his trousers. 'One problem's solved by the trip, anyway.'

Michael looked at him questioningly.

'I won't have to lunch with your father.'

'You're joking.'

'No. He asked me yesterday. A quiet chat, he said. Talk to him frankly about the position of our companies, discuss my experiences in America – that kind of thing. I can't say I was looking forward to it.'

191

'Why particularly?'

'I might have had to tell him I couldn't be bought.' Sanger pulled out an inhaler and sniffed it vigorously. 'Not at this time, you understand. Not at his price.'

He was on his way to the door when he stopped suddenly. The gesture was deliberate drama, beautifully timed, and both men knew it. This had better be good, thought Michael.

'I almost forgot,' said Sanger. 'That other project I was working on. There's not much to report, but the digging's started. Michael, has it ever occurred to you that one of your fellow directors might – very discreetly, of course – be a goddam fairy?'

9. The going price

It took Earl Sanger many hours to persuade Corsino that his journey to America had really been necessary. When, finally, he came up with his plan, Corsino was even more reluctant to agree. But Sanger argued with endless patience, sucking up objections with the dogged efficiency of a vacuum-cleaner picking up crumbs from the carpet. He won. Now he was on his way.

Not that the going gave him much pleasure. On this journey it was better to arrive than to travel, with or without hope. For even to Sanger, who accepted most things which made money as part of some grand, inevitable design, the scruffy New Jersey landscape on the west bank of the Hudson was depressing. He sat in the back of the limousine and watched the scrabble of diners and motels and gas stations peel past. Cars were littered around department stores like abandoned toys. Then, across brown dead grass, the fires which came with foundries and chemical plants burned off the inevitable waste. It reminded him of Ohio and the steel mills, and that was what he never wanted to go back to.

A blue-collar neighbourhood they called the part of town where he'd been raised. It was a soft sociologist's phrase. Sanger remembered nothing about the collars, only black fingernails and necks seamed in purple and winter snow that turned grey inside an hour under a hail of cinders from the polluted air. Once, when asked, he said he'd learned a lot there; like how to run fast. The street where he lived, in a no-man's-land between territories held respectively by blacks and first or second-generation Poles, had been surfaced in brick. That marked you out. Brick streets were old, lined with property that was poor and peeling. In those days, always in fear of the gangs of kids who liked victims who were small and wore steel glasses, he longed to live on a street made of concrete. Concrete streets were middle-class, respectable and safe. Sanger had devoted his life to getting away from brick streets.

Now he could afford the luxury of drawing other pleasures from his work: the feel and stimulation of power, which sometimes men truthlessly denied excited them, and the satisfaction of creating systems which worked. It was an art and a science, the best of all possible worlds. But he never fooled himself about the yardsticks by which he might judge his progress. If, at each December's end, he could count dollars in the bank, along with shares and options he had gained, then it had been a good year. He dismissed those who quarrelled with such a simple accountancy of life. You had to have lived on a brick street to understand the motivation or the arithmetic of the few who were ruthless enough and bright enough to claw their way out.

As the car waited at a stop light he watched a middle-aged couple, expressionless weekend people with unoccupied eyes, tipping groceries into the trunk of their shabby Plymouth. The woman dropped a can and looked up almost fearfully to see what the man's reaction might be. He was gross, in a worn leather jacket, the woman thin and pinched, black-coated, an archetypal survivor of endless pregnancies. The man half-raised his hand and shouted without sound, his thick lips distorting. Sanger knew all about that too, for people like these had once been his neighbours, the hard gut of America. He fingered the small scar above his right eye. He had got that when he was twelve, from the stiff edge of a five-and-ten vase. When the old man had been lapping up cheap booze and his mother screamed about the latest waitress his father had picked up, things usually got thrown. The *Wall Street Journal* had thought it was doing him a favour a year ago when it wanted to interview his mother. Normally, that was a sign you were making it. It had taken him a fortnight's hard labour to put them off the track. Unlike most Americans, he took no pleasure in his antecedents.

He was glad when the limousine, heading north, began to climb into the foothills of the Palisades. The communities they passed through might have their pretensions, skiing stores and antique shops sprouting thickly between the wooden houses, each with its porch for sitting on, but this was more prosperous country, heavy with trees and small streams and cascading slopes outcropped with grey-brown rock. Notices kept man and nature in order: threats of fines for litter-droppers, instructions on picnic places up ahead. He minded not at all that the landscape was thus constrained. He enjoyed it.

'How long, driver?'

'Another thirty minutes, maybe.'

Sanger thought it was a joke that the man he was going to see still chose to live in such classic robber-baron country. It was a world he had read about a great deal when he was young. Here in the hills, around the turn of the century, the merchants and bankers and railroad men built their palaces, separating themselves from the herd. Today Sanger regarded it as unfashionable to live so far from New York City. All the operators he knew clung to Manhattan Island where they made their bread, buying houses and apartments at incredible cost around the East Seventies and Eighties. Maybe Kerridge liked people to imagine his fortune was older than it was.

They passed through iron gates, down a long private road, soundless and dark. Sanger glimpsed deer through the trees. The house, when they arrived, was as imposing as he had anticipated, built in great slabs of grey stone, terraced and pillared. It stank of ancient power and wax polish. A manservant led him through a large hall, meticulously beamed in the fashion he would call English Tudor. Although it was not cold for early April, a log fire was burning in an open stone hearth. It was a very silent place and the crackle of wood seemed abnormally loud. Beyond double doors with great gilt handles, seated in a rocking chair which faced a tumbling vista of forest and lake, his host awaited him.

The old man turned, made no attempt to rise. His hair was black, as Sanger knew it would be, but his face looked even more astonishing than in his photographs, cratered and crossed with lines so deep they were more like razor scars, and pouches beneath the eyes big enough to hold dimes and nickels. Out of this wreckage jutted a magnificent nose – straight, long and unbloated. He waved Sanger into a deep, soft chair beside him and regarded him steadily before he spoke. His eyes were brown and hot.

'I've heard a lot about you, Mr Sanger.'

Sanger would have preferred to be sitting on one of the high-backed chairs which were littered around the book-lined room. He balanced on the edge of the uneasy chair, but still felt as if he were crouched at the old man's feet. It was not the best position from which to say what he had to.

'This man Gelson,' said Kerridge. 'How could he damage my interests?'

Sanger had already explained this part of the business at length to one of Kerridge's associates on Wall Street. He knew that the old man would have been briefed. Kerridge had a reputation for remembering very small facts and figures. That, so the *Time* magazine profile said, was one reason why he had kept such firm control of a vast commercial empire. A man like Kerridge, used to remembering the fine detail, would not forget big facts nor let big figures drain from his cash-register memory. But now he allowed Sanger to talk eagerly for almost five minutes. Then he was silent for a long time.

'You really believe my company's prospects of concluding their negotiations in England could be prejudiced?'

'The British are very touchy about the deal.'

'*Very?*'

'A lot of people don't go for any major extensions of American business interests in the country. It's a strong lobby.'

'But we're assured that the Government will not stand in our way,' said Kerridge. 'The argument is over.'

'In writing, sir?'

Kerridge grunted by way of answer. Sanger pushed ahead. 'My information is that it's still a delicate matter.' He stretched the diplomatic language lovingly. 'Opinion could change overnight if Mr Corsino's deal collapsed and a British company lost a major export order. The newspapers could make it seem like a gross example of American protectionism.'

'You would ensure that they did, I suppose?'

'They'd need no encouragement. There are plenty of precedents. Too many British politicians still view American business as a Big Brother wanting to take over the country. I wouldn't give your new textile subsidiary a chance of getting off the ground if the Prospero Group were given a kick in the teeth during the next few weeks.'

For the first time Kerridge rose. He crossed to the desk, leaned against it, and began to work a slim metal paper-knife in his hands. Sanger realised that he was a small man, whose face said that he was ancient beyond estimate, but whose compact, unflabby body could have been that of a man of forty.

'Your arguments are scarcely convincing, Mr Sanger.'

'There are others, sir.'

'Oh?'

Sanger enjoyed this moment. He knew how to balance a case. Start with the weakest arguments, build carefully towards the stronger. Business was rarely flair; just the willingness to amass detail, to take the trouble to put the pieces together or pull them apart. His approach to Kerridge had sprung from that process, nothing else. He and Corsino had spent two days going through

196

the companies with which Gelson had had associations. Then they looked among that list for those who might now gain from Corsino's present activities, the ones to whom any kind of further leverage could be applied. Everything had pointed to Kerridge.

'Mr Corsino wishes two of your companies to join a consortium concerned with a construction project he has in mind for Ecuador,' said Sanger. 'The business is impressive. Worth perhaps thirty million to them.' Corsino had wished nothing of the sort. He had his own ideas about the favours he would be handing out within the consortium. This was the part of Sanger's plan he had bucked at.

Kerridge smiled. 'Dollars or pounds sterling?'

'Dollars,' said Sanger. 'Thirty million dollars. I haven't forgotten my native tongue.'

Kerridge was still smiling. 'And the price is that I settle with Gelson? Why don't you pay whatever is necessary yourselves?'

Sanger paused, remembering his meeting with Gelson, the man's sly confidence as he sprayed hints like acid. Gelson could be bought, but not directly by Corsino or himself. The antagonism was too strong. Gelson needed also to be frightened, and Kerridge was perhaps the only man who had it within his power to do that; anyway, the only man Sanger knew, which was what mattered.

'Gelson is a man moved by motivation other than money, sir. He will, of course, take money – but only after another condition has been fulfilled.'

'Explain that, Mr Sanger.'

'He was one of the go-betweens some years ago in a missile project involving a certain company and three senior army officers. The project was an expensive failure, but the company was paid in full and when the officers retired they took up high executive positions with the company.'

'And?'

'You own that company, I believe.'

Kerridge was not at all disturbed. He might have known the point would be put. He tapped a fingernail with the knife before he answered.

'I did not own it then. My hands are clean. The men you talk about have been removed.' He dismissed the memory of them with a flick of his hand, as a man might dissuade a troublesome fly. 'Military sycophants. Men of no ability, deserving nothing.'

'Then, sir, why should you not show the world how you cleaned the stables you innocently inherited?' The old man still played with the knife, suggesting impatience, but Sanger rode on smoothly. 'The Senate would be very interested in that piece of past history. You have access to the documentation. You employ men whose memories might be, uh, stimulated to recall Mr Gelson's role in the affair?'

'I fail to see how it would serve my interests to rake all this up.'

'You may be right, sir. But I believe you alone could persuade Gelson that you had the power to initiate the investigation. If he was frightened enough, he would take quite a modest sum. For you the attraction is twofold. A major piece of business for your organisation – and no danger of your hopes in Britain being damaged. It's a strong case.'

Sanger allowed his body to relax, though his mind was still tensed, alert for signals from Kerridge. The old man put down the knife and returned to his chair, rocking himself gently. Sanger knew he must live with the silence. Additional words now would only spoil the architecture of persuasion he had built. He noticed the brown spots on the back of Kerridge's hands, the maculae which a woman would call her freckles, but which betrayed only the ageing of the body.

'How do you like working in England, Mr Sanger?' asked Kerridge. 'I'm told that the Prospero Group have been somewhat stagnant in the past year or so.'

Sanger knew how to handle gentle insults. 'Some of their executives believe in heading for the future at full speed astern, sir.' The joke wasn't his. Westbrook, who Sanger regarded as better at words than deeds, had made it. But it felt good to pick it up now. 'My job is to reverse the direction. You'll see big changes.'

'No doubt, Mr Sanger.' Abruptly Kerridge got up and extended his hand. 'I think we've gone as far as we can.'

'Gelson?'

'Don't ever try to force a decision too early, Mr Sanger. That is something you need to learn.'

He began to walk briskly towards the doors, leaving Sanger trailing uneasily behind him. As they walked into the outer hall, Sanger noticed for the first time the row of modern abstract paintings on the wall which had been out of his eye-line when he arrived. He appreciated that they might be worth a great deal, but he scorned the scale of values which made them so. He accepted Picasso, just; but the world of dangling wires and electrical movement and ketchup labels which now passed for art he rejected. Old men who bought such objects at ridiculous prices were simply conned through their fear of being thought obsolescent. It was like rejuvenating creams and cosmetic surgery; fortunes made from the endless quest to be young. It comforted him that Kerridge had his vanities and his weaknesses too, just like Bernard Grant.

Outside, the limousine's engine was running. Had the driver known he would be granted half an hour's audience only? He turned to shake Kerridge's hand again, increasingly concerned that the old man had given no hint of a decision.

'You look as grim as a mortician, Mr Sanger.' Kerridge leaned close, sourly whispering, enjoying his power as he always did. 'Most of your arguments are hogwash, as well you know.' Then, as Sanger dipped his head towards the car, 'But I like the sound of Ecuador. I think you have no need to worry. Have a happy Easter.'

All the way to Ed Corsino's home, he hugged the words to himself. The message he liked, but the patronising way it had been phrased he resented. They – the men who had made it – would not talk like that to him for ever.

*

Corsino had made it too, but he was not as big as Kerridge. Sanger felt more at home with him. There was nothing baronial about his house. It was kempt and modern, and the altar within it was not a hearth built to echo the culture of the old world but a bar, forty feet long, curving across one end of a sun lounge in which cane chairs were placed among tall green plants and soft-lit rocks. It was an echoing place, marble-floored, alive with the sound of water running through a series of linked pools. Sanger felt like a conspirator on an equal level with Corsino as they sipped vodka martinis.

'How fast will Kerridge move?' asked Corsino.

'Faster than the other side, pray God. Armfield will still be haggling with Talbot-Brown over the price. He's a conservative thinker.'

'You'd better be right.'

'Not my fault if I'm wrong. What more could we have done?'

'Leaned on Gelson ourselves.'

'Come on, Ed. How do you do that? We've been through it all. It wouldn't work.' He stirred his drink gently. 'You weren't thinking of anything really nasty?'

Corsino laughed and raised his glass. 'What do you take me for? I may live in New Jersey, but I'm not a mafioso. You've been

199

reading too many newspapers.' He munched his onion. 'We could still have leaned.'

'And made things worse. That guy hates you. He believes you unloaded him for doing just what you've done all your life.'

'Like hell he does. He was twisting *me*, not playing the system. There's a difference.'

As they sat quietly, the sound of rock music came faintly from somewhere deep in the house. 'My God, Earl, just listen to those kids.'

'Yeah?'

'They were supposed to do a school task today, would you guess? They have this astonishing talent for being able to do their homework while viewing TV and listening to a rock programme on radio at the same time. Sometimes I feel very old.'

You *are* getting old, Sanger thought. Probably still opening their mail or bugging their telephone calls to see if they're taking marijuana or worse. Old-hat. Not clever enough, not flexible enough. If we stop Gelson, you will take half or more of the credit, but the ideas were mine. I was the one who worked out *how*, the one who carried the ball. He would need to persuade Michael Grant about that.

'How's your job going, Earl?'

'Pretty well.'

'They'll make you a vice-president soon.' Sanger was not sure he liked the inflexion of the words. Corsino made it sound as though he ought to have been one already. He spoke guardedly in reply.

'There's a kind of arrangement.'

'When will Michael get to take over?'

Sanger was uncertain of his ground. He didn't know how much Corsino knew. He felt he was beginning to walk across a minefield, testing every footfall.

'His father has first to decide to give up.'

'Sure, I understand. But isn't Bernard Grant over the hill?'

'He's had a great record,' said Sanger, content to let Corsino make the pace.

'Michael will do well. Don't let him run too fast, Earl. You've got a fine opportunity there if you use it right.'

'I suppose so.'

'I want to do business with him, you see, but I can't give him a trouble-free ride.'

'No one expects that.'

Corsino took Sanger's glass and crossed to the bar to refill it.

200

Sanger was watching him all the time, fingers knotted around the cane arms of the chair, wondering what was coming.

'I've got the arrangement for progress payments on the control system job all buttoned up. But I can't do that *and* lay off on the delivery clauses. Brasserton's will have to meet the timetable we lay down, else the others in the consortium won't let the deal go through. Least of all Kerridge, if he plays to form. Will that give Michael any trouble?'

'I don't know all the details, but I wouldn't think so.' Sanger was still stalling, sensing that Corsino was building up a picture.

'Fine then. It's just that, well, there have been problems in this kind of deal with other companies.'

Sanger said nothing. Did Corsino really think he didn't know?

'There was a piece in *Fortune* magazine the other day. A company in Detroit, Michigan, got itself into strike trouble and hadn't taken the trouble to insure against it or get it excepted. They faced paying a penalty of 20,000 dollars a day for late delivery. The guys they were selling to didn't sue. They fixed a deal to buy into the company. Now they own thirty per cent of the stock.'

Sanger saw the point, and why it had been made. He knew how to play it. 'What,' he said smiling, 'would *you* want owning a chunk of the Prospero Group? I didn't know that was your line of country at all.'

Corsino walked over with the drink. 'Right. It isn't. Yet. I was just thinking. British companies haven't got the best of reputations for keeping delivery schedules.'

'*Some* British companies.'

'I know. With Michael it'll be okay.'

'Here's to you, then,' said Sanger, raising his drink. He realised precisely the option which had just been laid open to him. Persuade Michael Grant to sign a very tough deal which would leave all the leverage on Corsino's side. Corsino could stuff *that*. As of now, Sanger reckoned he had more future out of pushing Michael into the seat of power and sitting on the right hand than from picking up a few score thousand dollars in a Swiss account and a load of unwritten promises for letting Ed Corsino and his friends in through the back-door. But he'd bear it in mind.

*

When he came back to the office on the Wednesday after Easter, Armfield felt good. For once, he and his wife had not gone to the Cotswolds or Le Touquet or the house near Dartmouth.

He wanted to be close to London. He had work to do, decisions to make, and always in such circumstances he did not wish to stretch too far the umbilical cord that led back to Prospect House.

He could not have articulated the feeling as Westbrook would, but he felt at ease in his Surrey home. It was the perfect balance to the office, where he had to endure too much glass, where he prickled to the coldness of steel and plastic. In his house he could raise the symbols of a protesting past: small leaded windows, heavy mahogany furniture with ugly Victorian beadings, paintings through which cattle lowed and glowered as they surveyed empty forests and still waters. The place was stuffed with these confections, for since Armfield had taken to the idea that collecting was a good thing, it had become almost a religion with him. The walls groaned with pictures and visitors had to negotiate rather than walk their way through his lounge, the standing *objets* eager as rocks to catch their limbs and bottoms.

Here, during Easter, he had pondered and written, ignoring his wife's resentful scufflings and the heady aroma of her perfume. He could always tell when Mary felt neglected. Knowing she couldn't look good, she chose to smell like a scent factory to draw attention to herself. He was aware of the gambit, but no longer responded to it. He could lock up his mind and, as usual, the regimen had worked. The hurdle-rate analysis he had prepared showed suggestively, if not decisively, how much better life might be without either Michael Grant's American deal or the purchase of Lovelace's. Armfield had decided how much and in what fashion they might pay Gelson. His contingency budget could easily be manipulated to that end. And he knew now that he would fire Sims some time in the next six months, but keep Talbot-Brown. One always felt better, they said, once your course of action was determined.

From these fruits of a holiday weekend, he selected only the first to offer to Bernard Grant as yet another justification for the existence of Harold Armfield. It was late in the afternoon when they met, and Armfield thought how tired Grant looked.

'Of course I accept your argument,' said Grant almost irritably. 'It's not me you need to persuade. Sell it to Benjamin.'

'We've both got to sell it, Bernard.'

'I've discussed it twice with him by telephone. He doesn't want either project killed at this stage.'

'You're the Managing Director, for heaven's sake. And I'm your deputy. You could kill them.'

'Don't be simplistic,' said Grant with a trace of petulance.

Ten years ago, perhaps even two or three, he would have chopped up Michael's plans into small pieces. Now, after the weeks during which he had suffered this curious paralysis of will, every instinct told him not to be precipitate, in major matters at least.

He had tried to convince himself he had conquered the fear the thrombosis had induced. Now he suspected he was learning to live with it rather than conquering it. Even the argument he conducted within himself that illness need not destroy the will to act was not convincing. How relevant was it to him that Roosevelt had been a sick man surrounded by the sick, or that Jellicoe, like Napoleon, had piles? He dragged up a laugh at the thought and it rattled in his throat.

'Yes?' said Armfield, puzzled.

'Nothing,' said Grant.

'I still believe Benjamin will react sensibly to all this.' Armfield gestured towards the figures Grant had scarcely examined. 'It hasn't been spelled out at all clearly.'

'I expect he's already done the figures in his head, Harold. But you're right. We must try again. I appreciate what you've done.'

'You worry me, Chairman. We're losing time and position.'

Grant was impatient again. 'It's all under control.'

Armfield changed tack. 'You're looking very fit. I'm glad.'

'Of course,' Grant lied away the tiredness he felt. 'We'll do it, as we always do.'

Armfield left it at that. With Bernard in this indecisive mood, he would have to play the Gelson business on his own. Probably that was best anyway. When it came to the crunch, you always were on your own, weren't you? If only, he thought, I'd acted on that assumption back in the 1950s, there'd be no problem now. No playing as prop to Grant, no need to win over Lord Bender, no looking in all directions simultaneously to see which way the enemy might be advancing.

The chance had come to go solo, and he had ignored it. The play-safe philosophy imprinted from his youth had won again. Yet wasn't the property game one he could have played himself, without Grant, in the early years? The desert of the late 1940s, all austerity and ration cards and small-time spivs, had dulled the entrepreneurial senses of the nation. For those who woke up first once the Socialists were gone, who fastened on to the prime sites which lay around like diamonds in the cities, to make money out of property was a pushover. Grant was no miracle-worker, and Armfield always had this invisible bed-rock of resentment at what he saw as the man's inflated reputation. He also, from time to time, remembered that he had fought with Montgomery at Alamein whilst Grant was supinely obeying the Germans. Where was the equity in that?

As soon as Armfield was gone, Grant told Miss Harris he must not be disturbed, then lifted his private telephone. He had left the call late in the day, but knew he could not avoid it. He was finished with the weeks of defeat and indecision. If he forced himself to pick up again the mood for action, there could be no question that Lord Bender's loyalty would be reaffirmed. He was certain his old friend would respond, certain he could carry Armfield with him, knew he could grind the new men into submission. Then he would attend to Michael, but be magnanimous in victory.

'Frank?'

'Bernard. How are you?' Bartram's thick tones plugged the earpiece.

'There's something I'd like you to do.'

'Yes?'

'Get rid of Gerald Fielder.'

'You're joking.'

'I want him out of the company.'

'Have you been reading some bloody report on us? People have been poking around.'

'I know all about the activities of my son's trouble-shooters. Do you think I'm so much out of touch?'

'No, but. . . .'

'And now I also know that things are in a mess with your company.'

'That's not fair, Bernard.'

'Don't whine, Frank. I don't blame *you*, if that's what worries you. Your subordinates have let you down. Particularly Gerald.'

'How does that help us?'

'It doesn't. But it indicates we must act quickly. Westbrook and my son will want to make an issue out of Supergear. There'll be a report soon from – oh, whoever it is.'

'David Travis.'

'Travis, yes. And there'll be recommendations, Frank, in one form or another. You know what one of the recommendations will be. So – I want to get in first. Pre-empt the initiative. In the circumstances, what other course is there? *Think.*'

'I've had enough, Bernard. Honestly.'

'On the contrary, you have several good years ahead of you.

204

You are *my* man, Frank, given power by me, and if your company is in trouble, then that reflects on my judgement in appointing you. What's happened we cannot undo, but I refuse to have my son telling me how to get out of the mess. You have left the cure late, but not too late. Start picking up the pieces yourself. You will save some face at least.'

Grant let the words sink down the line.

'How do you want me to deal with Gerald?' said Bartram.

'Use your imagination. There are formulae to cover these things. You are reorganising, yes? And there will now be no room for a man of his calibre? Give him enough to set himself up in a small business. Whatever he wants within reason. I owe him that much. But keep him off my back. I don't want to dry his eyes.'

'I'll do my best.'

'Do your best tomorrow, then. I want it quickly, and Frank, I believe you need also to trim your labour force.'

'Why?'

'It will help your story about reorganisation. And it won't harm you. I've noticed your staff has been increasing. Thirty per cent in two years. Yet you turn out fewer coats. You used to manage three thousand a week. Now you're lucky to get much above two.'

'This high fashion stuff takes longer, Bernard. Special buttons, fancy buckles and facings – that's why. We sell them dearer too.'

'Too dear, I'm informed.'

'Not if the collection *takes*, Bernard. And this year it could. The store buyers have been telling me how much they like our autumn designs.'

'I don't care what they tell you, Frank. Have they actually *bought* much?'

'It's too early to say. Give us a few weeks until the middle of May or so. If my hunch is right, we could need all the labour we can get.'

'Nonsense, Frank. I've been talking to people in London. If you have to step up production, use out-workers.'

'That won't be easy. Not up here.'

'Of course it won't be easy. But why do you think you were made managing director?' Grant's voice had grown more taut and impatient as the conversation progressed. 'Just get on with it.'

'You sound as if you'd be glad to see me go too. I wouldn't much care, frankly.'

'Don't sulk, man. You'll stay, Frank, and that's an order. I expect some loyalty from you of all people.'

'Even if I accept that, you're asking a great deal.'

Grant might not have heard him. 'You can do one other thing to help yourself. Re-open your London showroom.'

'That would be a very expensive business. We closed it because I felt we had to cut costs.'

'A false economy. Buyers *like* to come to London. I don't wonder you've been selling less if you denied them that pleasure. They think it's the only place to be entertained. What you save on your production line will be more than enough to pay for setting up a base in London again.'

'Who told you all this?'

'I've been talking, as I said. It's not difficult to learn things if you have the energy to ask. Goodbye, Frank. Ring me tomorrow.'

Grant felt good when he put down the telephone. Less tired, less uncertain. I've been getting lazy, he thought. Now I'm making the decisions, fighting back. It would have been so much easier to manipulate a situation like this in the old days. He enjoyed the status which the size of his enterprises gave him, but he regretted the loosening of personal control that came with bigness, the panoply of directors and aides around him. Michael and Westbrook and the rest of them could beaver away and he scarcely knew what they were doing. From now on he *would* know, would be the master again. Even the fiasco at Supergear might be turned into a sort of wry victory for him, his foresight always one step in advance of his son's, better late than never. That might impress Benjamin.

Lulled by such simple self-deception, of which those who have made their own fortunes from nothing are strangely often capable, he rose and moved to the looking-glass. He was a little concerned that his eyes looked more sunken than usual, that his cheeks had assumed a more mottled appearance. But his face was still notably smooth, his hair vigorous, his shape unpaunchy. Nothing would be thrown away now, not after the years it had taken to achieve the summit.

It had been a long haul. In London you could have everything – the right address, a few millions up your sleeve, the ability to move the market or to give endlessly to good causes; and yet the financial establishment, the old-time alliances of names and money, could still ignore you. There had been the jokes about his methods, with Grant cast as Micawber, always relying on the hope of something turning up to keep his gambles with borrowed money going. There had been jokes about his Jewishness too, his personal tightness with money, one or two of the more vicious

206

overheard in the washrooms of clubs, which members seemed oddly to regard as secure. In face of the exquisite sneers he had learned to hold his tongue, and many of those who had laughed now sat with him on committees or accepted his hospitality. Two of those same men, with their unnatural wives, would tonight accompany him to see a new play by a writer he had sponsored. More importantly, they now invited him to their homes as well as to their favoured restaurants. It was a kind of revenge to see them surrender in this way, and he would give them no chance to laugh again. He would get out of the driving-seat when he was good and ready.

The telephone rang. It was Lord Bender.

'What's this story in the *Standard* all about, Bernard? I thought the Brasserton's thing was still secret.'

'Brasserton's? I haven't seen the evening papers.'

'They've both got it. Brasserton's are going to get a big slice of a contract arranged by a basically American consortium. More or less as we discussed it at the board meeting.'

'This is ridiculous. Nothing is settled. Who has given them authorisation to print?'

'They need no authorisation,' said Lord Bender drily, thinking it was not like Bernard to be so unrealistic. 'Only facts. They seem to have got them. Oh, it's a speculative story, full of *mays* and *mights*, but they've got the right line.'

'Why would they be interested, anyway? It's only a few millions.'

'They like the development aspect. They see as clearly as some of our own directors what this kind of deal could lead to – the new business that Brasserton's would be in line for. They also explain there's to be a big computerisation programme for the factory.'

'I know nothing of this. What the devil is Howland up to?' It was the worst thing Grant could have said. Lord Bender, remembering the aristocratic face of a chairman he had eased out the previous month, sat and wondered why Grant was so little in control of the politics of his own organisation. He suspected Michael Grant's hand in the leak, but was puzzled what advantage it might offer the young man. It would surely be better to keep the deal quiet until the trickier points, like the part-payment arrangements, were settled. Until the detail was right, Michael was in error to think that a piece of newspaper speculation would force the board's hand. It certainly wouldn't force Lord Bender's. He doubted Michael's judgement too often

207

for comfort: a man with the right ideas but perhaps not yet a skilful enough manipulator. Lord Bender remained, for the time being, inclined towards the devil he knew. His mind closed tight around the familiar metaphor. It gave him a kind of comfort.

Michael Grant was in no doubt what advantage there might be. A few hours earlier he had explained it to a nervous Westbrook, whose views had been much the same as Lord Bender's.

'Earl arranged it before he came back, Lionel. It's a necessary insurance against anyone getting cold feet in America. Now it's out in the open, it would look like the Americans were being beastly to Britain if they stopped the deal.'

'Why should anyone get cold feet?'

'There are reasons. Earl found problems there.'

In Westbrook's view, thinking of the meticulous papers he had prepared, there should have been no further problems, but he let the point go.

'I still don't like it. How will you explain it to your father?'

Michael shrugged. 'One of those things. The story came out in America first – with no named source. It's been picked up by the London papers. I know nothing of it. Nor do any of us. Someone has opened his mouth over there. My father may not like it, but we can't be accused of politicking.'

'Won't the papers check back with us? What's Howland going to say?'

Howland, confused by the errand he had run for Bernard Grant to Oldershaw a few weeks back, had stalled when the calls first came. He knew the Government contract for Brasserton's was now off, but nobody had warned him about an American deal. Who the hell was Ed Corsino?

He tried first to reach Oldershaw, without success. Then he rang back the newspapers to get them to hold the story till he could confirm or deny it. They told him it had been confirmed, but no one would say by whom. They were already printing it, and that was that, with no comment from the London end. When he tried to reach Bernard Grant, Miss Harris told him coolly that the Chairman was talking on the other line and had specifically said he was not to be interrupted. By the time Howland's telephone finally rang, it was obvious he had nothing to tell Grant which the Chairman did not already know.

'John, what *is* all this about Brasserton's? Are you asleep down there?'

'No sir. I've been trying to reach you. The newspapers came on earlier. They simply wanted the story confirmed. It came from their men in New York. I've been on to Brasserton's, but Older-shaw's not there.'

'Couldn't you stop them printing until we confirmed?'

'Sorry – but no. They said they had as much as they needed for a story. Is it true, then?'

'It might be, but it was *not* meant for publication yet.'

Grant felt furious that he had so little control over the situation. He could not deny the story. The newspapers, annoyed at being made to look foolish, would only start digging deeper. To confirm it would be to concede victory to Michael with the fight scarcely begun.

'What shall I tell the *morning* papers?' Howland sounded almost plaintive. 'They're waiting for me to ring back.'

'Tell them – dammit, tell them that such a deal has been discussed, but nothing is settled. What else is there to say?'

'You'll forgive my mentioning this, sir, but it was a difficult situation to be in – not knowing, I mean.'

'That's what you're paid for, John. To make bricks with no straw on occasions.' Grant was very quiet and very angry. He dismissed Howland with unusual curtness and asked for Armfield.

'Oldershaw will be furious, I expect,' he told Armfield. 'And that's only part of the problem. Michael's one up. No doubt of it.'

'That depends,' said Armfield, unusually calm, 'on whether the Americans manage to raise the finance.' He sat there polishing his gold-rimmed spectacles; a studied gesture.

'Don't play games,' said Grant with a sarcasm which these days he was using increasingly.

'This game, Chairman, is one I'd like to play on my own. You can rely on my judgement.'

Grant was scarcely prepared to do that, but Armfield was adamant in his secrecy. Lacking other weapons to fight with, Grant in the end let him have his way. He was, though, as piqued at Armfield's independence as his son was pleased with Alison Bennett's capacity to take her own line. She had assured her contacts on the evenings that the story they would get about Brasserton's was totally reliable, but that they would probably get no confirmation from the usual sources either at Prospect House or at Oldershaw's plant. There were reasons for that. Diplomatic reasons. They could take her word that they should print, but they must not mention their source for that assurance – not to anyone.

Michael rang her flat that evening. 'They must love your blue eyes. And trust you too.'

'I'm lucky,' she said. 'I haven't yet had to let them down. Not them or anyone. One day, I suppose, I will. Then I'll be reduced to distributing hand-outs for a living.'

✦

David's watch said 6.45. He looked at the papers surrounding him, decided to stay and finish the case. He sensed he was near to the answer. He lifted the telephone and told Sheila to expect him when she saw him.

He regretted his brusqueness as soon as he finished talking. It wasn't fair to take out his irritation on her, yet there were more times than he liked these days when his control slipped. He was annoyed with Westbrook for lumbering him with digging out more past history on some crumby deal done through Lymington in Africa several years back. Why was Westbrook gunning for Lymington so suddenly? They ought to give themselves time to get the Supergear business sorted out first. Then there was Brasserton's, which the morning papers had been writing about. He'd heard nothing of that from Westbrook when, with Hardy away, he expected to have been put in the picture. But half his mind was on Alison, not on business. He dug a nail into his scalp, testing for dandruff, as he tried to work out the next move.

Since the night he'd spent with her, she'd given no indication of what she now expected. They'd smiled twice in the corridors, once in a pub, exchanged words as formally as two embalmers at an annual convention. He wished he could make the point to Hardy. Hardy would appreciate it. The comparison was right. for was not their affair embalmed, a kind of cosmetic illusion, dead while retaining the appearance of life?

He was displeased at his uncertainty. Did he now ask her to dinner once weekly or fortnightly, with the assumption that bed was the final course? That would be too like taking things for granted. Or did they slink off to distant bars for drinks where no one they knew would be likely to see them, saving up the next tumble on the mattress for his birthday, or hers?

Logic told him he had made a mistake. The old adage: never on your own doorstep. His body, though, wanted only to make more mistakes. He felt he was just at the beginning of enjoying her. Between the two courses of action, and maybe a dozen more unregistered, he stood transfixed, doing nothing. His neutrality, and the feeling that to her he must look a fool, gnawed at his vanity.

He went back to the papers, flicking through one of the files

210

towards which Karian had pointed him. Karian was easy to manipulate. Go to him like a little boy lost, give him the feeling that he's a big man, long in service and wisdom, and he'll always help you. David almost liked Karian, certainly pitied him, and regretted conning him on Westbrook's behalf. Karian, knowing nothing of the reasons for dead history being disinterred, helped David because the boy was bright and open and respectful, even if he did belong to the new guard. Karian had, anyway, lost some of his faith in the old guard. He did not believe he would ever recover from Bernard's breaking of trust over his Burgham shares; nor would his bank manager, who was becoming distinctly obnoxious.

By 7.30, the problem was licked, David leaned back and whistled to the blank walls of the office. He saw how Lymington had been deceived. Hell, he thought. Why hadn't Sir bloody Giles picked it up?

*

When Fielder arrived home, screaming the Rover angrily across the drive, spurting gravel, he was angry drunk. He went into the house almost crying. He shouted 'Margaret' as he slammed the front door. 'Margaret, where are you? Margaret?'

There was no answer. He walked through the lounge, past the dining-recess, into the kitchen. The place looked as though someone had spent a careful hour working at giving it an air of sluttish untidiness. There was an emetic mess on the stainless steel top of the sink unit. Vegetable peelings, abandoned cans, lonely packets and breakfast dishes set with eggshells, butter smears and marmalade. Suddenly he felt more frightened than angry.

He found her on the bed. Despite the knowledge of their years together, he could not believe it was happening to him. She was dressed, after a fashion, and she must have knocked over the Scotch bottle on the bedside table. It had spilled on the wood, thence to the carpet. He had no idea how much she had drunk. Her mouth was open and she snored, stirring the strands of hair that lay across her mouth. Her ankles were crossed and her knees outflung, like someone frozen in action doing one of those neuter Scottish dances. Even through the wreckage of discoloured skin and heavy flesh, open-pored, he could remember how attractive she once had been.

When he struck her face it was more than a gesture intended to arouse her. He wanted to take out on her body all the pain he felt at the waste and disappointments of their life, at her uselessness to him now, when he needed strength and support, someone to reinvigorate him. He hit her again and she let out a small moan of pain. She opened her eyes, unseeingly, and closed her mouth. Slowly she focused on Fielder's face, not associating some dimly felt hurt with him. Here was her protector. She smiled with effort and croaked, 'Darling?' He saw that a thin trickle of blood was coming from her left nostril. The anger left him, pity for both of them flooding his body. He was crying as he sank on to the bed and cradled her head in his arms.

'Maggie, dear God, what have they done to us? The sods. The rotten sods.'

He fetched a face-cloth, soaked in cold water, and wiped her face. Then, sweating with the effort of moving her around, he took off such of her things as he could. Skirt and stockings he managed; the rest defeated him, except for some ear-clips he had bought her in celebration of his move to London five years ago. He really believed he might make it then, and Christ, how he wanted now to hurt all of those who had kicked him back into the provinces again. Especially Westbrook. But he knew, hopelessly, that Westbrook could not be touched by him.

He heaved his wife, in sweater and underclothes, beneath the sheets. All the time she smiled at him like an idiot, crooning indistinguishable words at him. He passed a hand across her brow and she closed her eyes again. The bleeding at her nose had stopped, the blood in a sticky dribble, shining. Then he ran downstairs, tearing off his jacket.

He went to a cocktail cabinet, all walnut and mirrors, and poured himself a Scotch from a heavy decanter. They had given him that when he left for London. Farewell present. He thumped a fist angrily on the wood, rattling the bottles, and for a moment put out a finger to touch the glass covering a photograph of himself and his wife, smiling expectantly. Years old, taken at a reception, when they still believed they might have a child.

Fielder sank very quietly into a heavy chair, covered with a creamy material, flower-studded. For a minute he chewed at the skin around his thumb-nail, and finally searched in his waistcoat until he found a folded piece of paper. He smoothed it, reached for the telephone, and began to dial.

Sheila, eating one of the steaks she had prepared for dinner, answered the call. Fielder's voice was so strained that she did not recognise it.

'Is Travis there?'

'No. This is Mrs Travis. Who is this?'

'Where is he?'

212

'Who's speaking, please?'

'One of the poor relations, out in the sticks.'

'I don't understand.'

'Fielder. Gerald Fielder. Remember?'

'Mr Fielder. How are you?'

'Bloody awful. He's not there?'

'David? No. He's working late.'

Fielder coughed into the receiver deliberately, pushing out laughter he did not feel, going on coughing abruptly, like a motor starting. 'More likely making it with that red-haired girl. Do you know her, love? Alison something. Very beddable.'

She didn't know what to say. She wanted to put down the telephone, but her curiosity was too strong. Feebly she said, 'What do you want?'

'I want *him*, the bastard.'

'Why are you saying all this?'

'He's chopped me, your golden boy. Given me the sack. They told me today. I'm too good for them, isn't that a laugh? Bloody Bartram, who couldn't tell a mini-skirt from a paper bag, sitting there and telling *me* not to take it hard. No room in the company for a man of your calibre. They're devising a new management structure – all that crap.'

'I'm sorry,' she said, and that only turned the screw tighter, compressing his anger and malice so that it exploded again.

'I don't want you to be *sorry*, Mrs Travis. Don't you know that's the game? You work your guts out, then *wham*, some jumped-up prick comes along and writes a report on you. That's the way it goes these days.'

'He hasn't given in his report yet. I *know*.'

'That's what he's told you, dear lady. Is that why he's supposed to be working late at the office? Doing his report? He'll be working hard with his trousers down, take my word. We all like a bit on the side.'

'Shut up,' she said. 'You're being ridiculous.'

There was a silence. Fielder sat morosely, almost drained of malice, bewildered, not knowing what he should do next. A dribble of sweat from his palm glistened on the telephone.

'Oh, Christ,' he said. 'What a mess.'

'Yes?'

'I don't mean all that. I don't know.' He half-sobbed the words.

'Are you all right?'

Again he was enraged by the tone of pity in her words.

'Oh, indeed yes.' The irony he used was almost histrionic. 'I'm fine. They're not cutting me off without a crust. Ten thousand they're giving me. And some shares. *Go and start a tea-room or something, Gerald, there's a good lad.* I don't know anything but Prospero, don't you see? I don't want to be on my own. I just hope they never try the treatment on your lad. The slow freeze-out. I haven't seen anything that resembles an important board paper in the last four weeks. No one tells me anything. It's like you're not there. It's been bad enough without David giving me the final shove.'

'He hasn't. I'm sure of it.'

'You keep your illusions, then. You're lucky to have that privilege. He's shopped me, and he's shopping you too.'

'*Please.* I'm sorry about what's happened, but I don't want to listen any more.'

'Wait a minute. Don't forget to tell him I called. Don't forget.' He was half-sobbing, half-laughing again as Sheila put down the phone.

She knew she should forget it, but she found herself dialling the office. There was no answer from David's extension. She couldn't eat any more. She sat looking at the unappetising steak, feeling the heaviness of her body. Aimlessly she switched on the television set. She watched the images blankly; a canned comedy show, American, featuring the fabled transatlantic double act of amiably cunning wife and rising executive husband. The outcome was, as always, predictable. Wife, using feminine intuition, worked out life. Husband, a cross between fond parent and doormat, acknowledged her immutable rightness, almost with gratitude. The American matriarchy marched on triumphantly, awaiting the fruits of alimony or widowhood, whilst the slave-male headed straight for his coronary at fifty-five.

She was in bed, trying to read a novel, when David arrived home. Sheila had rehearsed what she would say quite clearly, but what followed fitted the pattern of ten thousand town-house rows a week. She listened to herself with dislike, hypnotised like a person apart, speaking words which came from somewhere beyond her will.

'I rang you. You weren't there.'

'Umm?'

'You said you were working late.'

'That's right.'

'No one answered your phone.'

'I must have been having a pee.'

214

'Very convincing.'

David looked at her questioningly. The two words had been a sneer. He'd never experienced this kind of reaction from her before.

'Listen love, what are you on about? Don't I get any dinner, then?'

'At ten o'clock? I'm worn out.'

'What is all this?'

'There was a call for you. Gerald Fielder.'

'Fielder?'

'I gather you've done the deed, then.'

'I don't get it.'

'The deed, darling. The purge. He rang to say thanks for the size of his handshake.'

'Are you feeling all right?'

'Don't be bloody condescending to me. Gerald Fielder has got the sack. He's out. He sounded as if he could kill you.'

'You're joking.'

'It's not much of a joke.'

'Honestly? He's got the push?'

'Yes.'

'It's nothing to do with me, then. No one's seen my report yet. I've talked a bit. That's all.'

'Isn't that enough? The poor devil sounded out of his mind.'

'For crying out loud, Sheila – we've *done* all this. I haven't perpetrated whatever it is you're blaming me for. He was due to be fired anyway. He's no bloody good. I expect he's got out of it well – and that's more than a lot of the people who work for him would have done if he'd stayed. It *happens* like this, so don't keep on kicking me for it. The greatest good of the greatest number, remember? There are plenty of people involved in this. We've got to think about *them*.'

'What a perfect little corporation lawyer you sound, David. The pride of Prospect House. Fielder is *people* too, him and his wife. Don't you see what's happening to you? You're beginning to add up human beings like numbers.'

'That's balls. I'm involved with people all day long – talking to them, persuading them, measuring them. . . .'

Sheila snapped her book shut. 'Every day when you come home you look starved of people to me. Real people, I mean. Even I'm just the woman who gets dinner ready on time.'

'Don't be daft. You've been reading too many of those *Nova* pieces about dried-up wives left alone in the house.'

215

'So what if I have? Because they're six a penny, it doesn't mean they're not true.'

'Why can't you understand?'

'That's the cheapest trick of all,' she said. 'Accusing me of not *understanding*. I just want to know what you expect of me. I try to talk about your work rationally, and whenever I say something that doesn't agree with the party line, you infer it's because I'm not a big enough girl to understand grown-up things like business. What do you want me to be? Someone you talk with – an intelligent human being – or do you want me to be a Japanese wife, warming your slippers, scratching your back, opening my legs when you want me to and saying sod all about anything?'

He was still floundering, not understanding the reasons for her vituperative tone. 'I just want you to be yourself.'

'Myself? Do you know what that *is*? It's just like all the books say. It's staying at home waiting for babies to be born while you go out and kill meat. You like killing meat so much it's becoming your whole life. I can't compete with your work, can I? Your mind's like a searchlight. Everything it touches is lit up like crazy, but beyond the beam you see nothing. That's business.'

'What do you want me to *do*? I have to get on with what's to be done, that's all. How do you think we're going to pay for all this?' He swept his arm in a futile gesture at the walls, which remained pale blue and unimpressed. It was, he knew, an unfair argument; but he felt like being unfair. 'What keeps pushing me on?'

'Not me. I've never pushed.'

'You never say no – and isn't that the same? All you ever talk about is the people who get stuck in no-money jobs – or the ones like your father who got caught in a trap.'

'My father has nothing to do with this. Nothing.'

'All right – have it your way. But if you take the goodies that go with the job, you must take the crap as well. You've got to learn to live with the strain, girl. I'm having to – and, Christ, I don't like it any more than you do. I just *have* to like it. There's nothing much wrong with our life. We have our fun.'

'Where?' she said. 'Fun with the other rats in the race? Dinner here, cocktails there – and all you talk is business? You're just a company man, my love. We sleep here, but we don't *live* here. You've no roots, no friends, no interests here. God give us a few friends whose companionship you're interested in, rather than their potential usefulness to your damned business. This' –

and her arm was flung out – 'is just the place where we happen to have a mortgage on a house.'

'Bugger it, I'm going to get some food.'

'Got to build up your strength again after all the *work* you've been doing?'

He snatched at the inflection in her voice. 'What's that supposed to mean?'

'Just things people say about bright young executives. Using up their surplus energy on the side.'

'People? What people?'

'People we know.'

'Fielder, for instance? What's that poor demented bastard been saying?'

'That you have a good enough time.'

'With whom or what, for God's sake?'

She knew she should stop. He knew he should shrug his shoulders, laugh it off, make it up before they went over the edge. She couldn't *know* about Alison. No one could. Let them suspect what they liked. The proof was locked up for ever in the room with the snowstorm carpet and the toy balloon chairs.

But neither Sheila nor David made the concessionary gesture first. They were too stuffed with the pride of having to be debate-winners. That's what an ancient university education does for you until you learn wisdom. When it comes to words, you can't bear to lose. So she pushed on, beyond the point of return, almost helplessly, and he waited for her arrival, marshalling his sentences ready to fire back at her.

'Let's try that redhead for a start. The PR girl. Don't tell me you haven't tried her? Fielder knows it. Hardy knows it.'

'Hardy? He isn't even around.'

'He has been.'

'And he's told you all about my fantasy love life? Don't make me laugh.'

'You still haven't answered the question.'

'What question?'

'The woman. The redhead.'

'I'm damned if I answer questions like that.'

'Because you can't?'

'Because I don't bloody choose to. Not at this court-martial.'

He wanted to get away. He had known the scene would be like this, knew it had to come. He was furious with himself that he had to stand and lie, all because of Fielder, and confused too, not knowing how to defend himself, not having heard details of

217

the charge. Hardy's involvement he couldn't believe, or could he? He fiddled with his tie awkwardly as the words between them ceased. Then he walked out through the bedroom door, tossing the last grenade.

'The way you're going on, it would serve you right if I had a bloody harem.'

He regretted the sentence as soon as it was said; and the way his voice sounded. Sheila, he thought, was beginning to cry as he went down the stairs. She said nothing, but a moment or two later he heard her move, pad across the floor. The door slammed.

They had never had this kind of row before. He felt hungry but had no patience even to cut bread for a sandwich. He tipped cornflakes into a bowl, poured milk and sat at the cold formica-topped table gloomily munching, smelling the sour mixture of meat and soap around him. He wanted to go upstairs to bed, for he was too drained to work. But how could he do that? It was a situation where one or the other – or both – would have to creep low before the mending could be started.

Cheerlessly he drooped on to the sofa, put up his feet and closed his eyes, trying to squeeze some comfort from having solved the puzzle of Lymington's dealings in Africa. Then he started thinking again about Sheila. The baby was due in two weeks now. He'd been so preoccupied he hadn't even taken that into the reckoning.

'I am a shit,' he said to the empty sitting-room. It had bland walls and strangely mixed furniture – Portobello Road and Habitat churned together as the magazine vogues had moved Sheila and him to buy hurriedly over the past few years. In his gloom he began to hate the predictability which sprang from living with it too long.

He shut his eyes and shunted faces through his mind, drowsing: Westbrook, Grant Junior, Armfield, Hardy – bloody Hardy, what had he said to Sheila? The whole cast of Prospect House went trooping past. Even if his wife was right about him – and he knew the pitfalls of the business game as well as anyone in theory – what did she expect him to do about it? Society, his society, gave him few enough options.

He was veering towards self-pity when finally he drifted into sleep.

＊

Ever since Armfield had named the price, late in the afternoon, Talbot-Brown had been trying to reach Gelson in New York. The call was made half-hourly, and hard on the stroke the girl's voice rattled in the ear-piece. 'I'm sorry, sir, but your party doesn't answer. Would you like me to try again?'

It was almost eleven in the evening, Talbot-Brown drinking a fifth Scotch in his flat, when the silence at the other end was broken. Even from 3,000 miles away he knew the sticky drawl of Gelson's voice.

'Gelson?'

'This is he.'

'Talbot-Brown here.'

'Who?'

'Antony Talbot-Brown. The Prospero Group.'

'I don't believe we've met, sir?'

Talbot-Brown had no inclination for games after the hours of waiting. 'Listen, Gelson. Stop fooling. Are you frightened of this line?'

'I'm frightened of nothing, Mr – Talbot-Brown, did you say? I just want to know why the hell you're ringing me.'

'What we discussed. I have some figures for you. We're ready to do business.'

'You're wasting my time, sir. Yours as well. I haven't the faintest notion what you're talking about.'

Talbot-Brown breathed deeply, paused, pushing away the thoughts which began to drift across his mind. 'If you prefer it, I'll fly over tomorrow. We can see each other.'

'Just get this straight, Mr Talbot-Brown.' Gelson's voice had lost its easy note, its mockery. The words were no longer glutinously strung together; they came like separate steel darts down the line. 'I don't know you. I don't want to see you. We have nothing to say to each other. No business to do, no figures to be discussed. Nothing. I'm leaving town tomorrow anyway. I've got a place in Bermuda I want to look over.'

Talbot-Brown knew then that it was pointless. He knew why Gelson was speaking in these terms, though he did not know how the man had been suborned. He felt only the sour, frightening taste of defeat, which is almost as physical as the sharp prickles that afflict the guts of all losers. The hum of the transatlantic line was the only sound remaining, and then Gelson spoke again.

'Do you understand that, sir?'

'I understand. Why don't you just fuck off to your tropical island.'

Gelson was saying something more as Talbot-Brown put down the phone. For perhaps fifteen minutes he sat almost motionless, chewing his bottom lip with a nervousness which was not usual.

He added up the points on each side of the column, and, when he had checked and re-checked the answer, he knew what he must do. As he picked up the telephone again, he took a last swill of the warm Scotch. Half a minute later he was talking to Michael Grant.

10. Come in number seven

PROSSER took the train north on the third day of the strike at Brasserton's. He sat morosely in the overheated compartment most of the way, unable to summon any enthusiasm to open the newspapers or the documents in his briefcase.

Michael Grant had pressed him to go and look at the situation first-hand, but Prosser relished the prospect little. He did not believe in interfering so early in the affairs of a subsidiary company unless he was asked to by the local management, who would almost certainly – in the case of Oldershaw very certainly – now regard him as an inspecting officer rather than *deus ex machina*. Nor was this the kind of strike for which he had any notable appetite. It was, as usual, unofficial, also partial, and over no real issue except a feeling in the guts of the men that change was coming and they were afraid of it.

That wasn't why either they or the industrial correspondents said they were striking, of course. The walk-out had come when Colley, and then Oldershaw, refused to countenance a demand for revised overtime rates. But Prosser knew better than that and Oldershaw, bitterly cool on the telephone, had confirmed the diagnosis. It was going to be messy.

The plant had not stopped completely. There were strikers and what Oldershaw chose to call loyalists, whose numbers shrank steadily as the picket-line became more organised and more vocal. Prosser guessed that the men remaining inside the factory would be concentrating less on their output than on the problem of whether they should be there at all. It was all very well to talk of industrial democracy: once a strike began, with the insults splashing and the clichés about solidarity and class struggle fizzing around like bullets, it became increasingly difficult for individuals to hold out against the agitators. Strikes, in his experience, were usually emotive rather than rational, and outmoded words like *blackleg* never seemed to lose their aura.

221

Men responded to them as predictably as Pavlov's dogs to the bell; and this, he knew, was why any minority of militants always coalesced more easily than even a majority of those who did not care. The wreckers had a century or more of social history going for them, a conspiracy of memories which Prosser, bred in the Rhondda, could not ignore.

All this he understood, experiencing the customary division of sympathies in his mind. He had some fellow-feeling with the suspicious confusion of the Brasserton's men who sensed that their life-pattern was about to alter significantly, not knowing where their security or satisfaction on the job might lie and resenting their lack of involvement in the process of deciding how changes might happen. But he knew that involvement might cause only endless delays or total deadlock, since decisions cannot be happily made by committees, and that without changes these men would ultimately find themselves in a dead factory, stripped of customers, a useless artefact made obsolescent by more enterprising competitors. He hated, too, their crude way of reacting to the future, for once the bitterness generated by a strike was thrown into the equation, a solution inspired by his own powers of persuasion became all the harder to achieve.

Prosser was a businessman, but like most Welshmen he was by nature a teacher, an evangelical teacher, dressing like one too, except that he missed out on the leather elbow-patches. He saw himself as a leader with disciples who were neuter in mind, waiting to be instructed in the way they must follow. His negotiating methods were brilliant when he had the initiative, stepping in with programmes and panaceas in advance of trouble. With his pupils already rebellious, he was less at ease.

The car which met him at the station was a Zephyr, at least four years old, stained with muddy rain-spots. Prosser was not pleased. Automobiles should be a symbol to the world of one's position, proclaiming to those with whom he bargained that here was a man to be reckoned with, a man valued by his employers. But as they drove through dreary streets towards the factory, past rows of mean back-to-back houses and hunks of waste ground scrofulous with discarded junk and grey grass, Prosser decided he would not mention his annoyance to Oldershaw. The man was tetchy enough already, blaming the newspaper stories about the Corsino deal for all his troubles. On this assignment Prosser would be negotiating with the local management as much as with the labour force.

Feeling the black hair fringing his ears he was suddenly angry with himself. He should have had a haircut the day before. It was important for a prospective *deus ex machina* to appear impeccably organised in body as well as in mind.

Outside the factory gates there was action. From the car, Prosser saw two policemen trying to break through a heaving ring of men, some in overalls, others in incongruous sports jackets, fawns and greens and blues. Off-duty gear. Placards were leaning against the wall around the plant, parrot-slogans ignored now that a break in the monotony of standing and smoking and shouting was offered.

The car had to stop. Prosser got out and walked uneasily towards the men. The policemen, helmets still intact, had persuaded the crowd to spread a little. As the blanket of bodies loosened, he could see what was wrapped inside it. Two men were grappling tiredly with each other on the ground, the crowd neither urging them on nor dissuading them, but watching in a kind of numb, resigned silence. The policemen began to pull them apart, and no one moved to help or hinder. Even the fighters offered no resistance. They got up and stood hunched and helpless, as if relieved they had not to punch each other any more. One man's trousers had been torn, the frayed threads flapping foolishly below his knee. The other's face was bloody. An oozing cut at the side of his mouth gave him the appearance of wearing a sneer in lipstick.

As the policemen began talking to the men, the crowd pressed in again. Prosser waved the car away and walked through the gates of the plant beneath a new sign which gave the firm's name and also contained the modish logogram of the Prospero Group, the P and G overlapping into a figure vaguely suggesting computer script. Someone must have noticed him, despite the distraction at the gates.

'Piss off,' a voice called after him.

'And up you,' Prosser muttered in his mind.

There were more shouts, some boos, trailing away as he rounded a corner in pursuit of Oldershaw's office.

'Don't take it personally,' said Oldershaw. They were drinking coffee, ten minutes later. 'They let *anyone* have it – anyone who goes in or out of this place. They won't even know who you are.'

Or care, thought Colley. What a bloody situation. He looked at Prosser with careful suspicion. He didn't like men from head office. They made the mistakes which caused trouble for subsidiaries and then arrived, fussily self-important, demanding to know why local management couldn't look after itself.

Oldershaw, too, scarcely bothered to hide his scorn. 'I gather,' he said, 'they're very bothered in London about our troubles. Serves them right, if you'll allow me to give an honest opinion, Mr Prosser. It was a damn fool thing, the story in the papers.'

'No one's fault, Mr Oldershaw. Someone – God knows who – leaked it in America. We knew nothing about it.'

I knew nothing about it, rather, Prosser thought. He was certain Michael Grant knew more about it than he was telling, and Armfield's anger had been obvious for some days. Armfield had had some pet scheme cocked up, that was for sure. Prosser liked to see himself as no office politician and he resented those who spent their time in plots aimed at shifting the balance of power, especially when the balance shifted so much that a pile of trouble tipped on his head.

Troubles weren't coming singly either. The grapevine told him that the resignation of one of the directors at Supergear was only the beginning of a purge and of redundancies. He hoped Bartram could bring that off without involving him. Armfield's man, Sims, had come to see him off the record two days ago, seeking a transfer. Then Michael Grant had reacted violently over the Brasserton's strike, hinting intangible threats at Prosser if the mess wasn't cleared up quickly. Bernard Grant, to whom he was responsible, had seemed uninterested in the affair. Prosser, knowing the old man's hesitancy over his son's grandiose schemes for Brasserton's, understood why that was, as he also appreciated why Armfield had been unable to resist a controlled smirk when the news of the walk-out came through.

Even if he did his job, sorted out Oldershaw and the dissidents, Prosser realised he wouldn't get bouquets from everyone at Prospect House. He would be forced to take sides in the end, much as he disliked it, for that was the logic of all office politics. Did he really care who won?

Oldershaw was rattling on. Prosser hoped he hadn't missed much. 'There's not much point arguing over who's to blame,' said Oldershaw. 'But I'm getting tired of these situations where we have responsibility without power. London's idea of communications is bloody terrible.' He knew he was pushing his luck with a senior director, but though Oldershaw was developing a gift for dissembling, he sensed some kinship with Prosser.

'No management structure is perfect, Bill.' Prosser carefully chose this moment to switch to the Christian name. 'But let's get down to the meat. You agree with me, I know, about the real cause of the trouble here.'

'It's not about overtime,' said Colley. 'That's for bloody sure.'

Oldershaw laughed short and bitter by way of support, but he looked balefully at Prosser when the incomer asked: 'How much have you consulted?'

'I know the language,' he said. 'We're able to read up here. Consultation, involvement, participation – all the damned jargon. We don't *call* it that, but we do a bit of it. We weren't given anything to consult about. Hanging on and hanging on, waiting while London made up its mind. You know how I feel about all that, so I won't bore you repeating myself.'

Prosser saw no point in picking a fight. He needed Oldershaw. Where precisely was the line at which you slapped down a man for insolence even though you could scarcely do without him as an ally?

'All right, Bill. The main board had its reasons, but *you* know I understand your feelings. The point now, though, is whether you still want to go ahead with the modernisation programme, the deal with the Americans – everything.'

'We've no damned choice, have we?' said Oldershaw, and he was right. Prosser's implication of choice was a pretence, un-maliciously offered as a sop to pride. Oldershaw was also pretending, for he used his appearance of ill-temper to cover his ambition. He wanted the computer, the status, the vision of the future more than ever since his visit to London. But he needed to have an alibi if things went wrong. He wanted still to appear like a man pushed into plans laid by London. That way he could stay in tune with Colley, appearing to share his aide's resentment, and also maintain his lines to Bernard Grant and Armfield. He had sensed after the board meeting how the battle was shaping up at Prospect House – and he was determined to keep his options open. He intended to join the winning side, whichever it was, when it suited him.

'If we want this plant to stay in business, then perhaps we do have no option,' said Prosser.

He rose and stood before the diagrams on Oldershaw's pinboard like a master facing his class. The lesson was about to begin. 'We want to avoid a direct confrontation on the issue they've raised. So we approach it obliquely. Put up the idea of a whole new system of payments. That's inevitable anyway once the computer comes in.'

'They're worried about losing their jobs, that's all,' said Colley.

'Of course,' said Prosser sweetly. 'So offer to start talks at once. Let them know, as a fairly broad hint, that any savings from redundancy will be shared between us and them. That's usual, and conditions here favour it. Your men are pretty old, aren't they?'

'Nearly thirty years, some of them have been here. Never known anything else,' said Oldershaw.

Prosser said: 'Expensive to pay them off, but with the size of the handshake we can give them, they'll probably be glad to go. Labour's short around here?'

'They'd get other jobs all right.' Oldershaw looked quickly at Colley as he spoke. Surprisingly, his works manager nodded assent.

'That's the beginning of a package,' said Prosser.

'Nothing in it we hadn't thought of ourselves,' said Oldershaw.

Prosser smiled almost too dazzlingly. 'Great minds, Bill. There's a bit more too. I think you ought to have a joint works committee with the men. Something formal, but a place where they can come and let their hair down. And couldn't you do with one or two new chaps on the management side to help you look after your labour relations?'

'That's my job,' said Colley, flatly.

'You'll have your work cut out looking after the technical bits and pieces,' said Prosser. 'You could do with some help there.'

'All chiefs and no bloody Indians,' said Oldershaw sourly.

'Not really. Promote a bloke or two inside the factory. The more they have the confidence of the men the better. Good unionists, but not tearaways.'

Colley jumped on it. 'The men would only say they were selling out.' He believed it too.

'Tom,' said Prosser, in a tone which suggested the teacher was surprised to find a prize pupil slipping. 'This is the mid-twentieth century. It's quite a usual step these days. Poachers turn game-keepers all the time. I'll give you all the help you need.'

They talked on for an hour, Prosser soft and hard by turns, playing Oldershaw and Colley as an angler would play a moody trout. Colley disappeared for a time to check on the situation at the front gate. Prosser was disappointed, but not surprised, that the fight hadn't been between striker and non-striker: just two men, bored with waiting, falling out over some petty private matter – a woman, a football team, a bet, Colley wasn't sure.

In the end Oldershaw was pleased with his performance. Prosser could be useful to him, but he had played hard to get so that the man from London would have to keep on worrying, never allowing Brasserton's to become a second priority. That was the way Oldershaw liked his operation to be thought of: top priority. They went to lunch, and a first meeting with the strike committee, more or less aligned.

*

'The damage is done,' said Michael Grant. 'No matter what peace formula Barry achieves, it leaves a nasty smell. The consortium are bound to insist on the delivery clauses now. They'd be fools not to. So we run the risk or pay a damn great premium to insure ourselves. Either way we cut our profit margin.'

Earl Sanger sprawled on the black settee opposite Michael, not at all displeased with the way things were going. He had developed a fast respect for Prosser as a labour relations man and he sensed that the Brasserton's dispute would be settled quickly. Michael seemed to think they had no alternative but to agree to the delivery clauses. That, Sanger judged, was over-response, but he would not dissuade his superior from the assessment. It could still be useful to have Corsino think he had advised Michael that way. Double indemnity was the way he liked to play the business game.

'Makes no difference,' he said. 'They would have insisted on the dates anyway. Those guys are too sharp to give you money in advance on an open-ended contract.'

'I still feel watery in the guts when I think about it. If we hit trouble any time in the next year or so, it could cost us a packet.'

'The elements in the decision haven't changed, Michael. Maybe it's better to get *some* trouble out of the way before we start.'

'In my shoes, you'd advise the board to go ahead then?'

Sanger smiled. 'Unfair question – and you know it. All I'm saying is that if you were willing to sign the contract before, you shouldn't change your mind now. I think the balance is in your favour, yes – but it's still your decision.'

Despite his concern, Michael had to smile back, wryly. 'You Harvard boys never let anyone off the hook.'

Then he rose suddenly from the desk, his chair swinging away from him on well-oiled castors until it gently nudged the glass of the bookcase behind him. He stood looking down at the titles: *An Introduction to Marketing, Italian High Performance Cars, Organisation Man, The Cruel Sport, Human Aspects of Management, The Treasury of the Automobile.*

Business and cars. There were those who said he cared little about anything else. Let them believe it. He had worked out his rationale of business a long time ago. He could fulfil his duty to *people* by getting his business sums right. He had no time for sentimental so-called 'humanity' in business. Real humanity was to make the organisation work, to breed profits, and thus to ensure the security of employment for a lot of people in the future. It was an idea which, in its plain-speaking, he believed was more American than English. He knew where he stood, justifying his fascination with the razzle-dazzle of power-plays by an appeal to the simple rule: expansion equals employment. He came to a decision, turned to face Sanger again.

'Earl – I still think Brasserton's is a gamble. But it's only part of the game. It's all coming together.'

'Yes?'

'Don't say anything to Lionel – not yet. But there's something else. I'd like your opinion.'

'Be my guest.'

'Talbot-Brown came to see me last week.'

'Did he, by God!'

'Virtually offering to be a nark.'

'Nark?'

'Sorry – English slang, meaning informer.'

'You didn't believe it?'

'I've got an open mind. I don't think it's a double-deal – Armfield getting him to plant dud information or something. I'm pretty certain it's on the level. He's a very good motive now that Gelson hasn't come across. I wonder Harold hasn't pitched him out already.'

'Armfield hasn't so many friends he can afford to,' said Sanger gleefully.

'Don't you believe it. Harold has been around this place a long time. He's entrenched. Even I wouldn't be one hundred per cent certain who is or who isn't his man. Anyway, Talbot-Brown – he told me he's been working on the background to Lovelace's. Hinted he's on to something I might like to know. Something big.'

'*What*, exactly?'

'He wouldn't go any further, but he promised more news within maybe ten days.'

'Well?'

'I'd like to know what Talbot-Brown has to say about Lovelace's before deciding on Brasserton's. It would make me feel happier, that's all. More stacked up on our side.'

'What's the opinion you wanted, then?'

228

'About Talbot-Brown, I suppose.'

'I wouldn't trust him completely. But you've nothing to lose by waiting to hear what he comes up with. I wouldn't bank on being able to wait *too* long on Brasserton's, though.' Sanger was growing rather tired of indecision. 'The two aren't really linked, except you want reassurance that *one* of them will come out all right. You can't always buy that kind of insurance.'

Michael was a touch riled. 'I know that. But add up all of the score, Earl. There's Supergear too – and *that* isn't exactly the shining triumph we bargained for, is it?'

The taunt, suggesting that Michael was blaming Sanger for Westbrook's slowness in turning up the answers after David Travis's investigation, unsettled the American not at all. 'If you're worried about losing face because your father has stepped in first with a cure for Supergear, then forget it. There's another remedy.'

'Yes?'

'Shut the plant.'

'You're joking.'

'No jokes, Michael. When someone else achieves the kill before you, the only response is overkill.'

'We aren't playing nuclear strategy.'

Sanger shrugged, unperturbed. 'There are good reasons. The management at Supergear have screwed the thing up so completely you'd best cut your losses and start again on a new site with a new name.'

'You really believe that?'

'Yes. A lot of it is in the paper David Travis prepared – the rest I've deduced or discovered. Mainly it's that they tried switching markets instead of looking at how lousy their whole operation was – design, production, selling, everything. There's so much wrong it's hard to know where to begin.'

'Try, then.'

'Okay. Production. They could speed up everywhere if they automated more. You can get machines to do button-sewing, to put the interlinings in, to do the ticketing. They're still doing the whole damn lot by hand. If they'd produced more, they could have kept their prices down. Do you know they still *pack* the garments too? All the bright firms these days send the stuff out on coat-hangers. It keeps the clothes crisp – you know, nice-looking. Bartram acts like he's still running a schmutter sweatshop – but with no sweat.'

'And?'

'They buy cloth too dear from old suppliers. They can't keep good people because there are too many deadbeats at the top. That guy Fielder sits on his arse instead of getting out to the customers or pushing the designers. When he goes to Paris he spends more time at the Lido than he does wearing out the sidewalk in the Rue de Sèvres – that's where all the good boutiques are. Another thing – they threw out all their steady sellers, the coats for old dames, when they launched their new lines. They left themselves with no insurance at all, instead of changing their lines gradually. Need I go on?'

The way Sanger unrolled facts in an argument was like a salesman unrolling first-grade Wilton carpet. Impressive, but unemotional, letting the material speak for itself.

'Even so – shut the plant?'

'That's part of the trouble too. You can't expect to keep bright kids up there, away from London. Bartram loses all his best talent every six months. Who ever dreamed up the idea of opening the place in that dump?'

'Costs are low compared with London. We get development area grants – you know that.'

'What's the use of low costs and grants if you end up with no business? It doesn't make sense.'

'Besides,' said Michael, sitting down, acting as if he hadn't heard the words above the slow sigh of air from the cushion of the chair, 'my father wanted a place to hide Bartram in, and Bartram wanted to stay in the North.'

'Two more facts, Michael. There's probably a buyer for the site if we want one.'

'Who says?'

'David Travis.'

'What else?'

'If you're worried about your father's solicitude for Frank Bartram, then he may change his mind when he gets to know a bit about how Bartram's been handling Supergear's books.'

'What do you mean?'

'I mean that Bartram isn't too particular which heading he puts his costs under. I had the accounts checked out. There are a lot of strange items. I suspect he's charged a whole load of straightforward repairs to "improvements".'

'And?'

'And improvements go down as capital expenditure. Not deductible from revenue. It makes the profits look bigger. Without that bit of help, I'm not sure Supergear would have shown *any* profit last year. And isn't Bartram on a bonus linked to the profit figure?'

'Something like that. The old devil. Are you sure?'

'Pretty damn sure.'

Michael walked round the desk, stood with feet apart, looking down at Sanger. 'Why didn't you tell me all this before?'

'You didn't ask. Besides, I haven't been sitting on it for days, like you with the Talbot-Brown business.' He shot a bright glance at Michael, then switched it off again, not wanting to make much of the point. 'I only really pulled the pieces together this morning.'

Michael, sucking in the news, liked the taste too much to want to upset Sanger over a detail. 'It's fantastic if you're right.'

Westbrook was already halfway through the door. 'Sorry I'm late, Michael. I had an agency lunch. What's so fantastic?'

When Michael told him, he clutched his stomach in a mock paroxysm of laughter and lowered himself gently on to the bench, a careful yard or two away from Sanger. 'This organisation seems to have more than its fair share of fools and rogues.' The others didn't speak, merely asked questions with their eyes.

'Lymington,' said Westbrook. 'While you were away, Earl, we dug a bit deeper into the work you'd started on the African company.'

Instinctively he said *we*, which later became *I*, as he set out the details. Westbrook gave David Travis a supporting rather than a main role in this particular story. There was no malice or forethought about his way of telling the facts. This was simply how Westbrook's mind worked. He approached the end of his piece.

'He was taken in, simple old man that he is.'

'By an old gag like that?'

'No question of it,' said Westbrook. 'The assets were revalued a year before we became interested. It made the book value look marvellous, and the profits were inflated too. It would have been spotted, I expect, in this country – but in Africa, in a country smitten with the first hot flush of independence, a place that Lymington was supposed to know backwards? The decision was left to him, and he wasn't equipped to take it.'

Michael was back behind the desk. He didn't know whether to be pleased or desolated. Opportunities for blowing up the old guard were coming to him in almost lavish plenty, but at this rate, what wouldn't they find in the way of weakness as they raked their way through the Prospero Group? Yet the profits still bubbled, the market paid its respects to the organisation's

performance by a quotation for the shares which, in these uncertain days, might be termed buoyant. He had read a favourable
broker's assessment only that morning: purchase recommended,
but the market in shares is a narrow one.

He had heard the argument about conglomerates many times:
the possible weaknesses of a top management team who were not
especially expert in any of the multifarious businesses they ran,
but were merely providers of finance, seekers for best buys in
already going concerns. He knew, too, that in America the conglomerates were fighting against growing governmental hostility.
He didn't want to believe that the larger the whale, the more
parasites it attracted, still moving forward blindly and awkwardly.
But he was honest enough to review the possibility once more, the
likelihood of poor men and poor companies living off leviathan
simply because leviathan was there. His angry frustration with his
father grew. The tone came from the top. Size need not mean
cumbersome slowness if the leadership was right.

Sanger, for once, was working out no business problem, but was
biding his time to spice this substantial feast of damning facts
with a taste of gossip. Westbrook sat back, pleased with the way
things had gone.

'Lymington isn't only an innocent in business,' said Sanger.
'You remember what I said about one of our top men being maybe
a homosexual? That was Lymington too.'

Westbrook pushed out an unnatural laugh, one which half-said
he believed this was a joke, half-said he did not appreciate
Sanger's over-topping of his own narrative. Michael looked grim.

'He's been watched for a time, as we agreed,' said Sanger,
and Michael went on regarding him with hostility. He wanted not
to be reminded of his part in Sanger's ferreting, and his spirit
rebelled against having to accept the reality of what Sanger might
be saying, if indeed it were real.

'As *you* decided, off your own bat,' he said coldly.

'As you like,' said Sanger, undisturbed. 'Anyway – he goes
regularly to see a friend, rather younger. He stays maybe two
hours for no apparent reason. The friend has had trouble for a
number of years. Not notorious, but well known to those who
want to know about these things. The friend has been on holiday
with our noble knight three times. It fits well enough.'

'It's legal,' said Westbrook, trying to prick the balloon.

'Legal, but not likeable, wouldn't you say, Michael?' asked
Sanger. Michael answered only by leaning forward to push a
switch on his desk. A tapestry hanging on the wall began to roll

itself up neatly towards the ceiling. What was revealed was a useful educative toy, installed only during the last four days: a screen, glowing with light, a projected chart displayed upon it. He flicked another switch and a new chart appeared.

'We'd better look at those figures on Lovelace's again,' he said.

He could not be blameless in what Sanger had been doing, that was obvious. Yet this was one of the times when he loathed having to use Sanger and the methods which sometimes seemed necessary.

*

Neither David nor Sheila had been able to stand for more than twenty-four hours the atmosphere their first serious stand-up row had created. The morning after, they were sulky and silent. In the evening David made certain he was home early, cornily carrying flowers, not knowing quite what other token to bring. He was the first to say *sorry*, and his wife had gratefully added her share to the reconciliation. She needed him just now rather more than he needed her.

Not that either of them ceased to believe much of what they had said. It was the degree to which they had pushed the argument which was regretted. They refused to live with too sharp a realisation of the way necessity could constrain the pattern of their life. For the time being they would believe what they wished to believe, playing at being the agents of free choice, but always with the mid-century feeling of uncertain emptiness in their guts.

David was the uneasier of the two when they kissed and made up, for he had needed to lie. Not seriously, he argued to himself, but in the misty way of non-truth rather than falsehood. 'Please,' he said. 'No more about the red-head. You don't *really* think I've been spending my evenings in bed with her, do you?'

He was not called upon to answer his own question. Even if he had been challenged, the answer was that he hadn't. Not evenings in the plural. But Alison would, from his viewpoint, lie between them for a long time until the memory cooled. One day, he promised himself, he might even tell Sheila about the episode, drop hints about it at least. Some men comfort themselves in their procrastinations with such amiable fictions.

Now, a week later, the quarrel had receded, impelled into the background by two minds which wanted it out of the way of daily living and the immediate prospect of Sheila's baby. David did nothing about Fielder, feeling as unwilling to speak to the man as he was, for the present, to spend another night with Alison.

Hard-pressed at office and home, he found that a bit on the side offered no prospect of pleasure at all; merely over-commitment.

So he doggedly rode up to town and back each day, keeping to a predictable timetable, briefcase pregnant with work for Westbrook which Hardy should have shared. At Prospect House he avoided as far as possible those corridors and committee rooms where he might meet Alison. It would, of course, have been easier to make a date and tell her simply there was nothing doing just now for very good reasons – like Sheila and the baby. But some streak of vanity prevented him taking the step. He objected to having to *say* that his life was as mundanely circumscribed as most other men's. The confession would obliterate the fantasy through which their liaison acquired its aura.

Hardy's return from holiday touched off an impetuous resentment in David. Hardy was tanned and cocky, and after an hour's session with Westbrook seemed to know more about what had been going on in the past fortnight than David did. At least Hardy insisted on buying him lunch, so they went to their new bar to eat Scotch eggs and smoked salmon sandwiches and drink the standard carafe of undistinguished but harmless Chablis.

'Lionel thinks the strike at Brasserton's is bound to be settled today or tomorrow,' said Hardy. 'Then we'll really have our work cut out. Michael's itching to get the American contract signed, and Lionel insists that the long-range plan for Brasserton's is given a preliminary revision – but fast.'

'Didn't he tell you I'd already been asked to look at it?'

'No.'

'I could do with some help. It's not exactly my kind of company.'

'Supergear's more your style? Jesus, isn't that a terrible name?' Hardy sounded deliberately provocative.

'Get knotted.'

'I gather Gerald Fielder has folded his tent and stolen gently into the outer darkness. You are a butcher. I never thought you had it in you.'

'Don't think anything, chum. My report arrived *after* Bartram had fired him. Lionel Westbrook was not pleased. Now I get the feeling he and Michael Grant are hatching up something else.'

'You know, don't you?' Hardy was smiling in mock incredulity. David shook his head. 'Well, Lionel hinted we might close Supergear altogether. Either start again somewhere else or sell off the name to the highest bidder. Bartram's already laid off some people.'

234

Two images came almost simultaneously into David's mind. One was dinner with the Westbrooks on the day he became a director of Supergear, Lionel prating about the way he deserved his promotion. The second was the girl who had sewn the button on his coat at the factory, telling him how she liked working there. 'It's nice,' she said. 'You see, I've got all my friends here. We can talk and that. It's great really. There's not much else round here anyway. Not for girls.' She lived very close to the factory. So did most of the labour force; stuck in terraced houses that were like rows of decaying teeth, with gaps never filled in since the German bombs last rained down.

His tone turned ironic again. 'Thanks for telling me. I'm only a bloody director.'

'Lionel must have forgotten.' Hardy hadn't meant to push his advantage so far, yet he continued to talk with the sharpness which always marked his speech. He holed out as automatically as other men missed short putts on Saturday mornings. 'You can always start a board-room revolution.'

'For Christ's sake,' said David. 'Don't rub it in.'

'Nothing's settled. Maybe Bernard Grant won't let them.'

'Oh sure.'

David poured Hardy another glass of wine, a nervous reflex to fill the vacuum of words rather than a signal of reconciliation. Hardy made a rare gesture of apology.

'Look I'm sorry. I'm not Lionel's bloodhound. How's it been?'

'Confused. I'm just in the scrum. Head down and shoving. I'm not quite sure in what direction I'm pushing and I'm bloody certain I don't know where the ball is.'

'Aren't we all?' said Hardy. He sipped his wine. 'How's Sheila? Isn't it almost her time?'

'About a week.' David paused, considered, plunged on. 'You've done your bit, Colin. Keeping her posted on my office love-life.'

'I don't get it.'

'Sheila said you'd told her I was having it off with Alison Bennett.'

Hardy screwed up his face as if thinking hard. It looked like a face which had been used a lot, a mischievous Punch face. 'I don't recall. She talked a bit about Alison at that Christmas party. I didn't confirm or deny the rumour.'

'There wasn't any rumour. Not unless you started it.'

'We were just talking,' said Hardy. 'You know the way it is. Wives always take an interest in the local talent. It's only natural. It happens in every office.'

'And you helped the interest along, I suppose?'

'I honestly don't remember. Is it that important?'

'To me, yes.'

'In that case I'm sorry.' He smiled a wry, almost affectionate smile. 'Can't you cope, then?'

'Cope?'

Hardy phrased the next sentence carefully. 'Well, if Sheila knows enough to start stirring it. . . .'

'She knows nothing except what other people have told her. Fielder started it – and his motives I can understand. But you. . . .'

'I've said I'm sorry. All we had was a clever conversation. I never dreamed she'd take it seriously. Tell me about Fielder.'

David told him, all of it more or less. 'Christ,' said Hardy. 'Is Sheila back to normal?'

'No thanks to you.'

Hardy shrugged. 'I hope it was worth it. I mean, if you *are* found out, at least you've got your memories.'

'Very funny.'

Hardy laughed. 'I don't want the details. But I hope she's up to your fantasy of her.'

'How would I know?' said David, looking straight at Hardy, acting like mad.

'I don't believe it.' Hardy leaned across conspiratorially. 'You really mean you haven't laid her after all this time?'

David was trapped by the directness of the question. Either he would look sexually foolish, his pride impaired, or Hardy would be able to find some justification for whatever he had said to Sheila. He didn't want Hardy to know, not directly. To have a vague reputation as a successful ram was different from providing occasion and circumstance, court-room style. In the end, David gave an answer which Hardy could interpret as he wished.

'I don't fancy her as much as you seem to think.'

'You could have fooled me. I never knew you had principles.'

'Leave it,' said David, but Hardy was intent on making his crack.

'There comes a time,' he said, 'when every man must rise above principle. I've forgotten who said it, but it's very appropriate in your case.'

'Ha-ha.' David enunciated the two syllables precisely.

'All right – be miserable.'

'What other news of the great world inside? You seem to have everything sewn up.'

'Talbot-Brown, our young friend, is in the relegation zone, but hanging on grimly.'

'So I gather.'

'I don't know what it is he's done, or maybe not done. But the mob is waiting for his head to roll, struck off by Harold Armfield.'

David wanted to score one point, a good one. He shrugged off discretion. 'Do you know about Lymington too?'

'No.'

It was a careful version of his analysis of the African documents which David gave to Hardy, but it was enough. Suddenly Hardy was laughing, throatily, with no humour in the sound. 'Now I know why Karian was so jumpy,' he said.

'Karian?'

'I should have told you earlier. He rang just before lunch – I took the call. Asked me to pass on a message to you. Could he have back the files he lent you last week. He needs them urgently. He said you'd know the ones he meant.'

*

Michael Grant was warmly ebullient at first, almost too fulsome as he congratulated Prosser on settling the strike. But his tone changed when Prosser, in full pedantic flood, enumerated the reasons for caution.

'For God's sake, Barry, is this strike settled or not?'

'It's settled, Michael. But don't expect them to turn into computer-minders overnight.'

'We can train them – give them the best of everything. They're skilled operatives, not bloody navvies, aren't they?'

'They're also *people*. You can't push them too fast.'

'Can we sign or can't we? That's all I want to know.'

'It's a risk.'

'Crossing the street's a risk. Is it a *reasonable* risk?'

Prosser pondered. He knew the score, the factors in this decision. He could be riding a golden chariot or putting the skids under himself. He watched Michael Grant rubbing a hand against the silver car on the desk as if it were a talisman. The future was evenly in the balance, he reckoned, after days of working it out. Now, experiencing again the nervous energy which Michael exuded almost visibly, sensing the inexorable purpose in the man, Prosser felt the balance shift. Bernard Grant was nearly sixty-seven, his son just thirty-four. The only danger to himself was that Michael would not win soon enough. That was a chance he must take.

'Yes,' he said, 'it's a reasonable risk.'

It happens often when a struggle has been long and tortuous and exhausting that towards the end, within sight of victory, minor triumphs begin to taste flat. Michael felt no elation. Prosser was with him, yet oddly he wished the answer had been the other way. Then he would have needed to keep burning, to have argued again the rationale of the revolution of practice and attitudes he proposed. That would have fuelled his faith. Prosser's capitulation under pressure made him feel like a spoilt child in whom vanity and ambition for the self-fulfilment brought by power were dominant. He understood well that he would have pushed through the Brasserton's contract anyway. He was too far committed to withdraw.

'Thank you, Barry,' he said. 'I need all the confidence you've got.'

Ten minutes later, by-passing his secretary, he rang Alison Bennett direct. He asked her to get him on the first flight to New York the next morning; to do it quietly, outside the office. Later still, booking confirmed, he told Sanger what he proposed to do.

'I want to make sure Corsino hasn't got cold feet. I can't believe he hasn't heard about the strike.'

'I'll go if you like,' said Sanger.

'Sorry, Earl. But it'll be my hand that signs the papers. This one I've got to judge for myself, on the spot.'

'And the board? And Oldershaw? You wouldn't tie it up in advance of telling them?'

'That depends how strong I'm feeling after I've talked to Corsino.'

'You're taking a chance.'

'So I'll have to if necessary.'

'You have the authority?'

'My remit's a bit shaky. But there's nothing like a *fait accompli* to force through a board decision. They wouldn't want a scandal, my father least of all.'

'Good luck,' said Sanger, opening the file from which he would give Michael a final briefing. 'Brasserton's may even stay afloat next year so long as you give them twelve months to get that computer operative.'

*

Next morning, Michael huddled behind *The Times* as he waited in the departure lounge at Heathrow. When his flight was called, more or less on time, he walked quickly through the gate. A sharp wind was blowing across the airfield as he climbed the steps behind the nose of the Boeing. A male steward took his briefcase and led him into the dim, whispering interior. At the third row of seats, the steward leaning in to put down the case, his father smiled slowly up at him.

'Good morning, Michael,' he said. 'I thought I'd have seen you in the VIP lounge.'

Michael scarcely felt the steward remove his topcoat. He sat down like an automaton, searching for words. 'This is a pleasant surprise, father. What's it all about?'

'I thought I'd better have a look at your Mr Corsino along with you. A chief executive's duty, don't you think? He must be quite a man if you're so impressed with him.'

'I'm not sure I'll be seeing him this trip.'

Bernard Grant almost negligently began to flip the pages of *Time* in his lap. His grey hair was carefully brushed and waved, and his snowy cuffs protruded an immaculate inch or so below the sleeves of his dark jacket. He exuded a faintly scented aura of expensive confidence. Michael hadn't seen him so coolly cocky in weeks, almost an adman's caricature of the tycoon air-traveller for whom the going is great. When the pause had done its work, he spoke.

'That would be a pity, Michael. But I'm sure you can arrange it.'

His son did not answer. The first-class compartment of an airliner to New York was no place for the conversation he wanted to begin. For the moment he could not even decide what he would say or how he should play the next forty-eight hours. He tried to dismiss the idea that either Sanger or Alison had told his father of the intended journey. It made no sense for either of these allies to have betrayed him so obviously, yet how else could Bernard be sitting here now?

The answer was within so wide a range of possibilities that it was useless to grope after it without further evidence. He turned to the problem of whether his father was taking the ride to prevent him concluding a deal with Corsino or simply, like the politician Bernard could be, to grab some of the kudos for it. That, too, could only await the proof of events.

He looked at his father's hands manipulating the magazine, squat white fingers with the hair thickly upon them and bushy at the wrist; not artist's hands, despite Bernard's cultural pretensions, but hands meant for power and the manipulation of men and money. He supposed he would never resolve the compound of affection and dislike, admiration and scorn which he felt for his father. He was stuck with it, an immovable legacy of their personal history. Yet he believed that some kind of benevolent tolerance, superficially disguising the tension below, might spring on his side out of a victory which would show Bernard that he was now the inheritor. And no victories would be won in the next six hours. Armistice was dictated by circumstance.

'You won't mind if I don't talk much, father? I've a splitting headache. I'll catch up on some sleep.'

'You look tired, Michael.' Bernard Grant was enjoying this. 'I hope you haven't been overdoing it. Your devotion to the organisation's affairs is touching, to me particularly, but you have thirty years ahead of you. Pace yourself.'

The engines of the plane were screaming, then roaring as they shifted to full power. The captain's voice, faintly reading the usual script, oozed into the cabin. *We do a noise abatement procedure so as not to worry the people who live around the area too much, and this does necessitate quite a steep climb out.* Michael awaited his father's standard observation about airline pilots. Obsessions like this were all part of Bernard's imbalance of judgement.

'That man and others like him once went on strike and cost me a contract worth almost half a million,' said Bernard Grant. 'Ludicrous. Ten thousand a year or more for a fellow who's just a high-grade bus-driver? The world is going mad.'

'Yes,' said Michael, who knew also that his father thought of racing drivers as motorists with a dangerously irresponsible sense of fantasy. Bernard would never understand that the art of handling machinery was different from the brute science of being able to build it or knowing how it worked.

'I'm sorry,' said his father. 'I'm disturbing you.'

The truce was kept as they flew in sunshine, never glimpsing the land or ocean below, through the morning and early afternoon. Michael more or less slept, his mind working, while his father read and dozed. The life of the plane, an excess of movement and eating and drinking, swirled around them without touching their minds until they stirred to look at the approach to Kennedy. It was a poor greeting to a country which could be so spectacular in skyline. Offshore, Michael had noticed a vast area of water blacker in colour than the green of the rest, the notorious Long Island dead sea, so densely polluted after years of sludge-dumping, it could no longer purify itself. Crossing the coast, the yellow-white beaches looked scruffy, the soil around the jigsaw of lagoons and creeks too muddily brown. Even the mean white houses were in rows too predictably straight, broken by clusters of storage tanks that looked like abandoned hat-boxes.

240

'It doesn't change much,' said Bernard Grant, 'except for the worse.'

Kennedy was a mess, corseted and dusty with construction work. They walked through dirty temporary corridors, past a scrawl on a wall which said *Hail to the Mets*, and then were delayed thirty minutes by surly customs men hunting for drugs. By the time they took the highway to Manhattan, their limousine boxed in by mountainous trucks and rolling cars with unsmiling drivers, neither of them felt as certain as they had earlier that they would be able to maintain the peace.

'Do you really want to meet Corsino?' asked Michael.

'Why else would I have come?' said his father. 'I'd like to check your judgement before you commit the organisation irrevocably.' He continued to stare straight ahead. 'That is the idea, I suppose. You're going to sign the contract?'

'Not necessarily, father.'

'Let's not play childish games, Michael. I know it and you know it. I'm here to see that it's in *all* our interests.'

'If that's what you want to believe. I'll telephone as soon as we get to the hotel.'

'Thank you,' said Bernard Grant.

It's a brand-new taste experience, said the radio as they slowed to pay the toll at the Triboro Bridge. *Nine calories to the spoonful. No cyclamates. New jam.*

'Dear God,' said Bernard Grant, who had never been known willingly to acknowledge that advertising sold *his* goods.

At the hotel, as they parted to their separate rooms, he said: 'I shall sleep for five hours, Michael. Then we'll have dinner together. If Mr Corsino can see us tomorrow, so much the better. And don't do anything foolish in the meantime.'

They ate in a French restaurant on the East Side, the lower floor of a brownstone house, with a terrace and a tree as added attractions. Here the Manhattan dwellers with money forgot for an hour or two that they needed to put iron stanchions against their apartment doors before they went out to dine, gobbling martinis and leaving more food on their plates than a child in Cairo might get in three days.

'This is Pierre, your captain,' said a waiter. 'Would you like the menu, sir?' In his face was light without heat, a kind of regimented politeness learned from the book, rationed out carefully to each customer.

'The food's ridiculously expensive,' Bernard Grant said quietly.

Michael, softly angry, said: 'Would you prefer a hamburger?'

'Of course not. But fourteen dollars for an escalope?'

'I'm paying,' said Michael.

Bernard Grant was peering round the room. The faces looked greyer and grimmer and more tired than when he had last been in New York. He was glad he lived in London, which the newspapers told him was becoming a kind of refuge for New Yorkers these days. He had been tempted to come here years ago, looking for his first million. Now, beginning to experience what he had recently only read about – the crime, the dirt in the streets, the noise, the holes in the ground, the children killed by heroin – even the thought of the solid cataract of cash and cunning in these few square miles of Manhattan did not nibble away at his opinion. London could never become like this.

They began to grow really edgy during coffee. The food had been over-cooked as well as over-priced. Bernard Grant could feel again the slight pain in his chest which still concerned him. Michael was annoyed at Bernard's determination to remain sulkily unimpressed, all because his son was playing host at a place which was quite new to him. After a certain time it is no longer possible to converse on meaningless topics, to duck the subjects about which one most wishes to talk. The mind and the tongue grow tired of evasions. Michael, whose course of action was decided, began the careful process of attrition by which he hoped to undermine his father's confidence.

'I'm glad you've done something about Supergear, father.'

'Not I,' said Bernard Grant. 'Frank Bartram took the action he judged right.'

'Urged on by you, I've no doubt. We aren't playing games, are we?' he asked, deliberately echoing his father's phrase of a few hours ago. 'It's not enough, you realise that?'

'It's adequate for the present.'

'We should close the factory.'

What Michael hoped would be a bombshell seemed to have no effect at all on his father who simply shrugged and sipped his cognac.

'One day, perhaps. Why do you say that?'

'It's unprofitable, or very nearly so.'

'Nonsense,' said his father. 'I can't recall the figures exactly, but. . . .'

'The figures are wrong.' Carefully, he explained what had been happening, the complicity which Bartram must have had in the shape of the accounts, until finally he said, 'Your old friend Frank Bartram is on the fiddle, father.'

For the first time, Bernard Grant's voice turned sharp. 'I don't believe it. Even if he has been arranging his company's affairs to best advantage, then in the circumstances any one of us might have fought for our survival similarly.'

'And the company and the shareholders can go hang?'

'Don't be naïve, Michael. I know what my priority of loyalties should be. First, it's to those who have stuck by me down the years. To my colleagues, and not to the army of chief clerks and old ladies in Bournemouth who gave me their shillings to turn into gold. Without men like Frank, they would have had no gold at all in the early years. They can afford to allow him a luxury or two now.'

Michael was astonished. 'You've known what Bartram was doing?'

'Know? Don't know? What are you, Michael – some kind of inquisitor who requires things to be all black or all white? Things are in between as usual. If you say he has committed a small-time swindle, I will accept it. I've no doubt he was thinking of retaining outside confidence in Supergear too, which is in all our interests. His loyalty has earned him the right to my understanding. It is a minor excrescence in our total affairs, a matter of no moment. No one would have known, the organisation would have rolled on.'

'I don't understand you.' Michael was genuinely incredulous.

'Your passion for truth in every circumstance is ludicrous. Sometimes the truth is dangerous. It destroys men and wrecks that happiness which otherwise would have been undisturbed. I have always been selective in the pursuit of what you call truth. The world is a much more pleasant place if you learn that wisdom is more important than truth.'

Michael said nothing for a full minute. He picked up the bill, added it over again, tossed a Diners Club card on to the plate. He would save the facts about Lymington for less obdurate ears, Lord Bender's perhaps. He did not intend to give his father the chance to spoil that particular trail as Bernard might now contrive to blur the issue over Supergear. There was more he needed to know about the old man's motives, and there was no point in not speaking plainly.

'Do you intend that Ed Corsino should be coming on a fool's errand tomorrow?'

'I am here to hold your hand, Michael, not to bind your arms. If the arrangement looks right, you can sign it – you alone.'

'I thought you wished to sign it too?'

243

His father smiled very victoriously. 'The responsibility will remain yours. And God help you if it doesn't work out. I intend to keep my options open. In the event it turns out well, I shall be the wise counsellor who was at your shoulder when the contract was agreed. If it goes badly, I shall very easily remind people of my scepticism over the whole thing. You will have signed, of course, despite my advice.' Then it was as if a thought suddenly occurred to him. 'Did you have a good sleep, by the way? I don't suppose you did. That's a mistake. One should always go to bed immediately on landing in New York. The time change can murder your digestion.'

'What part do you *really* mean to take in the meeting, father?'

'I might even be able to help you in earnest,' said Bernard Grant. 'I'm rather good at spotting things among the fine print.'

On the way back to the hotel, Grant continued to dominate the conversation. Michael learned that Armfield had found the organisation some more money: a medium-term euro-dollar loan which would greatly ease the cash position, and at the bargain rate of nine and a half per cent. Within his speciality, Michael had to admit, Armfield was very good.

'That will enable one or two schemes of my own to come off,' said his father. 'Not before time.'

'And Lovelace's?'

'Not Lovelace's. Not at any price. You may have your way over Brasserton's and Mr Corsino – but I'm not going to have the organisation paying out a few million just to buy you a new toy.'

'That's unfair.'

The older man shrugged.

'I shall fight you,' said Michael.

'I expect you will. And your honest, honourable nature will not worry especially what tactics you use, what lies you tell, will it?'

'They won't be lies.'

'To you, no. I've noticed that your conscience is very flexible, Michael. It expands and contracts as the battle drives you. I've no doubt that when the time comes to cut my throat, you'll talk yourself into it. You wouldn't want your conscience to trouble you at nights.'

*

Lymington kissed his wife goodnight, a casual brush of dry powdered cheek, and watched her walk straight-backed towards her room. At the door she looked back for a moment and smiled. She felt relieved. It had been the best evening for weeks: Giles laughing, recalling the gaffes of other men and women at posts around the world. She wished he would more often see friends like those with whom they had dined, people of the service, whose past was as diplomatic as their own. Their kind of people.

His recent melancholy she had been unable to peel away. There were perhaps two causes which she suspected, but she could find no way of bringing herself to mention them. When she asked him about the worry in his eyes he simply said: 'A few business things, that's all. But they'll work out.'

Tonight she really believed the worst was over. He was like a patient recovered.

'Don't stay up too late, my dear,' she said.

He smoothed out the velvet of his smoking jacket and walked downstairs to the study. For half an hour he sat in his favourite wing chair, taking books from the pile at his elbow, leafing through their stiff pages, remembering the episodes of expertise which had brought him these things.

The chair itself: Queen Anne, with petit-point embroidery in the usual lightning pattern. He had bought that for fifteen pounds years ago, in the Portobello Road, before it became a snare for tourists. The man in the shop had pretended horror when Lymington ripped off the sacking underneath the seat, searching for the small struts which would confirm its authenticity. Then they had smiled understandingly at each other, the sharing of experts. Lymington had been glad to teach Bernard Grant much of what he now knew about antiques.

His Swifts, though, he treasured more. Several pamphlets in excellent condition; among them *The Importance of the Guardian Considered*, *A Letter to a Young Gentleman Lately Entered into Holy Orders*, *A Modest Proposal for Preventing the Children of Poor People from being a Burden to their Parents or the Country*. And a superb first edition of *Gulliver*, in two volumes.

To feel the pages, smell them, look at the shape of the words rather than to read them was what he had always enjoyed in the evenings. It was a kind of rejection of the modernity he distrusted, a gesture in himself whose significance he understood. Lymington had looked backwards all his life, clutching above all for the privacy which the new world was ruthlessly eroding around him.

Finally, he stood up and poked at the embers which, although it was mid-April, glowed feebly in the hearth. He loved open fires as he loved old books. He poured himself a brandy, added a little water, and as he walked to the desk he put out a hand so that he trailed a finger across the warm glass of the fish tank. The slow, graceful, silent movement which the swimmers inside provided had been a therapy to his mind for years whenever he sat working in this room.

From his pocket he took a key, bent down towards a drawer, then seemed to change his mind. Straightening up, he consciously thrust out his chest and went back to the chair by the hearth. Three large brandies later he went to bed, feeling better than he had felt for weeks. He had thought a great deal about his problems and he knew he could survive them.

He slept dreamlessly despite the alcohol, but he awoke early. He closed his eyes for maybe five minutes before he realised quite clearly that he was not going to fall asleep again. He got out of bed, coldish, pulled on a dressing-gown and quietly walked towards the study again.

The fire was dead, but the central heating had kept the room warm. This time he did not hesitate as he sat at the desk. He unlocked the third drawer down on the right, pulled out an envelope, and spread its contents before him.

The communication from the club, blandly phrased, was the third he had received since they had changed from making telephone calls to putting into print their reminders which never mentioned money, only the need for 'urgent settlement of the matters which we have discussed'.

To this he added the bundle of documents, letters, sheets of figures and memoranda which he had extracted from files at Prospect House since Easter. He had hesitated to destroy them, pondering Karian's news, imparted without its significance to Lymington being realised, that the files had been missing for a period. He wondered, without hope, how the borrowers had viewed the history of the African affair.

Finally, there was a photograph – not a good one, heavily grained, but recognisable – of himself and a friend, whose relationship had lasted seven years now, taking them to Rome, St Moritz, Nice and, more regularly, to a particular address in SW3. It had arrived in an envelope marked 'Personal' four days ago. There was no letter with it and none was needed.

He rubbed the stubble on his cheek and came close to a wry smile as he thought back just five hours or so. Could he really have believed, after the balm of the dinner and the drink, that there was any way to avoid disaster in this jungle of combined circumstance?

His mind scarcely bothered to reassess the evidence and the endless adjudication of the past seventy-two hours. He rose and placed the first papers on the grey ash in the grate, struck a match

246

and set fire to them. Sheet by sheet he fed the flames for ten minutes. Then, pouring himself a brandy, topped generously with water, he sat at the desk and wrote vigorously on a sheet of paper.

At the hearth again, he stirred the ashes, mixing the black of the paper with the grey of the embers, over and over. Then he sat down, stretching his legs.

As he placed his long white fingers, virtually hairless, in a steeple before his face, he thought about Esther. Nothing was left there, no feelings of substance. True, he felt a hazy debt of gratitude that she had let him follow his own way for so long, playing charades with the world meantime. He was ashamed, though not in any determined way, that this was another obligation he could never repay, with or without honour. At least there were no children to complicate the decision further.

He believed for a full minute that he would cry, but there was only a slight irritation in his eyes, like sand which the tide never quite reaches. His hands were slightly uncertain as he unscrewed the bottle.

The capsules were cylindrical, like bombs without fins, coloured turquoise at one end, red at the other. There must, he reckoned, be around fifty of them, cradled in the lap of his dressing-gown. He began putting them into his mouth two at a time, without haste or drama, each pair washed down with the dull taste of over-watered cognac.

11. Virtue wasn't in the contract

Naked into the council chambers of the world. A politician's phrase, from an age that was dead, the years when he was just beginning. Bernard Grant scarcely liked himself for remembering it, but it hovered in his head as his son led him into the room where Corsino awaited them. He hated being led.

A long table; rosewood. Solid or only veneered? As he sat he looked for a tell-tale chip at a join, found one, beamed inwardly. The disposable society at work again. Around him were pads and pencils, cigarettes and water, a mountain of documents and law-books. With Corsino were five men, two of whom were introduced as company lawyers, neat-suited and sweating case-histories from every scented pore. Their handshakes were sharp and un-committed. The remaining three, men with careful smiles and studious eyes, were vice-presidents of Corsino's and two other companies. There were also two girls who seemed to have come from the same Vassar mould: around twenty-five, dark-suited, white-bloused, tall, brunette, good-looking, with pale pink lips and brittle faces. Their eyes were cool and they showed too much of their upper limbs for a meeting such as this.

God knows what they are here to do, he thought, though he minded them not at all. Bernard Grant was more realistic than Armfield. The days were long since past, he knew, when business-men would trade in any three micro- or macro-skirted girls for one little old white-haired lady who could type. Girls who emitted sexual vibrations meant status and modernity; packages to be used in many ways. It was also a fact – and he knew Armfield would not understand this either – that sexy secretaries were probably less of a security hazard than ugly girls, terrified at the prospect of spinsterhood, who would open their arms and their legs and, distressingly, their mouths for any halfway-handsome man who wanted to find out the secrets of an organisation. He noticed that each of the girls in the room carried what looked like a small tape-recorder.

248

Grant and his son bore to the conference table the clothes they stood up in – in Bernard's case a high four-button single-breasted which he fancied made him look very Edwardianly severe – and one briefcase, Michael's. A New York lawyer was with them too, to watch for traps. Ranged against Corsino's flotilla, it didn't seem the Britons could make it a fair contest.

Corsino spoke first, relaxed and in command, beating his handsome head in time with the compliments he dispensed. It was, he said, a real honour and privilege for them to meet Michael's father. They had greatest admiration for his organisation and what it had achieved. Out of nothing. Rather like the American Dream, was it not? Rags to riches. Log cabin to White House. Virtue rewarded. He went on, like a man handing out improving literature at a prize-giving, while Bernard Grant kept his nose above the flood of flattery and itched to get his eyes on the small print of the document which lay in front of Corsino. Grant neither liked Corsino nor disliked him yet. He just sat there weighing up the style of the performance and scored it pretty high, since he was not averse to flattery, but unspecial, since he had heard most of it before, sometimes better done.

'Well, gentlemen,' said Corsino at last, handing his honest-broker look to Bernard Grant as well as Michael, 'do we have a deal?'

Michael shifted in his chair, inclined his head slightly towards his father with a suggestion of asking permission to speak. But he omitted to wait for an answer. 'I think we all know this contract pretty well by now, Ed. On our side it's been finally checked through, but I've a few minor points to request rewording on, and one more important change which our lawyers insist is made.' He slid a sheaf of documents from his briefcase, selected a photostat for his father, retained another for himself. 'I have the phraseology for the changes right here.'

One of the girls jumped athletically from her seat and distributed the copies which Michael gave her.

Bernard Grant looked fiercely at the papers before him as if they were a cabal of complaining minor shareholders, then smiled acidly at his son. Michael was trying to rush him. He had seen the draft only this morning, was not familiar with the emendations. He fidgeted, unwillingly ensnared in the strands of circumstance.

'Okay. Let's go through it,' said Corsino.

'Then,' said Michael, 'if we're agreed, I know my father would like a last private discussion with me to check out any points you raise. Mr Amstein' – he motioned towards the lawyer sitting on their side of the table – 'will also assist us. After that, we'll be all ready to close it.'

This time Michael smiled at his father, warmly, with a touch too much light from the eyes. Bernard, despite his annoyance, had to admit the boy had done it well. He was going to get his chance to shout, if he wanted to, but strictly at a time of Michael's choosing. For the next twenty minutes he had a chance to admire his son's command still further.

Michael dissected the contract with swift, undeflected skill. He built in small safeguards at several points, slightly shifting the order of adverbs and qualifications, even deleting a whole paragraph on the third page. The lawyer on Michael's left seemed unemployed. Everyone in the protective screen around Corsino was, by contrast, taking notes, like anxious students at a lecture, Michael dictating the pace. Except for the girls. They played with their battery toys, happy but unsmiling. Bernard Grant wondered whether he should complain about the meeting being on the record in this fashion. It was not his style.

Corsino said little, cocking glances at the lawyers whenever an opinion was wanted. They looked very judicial behind their thick-framed spectacles. After appropriate silences, they nodded or grunted quick assent to most of the changes.

The major point which Michael raised took longer to deal with, however. He sought to protect Brasserton's against the consequences of any delay in the delivery of the component computer which was to be built into the complex process control for the plant in Ecuador.

'We've allowed twelve months from placing our order until delivery. But if we're let down on the date by the computer people, we run a big risk of completing the whole job late.' He laughed as if he wanted to share a grim joke with Corsino. 'And Ed, your penalty clauses are tough enough without giving us *that* problem. Have you heard about some of the computer hold-ups there have been this year?'

Corsino was trying to look unmoved. Clever man, thought Bernard Grant. 'We're all taking some chances, Michael. I think that should be yours.'

'Our advice is against that,' said Michael. 'Surely it comes under the category of *force majeure*?'

Corsino frowned. 'We've given you a get-out in case of strikes at your plant. *Some* strikes, anyway.' He beamed ironically, suggesting that thus far the track-record of Brasserton's on disputes

250

hadn't been promising. 'You're safe against everything from piracy in the air to goddam earthquakes. Did you ever hear of an earthquake in England, Carl?' He questioned the man at his side, plump and bald, who emitted a blunt bray of laughter and looked at the next vice-president in line. 'What more do you want?'

'I don't want us to suffer because of inefficiency on the part of another company whom *you* suggested we should rope in on the deal. You know that getting Brasserton's to put the whole control unit together for you is a smart move. You'll save on installation costs, *and* we carry the can for making sure the whole thing works before you accept delivery. That's enough of a risk on our side. The delivery date for the computer won't really be within our control, will it? I reckon that's *force majeure.*'

'It's a lot you're asking,' said Corsino. 'Do you expect a full week's grace for every week they might be late in giving you the computer?'

'That's it,' said Michael.

'Open-ended?'

'Open-ended.'

'Christ,' said Corsino.

They argued on without much heat. Bernard Grant considered the scene impassively. Horse-trading; the same old routine, the combatants warily circling each other, striving for position. He remembered the scores of contracts he had signed in his time, the conferences where weaknesses were probed and strengths disguised. Who were the men whose judgement could be swayed by more money in exchange for a riskier situation? Who was amenable to a night on the town and a girl, or objects more bizarre, at the end of it? Who were the powerful, the craven, the time-servers, the honourable, the potential traitors?

Today's meeting was too late for all that and maybe, with Corsino, it was always too late. The more modern concepts of management, cool management, all computers and critical path analyses – that probably was Corsino's way as it was his son's. Yet Corsino could not be *so* clinical. He was, too, a politician and a conspirator, which similarly was the extra element in Michael's make-up.

Grant assumed that it was one of Corsino's men who had telephoned transatlantic to warn him that Michael was flying out quietly, probably to complete the deal. He liked the touch. Corsino, wanting to be safe all ways, unwilling to complete an undercover deal for fear that the old guard at the Prospero Group might still sabotage it. He sat there, impatiently waiting for a sign from Corsino that would admit complicity, and when it did not come he dragged his mind back to the point, thrusting his eyes over the document whilst the talk flowed on.

The penalty clauses: they looked like a dangerously volatile bomb, but Grant believed there would be little chance of defusing it – not with the generous part-payments which were due to be made during the course of the work. To him it looked as good a contract as even he could have achieved in the circumstances, though some of the technicalities of the product were beyond him. He was disturbed that he had been able to place no more than three question marks on the twelve pages of the document, and each of them a quibble.

Finally, Corsino said: 'Let's recess, shall we? I guess my side would like to talk privately about this. Maybe you would too.'

When the Grants were shown privately into a side-room, Bernard quickly got rid of the New York lawyer. Politely, but with patent impatience. Then he let the urge for sarcasm run free.

'Can we talk openly, Michael? Or do you think it's bugged?'

Michael acted as if he took the question quite seriously, refusing to be drawn. He lifted up the single picture on the wall and lowered it, opened a cigarette box, then looked beneath the table. It was a pantomime for Bernard Grant's benefit.

'It seems all right to me. But is there anything important to say?' His father let the silence hang ominously as Michael sat down. 'Well, father. What do you think?'

'I think you need to win your point about the computer. And I think you have insulted my intelligence and my trust in you by not taking me through the document earlier, and by keeping the changes to yourself. But' – he grudgingly smiled – 'it's a contract that in the circumstances is fair. I want to raise three points.'

He showed Michael the marks he had made. With each of Bernard's judgements, his son agreed. Grant had the uncomfortable feeling he was being humoured. It made his temper rise again.

'I also think,' he said at last, 'that I shall squeeze you like a lemon if this deal does not come right.'

'I expected nothing else,' said Michael. 'That's the risk I run.'

'And remember,' said Grant, as they rose to go back to the main conference room, 'that the organisation runs it too.'

Half an hour later the contracts had been amended, exchanged and signed. Cool management again, Bernard Grant reflected. No photographer, which Howland would certainly have laid on in similar circumstances. Michael had won, or half-won, his point.

The contract had been changed so that delay on the computer delivery would mean an extension of the final date for completion, day for day – but only up to a maximum period of two months. Michael had pushed it up from one month, had not quite managed to make it three months. It was a compromise weighted on the side of the Prospero Group. Bernard Grant knew he would growl some more at his son, but viewed the prospect without conviction.

They were shaking hands, laughing like men who had done a great morning's work, sipping martinis or milk to taste, when a messenger came in looking for Michael. As his son left, Grant saw Corsino approaching and quickly and quietly they agreed to talk by telephone later. Michael, meantime, took a telephone call of his own, sitting on the edge of a desk in a room full of shining secretaries. Very soon he stood up, instinctively looking towards the door which led to his father. It was Sanger, calling to tell him about Lymington.

*

Armfield and Westbrook were drawn together by the crisis, seeking mutual strength in the absence of the Grants. They sat talking in Armfield's room, with a cold April sun touching them.

'I suppose there's no doubt it was not an accident?' said Westbrook.

'We can't be sure. But my advice is that it must have been deliberate. Barbiturate poisoning, they say. Rarely accidental.'

'Could anything more have been done to save him?'

Armfield's eyelids drooped mournfully. 'They tried forced respiration for an hour. Either they were too late or his heart wouldn't take it.'

'There's bound to be a post-mortem?'

'Unavoidable, I gather.'

'Dear God,' said Westbrook, wondering how much Armfield might know or might yet guess about the investigation of Lymington's history and predilections which had been going on. He was afraid, and a feeling of guilt contended with a sense of compassion which ran deeply within his nature, but was easily overwhelmed in the pattern of his normal living.

'It's unfortunate,' said Armfield. 'And tragic. He was a good man. The organisation will suffer.'

'Yes,' said Westbrook.

They were neither of them speaking cynically. Outside this room and this context they might both, in varying degrees, have wished good riddance to Lymington. Now that he had gone, so brutishly, the loss touched them, and a kind of grief came naturally. Sorrow is often compounded of uncertainty and unease.

'Why are they in New York?' asked Westbrook. 'I had no idea.'

'Nor I,' said Armfield. 'It's a mystery.' By now both of them knew something of what had been happening across the Atlantic. But they were on different sides, and the habit of secrecy survived even the shock they had suffered. Westbrook, who was always most at ease when he could talk expansively, considered the possibility that alliances might change, else why had Michael been with old man Grant? But on the issue of the Corsino contract he scarcely saw himself lining up with Armfield in a boardroom revolution. Ridiculous. Yet – and yet – why was Bernard Grant in on the signing of the contract? Even Earl Sanger had looked worried over that.

'They're catching a plane tonight, I suppose.'

'No,' said Armfield. 'Bernard can't take that kind of nonsense these days. They leave early tomorrow.' He looked almost pleadingly at Westbrook. 'I'm worried about Lady Lymington. Not sure what we should do.'

'Do?'

'I think someone should go to see her. I think that would be right. They've no children and I don't know about other relatives.'

'Not me, Harold. I scarcely know her.'

'Nor do I for that matter. It should be someone senior. You do these things so much better than I.' Usually, Armfield would have resisted the suggestion, spoken or tacit, that Westbrook could improve on his own performance in any sphere. But his unease of conscience overcame his pride. Besides, he hated the trappings of death and mourning.

Westbrook carelessly crossed his knees, forgetting to adjust the crease of his narrow trousers. 'Is it really necessary? I mean, perhaps she wouldn't want to see *anyone.*'

'I'd be most grateful if you'd go. I believe Bernard would want it.'

Westbrook was driven to Westminster next morning. He had chosen the darkest top coat he possessed: a lightweight blue Melton, knee-length and belted. After some hesitation he stopped en route to buy a black tie. Death to him was as much the dirty modern secret as it was to the society around him, the twentieth century's substitute for Victorian sex. What would he need to say?

Lady Lymington opened the door herself. At times like these there was a drill. She had been trained to it, and the training stuck. She wore black, long and smart. No tears, nor sign of them.

254

That would be for others, uncontrolled in their emotion, not for her. The dark eyes were firm, glacial, narrowed as if by cigarette smoke. The coarse skin, which had once been fine, was spotted like pebbles and just as solid. Her head was held unnaturally high. It was the only touch that betrayed her, showed that even she faced this moment with effort.

'Come in, Mr Westbrook.' There was nothing friendly in her words. He walked into the hall. It was the first time he had seen it. Ancient portraits, eighteenth- and nineteenth-century gentlemen, hung on smooth cream walls. The furniture matched them: two chairs which looked good enough to be Chippendale, a heavy black chest, and metalwork in brass, silver and copper that shouted Cairo, the kind that travellers bring home unthinkingly but which needs careful choosing. There was about the place a gloom as if the house felt a loss, an atmosphere already of disuse and emptiness.

He followed her silently into a drawing-room similarly furnished, dominated by a huge display cabinet full of china and objects made of ivory and crystal. It was like a set for Somerset Maugham, circa 1933, old-colonial, on TV. He waited for her to sit down, then perched on the edge of a leather-covered armchair. She said nothing, and he blundered nervously into the silence.

'We thought – we felt – that we should come.'

'We?'

'Mr Armfield and I, on behalf of our colleagues. We really are very sorry. . . .'

'Where is Mr Grant?'

'He is away, in America. He is coming back today.'

She looked at Westbrook with undisguised hostility. 'And why are you really here, Mr Westbrook? To console me or to discover what I might say at the inquest?'

She had found her husband just before ten the previous morning, sitting peacefully, when she awoke from a deep sleep. As she waited for the ambulance she read the note and felt an icy anger engulf her that he should have died for reasons so unnecessary. She knew so much more about him than he guessed. He had played his artifices down the years like a confident schoolboy, never believing he could be found out, she resisting without difficulty the temptation to leave him since it had never really been a powerful lure. The habit of love dies hard.

'I'm sorry. I don't understand.' Westbrook's fears grew more tangible, and the woman opposite him read them. He controlled his mouth and hands, but his eyes were alarmed.

She had burned the note. No one would know. And now this vulgar man stood before her, one of the new inheritors; intelligent but without class, without guts, without taste. She wanted to hurt him, but knew that it would be difficult. Her silence could shield him and his kind as it would also protect the memory of her husband; provided she stayed silent.

She hated Westbrook. Suède boots and a black tie. Typical. Whether he was the leader of those who had hounded Giles she did not know. But Westbrook stood for the system which had destroyed Lymington. Tradesmen, all of them. Common little tradesmen, strutting around as if they owned the world, which in truth they virtually did.

'I believe you do understand, Mr Westbrook. Why did you not leave him alone, all of you? He did not betray *you*. Only himself.'

'I know how upset you must feel,' said Westbrook, driven to cliché.

'You know nothing of my feelings or you would scarcely have the nerve to be here. Let me tell you what you *do* know. You know you have been intriguing against my husband: turning over files, intruding upon his private life. Do you think I am afraid to say all this?'

Westbrook did not reply, and she persisted, mocking him. 'Come, Mr Westbrook. We're alone. No one else is here. I can face the facts. Why can't you? Are you afraid?'

Then he began to feel angry. He had come, against his will, to see if this relic wanted sympathy. Who did she think she was?

'I'm not afraid of doing my job.'

She spat the words. 'For one moment I thought you might say *duty*.'

'All right – *duty*. Why not? I'm sorry for what has happened. Your husband was in trouble. But don't try to shift the responsibility on to me.'

'You really *are* vulgar,' she said. 'Will you tell me now that Giles was dishonest or immoral or whatever other claptrap is in vogue? He lost you some money, that's all. Is that criminal? As for what else he did with his life, that was his affair – and mine.'

The truth was seeping through to Westbrook. 'And you didn't care?'

'As if *caring* matters, except to savages unused to decency and self-discipline. It was my *choice*, don't you understand? Living for myself and ourselves, Mr Westbrook, because that was the present and the future I wanted. To survive. It's enough. That's the lesson which diplomacy teaches you.'

He was staggered, unprepared, and the words which came were not as he would have chosen them. 'You've no need to tell me this. You're upset.'

'If you believe that, then appearances are indeed deceptive. No, I am not *upset*, as you call it.' Fishwives got upset. Not people like her. 'I see things rather clearly just now, and I want you to do the same. I shall force you to face yourself, Mr Westbrook, because that is the only revenge I can take.'

He wanted to get back at her. 'I can face myself. Some of us don't live only on the surface.'

'Then you are a fool as well as a murderer. Survival, Mr Westbrook. *That* is our duty. And when we are all so rotten inside, the surface is important. It's our proclamation of what we would aspire to be. Our only symbol of goodness. If you excrete all over the world because you *feel* like doing it, how are you different from the animals? That's the trouble with the vandals who run your brave new world. They behave like yahoos on the excuse of being true to their natures. Being true to its nature is the last thing mankind should be.'

'I'd sooner have things out in the open.'

'Spoken like a bourgeois, Mr Westbrook. How would a trades-man know about duty or honesty or corruption?'

'I've said nothing about them,' said Westbrook lamely.

'Because you haven't the fibre to do so. The words whirl around in your head, but like all your kind you wait for someone else to take the responsibility of actually speaking the truth.'

Westbrook rose. He had heard enough. But he made no move for the door. He hadn't got the guarantee he so badly wanted.

'Yes,' she said, 'for God's sake go.'

Suddenly she looked very tired. Westbrook tried to make some kind of gesture, impulsively. 'I'm still sorry it has turned out like this.'

'Not really. Face it, young man. You believe in your virtue, don't you? You're glad you've smashed the screen we built around ourselves. The remainder of what you feel is only sentiment. Slop. I can do without that.'

She led the way from the room, not quite at full sail. In the hall she turned and spoke again. 'Be careful that you know what is expected of *you*, Mr Westbrook. Giles did not contract either virtue or honour or duty to your damned business. He promised only his contacts and his expertise in the field which he knew. That was the bargain. You have crucified him for failure in a game he did not even understand you expected him to play.'

'The inquest. I'm sorry, but I have to mention it.'

'Why ask such stupid questions? My husband had been concerned about his health. Very concerned. He was afraid of cancer.'

To Westbrook, the statement smelled like victory. He softened. 'If there's anything more we can do. . . .'

Ignoring him, she said: 'But I may not tell the inquest about cancer. And if you're worried what exactly I'll say to the coroner, then I have one word of advice to you: Worry.'

'But Lady Lymington. . . .' Dry in his throat, defeated.

She looked at him bleakly. 'Go to hell,' she said.

*

The only problem for Michael Grant, flying into London with his father later that day, was one of priorities. Earl Sanger he had asked to stand by; and on the recording-machine at his flat were messages from both Westbrook and Talbot-Brown, wanting him to ring them urgently. He also would like to have spoken to Alison Bennett, to see if she knew what the papers really believed. Their reporting that day had been non-committal: medium-sized headlines and no heavily veiled inferences. Lymington's death had had no apparent effect on the market price of the shares either. That was something.

Alison, he regretfully decided, could wait. It was difficult to put the questions he wanted to ask over the telephone when she was so much in ignorance of everything that had been going on. He felt a strong desire to confide in her, wondered why he did so, and told himself it was because there was no one else. Yet could he ever do so? He was becoming dependent. Not good. Not the way he wanted to be. Had she tipped off his father about America? He was strangely undecided.

Talbot-Brown, too, he would leave till the next day or the day after. He got through to Sanger and Westbrook. Then he rang the restaurant across the street for sandwiches and stepped into the shower.

Sanger was the first to arrive. He looked less sure of himself than usual, Michael thought: he kept pushing nervously at the nose-bridge of his spectacles and his face beneath the black evening bristles was even paler than usual.

'You look as if you could do with a drink,' said Michael.

'Thanks,' said Sanger. 'It's been quite a day.'

He sat down, without being asked, on the window-seat, looking out over the Thames. The light was almost gone and the river ran black, tipped with gold from the lamps which pricked its banks and bridges. A gust of rain freckled the window.

'Cheers,' he said, lifting the Scotch woodenly in Michael's direction.

'Not much to cheer about,' said Michael.

'Who would have guessed it would turn out like this?'

'Once you begin this kind of game, you never know where it will end.'

Sanger glanced nervously up at him, threatening to be angry. 'You blame me, then?'

'Of course not. In a way we're all to blame. It's not simple. There are too many facts I don't know. But you haven't helped.'

'Thanks.'

Michael waved his hand impatiently. 'We haven't time for moods, Earl. You know what I mean. We all feel unhappy over this, wondering if we've been fair, wondering what Lymington's said or written, wondering if we pushed too hard. You pushed hardest of all, didn't you?'

'In the interests of the group. In *your* interests, for Christ's sake! Just because he's dead, it doesn't change what he was.'

'All right.'

'And don't listen to everything Westbrook says. He's like goddam jelly at the moment.'

'What do you mean?' asked Michael.

'Hasn't he told you? About his condolence call on the widow?'

'Not yet,' said Michael. 'He'll be here at any moment.'

'It's a big drama. I'll not spoil the impact.' Sanger rose, holding up his empty glass, and when Michael nodded, went to the decanter and poured himself another drink. Then he turned and said: 'Look, Michael, whatever happens, we're in this together. I think it will work out.'

'Worried about your own skin, Earl? Is that it?'

'I'll not fight with you. Tell me about New York. Did you sign?'

'Yes.'

'And what the hell was your father doing there?'

'You tell me.'

Sanger looked at Michael incredulously, then laughed. 'You think it was *me*?'

'Only two people knew. You were one.'

'Your confidence in me is very gratifying. No, it wasn't me. Have you asked *him*?'

'He just smiled and said he had his sources.'

'How did you book your flight?'

'Very discreetly.'

'They have name lists, you know. If your father has a contact at the airline. . . .'

'A long shot.'

'But possible.'

'All right – possible.'

Again the question. Could it have been the girl? Michael still could not accept that, did not *want* to accept it. But he didn't see himself testing out the hypothesis on Sanger. He intended to preserve the knowledge of his special relationship with her for a time yet.

He told Sanger about the negotiations in New York. He was explaining Bernard Grant's strange behaviour over the deal, the threats his father had made about the future of the contract with Corsino, when the doorbell rang.

Since he had visited Lady Lymington that morning, Westbrook had spent most of the time in his office. Apart from seeing David Travis and Hardy and telling them to keep quiet about the investigations into Lymington's African affair, he had refused calls, pretending to be immersed in documents. What he had really been doing was to play over in his mind, like a repeating record, every detail of the interview.

He would have felt more compassion for the woman had she not been so aggressive. The shreds of pity which remained were overlaid by fear and indecision. Again and again he asked himself whether or not she would cover up the details of truth at the inquest. She had been so enigmatic, he could not tell. And how much was he to blame for Lymington's death? Was he not the victim of circumstances? He had convinced himself by now that Sanger was to be held more responsible than anyone. As he told Michael the story of the interview, the prejudice showed.

Michael sat very still, gripping his empty glass tightly. 'How did she know it all, *how*?'

'I'm not sure she knew it *all*,' said Westbrook. 'But enough. It was ghoulish. How could she live with him knowing about his boy-friend?'

'Grow up,' said Sanger. 'It's happened before. You don't have to roll in the hay to stay married.'

'Shut up, Earl,' said Michael.

The three men sat silently for a while. None of them loved each other very much at this moment, though for different reasons.

Michael was angry with himself for giving Sanger so free a hand in the investigation into Lymington. He was no child in appreciating the ethical conflicts which might arise in modern business; but he had little taste for the fine detail of espionage, and he knew he had deliberately ducked his responsibility in wanting Lymington undermined without involving himself in the methods to be used. It was not easy to live with himself just now. Lymington deserved to be chopped, even disgraced. His death was something else.

Westbrook, still flinching from the unhappy memory of the morning, believed that both Michael and Sanger had so far escaped lightly. He felt mangled, with a taste in his mouth as if he had been sucking pennies. Sanger, angry with Michael's attitude towards him, despised both men opposite him, believing that neither was honest or adult enough to face up to the game they were in. It was Sanger who finally broke the silence, speaking with blunt sarcasm.

'May I?' No one interrupted. 'She can only have known what she did because he told her. That seems obvious.'

'When?' Michael's voice had lost its anger, was flat and husky.

Sanger opened out his right hand. 'Maybe face to face, maybe not. I don't suppose we'll ever know. Or he could have left a note.'

'Did she say anything about a note?' Michael asked Westbrook. 'No.'

'Supposing there was one.'

'Michael, I've been telling you. We just have to hope she's going to keep her mouth shut.'

'You really think she will?'

'I *think* she will. I don't know.' Westbrook was over-optimistic to keep his own spirits up, as well as those of his companions. 'The thing no one's yet asked is how Lymington knew we were on to him.'

'Not difficult,' said Sanger. 'Not with your young lions trampling around in the undergrowth.'

'And you,' said Westbrook. 'What about *your* operators? You haven't even told us exactly what's been happening.'

The sneer in Sanger's voice was quite patent. 'I thought neither of you wanted to know.'

'We'd better know now,' said Michael calmly.

Sanger told them about the inquiry agent who had watched Lymington for a month. He told them about the reports he had received and the conclusions he had drawn. What he didn't tell them was that the agency he used had reported during the afternoon that their man was no longer around. He had not checked in for three days, had left his usual address without giving any new one. Sanger kept thinking about other cases he had heard of where agents had tried a touch of blackmail on the side.

'You played it too rough,' said Michael.

'You didn't tell me not to,' said Sanger. 'You're as much responsible as I am.'

Michael could not deny to himself that Sanger was right. He put down his glass and said: 'We'll just have to hope she does it right at the inquest.'

'And that she doesn't tell your father,' said Sanger.

•

Simon Dickson, MP, sat brooding over *Private Eye* in the mid-morning gloom of his club. Once he had enjoyed his fortnightly dose of scandal-sheet; now he felt it to be obsolescently trendy and boring, its barbs cruder and less witty than during its very early days. He had, nevertheless, four times gone through the paragraph which described a contribution he had made to a recent debate in the House. *Parading his innermost conscience with the practised panache of an ageing stripper. . . .* He was sure it was actionable. But should he bother? Perhaps he needed to worry only when *Private Eye* wasn't writing about him. Yet even that sentiment seemed years out of date.

He tossed the thing aside. He had matters more important on his mind. Only two days earlier he had heard, from a normally impeccable source, where the new Hampshire development might be sited.

It was not *certain*, of course. It would be some time, even, before a preliminary announcement could be made. There would follow the usual round of hearings, of objections, of studied argument and counter-argument. The conservationists and those who owned desirable residences with woodland views would say their furious pieces. The government side, backed by the full panoply of wise men from Whitehall, would illustrate how a score of different areas had been considered, how the logic of the chosen place was irrefutable, how people in the overcrowded urban jungles of the South-East must be found decent homes in decent surroundings with work on their doorsteps.

In the end the developments would happen, as such developments usually did, partly because the civil servants *were* meticulous at finding the best sites, partly because too much ministerial pride and Whitehall obstinacy were committed for it to be conceivable that the objectors could be allowed to win. In the latest case, the planners had made even more sure of victory by choosing a stretch of countryside in which some industrial development had already taken place. There was a small plant in existence close to where a major new road would run and a new estate would be built. Not an unsightly plant, he gathered: compact, clean, interesting, with a history that went back to the early years of the automobile: called Lovelace's.

Dickson savoured the thought of his talk with Michael Grant before Easter, rationalising his plan of action for the benefit of his conscience. Had he not said then that he was interested in Michael's ideas about a car company deal? He was more than interested now.

The call from Dickson, enigmatic but full of promise, was not the only titillation which Michael Grant received that morning. A note from Talbot-Brown, strictly confidential, asked him to telephone an outside number to confirm whether he could make a dinner appointment in the evening. He called, told the woman who answered that he would be glad to see his friend not for dinner, but a drink, at a small pub in Chelsea not far from his flat.

During the day he saw his father for only half an hour. Bernard Grant was grave-faced, apparently genuinely upset by Lymington's death. 'It was good of Lionel Westbrook to call on Esther,' he said. 'She appreciated it, I think. I telephoned her this morning, but she said she really would sooner I didn't go round. She wants to be left on her own. I understand how she feels.'

The words eased Michael's fears, if not his conscience. 'Will you go to the inquest, father?'

'I feel I should. I may be called upon to speak. It's strange. I'm no further forward than when we discussed it in New York. He'd seemed a bit down lately – but to kill himself. . . .'

'Did you ask Esther Lymington?'

'I didn't ask, Michael. How could I? But she volunteered the information. He thought he had cancer.'

'Poor devil,' said Michael. The words were in a way relieving to his fears, yet for the first time in several years he wished his relationship with his father were different. It would have been so much easier had they been on the same side, able to confide in each other. Deception as a way of life, ever more tortuous, inhibited his natural enjoyment of the processes of business.

In his ultimate purposes, he remained confident. There would be no guaranteed future for the Prospero empire, for its men and women or its machines, if change did not creep up on it. Bernard's flabby power, his easy assumption of the role of *grand seigneur*, were dangerous. There must be a new command at the top. Michael did not even shrink from the means which were necessary to the end, though he wanted no more unforeseen serious casualties like Lymington on the way.

The events of the past month or so *had* changed him. He was still in the game, still determined to win; yet he had lost much of his capacity for enjoying it. The appetite was blunted. That was how he felt now, as though he were being carried along by forces he did not truly control. He wondered, however, if he would change again once Lymington's death began to recede. He understood what the feeling of power could do to judgement. It was a narcotic he was not yet addicted to, but whose surging strength he had already learned to appreciate.

'We mustn't get too depressed,' said Bernard. He flashed a quick look of challenge at his son. 'New York was interesting. Harold Armfield is after your blood.'

'You've told him?' Oh God, Michael was thinking, you won't let go, will you? You want to push me, make me keep on fighting you.

'Naturally, I don't think he likes *me* very much either, but I explained to him that my presence in New York with you was in no sense collusive. I *think* he believes me.'

'Keeping your options open to the end.'

'As you knew I would. Brasserton's is your problem now, Michael. I think Harold will try to persuade Benjamin Bender you ought to be severely reprimanded at the next board meeting.'

'I expected that.'

'But I don't think even Harold imagines he can get you voted out of office.'

Michael looked curiously at his father. He knew the rules. A straight majority to bring about a change of office: total unanimity to wipe a director off the board completely. Would Bernard try the first ploy one day? Even with Lymington dead, an alliance of Bernard, Armfield, Lord Bender and Bartram would cost him his office as deputy managing director. Westbrook and Prosser – if he could count on Prosser – added up to only two votes.

His father smiled at him. 'I hear you've talked to Oldershaw. Is he pleased?'

'You know the answer to that as well as I do, father,' said Michael, and walked out.

Talbot-Brown was waiting for him at the pub that evening, drinking beer with a fresh-faced man of maybe thirty-five, dressed in a rough-knit white polo-neck and belted safari jacket. Michael half-recognised him, but before the name clicked into place, Talbot-Brown was eagerly making the introduction. 'Mr Grant – this is Philip Lovelace.'

Michael looked questioningly at Talbot-Brown whose smile was smug. 'Let Philip explain, sir.'

'There's no sense in beating about the bush,' said Lovelace. He grinned attractively, pushing at his fair hair with stubby engineer's fingers. 'My father knows I'm here.'

'I always understood he wanted to stay independent,' said Michael.

'So he does. But something else has come up.'

Michael looked around the bar. There were two other people there: a man and a woman who only had eyes, and hands, for each other. He still worried about their ears, and raised his brows at Talbot-Brown and Lovelace. They nodded, draining their glasses, and followed him from the pub.

'Do you mind talking in the car?' asked Michael. 'I'm sorry it's not one of yours.'

Lovelace laughed. 'That's the problem. It's people like you who *ought* to be buying them.'

They slid into the Jensen, Talbot-Brown in the back, Michael and Lovelace at ease in the front. 'Well?' said Michael. 'Tell me about all this.'

'Antony here got through to me. . . .'

'A direct approach seemed the best way once I'd discovered a fact or two,' Talbot-Brown said hastily, eager to please.

'Yes. All right,' said Michael. 'I left it to you.'

'He's a good digger,' said Lovelace, exhaling a quick laugh. 'I don't mind that. I wasn't born yesterday. As a matter of fact I'd heard you were interested. We both have our sources.'

'And?'

'For some time I considered going to you. I didn't because I knew my father wouldn't be interested. He has pride, a certain stubbornness.'

'What's the reason for the change?' Michael's edginess made him more direct than usual. His mind was so full of Sir Giles Lymington he almost resented having this new problem thrust upon him. But he knew he could not turn back now and, feeling the momentum of events working for him, had no wish to. He simply had no time for finesse.

Lovelace seemed to feel he was owed rather more understanding. 'I'm speaking in total confidence of course. This is a very critical time for our company.'

Michael's smile was rueful. 'I'm sorry. It's been rather an un-pleasant day. You know about the death of one of our directors?'

'It was in the papers,' said Lovelace. 'It's not the best time for us to talk.'

'Don't let it worry you. I'm a bit short on sleep and words, that's all.'

'Well – the change in my father. I've convinced him, because we're on the brink of something big.'

'Yes?'

'We have another business besides making cars.'

'I know you make small engines – motor-cycle type things.'

'Right. So around four months ago I was in the States, getting depressed about how few cars we were selling. Then one weekend someone took me for a ride in a snowmobile, to cheer me up. In case you don't know, a snowmobile is a sort of motor-bike on ice. They fizz over the snow, up to ninety miles an hour. You steer them by a couple of skis at the front. Streamlined bodies. They're selling like hot cakes.'

'You're going to make snowmobiles?'

Lovelace laughed easily. 'No thanks. I'm afraid we're a bit late in the field. But they need engines – very like the ones we've had a lot of experience in. So far the Germans and the Swiss have had the market, but there's plenty of room. I asked the makers in Minneapolis what they wanted. They told me, and when I got back to England our boys worked a bit on the specification. Frankly, they've improved it – and the Americans think so too. But they're only interested in quantity. To do that means tooling up to a level we've never reached before. We need money.'

'And that's why you're coming to us?'

'Yes. Even my father sees that this is our best chance to get back in the game – to provide the kind of diversification which may keep our cars on the map. We've been desperately short of cash for promotion and advertising these past three or four years.'

Michael, his brain working faster, asked a question to which he believed he knew the answer. 'Couldn't you get money from another source? The banks?'

'With our recent profit record? You must be joking. No one wants to know. Our overdraft limit has been raised three times already, and they won't give us any more. Not the kind of money we need.'

'Which is?'

'A million at least. Maybe more.'

'That's a great deal.'

266

'To you?'

'Even to us.' He was excited, the recharging of his interest overlaying his earlier fears. The habit of playing hard to get, of manoeuvring for the best bargain reasserted itself. 'We have cash problems of our own. We'd need pretty good guarantees.'

'So would we. My father knows he'd have to allow you a stake. But not total control. He wants to run the car side *his* way. You understand how he feels?'

They talked for fifteen minutes more, the car windows steaming up. Michael didn't object to that. At one stage he wrote a set of figures on the windscreen with his right index finger. It seemed appropriate. When they had finished he was pleased. He and Talbot-Brown said goodbye to Lovelace. Things were satisfactory; the door remained temptingly ajar for both sides.

'What will you say to Armfield?' he asked Talbot-Brown.

'I'll report on the subject I was asked to report on,' said Talbot-Brown. 'The prospect for Lovelace cars – now and in the future. It won't sound very encouraging; just the cars, I mean.'

'All right,' said Michael, thinking that if Armfield went into action this time appearing not to have done his homework it would be very useful. 'And thanks for what you've done. I won't ask how you managed it.'

Talbot-Brown grinned, knowingly. 'Trade secrets,' he said.

'Do you want a lift anywhere?' said Michael.

'No thanks. I'm mobile.'

'Good,' said Michael. Then he gunned the engine and drove to his flat. Half an hour later, Dickson was at the front door.

'There'd be no question of your having to sell the factory,' said Dickson. 'Not unless you wanted to. But if this scheme goes through – *if* – the land on which it stands, like all the land around it, will become much more valuable. It could be a nice insurance to have.'

'Is the scheme certain, though?'

'Nothing in this wicked world is certain, dear boy. But the buzz has it that it's highly favoured. I just thought you'd like to know.'

'And your part? What do you want?'

'You *are* becoming unsophisticated, Michael. It must be the strains of big business. You people usually talk more discreetly. The bland leading the bland.' He beamed in self-appreciation and sipped his sherry.

'Nevertheless,' said Michael. 'Have you anything in mind?'

'I expect nothing,' said Dickson sententiously. 'I am merely passing on gossip to a friend. You may remember that I expressed my interest in Lovelace's when we last lunched. I'm still interested in a piece of the speculation, naturally. I realise that anything to do with motor-racing *is* a speculation. But then, when it comes to the sport, I'm really an *aficionado*.' The pronunciation was precise, the dentilingual neatly turned. He prided himself on such things.

Michael scratched the back of his head thoughtfully. He had told Dickson nothing of his talk with Philip Lovelace. Nor, for the moment, would he. Everything was running his way so strongly at the moment that he was almost suspicious of his good fortune. He could afford the luxury of having qualms of conscience.

'Lovelace's might get to hear about this too.'

'Not if you move fast enough, Michael.' He detected a hesitancy in his companion. 'You wouldn't *want* them to, would you?'

'I'd have to live with them afterwards.'

'Dear boy – you know and I know. No one else. *I* feel no conflict. Why should you? It's a perfectly reasonable business proposition. We have certain information which they lack. If they had it, they might put their price up. Whatever we do, we are taking a chance – a speculation which may come unstuck. If we are fortunate, they'll still do well out of it – you'll ensure that. Why should you not share their good fortune? Or would you rather leave it to a property speculator who has no interest in the future of an automobile company as you have?'

'My father was a property speculator,' said Michael quietly.

'Years ago,' said Dickson. 'Water under the bridge. Now he's respectable. An export king. Helping the balance of payments, as you will be doing once you've put Lovelace's to rights. You're not leaping in solely because you think you're getting a prime site in a development area. You were interested all along, remember? So was I. This is just an extra piece of icing on the cake. And it will make whatever you have to do to Lovelace's that much easier. Frankly, I feel like a public benefactor.'

Michael enjoyed this lecture not at all. It was ridiculous that Dickson, more pregnant with pomposity by the day, should imagine it was necessary to spell out so simple a message. It was the perfect corner situation, the one you always dreamed of enjoying when you played business games. Inside information, the hidden ace, a row of hotels on the most desirable site on a Monopoly board. Why did he hesitate? There was no doubt about it, he thought, I *am* losing my appetite. When the fight's fixed, in the end you lose the fun of winning.

'I don't disagree, Simon. Blame my cautious nature. We'll come to an arrangement – if Lovelace's will play, that is.'

They had another drink, then Dickson glanced at his watch. He wanted to hear the last hour of the main debate before the division at ten. 'For a moment, dear boy, you had me worried. You sounded as if you were praising my proposition with faint damns.' He looked like an anxious comedian waiting for the re-assurance of applause. As Michael laughed, he continued. 'I know that the business climate is changing. You're all so responsible and full of ethics these days you make a poor old honest entrepreneur like me feel I'm farting in church every time I make a suggestion. Don't overdo it. If you take away the rewards, no one will see any point in going into business. Might as well be safe and pension-able, like dons and civil servants.'

He stood up and put on his overcoat, light in weight, black and velvet-collared. 'The Americans have a lot to answer for. They've made so much money they can afford to be philosophical about it all now. In my experience grey-flannel suits encourage grey-flannel minds.'

12. No sinners, only survivors

It was an easy birth, which David almost missed. As April ran out, all Westbrook's men were working like mad, mainly on facets of the reorganisation at Brasserton's. Now that the deal with Corsino was complete, Michael Grant wanted no delays. David, kept late at Prospect House, reached the nursing-home towards the end of Sheila's labour. She said there were no problems; and the boy looked all right, as much like a corrugated gnome as David had expected.

'Kenwyn Travis? Where did you get that trendy name?' asked Hardy the next day.

'Nothing trendy,' said David. 'It's Cornish. Old Cornish. We thought we'd revive the family pride.'

They were having an untypical early evening drink. He looked carefully around before he spoke.

'Lionel had another go on Lymington this afternoon.'

'He needs something to worry about. The verdict was straight enough.'

'Trying to convince himself it had nothing to do with *him* by telling me it had nothing to do with *me*.'

Hardy shrugged. 'I should take it at face value. Maybe the poor old creep *did* think he had cancer.'

'I'd like to believe it.'

'Don't be so morbid, lad. If anyone has to carry the doubt, let the top men do it. You can't be responsible for the world.'

They sat silently for a while, not wanting to dig more deeply into themselves, yet unable to let the subject go. The inquest had been brief, undramatic. Apart from the formal medical stuff from formal medicos, Lady Lymington had given evidence. Her husband had become obsessed with his health. He was afraid of the pains he suffered in his stomach. There was, said a doctor, no sign of cancer.

The top men in the Prospect House hierarchy avoided talking

270

about the inquest; except for Westbrook. Three times he called David in to say, at length, that it was unlikely Lymington knew about the investigation David had been working on. David told him about Karian's message a couple of weeks back. Even so, Westbrook insisted, Lymington had no cause to suspect that the papers had been borrowed from the registry for other than routine reasons. It was sad that the man was such a hypochondriac. David had a duty to himself not to imagine things; and a duty to the company not to stir up further mud.

'It's a funny time, just now,' David told Hardy.

'How do you mean?'

'Apart from Brasserton's, everything seems to have ground to a dead stop. What the hell is going to happen over Supergear? Every time I mention it to Lionel, he tells me not to be impatient. It's weird.'

'Masterly inactivity,' said Hardy. 'The oldest trick in the book. Don't expect quick decisions in business today. The whole thing's too unwieldy to work that way. The gap between the taking of decisions and putting them into effect gets wider all the time. The barons today are specialists in taking decisions to defer decisions. There are too many people involved, all fighting for their piece of the cake. Even Michael Grant can't work miracles.'

'Lovelace's too. That seems to have been forgotten.'

Hardy poured the rest of his tonic water into the glass. 'The blood's got to flow at a board meeting before we get anywhere on that – if we ever do.'

He picked up a piece of lemon impaled on a toothpick and stirred it around the glass. He squeezed it and examined the rind like a prospector. Then he told David he intended to leave the Prospero Group.

'You're having me on,' said David.

'No. Lionel Westbrook will get a letter in the morning.'

'Honest?'

'It's not *that* surprising.'

'But why, Colin? Just when we're winning?'

'*You* may be winning, chum. I haven't noticed much happening for me.'

'Christ, you're not still on about Supergear?'

Hardy flicked his head impatiently. 'I'm not *on* about it at all. But it's indicative, if you want to make anything of it. I don't begrudge you your luck – but I'm fed up with the way Westbrook treats me, if you really want to know. I'm so bloody useful to him, he never gives me a chance to jump out of the nest. As far as I can see he wants to keep me tied to his apron strings indefinitely. I can't stay a sidekick for ever. Have another drink?'

David watched him go to the bar. It was the kind of shock he hadn't reckoned on. He hoped Hardy wouldn't be going too soon, else the work-load would be fierce. He had grown rather too used to having Hardy there: as senior prefect, Brain of Britain and father-confessor. He would feel a touch naked when Hardy went. At the same time he realised clearly enough that an important rival was getting out of his light.

'Where are you going, Colin?'

'QFN. I'm joining Barstow.'

David whistled. 'As what?'

'Sort of principal assistant to the Chief Executive. Barstow's left-hand man.'

'Lionel will love you for that.'

Hardy grinned. 'Quite likely. I know Barstow isn't exactly a bosom pal of the Grants, even though he gets invited to Bernard's parties.'

'It's almost like a slap in the face. They've beaten us to the draw too often for comfort lately.' David had heard a lot about the leaks of confidential information from Westbrook. Hardy was sipping his gin and tonic easily, amused, sweating slightly around the corners of his eyes. 'You haven't been telling them?' said David.

Hardy just went on with his drink, eyes moving up in surprise above the rim.

David persisted: 'How did you land the job?'

'As a matter of fact, I met him on holiday. In Tunisia. Wasn't I lucky?' Still he smiled a gradual smile and David realised that Hardy would go on talking if he was nudged. Hardy *wanted* to tell him, was enjoying the chance to show off.

'You were head-hunted?'

'Nothing so old-fashioned. I decided to reverse the roles. I went head-hunting for a new boss.'

'You knew he'd be there?'

'I wouldn't have spent the double fare to Tunisia otherwise. I've not got that kind of money. It wasn't difficult to strike up an acquaintance. All men are equal under umbrellas around a swimming-pool.'

David twirled his glass tetchily. 'I must say I'm surprised. Some people may regard it as positively suspicious.'

Hardy's smile faded. 'Are you trying to pick a quarrel?' Then

272

he laughed as the man opposite him tried to find words. The sound snapped something in David.

'It's a bit of a shit's trick. Getting out just now – and to *them*.'

Hardy put down his glass. 'Don't moralise at me, for Christ's sake. What do you expect me to do? Queue up with the rest of the first-class brains for my pension?'

'They'll be very glad to have you. With everything you know.'

'Oh, sure.'

'You could tell them a lot.'

'I can't forget the work I've been doing, can I? I can't be erased like sodding magnetic tape. But I shan't push it.'

'I wouldn't put money on that.'

'What is all this, David? You've suddenly grown a streak of loyalty to Prospero's as wide as the Champs Elysées. People do change jobs, you know. They carry information around with them. It's part of the racket. Prospero's lose a a little with me today; tomorrow they pick up a little from someone who joins them. So what? Do you expect me to take a Trappist vow of silence when I move? If I can help my new boss, why shouldn't I? Everyone does it.'

Hardy didn't often repeat himself so much. David sensed weakness. 'Not everyone. Not when you've been in a position of trust.'

'If I hadn't heard it, I'd never have believed it. You sound like the boardroom's Billy Graham. Learn what this racket is, for God's sake. There aren't saints and sinners – only survivors. People like you and me. When your moment comes you take it, else at forty-five you'll find yourself at the crossroads and you'll look down them and see they're all dead-ends.'

'Don't tell me,' said David. 'I know it isn't simple. No blacks and whites. It's a question of degree. You push it too bloody hard, that's all.'

'Harder than you? Be honest with yourself, chum. Maybe you don't like seeing me get away with what you'd like to get away with yourself.'

'I just thought there were limits, even for you.'

'You make a god-awful moralist. I've never misled you. In business your duty is to yourself, remember? Money for value.'

The phrases came floating back from their past conversations. David's emotions were confused. He couldn't accuse Hardy of not having warned him. Yet he was still riled by Hardy's easy assumption that his approval should be forthcoming without question. He could not dispel the feeling of betrayal.

'I hope the money's good,' he said, trying not to sound po-faced.

Hardy, in control again, wanting to close the break between them, laughed. 'I thought you were going to say pieces of silver. The going rate's more than thirty. It's okay. More of it. But it buys nothing I want.'

'I don't believe it.'

'I mean it. I've told you before. The only thing I'm interested in buying is independence. And until someone leaves me fifty thousand I can't have it. A big salary won't make me independent. It only makes me more dependent. As usual, we all live up to what we earn. We get seduced by the comforts money brings. You can't give them up. That's what I am. Bedded with a whore called comfort.'

David put down his glass. 'I want to catch my train.'

'I'm sorry if I've disappointed you.'

'Don't be bloody daft. It's your life. I don't mind.'

Hardy lifted his glass. 'Here's to Sheila and the kid.'

'Thanks,' said David. 'And to your job.'

'And to all survivors,' said Hardy.

*

Insurance men are traditionally suspicious of second genera-tions in business. To Lord Bender the proposition was elemen-tary. He had dealt with the situation too often.

An entrepreneur of genius builds up a company. The man gives his life to its creation, wins friends, influences people with big blocks of money to invest – insurance companies, pension funds, merchant banks – and everyone is happy. Then the pioneer grows old, loses his zest or health. The more autocratic he has been, the more acute the problem of succession.

Who should the major shareholders support? Their tendency is to play safe, to want to ensure that control is in the hands of professionals. Sons do not often possess the skills of their fathers. They are not hungry men. They have grown used to an atmo-sphere of success, sometimes have become soft in anticipation of their heritage. They lack the incentives to fight, that personal identification with the struggle which motivates the first begetter.

Fathers, however, usually want sons to follow them, though often – like Bernard Grant – they extract a shaming price in the paternalism they demand be accepted on the way. Directors, too, acquire this feeling of family, developing a hereditary strain of loyalty to the clan which has made them rich. Some sons can even

274

seem as good as their fathers; trained for the job and eager to take it. Yet the doubt remains. The decision is never easy for those who have the power to shape it.

All these arguments Lord Bender rehearsed as he waited for Michael Grant to arrive. He had not been overjoyed at the performance of the Prospero Group in the past six months. Not that the funds invested there could have done much better elsewhere. It had been a dull period in the markets both in Britain and abroad; analysts looking for jobs on Wall Street and portfolio supervisors hanging their heads in shame before they rolled. Lord Bender was concerned for deeper reasons. For months he had writhed uncomfortably as the tension on the Prospero board grew. Too much time was being wasted on the in-fighting. Opportunities, he suspected, were being missed. The crunch must come. Either Bernard must reassert himself and end the bickering, or there should be a redisposition of forces.

Lord Bender knew also that there was a weakness within himself. He had the power to resolve the deadlock if he chose to exercise it. But the arguments were so damnably balanced. To Bernard Grant he owed the memory of good years together; years which had bred profits and also loyalty, a relationship which transcended the straight rules of business. And Bernard was far from finished. He might have lost some of his old energy; but the flair remained if only he could be driven to use it. Michael was good, Lord Bender had to admit it. But Michael as *agent provocateur*, keeping the pot stirred, was one thing; Michael as leader, running the show, was another. Lord Bender still had not made up his mind, however sharply he understood that the judgement would have soon to be arrived at. He half-resented the pressure which Michael would be putting on him during the next hour.

Michael had sought the meeting, insisting on both its importance and its secrecy. Lord Bender could scarcely refuse, but this was an occasion when he had little appetite for conniving. He wondered whether he should tax Michael over the Lymington business. There was more to that than met the eyes or ears of the world, he would swear. But he had received no leads from anyone at Prospect House. He was surprised to discover he felt only a minor sense of loss at Lymington's death. He regretted the manner of it, but not the departure. Lymington had contributed too little for too long and lately had even seemed unable to operate in Whitehall effectively.

Damn Michael. He was late. Lord Bender was a time-table man, carving up the days into segments of thought and action whose disruption had an almost physical effect upon him. Sudden changes of plan needled his stomach and set his fingers scratching his crusted temples. That was the trouble with being a sought-after investment man: too many directorships, too many pies for too few fingers.

He pulled across a *Financial Times* cutting which announced a seven-year loan for an American electronic data processing company anxious to expand in Britain. He had watched their performance carefully for two years. It might be time for him to switch funds from one of their English competitors whose progress had disappointed him after a pyrotechnic beginning. He was about to ring an investment analyst he knew when Michael arrived.

Why doesn't Bender smarten up the office, Michael was thinking as he came into the room. The secretary outside was in her middle fifties. The paint everywhere was dark-brown, the metal of the filing cabinets scarred. Lord Bender's desk was old but without any special value, piled high with documents like a commercial compost heap, nourishing the wood. He imagined he remembered the titles on the spines of several pamphlets since his last visit, maybe a year ago.

Lord Bender waved him into a heavy leather armchair and came over from the desk to join him in its twin.

'They'll bring us some tea in a minute,' he said.

'Good. You're looking fit.'

'I watch myself, like your father,' said Lord Bender. 'Did you manage to shake off the car which was doubtless following you?'

'All right – have your joke. I don't mind.' Lord Bender liked to pull his leg about security; ever since Michael wanted the boardroom tested for bugs. 'It's important I see you, though. Quietly.' Michael was not out of countenance one whit. He had always been at ease with Lord Bender. His uncle-figure.

Lord Bender crossed his legs and leaned back, intent on the toe-cap of his shoe. It had the deep, grained shine of leather which has been hand-polished daily by servants for many years. But Lord Bender cleaned his own footwear. It was one of his things, a legacy of the northern grammar-school boy who had come up the insurance and actuarial ladder the long and hard way.

'Do you think it's fair to Bernard for us to be talking like this?'

Michael puffed his cheeks, momentarily. 'I need your help – the organisation needs it. I want to influence you, certainly. But you can make up your own mind. That's not unfair.'

Lord Bender felt, not for the first time, the attraction of the man

276

opposite. The enthusiasm was the main thing, magnetic and disarming. Michael wanted to go too fast, perhaps, but Lord Bender met too many businessmen who sat down on the job like cows in pasture, munching the usual grass and waiting for milking-time. Such men nodded abstractedly in the direction of change and action, but felt no commitment to them. The younger Grant's infectious pace he responded to. He wondered only if Michael was guilty of inflexibility in the pursuit of newness. Did he know yet which battles were too costly to justify the winning?

'It's Lovelace's, I suppose.'

'That and other things.'

'You got away with Brasserton's. Your methods didn't thrill me, but the principle – yes, I support that.'

'You laid down the conditions. I met them. Isn't that enough? Or has my father been at you?'

'Of course he has. As you might have expected. And he'll fight you over Lovelace's. Every inch of the way.'

'*You* encouraged me.'

'To make a feasibility study, yes. I didn't want you gnashing your teeth in an agony of frustration. That way you might have mislaid your judgement in the negotiations over Brasserton's. But *is* it feasible, this Lovelace take-over?'

Michael described his meeting with Philip Lovelace. His assessment of the prospects for snowmobile engines was very glowing. To Lord Bender, the profit forecast given by Michael seemed to grow a nought or two under the pressure of his enthusiasm. Tea arrived and Lord Bender found himself nibbling a chocolate finger without noticing. He put it down as quickly as a stick full of arsenic. He ate nothing between meals.

'That all sounds fine. But how honest are you with yourself?'

'I don't understand.'

'Harold Armfield will ask if I don't. You know that what you *really* want is some involvement with the motor-racing business again. Isn't that true?'

'I won't deny it. But I've got my priorities right. Good business first. I know there's a market for those engines, and I'm damn sure there's one for the cars too. If those criteria are fulfilled, where's the harm if I also get my kicks? You ought to be glad. How many men enjoy their work so much?'

No attempt at dissembling, Lord Bender noted. It was a technique to take the hearer by charm and by storm. Candour used as a weapon of ingratiation. Candour plus enthusiasm plus an appearance of commonsense. Formidable.

'There's still a problem. It will take a lot of money to get the snowmobile operation off the ground. I'd guess seven figures for a start. You know we don't have that kind of money just now, not even with Harold's loan. Bernard's got it all earmarked and he won't give way.'

Michael could have mentioned his talk with Dickson, the politician, but he knew when to conserve ammunition. Instead, he said: 'We can lay our hands on most of the money.'

'You're more optimistic than I am. How?'

'By selling Supergear.'

Lord Bender fired off a laugh which combined surprise at the simplicity of Michael's solution with scepticism about its feasibility. 'You don't have much time for your fellow-directors. Bartram might have something to say about that. So might your father.'

'All right,' said Michael. 'Let me tell you a few home truths.' Then he laid out the facts about Supergear, full strength: about its real profitability, its prospects, his reasons for wanting to close it. He handed Lord Bender an analysis of the balance-sheet which showed up clearly the suspicious nature of Bartram's dealings in the previous year. Lord Bender looked at it, sipping his tea, and there was in the room the kind of silence which is not caused simply by absence of noise. Two clocks in the City struck four and Bender did not even, as was his custom, glance at his wrist to make sure he was in time with the rest of the financial world. He just went on sitting, two fingers pulling at the scrubby hair around his left ear. When he looked up again, his eyes were curiously sad.

'You might be mistaken.'

'You know I couldn't risk that,' said Michael. 'In my position, I *have* to be right. And good. Bloody good.' He paused to let the words sink in. 'That's not immodest, Benjamin, and you know it. If I'm not on top of the job, you and the others – especially the others – would tear me into tiny pieces and feed me to the discount brokers. I know my father.'

'But why do you want to destroy him?' The question came suddenly, simple as a bullet.

'I don't. Not him. I want to destroy the myth he's created in his mind about his infallibility before it destroys me and the organisation.'

'Exaggeration, Michael. Ridiculous hyperbole. Business doesn't work like television soap opera.'

'I read yesterday about an engineering firm that made three

278

million clear last year, and is on the brink of closure this. That's how quickly it can happen. With our kind of organisation – all those bits and pieces of companies which father has picked up down the years – we're more wide open than ever. Haven't you seen what's been happening to conglomerates in the States? Nobody loves us. If you thought in six months' time we were on the slide, you'd whip your funds out faster than anyone. You'd have to, wouldn't you? Your responsibility is to Mondor first.'

Lord Bender pushed at his eyelids. The analysis was not unjust, except in being over-harsh on Bernard Grant. Who had made the money in the first place? The young didn't think of *that*. It was like the students who wanted to kick down everything without much idea what they would build on the ruins. Skinheads with government grants.

'I'll think about supporting you on Lovelace's, if that's what you want. And Supergear. I'd like to follow up your findings. I suppose that's not enough.'

'No.'

'You want Bernard out.'

'He'd make a good chairman. As a chief executive you *know* he's not doing his job. Mistake after mistake. First, fiddling about with Burgham's. The wrong kind of company to take over, plus that childish attempt to manipulate the market. Then the cock-up of the government contract for Brasserton's. Messing me about over Ed Corsino. Trying to block any move that isn't on his side of the house. Lovelace's is typical.'

'Burgham's. Yes. I keep hearing whispers about the Take-Over Commission wanting to look into that.'

'It's the whole thing, Benjamin. Nothing seems to work out any more.'

'And directors kill themselves,' said Lord Bender softly. 'Directors you don't like.'

'I can't deny I didn't like him,' said Michael. 'And I'm sorry it happened. But was Lymington's the kind of judgement we wanted?'

'Put like that, how can I disagree with you? I may not like you much for saying it, though, and perhaps I don't like myself either for going along with you.'

Lord Bender got up and went to his window. The dome of St Paul's filled a gap between two buildings. The queues at the bus stops were already beginning to grow. The early leavers. Once he had despised them. Now there were occasions when he envied them.

'God knows why you want it so badly,' he said. 'It's only a treadmill.'

'I've grown up an Englishman, Benjamin. Masochism is a national disease. We enjoy punishing ourselves.' He was at Lord Bender's shoulder. 'Like the people down there enjoy queueing.'

Michael patted the older man's back in an intimate gesture of departure. 'Besides, I have my principles. I never have believed in benevolent despots.'

Lord Bender knew what he meant, and Bender knew he wasn't joking.

*

When Westbrook learned that Hardy was leaving he felt a personal sense of betrayal, for he had brought the man to Prospero's, had nurtured him. When he learned where Hardy was headed, he worried what the news might do to his standing in Prospero's. Barstow's twitting of Bernard Grant at the party was known to several people at the top. Rather more knew that QFN companies had stolen a march on those in the Prospero Group several times in the past few months. To have a member of his personal staff going over to so identifiable an enemy looked not good at all.

Earl Sanger, typically, made the point for him, in front of Michael Grant. 'I'd better reactivate my forces,' Sanger said cheerfully. 'Maybe we haven't been looking in the right direction for those leaks.'

Sanger hadn't taken long to recover from his uncertainty after Lymington's death. Around a week, that was all. Now he was back, playing truer to form than ever. Dancing on the grave, thought Westbrook.

'What do you think about Hardy?' asked Michael.

Sanger chipped in. 'Triviality has always struck me as his flaw. Not treachery. A pity, though. He's a guy with a first-class brain.'

Westbrook found himself in the position of having to support Hardy. He could scarcely do otherwise since he had employed the man for three years. He didn't like it at all. Supposing Hardy *had* been a traitor? No, that was unthinkable. His brain rejected the idea because it wanted to. Westbrook desired no further doubts about the train of events which had led up to Lymington's death.

The action he took was immediate and defensive. He ordered Hardy to return all confidential documents the same day. He handed over to David the work Hardy had been doing on Lovelace's. Then he told Hardy to go away for a week while he thought about what he would do with his subordinate during the period of notice. Westbrook, like every other businessman, had no answer to this kind of situation. If Hardy wanted to carry away information with him, he would have laid out the ground and the documentation long ago.

It could not, Westbrook reckoned, have happened at a worse time, even though he knew that when good men quit, any time is a bad time in business. The pile of routine stuff in his in-tray and diary multiplied like cobwebs every day. Michael Grant now had the whips on for Lovelace's after telling Westbrook and Sanger about the meeting Talbot-Brown had arranged. To Westbrook, Talbot-Brown looked like another threat; the threat of the unknown quantity. Brasserton's was still a problem, with Oldershaw shouting for answers to everything and Prosser steaming round like a demented locomotive wanting to know the detail of each document which went out in case it might upset the precarious peace he'd bought at the plant. There were times when Westbrook thought he'd scream if he heard the words 'joint consultation' again.

But he coped because that was what he was trained to do. Take pressure, absorb punishment, keep the wheels moving. Driving home to dinner, which these days he often ate alone, he sometimes revelled in the way his mind devoured the work. Maybe he did react to pressure with flap and flail. But he managed, he got through, and that was the test. No one could say he didn't deliver.

He'd survive the early summer somehow. Then he and Diana would go to Portugal. He might even make that work. He hadn't realised before that he had such a capacity for going without the feel of a woman, any woman, in bed. It was her fault, too, wasn't it? She seemed to have no capacity for limiting *her* work either.

One night, when he had been drinking Scotch, he'd gone up to their room almost hopefully. She was sitting naked before the mirror, holding her breasts in her hands, examining them.

'Very nice,' he said, but his heart wasn't in it. He felt like a conference delegate at a strip club, the pre-lunch session for the belted-raincoat trade.

She spoke sourly. 'See what I'm reduced to? Playing with myself.' He pretended he'd come for a clean handkerchief and went back downstairs to his briefcase.

At the office, he worked insanely, sensing that some kind of crisis was coming, the contest his side must win. He piled the work on those he commanded so that they had to keep pace with him. And mostly David was where the buck stopped.

David enjoyed these early days of May not at all, when usually

281

it was his favourite time. Cornwall and Cambridge alike had done that for him, encouraged him to fall in love with rain-scrubbed early mornings which suddenly came up warm and sunny, an end to April's cheating.

London last year, and the year before, had seemed a tolerable shadow of May in the country or by the sea, though he still missed the frenetic seagulls and the comic relief of moorhens skidding flat-footed on rivers. This year it was different. At the office he was hammered by a landslide of paper. At home, no one took much notice of him. The female relatives who trooped in and out were paying court to Kenwyn, to Sheila, and to Sheila's mother in that order. He was an incidental object. The fact that he'd been prepared to be neglected when the child arrived did nothing to make him feel any better. He tried to laugh at the pre-dictability of it all and found he couldn't. He was learning that preparing for the worst often serves only to sharpen its flavour upon arrival.

When, finally, he stepped into a lift on his way home and found Alison in it alone, he was in no state to resist. They said hello, then froze into formality as the doors opened and two men from the accounts floor joined them.

'Personally,' said one, 'I agree with him. How can you have any faith in the kind of management education that merely gives professors the chance to bend your ears with their eloquence?'

'Right,' said the other. 'Never had to make a profit in their lives.'

They looked at David and the girl awkwardly, suddenly curious who might be listening. For the rest of the way down one watched the flicking lights of the floor numbers as if they were some abstruse example of pre-Christian paleography. The other gently stabbed his umbrella ferrule at a fragment of paper, office confetti.

Out in the street, she said, quite cheerfully: 'You are a bastard, David. I know what we agreed, but I didn't mean hello and goodbye for ever.'

He felt dominated by his briefcase. It is difficult to walk with any nonchalance carrying twenty pounds deadweight. 'I know,' he said. 'It's been murder the last few weeks.'

'Even so.'

'You know how it is.'

'Yes,' she said as they stopped at the kerb. 'I hear you're a father.'

He gave her a look that should have split a plank, then quickly

282

tried to turn it into a laugh. The result left his jaw hanging awkwardly so that he felt it was coming away from his face. He
hadn't practised the sequence much.

'Don't look so pleased,' she said. 'I don't exactly stop my ears
whenever you're mentioned.' And he thought, What the hell, I
might have known.

'Like I said. It's been murder.'

'And now you're racing off home like a good lad. Real nine-to-
five.'

'Except it's twenty to bloody seven.'

'That doesn't change the principle.'

He didn't even know which way he was walking at that
moment. He was just following her. The sun was burning off the
glass in a new block across the road and the wind was whipping
her skirt hard against her thighs, outlining the curve of her bottom. God, he thought, here we go again. He could feel dust
irritating his eyes and he was too hot. She looked to be enjoying it.

'Okay,' he said. 'So I'm taking you home – or wherever you're
going. Didn't I mention it?'

'Let's get a cab, then,' she said. 'Home.' And he thought that
she was getting her own back, the lovely bitch. Cabs to Holland
Park from close to Lambeth Bridge cost real money.

She settled back into the seat and stretched her legs. 'My treat,'
she said. 'I just felt I couldn't face the tube. Not on this special
occasion.' She opened the jacket of her suit and slid further down
into the seat so that her stomach was bunched and ugly. 'This is
only the second time I've been in a taxi with you, do you realise
that?'

'I'm not likely to forget the first time.' He was wondering what
she wanted and simultaneously speculating how late home he
could be without search parties setting out.

'Boy or girl?' she said.

'Boy. Look, I'm sorry not to have seen you. But I felt – it's
difficult to say – I felt probably you wouldn't want to be
bothered.'

'Don't make alibis for yourself. There's no need. I *know* something of what's been happening in your neck of the woods.'

'Thanks.'

'But I still think you're a bastard.'

'Thanks again.'

'If you'd *really* wanted to, you'd have found the time. Just a
talk – you know. I don't like the feeling I was only a one-night
stand. Not good for the ego. So tell me what's your hang-up?'

'No hang-up. Just lack of opportunity.'

'Crap.'

He put on his injured, silent face and she laughed. 'I'm sorry. What's the big news among the decision-makers?'

He was slow starting, but by the time they passed the King's Road he felt more relaxed; still alert to danger, because he was always skirting her questions, trying to gauge how much she knew about Hardy and Lymington and Westbrook, but increasingly confident that he could survive and even maybe enjoy himself too. Her body, which looked slack and broken, curiously boneless, seemed inviting again. Her breasts moved slowly with her breathing and her thighs trembled whenever the cab slowed down quickly. What was it she'd said? No hands up my skirt in taxis? He laughed in the middle of a sentence and she asked why. He told her.

'You're a randy sod,' she said.

The flat was the same, but smaller than he'd remembered it. Untidier too. Dresses in a heap, papers scattered about, a dark stain on the carpet. This time he didn't grab her. He put his briefcase down and, following her permissive wave of the hand, sat almost decorously on the chaise longue, ignoring the balloon chairs.

'You look tired,' she said, 'or shouldn't I say that?'

'It's not vitamin pills I need.'

She brought him a Scotch, unasked, and he sat silently while she scooped up some of the debris and carried it off into the bedroom. The glass was dusty, he noticed. He quietly pulled out a comb and ran it through his hair. He could not believe she was about to repeat her ploy of two months ago, and she didn't disappoint him. When she came back she had shed her jacket, though, and her nipples were too firmly outlined beneath the white sweater; almost tarty. She lit a cigarette, put it down immediately and spoke over her shoulder as she poured a drink.

'I know why you didn't,' she said.

'Didn't what?'

'See me. *Want* to see me.'

'I did want to see you.'

She acted as if she hadn't heard him. 'I said it last time. We can't compete, can we, not with your work? Maybe in three months' time, or six months, you'll manage to have caught up. There'll be a spare evening. Then you'll find some excuse to ring me. But while you're busy making it at your work, that's all the sex you need.'

'You're wrong. But have it your way.'

'Come on, David. Own up. I'm being a bloody bore, aren't I?'

She doesn't have any idea, he was thinking. Not that he could totally rationalise the situation, even to himself, though he had groped for the reasons long enough. The feeling he had was close to resentment; that she should start to complicate his life, that he hadn't been able to stop himself wanting her to, that the decision whether or not to go on with it had never satisfactorily been resolved. And always at the back of his thinking was the suspicion that what he really wanted was the fantasy of it without the aggravation of having to make dates, buy time, fabricate stories and actually go to bed. Sheila, as a person, didn't come into the argument. It was the disruption of his total life pattern – home, job, the time and disposition of his days – which he kicked against.

'Don't be silly, Alison.' It was the first time he had used her name that evening. 'I'm not another specimen to stick in your butterfly book. Not one of the collection of management stereotypes.'

'That's not the point,' she said. 'It's just the sheer inconvenience of it all for you, isn't that it? It's a pity I'm not a blue movie. Then you could run me when you felt like it, and afterwards put me away in a tin with no label.'

He realised now that she *did* know. She'd summed him up perfectly. A jokes-with-the-boys man, but afraid of the action. And he wanted to hit her. Instead he faked words.

'Stop it, you daft bitch. I'm tired of this game. Come and sit down.'

Surprisingly, she came without a word. She sat down very close, put her head on his shoulder and looked up. It was a kind of mockery. She kissed his cheek and said: 'Hey-ho.'

'What do we do?' he said.

'Try a little harder.'

'I'm trying.' He put an arm around her, but this time it felt awkward. Calculating love leads often to loss of touch.

'Darby and bloody Joan,' she said, and he was looking across at the clock on the wall. 'I know you can't stay. Don't count the minutes.' He felt incredibly foolish. Then the telephone rang.

He followed her across the room and when she lifted the receiver he slid his arms around her and gently squeezed her breasts. She was trying to wriggle free and speaking into the phone.

'Hello,' she said. There was a pause. He couldn't hear what

the voice was saying. It sounded male. She hacked him on the ankle. 'Look, someone's at the door. They're just leaving. Hang on a moment.'

She put her hand across the mouthpiece and still managed to jab her elbow hard into his stomach. He winced, let go and stepped back.

'Me Tarzan, you Jane,' she said with her back to him.

'Okay,' he said, and thought how very bored her back looked. And he admitted that she had cause.

She turned. 'I'll see you, I suppose.'

'I'm still trying to work out why you asked me here.'

'I thought you asked yourself. Still, it's no one's fault. Perhaps both of us believed it was a good idea.'

'Yes – well, your friend's waiting.'

'I do have them.'

'I'll bet,' he said. 'And why not? See you around.'

He picked up his case and went through the front door, closing it softly. By reflex, she smoothed the sweater over her breasts with her free hand and began to talk softly to Michael Grant.

*

Board meetings at the Prospero Group, as with most other companies, had developed their own ritual down the years. Since he had joined the organisation, Westbrook was always first to arrive. A brief contest with Armfield on this unspoken point of punctilio had ended when the financial man was named a deputy managing director. Armfield told himself that now he had no need to compete.

Whoever was second in the room would find Westbrook already seated at the table, surrounded by papers, as if he were afraid that should he show up late he might find his place taken over by someone else. Westbrook rarely rose to greet anyone, but he would stand up, half bending, when the Chairman walked in, like a man doing his duty by the National Anthem in the theatre but desperately wanting to go for a pee.

There was a lot of room around the table, which had always been circular, both in the old days when it was oak and since its replacement by modish plate glass and steel. Fourteen men could have found room around it as easily as the eight who formed the board before Lymington died. Each one of them had his appointed place, conceded as new men had joined, and automatically filled thereafter. There was none of that sly jockeying for position which exercises the ingenuity of power-players around other tables. Nor did anyone deliberately arrive late, emphasising his importance by speaking of urgent phone calls from New York City or Caracas. Earl Sanger would have been disappointed at these guileless preliminaries.

The morning of the first board meeting after Lymington's death was, however, different. When Bernard Grant strode into the room – deliberately brisk, smiling broadly, to let the world know that today was a winning day – he found everyone standing, sipping coffee. There was little conversation. They seemed nervous about sitting down. Everyone was looking at Grant.

'Good morning, gentlemen,' he said. 'Let's begin, shall we? Bring me a coffee, would you, Michael?'

He waved his hand around the table and moved towards his seat. There was a drifting of bodies, still uncertainly, in the direction of the other chairs. 'Perhaps you'll sit with me today,' said Grant, taking Lord Bender's arm; and Bender obediently lowered his grey frame on to the Hepplewhite which Lymington used to occupy, immediately to Grant's left. The decisive gesture had been made, and the circle closed up according to the sequence it had followed before: Bartram next to Lord Bender, then Michael Grant, Westbrook, Prosser and Armfield, who sat on the Chairman's right.

Bernard Grant opened the file before him and gazed seriously at the men around him. He felt good, his face masking the cheerful confidence with which he contemplated the morning ahead. He knew there might be some tough argument over Lovelace's, but Armfield had prepared him with a trunkful of helpful statistics on *that*. Supergear would need delicate handling too. Would Michael ask awkward questions? There was no means of knowing. The Supergear balance sheet was not, however, as vulnerable as his son imagined. Frank had convincing replies on the details of the previous year's capital expenditure should they be called for. Grant was certain he could hold the ring, though he had judged it unwise to go round canvassing support from Lord Bender and Armfield before the meeting. That would have looked suspicious. Better to leave it and see if Michael made a move, while still preparing oneself for counter-attack if necessary.

Those problems, however, should diminish under the impact of the good news which he knew he had to give. Most of the reports he had from the companies in the group looked promising. They were, by and large, on budget. Some of the subsidiaries had, he felt, modest targets. Still, no one expected it to be a great year. They'd agreed on that last autumn when the budgets for the coming twelve months had been laid out and chewed over, the board wallowing in a welter of charts and diagrams and risk analyses prepared by Westbrook's statisticians. Things were going as well as could be expected, and the cash-flow position had been revolutionised by Armfield's recent work. The loans were guaranteed. At last they had some elbow-room, some cash to invest in those subsidiaries which needed it. He felt happiest in such a position, able at last to play financial chess again. It was his move.

Grant coughed, laid his beautifully manicured fingers across the file, and began to speak.

First, he talked of Lymington: formal words of regret, which told nothing of his deeper feelings. The other directors looked down at their papers as if they were praying. What does he really think, Michael wondered. During the past fortnight, Bernard had scarcely mentioned the dead man. Nor had he discussed the question of a successor, if any. Sanger had begun to drop plain hints in Michael's direction; so had other contenders inside the building to their various lords. Michael believed his father might even be relieved about Lymington. Pride would never have allowed Bernard Grant to admit that one of *his* men was no longer earning his corn. Secretly he might have realised it.

Grant moved on to the financial reports. The other directors stirred, relieved to escape the inconvenient reality of death. They turned pages back and forth learnedly as their Chairman bored on. There was a question or two, even a laugh. Then, after fifteen minutes, the name at the top of the sixth page was Supergear.

'Our reorganisation of the business is going according to plan,' said Bernard Grant. 'Perhaps you'd like to talk briefly about that, Frank?'

Bartram explained the top management changes they'd made. They were negotiating redundancies successfully. Costs had already been reduced. By late summer the measures should begin to show results in the profit-and-loss column.

'It's very impressive,' said Michael. 'But I have some points to make.' His father scowled and Bartram dug chin into chest like a boxer covering up.

'We've been trying to project the next five years for Supergear, Frank.' His voice wasn't cocky or hostile. It had the right, well-modulated note of concern. 'Your economies are shrewdly chosen and necessary, but they're essentially defensive. Unless you get your market right, I honestly don't see how you're going to make much progress.'

288

Bartram could take offence only at the content of the remarks, not Michael's style of making them. 'We decided on a new market position three years ago. A younger approach. Higher-quality design. I believe that was a right decision.'

Michael shrugged. 'You did fine when you were designing for matrons. All those Harris tweeds and topcoats – great. It's since you began neglecting that end of the market that things have gone wrong.'

'Frank's shown a lot of adventure in what he's done, in my view,' said Bernard Grant. He was enjoying this; it was not often he found himself in the position of being able to accuse his son of being old-hat. 'I'm surprised to see you displaying all the initiative of a junior pay clerk.'

Michael's tone grew harder. 'Supergear hasn't got the right people designing for them if they really want to crack the swinging mums market. Stuck up on Merseyside I'm not surprised. They're not producing clothes fast enough or sharp enough – and that's partly a factor of Frank's machinery. What he's got is pretty clapped out, and he needs a lot more investment in new machines if he's to make any impact at all. I'm sorry, Frank, but I question the whole way the company is going.'

'Sometimes you have to take chances,' said his father. 'What do you want, Michael? An insurance policy against failure? You can't approach any venture like this on crutches.'

Westbrook handed Michael a small sheaf of papers. Michael placed them on the table, and offered one sheet to each man. 'Perhaps you'd care to look at this.'

It was a Westbrook special; a diagram full of square boxes linked by lines of differing colours. It showed the effect of alternative levels of sales and expenditure for Supergear. It looked very pretty.

Bernard Grant hesitated and glanced questioningly at Bartram. 'I don't mind,' said Bartram. 'I think the board would like this to be thrashed out.' The board said it would. Grant put on his half-spectacles as if the action were an immense labour and peered at the paper. After a long silence, he said: 'These colours are very confusing. The two shades of blue aren't differentiated clearly enough.'

Westbrook spent five minutes clarifying the Chairman's misunderstandings. Everyone around the table knew it was a game, a skirmish about inessentials for the purpose of distracting attention from the main issue. Grant played it well. He was a master of obtuseness when it suited him. Finally, he said: 'Even if we accept this assessment – and Frank doubtless has his own views – all you're saying is there will be investment needs?'

'That and more,' said Michael.

'Capital, for once, isn't any problem,' said Armfield, dead on cue. 'We've enough to look after our needs for the next twelve months at least.' He sat back with the air of a man who hears applause rising.

'My point is more fundamental,' said Michael. 'I can't see that the return on capital is ever going to be worth it. There are better ways of using our money.'

Bernard Grant wrinkled his mouth like someone biting on a lemon. 'I think we know what you mean, Michael. We'll look into all that later. It's always been the policy of this board to allow chief executives of subsidiary companies to work out their own strategies. This is becoming a drumhead court martial. I don't like it.'

Don't like it because you're not running it, thought Westbrook. Prosser picked at a fingernail, keeping his head well out of the firing line, rehearsing his statement on Brasserton's. Armfield sharpened the points he would lay out when Lovelace's came up. None of them, not even Lord Bender, wanted to be discovered taking sides too firmly. Supergear wasn't worth an explosion.

Michael smiled, trying to turn away his father's anger. 'I don't think Frank feels especially attached to Supergear. He's done a good job with a business which, to be honest, was run down.' Not a flicker of irony showed. 'Perhaps we should use his talents in a more profitable field.'

'And who would you suggest to run Supergear?' asked his father sarcastically.

'Not run it. Sell it. For us, it's outlived its usefulness.'

Armfield tried to smile too, thinly stretching his lips so that the acid dripped slowly. 'Who would want it if its prospects are as poor as you say?'

Bernard Grant turned his head and regarded Armfield coldly. His ally had made a tactical error; so keen to score a palpable hit that the possibility of selling the company had been conceded.

'There may be a buyer,' said Michael.

'Who?' said Bartram. 'I've never been approached.'

'For the site, not the business. Bettleton's. Your engineering neighbours, Frank. They want to expand. It would suit them very well to add on your place to their existing plant.'

Lord Bender spoke for the first time; shrewd and damaging

timing. 'If that made money sense, we could move the business elsewhere. Come south, perhaps.'

'We'd lose the development area grants,' said Armfield.

'I think we should take our money, if we can get the right price, and forget it,' said Michael.

Prosser frowned. 'Close down completely?' He was considering which would be the trickier: the phased redundancies in which Bartram had recently got him involved, or the negotiation of a shut-down.

'There comes a time when a business has run its natural cycle,' said Michael. 'These days the cycle gets shorter all the time. The president of General Motors was saying it the other day: you need to re-think what business you're in every ten years – or less. Supergear seems to be in that position now. It's run out of steam. If Frank can face it, we've got better things to do.'

Bartram didn't give a damn about Supergear. Who was it who'd dreamed up that god-awful name? He couldn't even remember, and now all he knew was that he had no stomach for a fight. Almost twenty years of working with Bernard Grant was a gutful for anyone. He still liked the man who had given him his chances well enough. It was the game he was out of love with, not Grant. He had meant what he said to David Travis. No considerations of pride could move him now. He was tired of fighting, of sweating to make the books look good, of dreaming up new tricks to keep tomorrow bright. He wanted only to take his rewards and steal quietly away. But he would need to persuade Bernard that he wasn't opting out, else he feared what the Chairman's reaction might be when the financial settlement was due.

'I think we know what we're doing, Michael,' he said. 'We can make it work. I'm sure of it. It's not that I love Supergear.' He smiled at Bernard Grant. 'It's the tenth company I've worked with since I joined your father. I just believe it would be a silly business decision to give up so easily. Morale's still good. Help us to have a bit of success and the company will be all right.' He had said his piece. It sounded good. Was it enough? He watched Grant.

'I agree with that,' said the Chairman. 'I'd hesitate to preempt the power of any local chief executive when he's in the middle of a reorganisation as Frank is. I suggest we leave it over.'

'I'd support that,' said Armfield dutifully.

Michael looked across the table. Lord Bender was already turning the page, eyes averted from any commitment. You old turncoat, Michael thought: you won't do it, you're going to sit on the fence, leave me without support. He sensed Westbrook stirring in his seat, embarrassed at the silence. Prosser wasn't going to stick his nut above the trenches on this one either. His father was gazing at him almost challengingly, and at that moment he stood at the brink, ready to accuse Bartram of being a fraudulent operator.

Then Lord Bender spoke softly. 'Decision deferred, Chairman. But not forgotten. It would be wrong to sweep this under the carpet.'

Bernard Grant, still believing he had won, said: 'Of course. Shall we move on?' His son, reading the signals loud and clear, nodded and tried to look displeased. Lord Bender was with him, but warning him not to break up this morning's meeting. The time would come.

'Brasserton's,' said Bernard Grant. 'The American contract has been signed, as we all know. Is progress at the plant satisfactory?' Prosser spoke this time, at Michael's suggestion, explaining the local labour agreements he hoped to negotiate. Westbrook added a report from the computer consultants. Michael knew that Oldershaw should be here for this. Five days ago his father had refused point-blank to issue the invitation. 'I'll not have the main board wet-nursing him. It's up to you to make things tick without continually dragging us all into it. You wanted it. You look after it.'

Now, speeding up the pace of the meeting, Bernard Grant brusquely said: 'We'll leave it in your court, then, Michael. It's a lot of development capital we're tying up.' The words hung on the air like mines floating on parachutes. Michael sat quite still, experiencing the kind of humiliation he had endured as a teenager when his father forced him to wear school uniform in his youth club one special night, the night he was taking a new girl home. He had stuffed blazer and cap beneath a hedge, shivering in shirtsleeves when she let him put his hand down the front of her dress – though never up her skirt – and when he got back some bastard had stolen his clothes. Life had been hell with Bernard for seven whole days. Yet now his feeling of acute discomfiture was mingled with admiration at his father's recovery of form. Both of them were fighting for their lives, Bernard Grant with more of his old panache than he had shown for months.

For the next hour, the Chairman scored most of the points. It was a bravura performance, enriched by Armfield's financial orchestrations. Property and restaurants, electronics and frozen foods, books and helicopters: all this was only a sampling of the interests which Grant had placed under Prospero's umbrella.

He summed them all up, indicating his recommendations for capital investment. It was like an annual report for shareholders, plump with good tidings, speckled with the fruit of optimism. At the end of the recital, Michael reckoned that Armfield's borrowings had been more than used up. Even Lord Bender had looked curiously at Michael from time to time, obviously surprised that he was offering so few objections. Michael almost surprised himself. He was holding his fire, but was vaguely concerned lest the bullets were rusting.

'Any other business before lunch?' said Grant.

'Yes,' said Michael. He was not going to have Lovelace's discussed in the somnolent mid-afternoon. He had watched his father's deft manipulation of the brandy decanter on other occasions. When the brain throbbed and the sweat prickled after too much food and drink, judgements could be fudged and decisions too easily evaded. 'There's been a very important development on the Lovelace's front. Before we wrap up the group's capital development plans, I'd like to tell you about it.'

Armfield reached for the summary of the paper Talbot-Brown had prepared for him. He had annotated the document heavily, adding firepower to the case against purchase. But within five minutes the columns of ammunition before him seemed almost irrelevant. Michael Grant was so enthusiastic about snowmobiles, he scarcely mentioned cars. And cars were virtually all that Talbot-Brown's document for Armfield dealt with: car sales, car production, analysis of the market, country by country. There were some good phrases about the Japanese competition in America: 'the favourite Japanese sport – poking their nose into someone else's technology.' Armfield had looked forward to deploying some of these words as his own. He was dismayed to find that the contest was being fought on entirely different ground. Lamely, he listened to Bernard Grant take up the fight.

'Moonshine, Michael. You're asking us to divert huge resources into a gamble on a product which Lovelace's have only handled as a sideline before?'

'We haven't the money,' said Armfield. 'Not if we're to go ahead with the other sensible investments we've decided on.'

'Maybe Lovelace's should take priority,' said Michael. He wanted to push hard, almost recklessly. 'We could always sell Supergear.'

The sudden deflation of the euphoria he had enjoyed for the past hour seemed to drain Bernard Grant's stomach. The closeness of total victory made him almost desperate. He had never felt so angry with his son. He wanted to win and to hurt Michael as he did so.

'You're being irresponsible, Michael. This organisation is not in business to subsidise your automotive fantasies.'

There's the weakness, Lord Bender thought. Five years ago, Bernard wouldn't have done that. He would have kept his control, destroying an opponent with reason and sharp irony. Bender looked blandly round the table. Most of them need not have been there that morning. Bernard had transformed the whole discussion into a personal confrontation with his son. It was all so needless, so wasteful.

Westbrook was speaking. Industry of the future ... growth market ... the two-snowmobile family. Armfield could scarcely contain his scorn. It sounded like a piece from one of those bright young business journalists who write up companies in prose so lasciviously entertaining it belongs to the centre-spread of *Playboy*.

The squabbling, hidden mostly behind a smog of business jargon, went on for a further ten minutes: nursery games with knives. Michael was as tempted to mention his knowledge of the Hampshire development area, which must have settled the thing, as he had been earlier to put the case against Bartram's conduct of Supergear's affairs. But he stayed silent.

Bernard Grant, imbued with growing confidence, added up the odds. Should he push it to a formal vote? Armfield, Lord Bender, Bartram and himself. Four of them. Even with Lymington gone, even with Prosser an uncertainty, he must still win. With what he imagined to be a cold edge on his brain, he plunged.

'We must take a decision. We can't keep spending the resources of our planning departments on it. Harold's investigation has taken weeks. I imagine you and Lionel have used up a few hours too.' The sarcasm was strong. 'Who believes we should make a bid apart from Michael and Lionel?'

Prosser knew there was no escape. When the chips were down, he had to declare his support. Like a boy reluctant to own up, he slowly raised a hand.

'It sounds a good idea. Let's not throw it away now.'

The Chairman waited ten more seconds, his heart thudding. Then he knew he had won. Four to three.

'That's settled, then.' He could, as always, afford magnanimity. 'I'm sorry, Michael, but I think it would have been madness.'

Lord Bender said: 'No, Chairman. I believe we have deadlock.

I withhold my vote until I know what terms Lovelace's might be ready to accept. It depends entirely on the price.'

*

Westbrook went home early. All through the board meeting the pain of the migraine had grown. By three the agony was all over his forehead, just as though his skull was on an anvil. He felt nauseated and hungry simultaneously. He left unwillingly. He wanted to talk over the morning with Michael. It was one of the pleasures of business life to recall the detail of engagements won. When they had been cliffhangers, the enjoyment of recollection was total.

But there was nothing more to be done that day. Far better to catch one's breath, get some sleep, and take stock.

London was dusty. A haze hung across the sunlight as the Daimler floated round Marble Arch, homing in on the Edgware Road. He slumped in the back compartment, closing his eyes for seconds at a time against the light.

For some absurd reason he wanted Diana to be at home. Absurd because it defied the pattern of their life and their present expectations. Once she used to ask him to try to get home early some evenings, though she hadn't mentioned it for long enough now. Perhaps he wanted to expose her to a dagger joke about it. How else could they celebrate, these days, what they had lost?

He asked himself, for the umpteenth time, what he should do with Diana. For several years he had been a tomorrow man about their marriage; let's get this bit of business wrapped up, this deal sorted and secure – and then we'll catch up on what we've missed out. Later he had tried to rationalise their relationship as typical of second marriages. Love – the idea of love – was for adolescents, wasn't it? What they had was togetherness, in the sense that they formed a unit. They enjoyed freedom and self-fulfilment within a stable structure, as well as a certain convenience.

Finally, that had seemed no answer either. They now saw each other only if their timetables overlapped: like teachers passing in corridors on their way to lessons, or talking shop over chalky common-room tea. Westbrook was an intelligent man, viewing his life this killing London afternoon with a kind of dumb self-clarity. He realised that he could see no reason to his marriage, yet was fearful to break the pattern because he could not see beyond that either. It was all very modern, appropriate and hopeless. He clung on, hoping that something would turn up to change it all. Perhaps it would be the next holiday. Perhaps Diana would grow tired of being in business for herself. It was even possible that she didn't sleep around after all, not even occasionally, but only chose to use the assumption that she did as a sophisticated weapon against him. He himself had not been to bed with another woman for eighteen months. It somehow gave him hope. When self-delusion is so rampant, hope becomes pathetically over-important.

They were winning, he knew it. He and Michael. Lord Bender was coming round, it was obvious. Winning. Grant Junior and Westbrook. And Earl Sanger. Must watch Sanger. Eternal vigilance. Price of power. Westbrook was almost asleep in the car. He opened his eyes and sat up, pushing a clammy hand across his forehead, trying to squeeze the pain away.

Sanger confused him. Michael appeared sometimes to view the American with all the distaste which Westbrook felt. Michael might grow tired of Sanger or Sanger might weary of London. Westbrook feared an arrangement between Michael and the incomer. He questioned whether Sanger had not harmed their cause more than he had aided it. Typically American; typically *Manhattan*. A policy of overkill.

Again, unwillingly, Westbrook was thinking about Lymington. The arguments clumped through his head in well-drilled columns. He had, in the past few weeks, assembled and refined them, because it was necessary if he was to live with what had happened. They proved that although Sanger could not be exempt from suspicion, no direct causal link between Westbrook's activities and Lymington's death could be established. Westbrook had to accept this as adequate. Elsewhere in his mind a nastier advocate's voice rebelliously argued. It said that if Lymington killed himself because he knew his various frailties were about to be exposed, the fault lay with the begetter of the sins and not the inquisitors, so serve Lymington damn well right.

Automatically he thanked the driver and walked the few yards to his front door in the sunshine. The road was quiet. He felt as strange coming home to this kind of brooding quasi-suburban tranquillity as if he had been dropped by parachute into the Cambodian jungle. Mid-afternoon early-summer England away from the routine of business was totally foreign to him. He felt like a sticky truant.

He let himself in. The house was silent too. He dropped his briefcase in the hall and walked into the sitting-room. His forehead was damp with the pain and he still felt uneasily like vomiting. Two used glasses stood on one of the low tables, a half-finished bottle of wine between them. There were cigarette ends in the ashtray, a fan of typewritten papers beside it, a worn leather topcoat slung across a chair.

He wanted to call his wife's name. Instead he walked slowly and still hopefully towards the study. It was neat and unoccupied, heavy with that hygienic imprint of Lucrezia's presence which he had come to recognise; a kind of disembodied tidiness. He went to all the downstairs rooms and they had the same antiseptic air. He stood at the bottom of the staircase and climbed a dozen steps. Through the stillness of the house, inturned upon itself, he heard soft sounds from one of the rooms. A foot treading gently, a low female voice, the swish of curtains being drawn. He didn't want to go any further. He shouted 'Diana!'. Then he went into the sitting-room and waited.

When his wife walked through the door perhaps three minutes later she said: 'Hello, Lionel. What brings you back to the nest?' She was like an actress who had just learned the opening lines of a lousy script. A girl stood beside her, scruffily gamine, slim hips in jeans, big breasts stuffed untidily in wrinkled T-shirt and sliding about as she walked. Her face was flushed and her blonde hair was a halo of frizzy spikes. Westbrook was thinking of an agency man's joke: more like nerve-ends than hair.

'It's been a hell of a morning,' he said. 'I'd had enough.'

There was a nervousness in the air. His wife's eyes were averted and she kept twisting the big ring on her right hand. Awkwardly she half-turned towards the girl.

'You don't know Lucy. My husband. Lucy designs interiors. We were looking round to see what ideas she might have.'

'Ideas?'

'For the house. She says we need a bit more showbiz in the kitchen.'

He looked up at them through eyelids creased against the pain. 'What did she say about the bedroom?'

'Nothing much.' The girl moved quietly behind his wife and picked up the leather coat. Then she stood with one hip jutting, waiting and challenging. Her eyes, black, overflowed with what he took to be scorn.

'I'm going upstairs,' he said. 'My head's killing me.' He stood, wanting to get out. The atmosphere in the room could be felt but not yet understood by him. It was conspiratorial, secret, disturbing. He knew only that he couldn't take it.

'Are you all right?'

'Just leave me alone. I want to lie down.'

His wife was blocking the doorway. The girl stood very still. It was the first time in his life he had sensed panic in Diana.

'Sit down, Lionel. I'll make some tea.'

'I don't want any.'

'It won't take a minute.'

'For Christ's sake let it be.'

She was still immovable. He reached out with both arms and pushed her aside. As he went past her she tried to grab him and he chopped viciously at her arm. He was climbing the stairs and she called out after him, desperately.

'Lionel!' An animal's cry. 'You're not well. I understand. Don't you see?'

He ignored her and almost ran into the bedroom. The scent of his wife was still there. Two crumpled tissues lay beside the bed and on the dressing-table were a pair of earrings and an open compact. The bed was neatly made, but when he pulled back the coverlet he saw the indentation in one of the pillows.

He went out on the landing and stood silently. The two women were standing by the front door whispering; why should that simple act seem, to him, so evil? He thought he understood everything, yet even at this time he wanted to be argued out of his conclusions. The men he had seen his wife trying to make in the past were real enough, weren't they? Not fags, not all of them. That, he realised, meant nothing. Old jokes came back to him. Mister facing both ways. All that. But never about a woman. Did women tell jokes about dykes as men did about queers? Women don't tell jokes. Why? And all the time he was also conscious of his interview with Esther Lymington and Sanger's words afterwards. *Grow up ... it's happened before.*

Diana and the girl suddenly looked up towards him. He looked down at them. The girl had an insolent air of victory about her and he was devastated to realise that he was stripping the clothes from her in his mind, wondering about her breasts and her belly, touching her, wanting to strike her, and imagining he would already find the body marked.

They remained immobile, watching. Like a waxwork tableau. Still he could not bring himself to speak. The whole precarious relationship of his marriage, existing almost by default, could finally be destroyed or somehow preserved at this moment. He was amazed that he felt no conscious revulsion, not even at himself; only an exhausted bewilderment.

298

'How about the bed, girl?' he called out at last. 'Would you advise us to change it?'

Diana put her arm around the girl. 'Leave it, can't you? Get some rest.' It was the protective gesture, insignificant in itself, which pushed him over the edge.

'Get that dirty bitch out of my house,' he shouted.

Even in the shadow of the hall he could see how pale his wife looked. 'We were going anyway,' she said and turned to open the door. The girl looked up again, lascivious and sneering.

'Do you think I can't *see*?' he said. 'And bringing her here. You're disgusting.'

'I think you're going out of your mind.'

He screamed. 'You know, you know! Admit it!'

The girl spoke for the first and last time. 'Get stuffed, darling.'

The door shut. Westbrook went back to the bedroom, took off his shoes and jacket, drew the curtains shut, and lay down on top of the coverlet. He felt cold and he fetched a heavy dressing-gown to cover himself. He could not imagine whether his wife would return soon or not at all, nor what his actions should be. His mouth began to form words; alternative speeches he might make to her. In the end they were a desolate logjam in his mind. He surrendered to a feeling of hopeless numbness, postponing every decision he might have to take. Thank God, he thought, that things at Prospect House are working out. Deputy managing director? Yes, he ought to make that now. He laughed aloud, deliberately theatrical, and spoke to the empty room. 'You can't have everything, can you?'

13. Even rattlesnakes are moral

LORD BENDER learned what price Lovelace's would be prepared to accept a week after the board meeting. It was higher than he had anticipated; not by much, but still high. On the telephone he told Michael Grant he was disappointed but would make up his mind only after he had fully studied the documents. Later that afternoon Bernard Grant rang him.

'Are you satisfied, Benjamin?'

'No.'

'I told you. Harold agrees with me. It's a ridiculous proposition.'

'Have you seen all the documents?'

'As many as I need. The price is out of the question, even allowing for what seems to us like a very optimistic profit projection.'

'I'm seeing the papers tonight. Michael is sending me a set.'

'Naturally,' said Grant drily. 'However great your affection for my son, I don't see how you can disagree with me.'

'Don't be silly,' said Lord Bender. 'It's an exercise we had to go through.'

'For once, I can't see your line of thinking. I'm sorry you've lost faith in my judgement.'

Oh God, Lord Bender thought, as he put down the phone; now he's sulking. For the next twenty-four hours he dropped everything, turning the figures Michael had produced on their head, making discreet calls to several friends gleaning information. It was the kind of operation he was very good at, which he liked as much as folding money. Oblique questions to an export man in the Board of Trade; a low-keyed, almost social, conversation with the chairman of a company whose performance in the American market had brought great joy to Mondor Insurance over many years. In the end he knew as much as he wanted, but it made no sense. He still couldn't see what Michael was about. The price *was* a touch on the high side.

300

Michael changed Lord Bender's mind in one minute short of a quarter-hour. They met in the Mondor building and after Bender had taken the figures apart, the younger man leaned back and smiled ruefully.

'All right, Benjamin. I might have known.' He meant it too. He had hoped to have a bonus in hand on the deal, but had not really expected to gain Lord Bender's support on the figures as they stood.

'There's a good reason why the offer looks generous. I want to make sure Lovelace's accept it – quickly.'

Lord Bender listened to Michael's exposition of the Hampshire development plan. It wasn't merely the plant, Michael explained. Lovelace's owned land around it too. There was no question that values would soar if the plan went through. He mentioned an estimate. This time Lord Bender thought the figure was conservative.

'Lovelace's won't love you,' he said. 'Not when they know.'

Michael shrugged. 'They'll be sharing the fortune of our joint company without having taken any of the risk. Besides, I assume they'll *never* know.'

'They'll suspect.'

'But they won't *know*. My interest seems natural to them. Comes of having been a boy-racer.'

Lord Bender pursed his lips in an expression that for him was close to humour. 'You remind me of your father quite staggeringly sometimes. By good luck or judgement he made some very shrewd buys in the fifties. Even I never knew quite how he got hold of his information. I take it yours is sound?'

'Gilt-edged.'

'Not exactly the metaphor I would have chosen.'

Michael laughed. 'Right. Yes, it's good information. As good as you can get. There's always an element of chance. But I think the risk should be taken.'

'Have you told your father?'

'No. I was hoping you might do that.'

'Why?'

'Take the credit if you like. I'm tired of fighting him. I've got to live with him, whatever happens.' He rose and sat easily on the edge of Lord Bender's burdened desk. 'Just get us Lovelace's, Benjamin. That's all.'

'Not all,' said Lord Bender. 'I know what you're thinking.'

'Frankly, I'm thinking that if things don't happen soon, I might get out. Start something on my own. I want to be my own boss.'

It sounded unconvincing, and Lord Bender was moved only to pick at his nose. 'No, Michael. This kind of emotional blackmail doesn't work with me. I don't believe you.'

'You must believe what your good sense tells you. I'm tired, that's all. Tired of demonstrating over and over what you know in your heart is true. Tired of being the favoured son who can have anything provided it's not an opinion the organisation should act on. I've grown up, and Bernard hasn't noticed. Nor has he even begun to recognise that he's free-wheeling.'

Lord Bender said: 'That's a harsh judgement. Too harsh.'

'It's realistic. It happens to the old.'

'I'm old too.'

'And willing to let me go ahead if you judge I'm right. Without prejudice. There's the difference.'

'Flattery will get you somewhere.' Lord Bender had risen, smiling; the first joke he had made in the last two months. It was essentially a defensive gesture. He wanted to end the conversation, seeking time to think away from Michael's persuasive aura. Charisma was the vogue word, wasn't it? Michael Grant had it. Son of his father, with much the same morality and a similar ruthlessness within the rules. In business one competes, company against company, man against man. But often the rules were far from clear. What could be defined as sharp practice and what as an intelligent garnering of available information? At what point did the end stop justifying the means? Lord Bender distrusted those who pretended to lay down general principles. He was a pragmatist, accepting the uncertainties and knowing that his decisions would sometimes prove to be wrong. There were times when, as a finance man, he regretted such imprecisions. But he lived with them and would have sought justification, if challenged, in the fierce loyalty he felt towards the customers who entrusted him with their money and the employees who looked to him for their careers. No man could serve too many bibles.

'Goodbye, then,' said Michael. 'I rely on you.'

They shook hands, Lord Bender reflecting that it must be intoxicating to be young and so convinced of one's rightness. Michael would also come to learn that the rules were ill-defined. Probably he knew it now, but like his father was too proud to admit it.

'All in good time,' said Lord Bender.

Michael slid a glance at his watch as he turned to leave. 'It's later than you think,' he said.

*

Two days afterwards, Lord Bender lunched with Bernard Grant at the Savoy Grill. They went there perhaps four or five times a year, for no fashionable reasons. The newer restaurants in London, full of yelping men in flowered shirts, jammed everyone so close that private conversation was impossible. At the Savoy, each table was its own island. They also liked the food.

Lord Bender said quietly that he wanted neither onion nor anchovies with his steak tartare, a peccadillo which was plainly not approved despite the immobility of the waiter's face. Bernard Grant gloomily surveyed his entrecote. During the smoked trout, Lord Bender had told him precisely why Lovelace's was a good buy.

They sat in silence while the waiters swirled around them. Grant wondered if he might challenge the soundness of Lord Bender's information on the Hampshire scheme, but judged the risk of exacerbation too great. He had always thought of Bender as a friend, though he would have been hard put to define the word. But Benjamin was not the ally he once had been. There was a wariness in their conversation which was alien to the relationship of a year or so ago. He felt no longer able to judge Lord Bender's moods.

Since the board meeting, Grant had been hustling, spending long hours with Armfield deciding how their new-found funds might be deployed throughout the group in the coming year or so. He would have liked to use Westbrook and his department more, but was fearful lest his plans should become known to his son too soon. So he fell back, not unhappily, on his entrepreneural flair. The marketing detail could come later. First, he had to have a strategy, one that came from the guts. Harold backed him up loyally, occasionally calling on Sims and the new young man Talbot-Brown to provide background. He had never felt more confident as he rode to luncheon. Now, he was deflated, struggling to summon up his reserves.

They were alone again, the last dab of mustard placed upon his plate. 'I can't argue with you about Lovelace's,' he said. 'In theory it looks good. Michael will crow, but that I'll have to live with.' He frowned at his knife and cut the first piece of steak. 'God knows where the money's coming from.'

'Supergear?'

'I'm not selling. Not yet.'

'Why is it so important to you?'

'It wouldn't be fair. Not to Frank, not to the people who work there. They should have their chance to pull it round.'

Lord Bender smiled wryly at Grant. This was the moment when he would have to start breaking eggs. 'It will hold us back, Bernard, maybe damage us. And that's not fair either. There are more people involved here than a few girls at Supergear.'

Grant put his knife and fork neatly together, wearily dabbed a napkin at his lips, and pushed the plate discontentedly from him. There was no spark in his eyes when he spoke.

'Why, Benjamin? Why are you trying to destroy me?'

The question did not surprise Lord Bender. He had anticipated this kind of emotional pressure from Grant. The timing, though, was premature. He had hoped to build towards a climax over coffee. He studied the face opposite him, resentful and sulky, and knew he must speak at last with directness.

'You're destroying yourself,' he said. 'If things don't change, the contest between you and Michael will tear the organisation into pieces. That's what I want to prevent.'

'And to do that you'll ditch me?'

'No, Bernard. You can't go on for ever. Don't you see that? Michael is ready to become a chief executive. With you as Chairman, not bogged down in day-to-day detail, the group will be stronger than ever.'

'Don't you realise what Michael would do to the organisation if he had a free hand? He's like a child. He's swallowed the whole damn library of textbooks from those American professors who taught him. He thinks he's tough, but in fact all he wants to do is draw marvellous charts – like Westbrook's – which will convince him he's got the thing planned. Planning – huh! Look where it's landed this country.'

'You exaggerate, Bernard. Michael is older than you think.'

Grant ignored him. 'Do you know he was talking to me the other day about industrial democracy? Every half-baked idea those American reviews of business ever put into print – he's got them all. I'm not going to have the organisation I created turned into a stultified case-history of decline for simpering Harvard egg-heads to leaf through. Michael – dammit, he hasn't had the experience.'

Grant, to Lord Bender's ears, had never sounded more English, in both accent and philosophy; like some baffled colonel protesting that his regiment was going to be merged with another in the next county, just to satisfy the itch for rational streamlining of a faceless planner in Whitehall. He spoke to Grant in a voice of infinite softness and patience.

'Perhaps Michael hasn't had all the experience we would wish.

304

But nothing in life is ever perfect. When this country got out of Africa, many of the new nations there weren't ready to govern themselves. But we had no choice without inviting a blood-bath. We had to let them make their own mistakes.'

'People would lose confidence in us if I went. There's an aura of success about the Prospero Group because there's an aura of success about me. I have seventeen cuttings books filled with the successes you and I have created. The organisation needs me.'

'As Chairman you can do all that needs to be done about our image. More, in fact. You'll have a freedom I think you'd enjoy.'

'Freedom but no power.'

Lord Bender sucked gently on the minced raw meat. 'Power can be a delusion. Michael and the new men are chipping away at it all the time anyway. You're losing battles, Bernard, and frankly you deserve to lose them. Brasserton's, Supergear, Lovelace's. All won by Michael, and for good reasons.'

'And you don't back losers.' Grant's voice was scornful and weary too. 'I never thought you would turn out to be disloyal.'

Lord Bender flushed, the parchment face suddenly alive. 'I can't accept that from you of all people, Bernard. You've chopped dozens of men to pieces in your time. By your standards you did the right thing. Now you're older, you think you can relax, try to salve your conscience by handouts to men like Frank Bartram. It's not good enough. I don't confuse my loyalties. In business my duty is first to my own company, then to yours. I'm losing confidence in the Prospero Group, and I see clearly why that is. Don't you realise how ill you were?'

'I'm all right now,' snapped Grant. 'Everyone knows it.'

'You mean you have spent six months trying to demonstrate to the world that they *ought* to know it,' said Lord Bender. 'That's not quite the same thing. In fact it can be damned dangerous.'

'You're frightened I'll drop down dead?' Grant raised his eyes to the distant ceiling in an ill-timed attempt at comedy.

'No,' said Lord Bender. 'But this continual striving to show people you're still a boy wonder undermines your judgement. You want to justify your rightness all the time, and you force Michael to do the same. It's crazy. I'm suggesting a way out which is not only easy but also happens to be right. What would you sooner have me do? Try to persuade you to give up being managing director – or let things slide and, in the end, pull out Mondor money? You'd be finished if I did that and you know it. The market would murder you.'

'That sounds suspiciously like blackmail,' said Grant.

'It's a formula for peace, rather. No more fighting. Except against the enemy outside. You can't be Napoleon for ever.'

Grant tried one final argument. 'None of Michael's ventures has yet actually made us a penny. I hope you know what you're doing.'

'They'd stand a better chance if you two signed an armistice.'

Grant looked round the restaurant. Grey men, bald men, eager men, sullen men. All dealers in one way or other, shaping the world under a cloud of cigar smoke. He wanted to stay in it very much.

'I'll think about what you say.'

'I'm sorry,' said Lord Bender, driving in the final nail. 'But it would be better if we did this without involving a vote by the board.'

Grant laughed sadly. 'You *are* a bastard, Benjamin. I believe you'd do that too if you had to.'

*

Westbrook hadn't the time for scandal. Not at present. He hadn't the time for inconvenience either. There was too much at stake at Prospect House. So when Diana came back and looked as if she intended to stay, he didn't move out. Instead he asked Lucrezia to make up the bed in the spare room. He had been sleeping badly, disturbing his wife, he explained. After two days of abrasive silence, the arrangement lost its necessity. His wife flew to New York. The note from her office said she would be away for some weeks, on business for her clients.

He needed a fast trip to America himself. Michael was still pushing him on Lovelace's. He had met Philip Lovelace. A bright boy, but naïve. Westbrook wanted to look at the transatlantic sales operation for the Lovelace Specials himself. And he didn't know a snowmobile from a combine harvester. Not at first-hand, anyway.

But he wouldn't take the risk of leaving, even though he could forget about Brasserton's now. There was not much more his department could do except watch and hope that Oldershaw and the machines didn't cock it up. What held him back was more intangible. Michael was withdrawn and secretive. Earl Sanger looked like a satisfied stoat. Westbrook had the feeling that something big was about to happen, perhaps the end of the war. He aimed to be around for the victory parade.

He called in Hardy for the last time ten days after he had sent him on indefinite leave. It was a brief, edgy interview during which Westbrook raised his voice too much while Hardy sat unperturbed, one arm loosely poised on the back of the chair, fingers pressing his forehead like some disinterested don on a TV panel. When it was over, Westbrook was more than ever convinced that Hardy would have no scruples about feeding useful information to QFN.

'I saw Hardy around today,' said Sanger later that afternoon when he and Westbrook were sitting in Michael Grant's office. 'Hasn't he gone yet?'

'As of now, yes,' said Westbrook. 'I got back all his papers the day he resigned.'

'Too goddam late,' said Sanger. 'He could have been servicing Barstow for months.'

'You've no proof,' said Westbrook. 'There was Lymington.'

'Sure. Both of them.' Sanger stood up, hitching his trousers, ritually tucking in his shirt. 'It occurred to me that if Hardy was that kind of guy he might be prepared to keep us in touch with what Barstow's doing.'

'You've seen too many Bond movies,' said Michael. 'You're not serious?'

Sanger could afford to smile. Only Westbrook could lose face in this situation. 'Maybe not. But he was Lionel's guy. What do you think? Maybe you've already asked him?'

'I haven't, and I won't. He's very clever, perhaps a touch too ambitious. But not a traitor.' Westbrook hated committing himself, detested Sanger for yet again setting the trap. Michael did not comment. They began instead to talk about how Armfield and Bernard Grant were planning to spend money around the group.

Talbot-Brown's service, Sanger observed, was really on the button.

*

David was surprised to see Hardy.

'I'd given you up for lost. Why didn't you tell me you were coming in?'

'I tried to reach you. Didn't you hear?'

'No.'

'Sorry. I really did ring. A girl took the message.'

'What's happening to you, then?'

'Hello and goodbye. Lionel's told me to bugger off forthwith.'

'Seriously?'

'He's developing delusions of spirituality. Today he wore an evangelical look. As if he had a private line to God and the word said my place was down below. He got very worked up.'

It was the same as the last time they had talked. David was no longer finding the script funny. He knew that envy – his envy – was in there somewhere. He hoped there were other, more acceptable reasons for his sourness. At this moment he couldn't find any.

'He's under a lot of pressure,' said David.

'So are you. So are we all.'

'Not you.'

'Not yet.'

They seemed to have run out of words. David had unravelled a paper clip. He was bending it backwards and forwards, untypically busy with his hands.

'I suppose it's no use asking you to come out for a quick beer.'

'I'm a bit tired of quick beers. That's all I ever drink these days. Besides. . . .' David waved at the pile of paper around him. 'In an hour maybe.'

'We've got people for dinner tonight. I can't wait,' said Hardy.

'Will you be coming in again?'

'Depends when Barstow wants me to start.'

'See you at your farewell party then.'

'No farewells. I don't believe in them.'

'The others will be disappointed. There's a move to pass the hat round for you.' David coated the words with uncontrollable malice.

'Thanks. But I can do without a pen and pencil set. No offence.'

'Give me a ring. We'll have a drink on our own, then.'

'I'll be in touch. Maybe next week.'

Hardy picked up his coat and stuck out his hand.

'Good luck,' said David. 'Not that I think you need it.'

'Look after the shop,' said Hardy. 'And remember the school motto.'

Even at this point in their relationship David couldn't defeat his reflex. 'Go on,' he said feigning weariness. 'Tell me.' Like one half of a double-act; the stooge, feeding the star.

'Having lost sight of our objectives, we redoubled our efforts.'

'Oh Christ,' groaned David.

'Take care. Remember me to Sheila.'

He walked out. Hardy on his way up; shedding friends as he reached for the next rung of the ladder. David suspected that he wouldn't get a telephone call next week; nor the week after that; not until Hardy wanted something.

*

After all his years at Bernard Grant's side, Karian should have known how to read the signs. But no one could really have blamed him. The situation was unexpected and almost unprecedented. Grant came back from lunch flushed and loud, walking stiffly, as if some inexpert cobbler had been repairing his ankles. He seemed to want someone to talk at. Again, unusual.

Karian followed him obediently into the inner room, cool despite the brash May sun hammering at the blinds. There were three messages to deliver, one from the Ministry of Arts.

'Let them damn well wait,' said Grant. 'I've had a bellyful of politicians already.'

Karian did not comment. He waited uneasily, but Grant waved him into a chair opposite his desk. Then he roared with laughter. 'Don't you want to hear?'

'Sir?'

'You wouldn't know the works of e. e. cummings, I suppose.'

'I'm afraid not.'

'*A politician is an arse* – how does it go? – *is an arse* – yes, that's it – *upon which everyone has sat except a man*. Perfect. One of them at lunch today. Pitiful creature. I was very rude, Joseph. Very rude.'

'Yes, Mr Grant.'

'You're a damn poor audience, Joseph. I told him. Today Britain is not a nation of shopkeepers. It's a nation of shop stewards. He didn't like it.'

A faint haze of wine floated across the desk. Karian knew Grant might take a glass with his lunch. But he had never smelt drink around the Chairman in this way before. Grant was talking on, but Karian scarcely took in the words.

'What are we going to do with you, Joseph? Tell me.' Grant smiled. He looked like a playful cat. Karian, misled, allowed the problem which these days was always in his head to move to his mouth.

Nothing had happened for him in the last six months. His money was still locked in Burgham, now more lowly priced than ever. Still showing on the shares page of his newspaper, tantalisingly, was the high level the shares had hit for the seventy-two hours during which the Prospero Group had been rumoured to be interested in them; the three days when Karian, typically, had failed to sell.

He was in trouble: the usual reasons from inflating school fees for his three children to over-heavy mortgage. Every day he asked himself why he was on the hook when he lived and worked so close to the scent and gift of money. So did his wife.

'Mr Grant, I haven't had the chance to talk to you for a long time.'

'Mm?'

'I've been wondering whether you could – would consider – the company making a loan to me.'

'You're not listening, Joseph.'

'It wouldn't be for long.'

'What is all this, Joseph? I'm telling you about these people. The people at lunch. How can I believe in the collective wisdom of individual ignorance? Thomas Carlyle. Did you know?'

'But, sir, this is important.'

'Not now, Joseph. What's happened to your sense of timing?'

'I thought in view of my long service. I've not asked this kind of thing before.' He was beginning to lose hope.

'Well-paid service, Joseph. Good fringe benefits. Generous pension. What in God's name do you want a loan for, living the way you do? Money is tight.'

As he spoke the words, Grant realised he was being unreasonable. It would have been easier to say yes and forget it. Karian's supine nature was the block. It drew from Grant a contempt he could not control. The habit of years in his attitudes to Karian asserted themselves, exacerbated now by his unease. He had been too waspish at lunch, buoyed by the wine. What he had drunk was a symbol of his decision. In victory, he would have taken Evian water, with the strong adrenalin of success potent enough in his body for celebration. With wine he celebrated defeat. Now Karian was spoiling even the purity of the confession which Grant felt the need to go through, a kind of religious ceremony with Karian as priest.

Grant looked at his watch. 'My son will be here.'

Karian stood, licking his lips uncontrollably. 'Will you think about it, sir?'

'See Prosser. That's his job.'

'I thought – well, Mr Grant, it didn't seem dignified.' Karian had resisted the idea of having to say this. Now he sickened himself. He was also aware enough of office procedure to know that any request for such a sum as he had in mind would automatically come back to Grant for approval. He heard the Chairman exhale a laugh through the teeth, a siphon sound.

'Dignity, Joseph? Do you believe that asking for money can be dignified, whoever you put the question to? Never ask for anything. Not even understanding.'

Karian brushed harshly at his shoulder in a nervous gesture

310

which released the locked-in humiliation and anger. 'You won't forget Sir William at four.' Then he was gone. Grant leaned back in his chair. He erased Karian from his mind. Karian was easily forgettable. He tried again, unsuccessfully, to argue to himself that the future would hold a new, more subtle flavour of fulfilment.

'I met your friend Lovelace this morning,' he told Michael when his son arrived.

'What did you think?' Michael was genuinely surprised. Why hadn't Philip told him?

'Not the son. The old man.' Typical, Michael thought. Lovelace senior was four years younger than his father. 'A dull man. I hope you know what you're about.'

'He's a good engineer,' said Michael.

'No breadth. I've never understood how a man can spend a lifetime on one thing. Engineers and scientists. They're so in-turned. So cut off. Scruffy men in white coats and overalls playing with their Meccano. This obsession with *contraptions*.'

'He created a classic line of cars.'

'And now he needs us to sell them. *Hopefully* to sell them. The real gift is with people; not with nuts and bolts.'

It was not a new conversation. Michael was bored as hell with it. He shrugged. 'Both gifts are important. You know what I believe. I know what you believe. You seem to take a perverse pride in not understanding how a motor car works.'

'Unimportant detail. You pay other men to know these things. Like Oldershaw. Where would he be without us?'

'I know all this, father. Why say it again?'

'Oldershaw's been on to me.' Michael didn't know that either. 'Trying to blind me with science. Do you really intend to give him a computer terminal in his office?'

'It's a possibility.'

'I heard at lunch that a graphic terminal, if that's the name, costs upwards of thirty thousand pounds. A ludicrously expensive toy.'

'Oldershaw won't get anything as sophisticated as that. A much simpler system.'

'Is it really necessary? I'll not have extravagance. The whole contract with Corsino is enough of a gamble as it is.'

Michael looked steadily at his father. This laborious build-up was too obvious: the Chairman and Managing Director reminding a subordinate of the ultimate source of power if he cared to exercise it. Between board meetings, his father could still say no.

Always watching, waiting for a mistake. Able to hold things up. There was also an excitement in the old man's eyes which was more uncontrolled than usual. If he hadn't known his father better he would have said the old man had been drinking. What do you want me to do, he thought. Go on fighting? It's not what I really want. Despite the past, despite what I intend the future to be. Let's stop it.

Bernard Grant picked up his Parker 61, was examining it closely. It might have been an object as precious as the Hepworth or the Dufy. 'Don't imagine your computers and management systems can ever replace judgement or flair,' he said.

'My education taught me about judgement too. I haven't forgotten.'

'I've been to see my doctor.'

Michael was lost. 'Are you all right?'

'Yes. A new doctor. He's called Lord Bender. It seems the job's too much for me. I need a rest.'

There was a nerve twitching in the base of Michael's neck. He said nothing.

'Naturally I'm disappointed. But being just Chairman will be interesting. You can have the rest of it.'

'I don't understand.'

'Nicely ingenuous, Michael. I'm not bitter about Benjamin. But I hope you've taken note of the lesson.'

'It's not very obvious,' said Michael.

'You think you have deserved loyalty. Then someone lets you down. How can you ever trust that man again? If he betrays you, he will also betray others.'

Michael had no appetite for argument because there was none. His father was right.

'You mean you're resigning as Managing Director?'

'You know better than anyone I've no choice.'

'I believe it's a right decision, if that's what you mean,' said Michael.

'You can have it. All of it. I'll watch you with interest. So will Benjamin. Don't forget it.'

'You're not likely to let me.'

His father held up the pen, didactically. 'I was reading about rattlesnakes the other evening. When two of them fight, they never use their poison fangs, not even if they're being beaten, perhaps dying.'

Michael just sat there, waiting for the end of the story. 'They're a damn sight more moral than human beings,' said his father.

312

Then Bernard Grant pushed wearily at his hair. 'Poor Harold,' he said. 'I suppose he'll be disappointed.'

*

Howland sat in his office reading the press release yet again. It was unlike him to be so obsessive. There was nothing wrong with the words. They had been checked and re-checked, approved by both the Grants. It wasn't the accuracy of the facts which gave him these twinges of nervousness in his stomach, but their implications. And though he had written most of the typescript himself, he looked at it with detachment, straining to see what might lie between the lines, trying to crystal-ball his own future.

The first of the expected telephone calls arrived. One of Howland's usual contacts, complaining.

'You might have given me some idea.'

'Not on,' said Howland. 'Not in a case like this. Anyway, it was rather unexpected.'

'Dad must like the boy more than I thought. How did it really happen, or is that asking too much?'

Howland wished he knew the answer to that himself. He couldn't miss the fact that Bernard Grant hadn't been winning all along the line recently, but in the past month the Chairman had seemed perkier, more assured, more like the old Grant, talking of the stories Howland would be writing once the division of funds throughout the group was worked out. When he had revealed to Howland his intention to give up being Managing Director, his words and his mood seemed unreal. He had joked about his age, which normally he hated being referred to. He had even spoken of approaching senility and the relief which non-involvement might bring in a way which was totally untypical.

'Why don't you just believe the words for a change, Dennis? He's sixty-seven next month. He's ensured the succession. He wants a rest. It's natural.'

'For your boss to give up anything is unnatural. He's the original one-man board.'

'He's also had a thrombosis. That's not in the hand-out, but I'm sure you haven't forgotten it. Make something out of that.'

'Remember that night we talked? After the body-snatchers had got him?'

'Yes.'

'You didn't know his son would be the successor then. At least you *said* you didn't. Where does this leave Armfield? And Westbrook?'

Where, Howland was thinking, does this leave me? Grant was evasive about the future. Howland worried to what extent the old man was going to become a sidelines chairman, leaving his son to get on with it. Howland still found it difficult to assess Michael Grant's attitude towards the Public Relations office. The Chairman's son rarely called him, rarely used him. There were occasional messages which Alison passed on. She was damned good, that girl. The office had run like a bomb since she joined. Maybe that wasn't helpful either. If his face didn't fit with Michael Grant, he had created his own successor. How hard would Bernard fight to protect him? That morning, for the first time in years, Howland had spent twenty minutes on the job ads in *Campaign* and other trade magazines.

'Status quo, dear boy,' said Howland.

'I can read. But when will the blood start flowing? And whose?'

'I hope you're not going to write one of your power-game stories. I expect there'll be a decision on new board responsibilities within the next fortnight.'

'Can I quote you.'

'No. But it's a reasonable speculation. I leave it to you.'

'Thanks for nothing. I'm beginning to believe PROs are in charge of *not* handing out information.'

Howland ignored the irony. He had, years ago, tried journalism himself, and was under no illusions how newspapermen regarded his trade. The old love-hate relationship. Make use of PR men and scorn them too. He had a defence mechanism in face of this. He got the sarcasm in first, taking the steam out of attackers by knowing more anti-PR cracks than they did. *Organised lying* – the definition of PR according to Saint Muggeridge. And Harold Wilson: *A most degrading profession.* Streams and streams of jokes. Self-depreciation employed both to defend himself and to attack the knockers from the flank. It was neat and effective. That way he kept his cool and his contacts. Now he tried a joke to ease the pressure.

'You must have heard that story, Dennis.'

'Which one?'

'The guy who's saying it's not that he doesn't trust PR men, but after shaking hands with them he always counts his fingers.'

The man at the other end of the line laughed. 'I suppose that means you've nothing more to tell me.' He had spoken with Howland too many times not to read the signs.

'What else is there to tell?'

'Maybe who's going on a world tour prior to taking up new special responsibilities.'

'An outmoded formula, Dennis. We're more subtle than that.'

'Keep me posted. Especially if it's you who gets the airline tickets.'

Howland didn't think that was very funny, but he pretended he did. He sidestepped a final flurry of questions. Then he put down the telephone and walked along the corridor to the men's room. Inside he found Karian. He said hello and the little man grunted. They stood at adjacent basins, washing their hands, and in the large mirror Howland watched Karian's face. It looked like a face that had very recently been walked over, haggard and creased and grey, with the black of the beard pushing through. There were specks of dandruff in the thin eyebrows. Howland took a drop of comfort from the thought that here was someone who looked more worried than he did. Howland's dark striped suit was pristine, an Identikit smoothie. He adjusted his pale violet tie. Karian did not touch his clothes. He straightened up and jerked at the continuous towel, his expression fixed and miserable, then left Howland without a word, like a man walking under hypnosis.

Karian's lips moved as he trod the carpeted corridor towards his office. Howland would be all right. Bernard Grant would look after Howland. He had been a favourite of the Chairman's for years. With the change of regime, Karian feared for his job. What if Grant decided to be an absentee landlord? What would there be for him to do?

Earlier that day he had tried to speak again with the Chairman. Grant had laughed and told Karian he worried too much. What kind of answer was that? He had also been to see Prosser twice. On the second occasion the personnel director said that in the present situation there was no chance of a company loan.

Karian knew what he was going to do. He almost surprised himself by the strength of his resolve, for he had never experienced so intensely this feeling of wanting to hurt someone, to lash out at the indifferent injustice he felt around him.

After supper at his home that evening – his wife never would call it dinner – he said he had some work to do. He took the cover off the old Olivetti, inserted a sheet of plain paper, and began to type, single-fingered, a statement setting out everything he knew about the movements in Burgham shares six months ago.

It was cleverly written. The information was all there. The suspicion that must now fall on Bernard Grant's operations was firmly implicit in the text. Karian was sure that no one would be able to trace the source back to himself, though for a few minutes he sat with knuckles pressed against his forehead wondering if the typewriter might betray him. He had read about that kind of thing. Finally he decided that no one would conduct such an investigation. His note would simply set inquiries in train. Anyway, it was a risk he'd have to take.

Finally, he typed an envelope – plain, blue and ordinary – addressed to the City Panel on Takeovers and Mergers. He put the letter in his briefcase to post in the morning at some place in town, far from his home. Karian felt no burden of treachery; only a sense of resentment mingled with self-pity. Bernard Grant had gone too far in his indifferent vanity, and now Karian would damage him if that were possible. He slept well that night, after wondering for a time whether the Panel would really take action on the basis of an anonymous letter. And if someone had questioned him, he would not even have asked for understanding of his actions. Only help.

14.   We have each other, haven't we?

SECRECY breeds secrecy even if the need for it is largely gone. So when Michael Grant rang the girl and suggested dinner they did not choose Soho or the red plush of St James's or even the candle-lit and intimate rooms of Chelsea, where occasional actors and artists turn to being restaurateurs. They drove out of the city, in the dusk, warily assessing what new stage their relationship might be reaching.

The basis hadn't changed during the last few months. No sex, no unspoken assumptions on either side. They were still con-spirators, working together as circumstances drove them for busi-ness ends: boss and employee brought to the same level by their need for each other's services.

Neither was certain that everything they did was either like-able or even necessary. Michael rationalised it to himself as an unavoidable evil, the end justifying the means. His dealings with Earl Sanger he placed in the same category, arguing that once the shape of his father's empire was changed, the political neces-sities might also be different. He felt no deeper conviction of this than did Alison Bennett that she might in the future opt out of the role of office sneak.

For her, ambition excused her pettier actions; ambition for position as well as to be needed and admired by men she coveted. Yet even this, she felt, was an explanation to her intellect rather than ultimate truth, if that was not too dignified a name for what her existence lacked. The fact was that, despite her air of pur-pose, a clear objective in her mode of living eluded her. She took the path of least resistance, laying out her gifts of body and brain for others to use at will, waiting for them to suggest how. She enjoyed the exercise of her talents without ever knowing what lay beyond the enjoyment. Her drifting had an apparent end, but was in essence purposeless, and she supposed that many people of intelligence behaved in this fashion. For Michael, the compulsion to justify himself was a kind of sentimentality, similar to his father's. He strove to hide from himself how tough he really was. To seek control – ultimate power – was simply an intuitive way of life with him.

'Is everything okay?' he said as they drove carefully, the low sun in their eyes between the trees.

'I can't say I'm not enjoying it,' she lied, for she was as yet too unused to his company in this social context to be at ease. 'But why, Michael? I was surprised to get your call.'

She had this directness which was both refreshing and presumptuous, like the first night he had gone to her flat and she had signalled her availability so clearly. He glanced at her face, half-masked by huge-lensed glasses, fashionably tinted, but it told him nothing. He had no idea whether she was acting or not, whether she wanted now to use him as he had used her. He was caught in that modern snare which makes us suspicious of everyone and then, out of our desire to believe *something*, lays us open finally to every kind of con-man.

'I felt I had something to celebrate,' he said.

'I know. I'm not clear why you should have chosen me to celebrate with,' she said.

'Who else is there? I don't think my father would want to crack a bottle of champagne with me just now. Except across my head.'

She laughed, and he felt slightly ashamed to be speaking lines like that about Bernard. To this girl. The reason why he had rung her was apparent to him. With Westbrook and Sanger, even with Lord Bender, he had felt almost claustrophobic in the past few days. He had seen too much of them, so that in victory he experienced a feeling of staleness and of disappointment to which he was becoming more and more accustomed. Now he wanted someone to talk to, and not the praetorian guard who had surrounded him while the engagement was fought. He needed an audience, not competing actors. In the aftermath of the announcement that he was the new chief executive, he recalled again how few people he had been in contact with during the last year or so for other than business reasons. He was not the kind of man who could exist on hugging good news to himself. And the girl was a rather riskier audience than usual. It felt good to take a different kind of risk.

'Do you think we ought to be seen together, though?' she said.

'I don't really care. But preferably not.'

318

'Well?'

'Stop worrying, girl. I wanted to do this so I'm doing it. It's unlikely we'll be seen by anyone who matters.'

'But if we were?'

'It has certain advantages.'

'Such as?'

He slid the car through an S-bend, concentrating hard, before he answered. 'I *am* allowed girls, you know.'

'I thought you were trying to give it up.'

'Strictly temporary. If I go on like this much longer, people will be saying I'm queer. That's what Freud has done for us. No man can live without sex – without a public display of sex, anyway – even if he wants to. The talk starts. So I'll have to make the gossip columns soon, escorting some girl or other. You must have seen some of the stuff the papers have written about me in the past. Since I gave up driving, anyway. I'm seen as a sort of cross between a head prefect and a computer. Very grey.'

She knew. She had read everything in the cuttings libraries of two Fleet Street newspapers. Part of her preparation for the job. She knew about the yeh-yeh girls who had followed him around the race circuits of the world, the girls you blew up like inflatable sex queens for the season, then folded up once the photographers had gone home. She also knew of the embryonic engagement with a girl of old Boston stock whilst he was at Harvard. The cuttings had built towards a climax, and suddenly stopped, without explanation. She wanted to push him into telling her about that some time.

'I'm not sure I like being *some girl or other*,' she said.

He was, he acknowledged to himself, out of practice. He used words clumsily. He took one hand from the wheel and squeezed her arm. Again, he was suspicious, yet wanting to believe that she meant only what she said. His indecision over her mood and motives revealed just how little he really knew her.

'I'm sorry. Tonight's different. Is this where we have to make the left turn?'

'Yes.'

'What's it like, this place?'

'For you, a bit down-market. But you said you wanted it anonymous for preference. Don't say I didn't warn you.'

'Fine. Do you go there often?'

'I've been twice.'

'With whom?'

'Men. Who else? You wouldn't know them.' The slight sharpness of her tone warned him off. He was being clumsy again, yet he couldn't get rid of the feeling that he did, in a way, half-own her. He wanted to take it gently, to explore his feelings and hers with a luxurious slowness he had not had time for in some years. If the feel came out right, it would be beautiful to sleep with her. She had leaned back, tilting the seat, ankles crossed and coat open so that the outline of her body was quite tangible beneath the loose silk of the kaftan. Her style combined modesty with a provocation that was almost lascivious. He wished he knew whether that was natural or a further affectation.

'John Howland is worried out of his life,' she said. 'He thinks you don't like him much.'

'I don't.'

'He's all right,' she said. 'Really.'

'Do you want his job?'

'No.'

'You mean that?'

'In all the circumstances it isn't on, is it? Not seriously.'

'You'd be good at it.'

She shrugged. 'If we *are* noticed out together tonight, that's not what people would think I was good at. Private relations rather than public.'

He didn't answer, though he recalled that he had made a similar crack months ago, when they had met in her flat after the party. They drove on, with low-toned rock on the radio killing the need for conversation. She found herself wishing they were in London. They were perfect; the success image the city lived on. Sleek car, rich tang of leather, far sexier than either his after-shave or her Madame Rochas. Two beautiful people in a beautiful box on wheels, driving out to do nothing in particular.

The club was improbable, created in the restored remains of what had sprouted as a roadhouse in the 1930s, all Cunard architecture and white concrete. It had in its early days done as much for the British way of adultery as the motel did for the American, but fell into sad decay after the war, run by ex-officers with puffed red hairy faces and strangely bent moustaches who did not realise the 1930s would never return.

Food, and the affectation for places in the country with special menus and unusual cellars, had saved it. It could also, once the thirties vogue arrived, be regarded as faintly high-camp. In the early 1960s its name was whispered around London and it was, in truth, rather good if ludicrously expensive. Once it was written up in the papers and the trendy mags, its standard slowly de-

320

clined. But it was still tolerable, and the age of its clientele moved sharply downwards when a discotheque was added to its other delights. No one slept there any more, except the owners and the staff, whose sleeping was more or less blameless. A society which has New York or Cannes available, and which smiles at the stealthy pit-a-pat of wife-swapping in Dulwich, has no need of Maidenhead or Reigate or even Brighton. The age of the dirty weekend in the Home Counties was dead for ever.

This Friday evening it was busy. As they walked in no one looked up, though their appearance was good, very good. This crowd, young and relaxed and very well cared for, admired only themselves. At a small alcove table they ordered avocado and steak, dismissing the idea of an aperitif. Alison didn't want the problem of thinking about food. Tonight he would talk. He had come for that and so had she. She was content to let him make the pace in whatever way he wanted. He began to make it once they were left alone.

'I'd almost forgotten what dinners which weren't the sauce on business deals were like,' he said. Corny, she thought.

'I don't believe you, but I know what you mean.'

'It's been a hell of a year.'

'And will be. I don't envy you.'

'Sometimes I don't envy myself. You know how it is.'

'Not really.'

'When you take over an organisation like ours, there aren't many left who love you.'

She raised her eyebrows at him. 'Are you asking me to feel sorry for you?'

He screwed his lips thoughtfully. She was always trying to emphasise her independence: as if she didn't give a damn for his job or his dinner. Although he knew that this quality of faint mockery was part of her attraction to him, it didn't curb his irritation.'

'No,' he said. 'I accept the rules of the game. I've needed to play it hard myself. I can't blame others for playing the same way. I'm just stating the facts, that's all.'

'From what I hear about the nineteenth floor, you're well prepared. Too many bodies round you for anyone to get the knife in.'

'I don't know,' he said. 'You choose the best allies you can. Sometimes they want too rich a share of the spoils. That's when the trouble starts.'

Michael paused. She was caught between wanting to push him

321

further and fearing that a wrong word would dry him up. She compromised, speaking as softly as she knew how.

'What am I supposed to do? Fill in the names?'

'You know them anyway. Earl Sanger and Westbrook, both very ambitious. Lord Bender, whose support I can't do without. Prosser – a bit of an enigma. They can't all sit on the right hand of God.'

She had no need to push him now. He wanted to bounce his thoughts off someone, and she wanted to be bounced at, her motive no stronger in the end than simple curiosity. The hunger to *know* is basic to all kinds, the intelligent as well as the slow-witted.

'Sanger I can satisfy – for the present. Westbrook, I'm not so sure about.'

'Too stratospheric for me. Come down a bit in the hierarchy. Antony Talbot-Brown, for instance.'

'I don't know.' He was becoming more indiscreet. 'I'd never be sure I could trust him.'

'You can't be sure you can trust *me*.'

'You have to believe you can trust *someone*. It's part of the human condition. But if you're wise you don't believe it will go on for ever. After a time everyone feels the need for treachery. That's human too.'

He went on talking business, editing his remarks carefully nevertheless. He was not going to give her the whole picture, not yet. Mostly he spoke about his feelings towards people, rather than the detail of deals. When they reached coffee he felt a tiredness from the strain of talk, but it was mingled with the relief he had sought in their meeting. The old remedy: to tell someone made him feel better. A steady grumble of sound came from beyond the restaurant, a thunder that touched nerves in his stomach, compounded of drums, guitars and baying voices.

'I suppose you know all about that?' he said.

'A little. It's difficult to live in London without knowing just that little.'

'Not my scene. Not for a few years. It went with the car days. Somehow it doesn't go with business.'

'Not even the new-image businessman? Why don't you have a look?'

It was standard discotheque: black as night, equatorial in climate, music loud enough to tear membranes, on this occasion from a live group rather than records. The floor heaved and bubbled stickily, like boiling jam. They found a seat at the bar and sat dumbly, watching. Michael wondered what the hell he was doing there. After five minutes he began to see the point. No one had to talk, and most of the customers looked as if they were glad to be relieved of the burden. They writhed away with smiling faces. The music beat every other thought out of the brain. There was simply no room for anything else except a marshalling of resistance to the monstrous noise. It was, he supposed, one way to relax.

The group, when it stopped, was greeted with a fashionable storm of apathy. Smiles switched off with guitars as the idiot dancers faced the strain of unaided human intercourse again. In the silence she bent and said, 'Do you want to go?' He nodded. In the car he said, 'Thanks. I needed that. Even the last ten minutes.' He wanted to touch her sweet body, immerse himself in her, to excite and to be excited, but he knew that would spoil everything. Managing directors don't make passes in cars; not, at least, until they are no longer thought of as managing directors. So now he wanted only to drive very fast and very well and let the speed sum up the way he felt about the evening. He had drunk two glasses of wine and a single brandy, since his present cast of wariness conquered even his desire to get drunk. He knew exactly what he had done: the risks he had run and the pleasure this had given him. She symbolised the release which had come with winning. He even, at one point of the drive, asked himself whether one got married to symbols.

There was nothing wrong with his driving. He timed every approach to every corner perfectly. Alison enjoyed it too. It was a change after the jarring progress to which young men misusing Sprites and MGs had often subjected her.

They were on the last stretch of the Guildford by-pass, moving more slowly to negotiate a final roundabout, when a small saloon skimmed out from an intersection at which the right of way was clearly theirs. He saw it in time and swung the wheel quickly so that when the impact came, hard on the side where Alison was sitting, pitching her forward towards the windscreen, the two cars drifted along almost parallel, locked together. He had been in crashes before, but the overwhelming noise still astonished him: as if the automobiles had been taken to pieces and dropped on concrete from a great height.

They finished up hard against the kerb. For a moment there was a great silence, then the sound of glass falling, then someone crying. He felt a pain in his leg, but he could move his arms and legs freely. Looking left, he could see nothing through the crazed glass of the door; the laminated windscreen was jigsawed too, with a bulge in it which his experience quickly read. That was where her head had struck it, shattering the inner layer of glass but restrained from bursting through into the open air, and certain death, by the tough central sheet of plastic around which the glass hung. Now her head was lying across the raised transmission tunnel, an arm trailing towards his left thigh, and there were glinting fragments of glass in her hair and sticking to her face. A tiny dark trickle which he thought was blood came from her left ear. He began to see if he could get out of the car.

❊

Colley looked at the men around him and wondered what way through to them there might be. At four to one he felt outnumbered. He didn't count the man at his side, an old union hand in the Brasserton's plant brought over to help him as labour relations assistant a month ago. So much for Prosser's advice, which Colley believed Oldershaw had too readily followed. The man was a neuter: distrusted now by his former mates on the shop floor, baffled as yet by the needs and duties of management.

They were concrete faces, set with suspicion. Though he was going through the motions, Colley expected to make no progress. Not until he had the figures. Why couldn't those damned consultants work faster?

'The fact remains, Mr Colley, that when we came back you were talking about ten per cent redundancy. Now it's fifteen. Some of my members have heard twenty.' The man who spoke was maybe forty-five; squat and black-haired. Not a troublemaker. Colley had known him for twelve years. There were worse around the table.

'We don't know,' he said. 'Not yet.'

'It's time you bloody did,' said another man, the youngest in the room. Oldershaw knew him too. Cocky: preening himself with the power his standing on the shop floor gave him; the kind of shop steward who stuck up two fingers whenever the branch secretary showed up from the local union headquarters. There were times when Colley surprisingly yearned for a bit more Americanisation in industry. He'd heard about the way the union bosses controlled their men on the New York waterfront; do as we tell you or end up with a broken head, or worse.

The young man went on talking: 'How much longer have we got to wait while management sits on its arse?'

Colley wanted to hit the sneering face in front of him. Instead, he said: 'We're going as fast as we can. Putting in a computer isn't like building an Airfix kit.'

'If it's twenty per cent, it's not on,' said the man who had spoken first. 'Not by a bloody mile.'

'I can't tell you what the percentage will be,' said Colley. 'But the terms of the agreement will still hold good. You get your share of the money from manpower savings. It could mean four or five quid a week more in every man's pay packet. More job opportunities for everyone. And better welfare arrangements.'

'It won't mean five quid for those who go, will it?' The voices ran into each other, angrily, until Colley cut through the sound.

'This is all speculation,' he said. 'Just give us a bit more time. Then we can talk sense.'

'We haven't noticed management saving much manpower,' said the young shop steward. 'There's your friend you've got with you. And all them fellas in nice clean suits running about like three blind mice. They seem to be doing all right down in London too.'

'What are you talking about?' said Colley.

'Plenty of time to spare up there. Taking out birds in cars. La dolce bloody vita. Didn't you think we could read, then?'

The newspapers that morning had said the girl was recovering. She had fractured the base of her skull. Colley didn't know which made him angrier: young Grant in London or the clever dick who now curled his lip across the table. He didn't give a toss what the Grants or any of the top brass got up to. But the incompetence of it all sickened him. Michael Grant was supposed to be a great driver, wasn't he? And he couldn't even keep himself out of trouble on the road. Hell.

'That's none of your business,' he said. 'They're bloody human beings, not monks.'

The phone beside him buzzed. He answered it curtly. Then he said: 'Gentlemen, I'll have to adjourn this meeting.'

'What about the big lathe?' said another of the men.

'We'll talk about that when we reconvene.'

'We're not having it, Colley.' It was the young one again, not bothering to call him Mister. 'It's not safe.'

'I'll not discuss it now,' said Colley. 'We'll fix a time this afternoon.'

He found Oldershaw talking to Prosser. Hotfoot from London to sort out the little spot of local bother the natives are having, thought Colley. The two men were speaking quickly, the impatience in Prosser's voice sticking through like a knife. Then they walked out on to the gallery which surrounded the main workshop. Their feet rang on the metal grating. Below them, the lines of lathes whined and screamed. In the middle of the floor, curiously detached, a man sat on a stool beside a larger lathe. His machine stood idle.

'It's the second day he's been like that. Yesterday he sat for five hours. Then he went home,' said Oldershaw.

'What action did you take?'

'Colley's talked to him. So have I. He just says he can't do it.'

'You haven't talked hard enough.'

Oldershaw would not have admitted this, but for himself it was true. Since the accident to Hannah he had increasingly side-stepped confrontations in the plant, pushing the burden on to Colley. Hannah had lost his hand. Oldershaw's fault – or so Oldershaw convinced himself. He wanted no more tragedies, believing that his handling of problems at the top, combined with Colley's negotiations at shop-floor level, could achieve his expansive dreams for the plant. He had withdrawn from contact with his men, they believing he no longer cared about them. It was a large part of what was now going wrong with Brasserton's.

'Talk doesn't seem much use,' he said.

'Bloody ridiculous,' said Prosser. 'I've seen the consultants' report. That machine can run at twice the speed you've been making. They've proved it.'

'I'm not denying it,' said Oldershaw. Colley couldn't either. They'd done another test run the week before, the swarf rattling madly against the protective metal shield which kept this dangerous spray of hot metal chips from peppering passers-by. They pushed the lathe so hard that the water cooling the cutting tool had gushed up steam like a miniature volcano. One by one the other lathes had stopped, the men gathering in groups to watch. Then, slowly, they had gone back to work, saying nothing. The machine could run all right, and safely. But who could they get to run it?

'That man,' said Prosser. 'He took part in the test?'

'He was the operator,' said Oldershaw.

'Then why won't he work it now?'

'He's been got at over the weekend,' said Colley. 'No one's talking to him. He acts like he's paralysed or something.'

'Try someone else,' said Prosser.

'We've tried,' said Oldershaw. 'No one will work it.'

'You've got to try again,' said Prosser. 'Unless that machine runs fast, and the others follow it, you'll never clear the decks of your back-orders in time. It's a test case, that lathe. You've said so yourself. And if the American deal gets held up, God help us all.'

It wasn't as bad as that. Not yet. Prosser knew it, and so did Oldershaw. But Prosser badly needed a victory to take back to Prospect House. The redistribution of power on the board was still awaited, delayed further by Michael Grant's crash. Each day he weighed the odds. There was still time to shift them.

That morning his wife had spoken about it again: *Why don't you think they'll lift you? If you can't beat Westbrook – well....* Prosser had unexpectedly found himself wanting the niche that Michael Grant had stepped out of. Deputy managing director, up there along with Armfield. He wanted it to shut up Frances and, he suspected, for his own satisfaction too. He had to be a bringer of good news when he caught the train back.

'I'll talk to him,' he said suddenly.

Oldershaw flushed angrily. 'What do you think *you* can do?' He didn't care if Prosser was a main board director. He wasn't taking interference on his shop floor, not from anyone.

'Perhaps I can do more than you think,' said Prosser.

'That's bloody daft,' said Oldershaw, and Colley shifted his feet, uncomfortable but silently cheering.

'I've got the mandate,' said Prosser quietly. He turned to face Oldershaw. 'And if you get in my way I'll break you, Oldershaw. Sure as God I will.'

Oldershaw turned on his heel and went towards his office. The strains of the past month were beginning to tell. They hadn't had a day without trouble. But he had driven ahead, grimly, hoping his luck would hold.

Prosser followed him into the room. Oldershaw controlled his temper with an effort. He knew what he stood to lose, and the knowledge weakened him. 'All right,' he said, 'we'll see him together.'

'I don't mind that,' said Prosser.

'What are you going to say?'

'Persuade him first. Then play it by ear. Offer him more money. Push him. Bribe him. I don't care. Only get him moving.'

'The shop stewards won't like it,' said Colley.

'Then they'll have to lump it. Have you lost control of them too?'

Too bloody easy for you, thought Colley. You don't have to get down in the dirt and the muck and talk to them. Prosser's suit was dark, clean and half a size too large; his homburg sat on the table.

You've been away from it too long, friend. You've forgotten, haven't you?'

'I'm still in control,' Colley said quietly. 'But if we don't have a few more answers soon, there'll be real trouble.'

'Let's see him then,' said Prosser. 'Now.'

'If he works that machine, the rest of them will give him hell,' said Oldershaw. 'You know that, don't you?'

'You've got to prove it can be done,' said Prosser. 'Then they'll fall into line. I've seen it all before.'

'And to do it you'll crucify that man?'

'If necessary, yes,' said Prosser. 'When will these people understand that they only make money if *we* do? They've got to learn the world doesn't owe us a living.'

❋

For three days after the announcement that Michael Grant was to be the new managing director Armfield turned over the thought of resignation or early retirement in his mind. Financially there was no problem; he had carefully stacked away the takings from the good years with Bernard Grant, and was still stacking. Mentally he was not so sure. In the end it was the prospect of the endless dreary days with his wife, cooped up with her, listening to her trivialities, which decided him against the big gesture. At sixty-five he might be ready to face it, but not so prematurely.

Thereafter his mind moved in other directions. In truth it was not so much his disappointment that Michael had managed to manoeuvre into the top job which rankled. Armfield was, at times, blindingly honest with himself and he had admitted for years that the Chairman's son must be the favourite, even more so when Michael began that self-willed, determined training in business, with years at Harvard and the increasingly prestigious European business schools.

Armfield was more undermined by the thought that one of the newer men would now ascend to equal standing with himself. It must be either Westbrook or Prosser; and both were unacceptable to him. It would have been so much more desirable for Bernard to bow out altogether. Michael as Chairman, himself as chief executive, he could have lived with, even revelled in.

The suddenness of all that had happened unnerved him. Bernard gave virtually no warning of his intention to hand over to Michael. The Chairman was evasive about his reasons and unwilling any further to discuss the plans they had laid for group investment. Lord Bender, whom Armfield had been to see, was serenely aligned with Michael, frigidly refusing any invitation to gossip. Even the news of trouble at Brasserton's gave Armfield no joy. It was too late to be used as a realistic weapon to stop Michael's ambition. Looking at the progress of their profit-and-loss sheets, Armfield was in fact concerned lest the future of the whole deal with Corsino should be jeopardised. Failure there would involve them all in the eyes of the outside world, and Armfield wanted no part of patent failure, especially since he rated the chances of a palace revolution against the new chief executive as thin indeed. Any new directors would be Michael's men, for what is the purpose of such incomers except to be friendly to the chief executive and maintain him securely in his seat?

Thus, slowly, he found himself compelled to support the new regime, a gesture made less unpalatable by what he regarded as Bernard Grant's turning away from him. His old colleague was not the same, nor could their relationship remain unchanged. As Grant seemed to be accepting the victory of his son like the realist he was, so he grew less concerned with old allies. Armfield felt very disorientated as he walked into Michael's office in late May.

'How's the leg?' he asked.

'A bit stiff. But it's better.'

'And Miss Bennett?'

'The news is good. No complications with the fracture. Her face may be marked. They expect her to be out of hospital inside three weeks.'

Michael gazed at him steadily. Not a flicker, Armfield noticed, to betray his feelings. Nothing had underscored Armfield's present attitudes more than the aftermath of the crash. He was suspicious of the relationship Michael had with the girl. Was it sex, an arrangement which Armfield would call an affaire, serious or casual? Or had they been plotting together for months to change the future of the Prospero Group?

He had, in the end, no answer – but he did not go on the rampage to either Bernard Grant or Lord Bender, despite his distaste. He accepted what had happened, carefully watching the shares to see if the market reacted, damping down gossip within Prospect House wherever he detected its beginnings, playing along with the official line that Michael and the girl had been heavily engaged on a batch of press releases about organisation deals. There were slight innuendos in the papers, nothing worse. She was a company employee, after all. She had every right to be working with Michael.

'I'm sorry about her face,' said Armfield. 'I expect she's fixed up, but if you need someone I do know an excellent plastic surgeon. Will you prosecute the other driver?'

'Yes,' said Michael. Abruptly he picked up a folder, plainly wishing to change the subject. 'Harold, I've come to a decision. I'd like you to continue as my deputy.'

Armfield felt his anger rise sharply. Michael said it as if it was a favour. But Michael's next words were of a different kind.

'And I don't intend to appoint another. It makes our organisation structure too complicated. There's no need for it. You'll have complete authority as number two to me.'

Armfield choked back a smile. Winning was immensely pleasurable to him, even though he could not yet see why Michael should act in this way. He tried to be calm as he spoke.

'If that's what you believe is best.'

'You know more about this organisation than the rest of them put together. I shall need every bit of help you can give me.'

'Thank you,' said Armfield, who was in no mind to refute either statement. 'You know you'll have my support.'

Now he allowed himself to smile briefly, and Michael understood him. Flattery, a concession, and the inevitability of events had won over Armfield. It was as simple as that. But their new alliance was fragile. Armfield would always be watchful, wary, ready to shift his ground again if the opportunity presented itself. In business you win no wars, only battles; and there is always another one on the horizon.

'Have you any plans for the board?' asked Armfield.

'Earl will have to join us, Harold. Else we'll lose him. I don't think we want that to happen at this moment.'

They talked on for perhaps fifteen minutes. As he rose to leave, Armfield mentioned that he would be making some changes in his own office.

'Talbot-Brown,' he said. 'He's been rather a disappointment. I wondered whether I might go into the market for someone else.'

Michael tried not to show his concern. 'I leave that up to you, naturally,' he said. 'But I don't think we want to make too many changes, not when the organisation's a bit unsettled. I thought he was rather good.'

Armfield looked curiously at him. 'I didn't realise you knew his work. He made a hash of a couple of jobs I gave him. Still, I don't mind waiting a bit if that's what you want.'

'Perhaps it would be best. But he's *your* man.'

As he sat waiting for Westbrook to arrive, Michael pondered the dangers which the Talbot-Brown situation now presented. Until the Lovelace deal was through he would have to protect Talbot-Brown. It was a problem he would sooner have been without.

Westbrook took the news from Michael badly. His plump face was spotted with sweat as he sat in the warm room, the sun streaming in. He had not been sleeping well since Diana left. Even he thought it ironic. A woman of dubious sexuality for a wife, yet he had grown so used to her familiar form beside him down the years that he missed it. There were other problems. The children would be home for the summer in six weeks' time and he had no idea what he, or his wife, should say to them. He found the strain of existing without the customary scaffolding which shored up his life intense. His face looked collapsed when he spoke back to Michael.

'I expected you to be telling me something different,' he said. 'I would have thought my work over the past six months deserved rather better.'

'I'm sorry if you're disappointed,' said Michael.

'Disappointed!' Westbrook's disgust exploded. 'You've let me down, Michael. What do you expect me to do? Congratulate myself?'

'I've had to think of the group. Harold would have fought you to be the *more* important deputy. And you'd have fought back. You know it and so do I. I can't take the risk. There's been too much in-fighting already. We should all take a rest; otherwise the market may start getting worried about us.'

'So now you'll just let the fight go on at a lower level. Earl and Barry and me. I admire your tactics.' Westbrook spoke with ironic resignation.

Michael thought, as he usually did, that Westbrook was smart. Perceptive, but unstable. He had decided against letting Westbrook fill his empty chair for precisely the reason he had stated. The man lacked control under pressure, and that would almost inevitably have led to damaging explosions in direct confrontation with Armfield. But it had also occurred to him that some healthy competition among the other directors would be no bad thing. He wanted to keep them striving, with a prize to compete for.

'Grow up, Lionel,' he said. 'You know this is the right way.'

'I notice that Earl gets his pay-off.'

'You too. But money-wise, not in position.'

'The Chancellor will be delighted,' said Westbrook. 'But I still

331

don't understand. Why have you treated me like this?' His mind grabbed at one of the many thoughts jostling within it. 'Because of Hardy?'

'It wasn't very clever to sit on his head for so long that in the end he wanted to leave.'

'It happens. People change jobs.'

'For God's sake, Lionel. It isn't Hardy. I've told you my reasons.'

'It wasn't my fault he left.'

'It doesn't matter now, anyway. Hardy isn't leaving.'

Westbrook's jaw slumped a fraction, like a parody of a man suddenly surprised. 'What does that mean?'

'He isn't leaving. I've persuaded him to stay.'

'*You've* persuaded him?' Westbrook slid into the trap which Michael had quite accidentally laid. He was so eager to point out the unwisdom of the move that he scarcely bothered how his words might reflect on his earlier judgements of Hardy. 'I know I've been able to prove nothing, but he must still be under suspicion of retailing confidential information to outside people – including QFN.'

Michael shrugged. 'The idea occurred to other people too. Earl, for instance.'

'Well?'

'If it's true – and I appreciate it can't be proved – all the more reason to keep Hardy here. He knows a damn sight too much to let him go off to Barstow. I made it quite clear to him we regard him as suspect. He seemed to find that amusing.'

'He could go on leaking our business.'

Michael shook his head. 'I don't think so. Not now he knows *we* know.'

'How have you persuaded him to stay?'

'Not especially clever. I simply upped the ante. More money – and a couple of directorships in the subsidiaries. Oh, and he'll be forming a special projects department. Responsible to Earl.'

An expression which was almost a smile flickered on Westbrook's face. He felt too weary to dispute any more. He had lost too many points to recover the game now, and he would only make things worse by further argument.

'Pretty good,' he said. 'I hope it works out. For all our sakes.'

'I think it will,' said Michael. 'I'm learning that nothing's ever easy. Not even when you're winning. There'll be something for you, Lionel. Don't worry.'

'I wouldn't bet on that,' said Westbrook. 'But don't think I'm feeling sorry for myself. The one I'm sorry for, if anything, is Giles Lymington. It's ironic that Earl is taking his place.'

'Yes,' said Michael. He didn't lower his eyes, but looked straight ahead, switching them fractionally from direct confrontation with Westbrook's gaze. 'None of us knows what responsibility we bear for that. We couldn't have foreseen it, that's all. So we'll just have to live with it. My first responsibility now is to make sure this business survives.'

＊

She was sitting up when he walked into her room at the hospital and her face, indeed her whole head, was a mess. He laid the flowers he was carrying across the foot of the bed. He had tried to rehearse what he would say en route in the Silver Shadow, chauffeur-driven, but now he had arrived, nothing would come together for him.

'I know,' she said. 'Like something out of the Chamber of Horrors at Madame Tussaud's. But I'm all right, really.' Her voice was quiet, husky with the effort of trying to sound relaxed, and she did not move her lips much. She had thin red lines all over her face, some of them intersecting, mostly around the orbital rim of her right eye. In one gash, across the bridge of her swollen nose, he could see the fine stitching.

'You poor dear girl,' he said. 'I'd say I'm sorry except it seems so feeble.'

'I'm all *right*. They used the very *best* horsehair on my face. Only thirty-five stitches, each one separately and lovingly done. I was lucky.'

They had cut hunks out of her hair to get at the scalp lacerations, and the patches of thin gauze covered with new skin glistened beneath the electric light over the bed. There were small crusts of dried blood still visible at the edges of the wounds. She looked like one of those French girls suspected of sleeping around with the Wehrmacht after the wives of the Resistance had finished with her on Liberation Day.

'How do you feel?' he said.

'Not bad. They've had me up. They won't allow me to think I'm an invalid.'

'My God.'

A small laugh escaped through the tight lips. 'Don't look so miserable. It wasn't your fault.'

'I asked you out. It was a piece of self-indulgence on my part. Not one of my best ideas.'

333

She eased herself against the pillows, turning her blue-green eyes full at him. 'I don't know. I was getting tired of all that hole-in-corner stuff. It's a relief we don't have to do it any more.'

'We won't be doing *anything* for some time,' he said. 'First we must get you better.'

'*Please*, Michael. Don't treat me like a little girl who has to be humoured. I know exactly what the score is. They've told me. My face won't be marked. Maybe a small scar from one cut, and I expect plastic surgery will do wonders if it matters. The skull fracture will be all right. When my hair gets back to normal you won't know it happened.'

Once more he marvelled at her cool. Reciting all this with the passionlessness of a weather forecast. The verdict on her face which he had been given was considerably less optimistic. It took some guts, he thought, even to face up to letting him see her like this; some guts or some indifference.

'Do you remember much?' he asked.

'No. They tell me it was forty-eight hours before I said anything that made sense. Amnesia. The usual thing with concussion. By that stage they'd done all this.' She waved a hand slowly at her head. 'They call the stuff they've brushed on my nut Nobecutane. It protects the wounds when I rub my head on the pillow. Smells like what my mother used to paint her nails with.'

'Perhaps you'd like to write a medical column for the house magazine,' he said, beginning to answer her mood.

'Good,' said Alison. 'And how have you been getting on back at the ranch? I gather most people have suspected the worst about us. And who can blame them?'

'My father asked me if you were my mistress. Lord Bender rang to say that now he understood a lot more. The rest of them keep inquiring about my bloody leg.'

'Your leg? What's wrong?'

'Badly bruised, that's all.'

'Poor Michael.' There was that familiar mocking tone in her voice again.

'I'll get by. Especially if people forget it. They ask about my leg, but usually they don't mention you. It's strange. Everyone's determined to pretend you don't exist.'

'That's understandable. All this must be rather inconvenient for the organisation.' The attempt at irony was deliberately gentle.

He shrugged. 'We'll survive it, I don't doubt. People will find something else to gossip about.'

334

'Seriously – has it made things difficult for you?'

His finger was tracing lines around the pattern on the counter-pane, and for a few moments he did not speak. He wanted to say a great deal to her, yet knew how unfair it would be to lay his problems on her mind, even to stay much longer. The nurse had said ten minutes. 'Not really, Alison. There are a few jokes going round the City. The sort they'd clip out and keep in their wallets if they could. But Prospect House is all right. Not that I'd say it was my best time just now. That's nothing to do with you, though.'

'Oh?'

'All hell's let loose in most directions at once. I won't bore you with the details.'

'I wouldn't be bored.'

'Not for your ears. On medical advice. But for a start there's been another stoppage at Brasserton's. I sent Barry Prosser to push them a bit. He got himself into a dispute on the shop floor. And out they came. Bill Oldershaw, the boss up there – you know? – he's been burning up the wires over it. He's also been on to my father.' Michael looked at his watch. 'Look, I'll have to go. I'm over my time already.' He also realised that it *did* sound boring to be talking shop in this particular room.

He took her hand and caressed it. 'It'll be great when you're better.'

'I doubt you'll have much time for me,' she said. 'But maybe you can give me a reference for a job.'

'What does that mean?'

'I'm not coming back. How can I?'

Michael let out his breath slowly, screwing his lips. He hadn't considered that particular piece of the future. Too many problems pressing in on him short-term, hour by hour, at present. 'Let's cross that bridge when we come to it. I don't see why you shouldn't.'

'I'm serious. John Howland was here earlier today. He was sweet. Like a maiden aunt visiting her favourite erring niece. Determined to cheer me up, but with a lot of tacit disapproval. Is he queer, that man?'

'Neuter, I suspect.'

'Don't be nasty, Michael. He was dying to know what I'd been doing out with you. I had to let him assume it was simple lust. But God knows what he really thinks. I couldn't work with him again. And I gather he's staying.'

'He told you that?'

'He said you'd talked with him.'

Michael had seen Howland the day before. The PRO, rolling a watch-chain endlessly between his fingers as they talked, had asked for reassurances about his position now that Bernard Grant was moving out. In the circumstances, Michael had had no alternative but to satisfy him. Howland remaining in office was the outward and visible sign that his dealings with Alison had been either sexual, which in one way was all right, or strictly business with her departmental chief's approval. There was another reason why Howland had to stay, and that he would be discussing with his father later in the evening.

'Yes,' he said. 'I've renewed his contract. You see how you influence me?'

'Not really,' she said. 'I can think of several reasons why he's bullet-proof just now. You need to use him, Michael. You know how to use people.'

He just stood looking at her, pulling together the words of protest.

She said: 'I'm not complaining. Just being realistic. We use everyone, even those people we like – maybe *more* those we like. One day you'll tell me I'm using you. And I probably will be.'

She slid down the bed, closing her eyes. The door opened and there was the nurse. 'I'm just leaving,' he said. The nurse disappeared, and he turned again to Alison. 'Why do you make it so difficult?' he asked. 'Now everyone knows, maybe we can have one of those nice normal relationships. You know. Male and female.'

'I'd like that,' she said. 'But don't make any rash promises. Thanks for coming, anyway.'

*

He had not been in his father's house in the evening for a long time. John, the manservant, gravely inquired after his health, then led the way past the Manets and Lautrecs to the library where Bernard Grant sat in a leather chair sipping sherry. When the door was shut, Grant put down his glass and poured one for his son. Michael waited for Bernard to speak. He could always tell when his father had something surprising to say. The old man stretched the silences before he spoke on these occasions, savouring the drama to come.

'I hope you won't expect me to hold your hand every time,' he said.

'Please, father. No play-acting. What's wrong?'

'Almost everything.'

336

'We've got our problems. I know that. We always have them. But I'm confident we have the answers.'

Bernard Grant roared with laughter. 'You sound like an annual report, Michael. All right, I won't be dramatic. By the way, how was the girl?'

'Fine. Getting better.'

'Good. Are you going to marry her?'

'I might. Do you want me to?'

Grant smiled. 'A trick question, boy. Whichever way I answer, I expect you'd take the contrary course. Make up your own mind. I'm rather enjoying the freedom of not trying to push you into agreeing with me.'

'Tell me what's on your mind.'

Grant said: 'Brasserton's is on my mind, as you so crudely put it.'

'We'll get that sorted. Barry Prosser has worked out a bonus scheme for extra output if they produce more by running the machines faster.'

'Not that,' said Grant. 'Our friend Ed Corsino has been on the telephone.'

'*Our* friend?'

'Mr Corsino and I understand each other very well,' said Grant. 'He was trying to get you, but you were out. So he came through to me instead.'

'You scarcely know him.'

'True. But I know enough. We had a short meeting the night the contract was signed in New York. Just the two of us. Do you think I'd let a chance like that slip by? Or that Corsino would not make sure his alliances are flexible? I was still chief executive then. I remain Chairman even now. Corsino knew he might need me. That was why he let me know you were flying to New York in the first place.'

There was silence. Overhead Michael could hear the creak of footsteps. It was an old house that yielded up secrets of movement easily. His father was smiling softly.

'Don't take it badly, Michael. You would have done the same. And you must see it's in the interests of the organisation that I acted as I did. Don't assume that all the cleverness and the foresight are on your side alone. *Were* on your side, I should have said. You and I are on the same side now, aren't we?'

'All right, father.' Michael knew he had no point to dispute. 'What did Corsino say?'

'There are troubles over Kerridge. Corsino wants to give him his share of the contract, but it means that Kerridge has to extend his interests to fulfil it. He needs to take over a quite smallish company in specialist engineering, a field where he is already strong. The Department of Justice in Washington have put the block on that. They can turn nasty these days where conglomerate organisations are concerned.'

'I know. The anti-trust laws.'

'Precisely. I've read that General Motors can't buy a shoe-shine stand today without Washington taking a look at it.'

'Sure.'

'Well, there it is. What do you propose to do about it?'

'I must talk to Corsino. It's his problem.'

Bernard Grant slowly put down his glass and then shook his head. 'No, Michael. If Kerridge loses interest, he could take the pressure off Gelson. That leaves Corsino vulnerable. And it places our order in doubt. In this situation we've got to help Corsino in order to help ourselves.'

Michael wondered if there was any circumstance surrounding the deal with Corsino which his father did *not* know. Corsino must have told Bernard everything. But he still didn't see the logic of what Bernard was saying.

'Our order's safe. The contract is signed and the down-payment guaranteed. If Ed Corsino reneges, we'd sue.'

His father shrugged. 'We could. But it would take time. Meanwhile what would you do with Brasserton's? Computerised, re-organised, everything. All set up and ready to go – but no orders. Down-payment or not, Brasserton's still needs to have *work*. Anyway, do we want to get a name as a group which goes round engaging in litigation against other corporations? It won't exactly encourage people to want to do business with us, especially Americans. No, it's easier to get Corsino off the hook.'

'You've thought of something. I know you too well, father. You're lecturing me, aren't you?'

'I have an approach to the problem, yes. First, we've got to get our diplomatic people in Washington to have a quiet word with the State Department. Point out that a British company may suffer badly if the whole deal doesn't go through.'

'It's a long shot.'

'Maybe. But it could work. The State Department are always worrying about the vulnerability of American firms in Europe. Kerridge himself has lots of interests over here. As I remember, it was one of the points at issue when Sanger had his tête-à-tête with Kerridge.'

Michael said nothing. His father really did know it all.

'So,' Bernard Grant went on, 'the State Department must tactfully suggest to the Department of Justice that if they bitch up deals involving British firms, we might do the same to their own people.'

Michael, his mind working quickly now that the way ahead looked promising, said: 'I leave it to you to deal with your contacts in the Foreign Office. Earl can speak with the State Department people direct. He has friends there. It will all help. There's one snag. They'll still want to know why it *has* to be Kerridge that Ed Corsino gives the contract to.'

'We can dream up a reason for that. Maybe his tender was the lowest. It's not difficult.'

The light in the room was fading, but Michael could see that his father looked pleased. The irony, he thought, was full-flavoured. For years he had fought Bernard. Finally he had won, but it was working out differently from what he had expected. Now that the chores that went with being chief executive were off his back, Bernard was finding more time for the finesse of conspiracy. On the evidence of the Corsino deal, his father was quite willing to work with him, to form an alliance – at a price. Bernard's approach thus far reeked of the old man's desire to establish a teacher–pupil relationship with his son, and Michael liked that very little. Still, he was surprised to find how easy the last ten minutes had been. They had sat in the dusk together, fellow-planners and plotters, quite naturally. They might have been doing it all their lives.

The telephone rang. Bernard Grant lifted it. Michael gathered at once it was Lord Bender. His father spoke little, mostly in monosyllables or short cryptic sentences, his face serious. When he finally put down the receiver, he switched on the light beside his chair. Michael waited for him to speak, noticing yet again that even when Bernard had something on his mind his face remained smoothly cherubic, unlined as a child's, except for the small wrinkles at the corner of the eyes.

'Benjamin's grapevine tells him we may expect trouble over our flirtation with Burgham. You know about that?'

'Enough,' said Michael.

'What you don't know, I'd better fill you in on.'

'What trouble?'

'The Take-Over Panel. They've been told by someone we were trying to fix the market.'

'*You* were trying to.'

'Of course, Michael. But as managing director you'll be under scrutiny now as much as I. This is a problem we'll have to tackle together.'

Michael knew he was right. 'How safe are we if they start digging?'

'Usually they're not much interested in this kind of allegation. The evidence is too tenuous. And what's illegal in anyone – including me – hazarding a public guess that a company is shaky? Especially if it's true?'

'There's not much danger then.'

'I'm not sure. Our reputation could be damaged. It depends partly on who's been talking to them. Howland was involved. I can't believe it's him.'

'I gave him a new service contract today,' said Michael. 'It was one of the things I wanted to talk over with you.'

Bernard Grant sat up and slapped the side of his chair. 'Not bad, boy. Not bad. I thought you might have eased him out.'

'We need him, don't we?' Michael said simply. 'The Burgham thing isn't the only reason either. I don't much care for him, but I decided we couldn't have him feeling disgruntled. I was generous. Five thousand a year – and fringe benefits. Was that enough?'

'I think so,' said Grant. 'Like most PR men he has his price and his principles are elastic. He has stamina too. Not much guts, but stamina, yes. He doesn't like doing things which are obviously dishonest though, did you know that? So I have to find plausible reasons for asking him to behave in certain ways. He certainly thought that spreading a tale or two about Burgham was fair enough. It was a bad, weak company. Still is. But I wouldn't relish him having to answer too many questions about it. He's more naïve than he imagines.'

'He'll put two and two together, father. He's bound to. If he didn't realise what you were up to at the time, he'll see it clear as daylight once people start asking questions.'

'I suppose so,' said Grant. 'But we can leave that until tomorrow. It was a good move to keep him happy. Well done.'

The inflection of the voice carried the same assumption as it had earlier. 'You might do something for me,' said Michael. 'Harold Armfield was talking about getting rid of Talbot-Brown. I don't think that would be wise.'

'Why?'

'Many reasons. The one you can give to Harold is that the organisation needs time to settle down after all that's happened

340

– especially with other squalls blowing up. Don't rock the boat any more. You know.'

Grant smiled a suspicious smile. 'You mean you won't tell me the real reason?'

'It's too involved.'

Both men were suddenly intent on their shoes. Michael realised quite clearly that Bernard's question marked a potential watershed in their relationship, not for its own importance, but because of the principle involved. If ever there was to be peace between them, his father would need to leave an area of privacy for him, scenes of action where he could make his own decisions and have them accepted without explanation.

'Would you like to stay for dinner?' asked Grant.

Michael accepted the change of subject. Still he could not be sure his father had conceded.

'Thanks, but no. I've another date.'

'All right. I'd like it some time.' No hostility, no sarcasm in the statement; only, perhaps, a faint aura of warmth and pleading. Michael relaxed enough to smile.

'Of course,' he said. 'It's been a long time.'

'I'll do what I can over Talbot-Brown. And your board dispositions – good, very good.'

'So you said at the time.'

'But I mean it. I want you to know that. Harold will serve you well if you lead him right.'

'Westbrook may not stay.'

'He'll stay. He'll scream a bit, but he's too insecure to leap into the dark just now. He has wife trouble, I hear. Don't worry about Westbrook. Sanger's the man you'll have to control.'

'I know that. Sometimes you have to ride a tiger. I'll watch it.'

'I'll be watching too,' said Grant. 'After all, I have the time.'

Michael drained his glass. 'I wanted to talk about Lovelace's. But that can wait until tomorrow too. I thought of putting Hardy on the new board. He did most of the preliminary research.'

'Think about it some more. Don't bribe that young man *too* generously. You'll find that with bribes the price gets higher and higher. Leave yourself room for manoeuvre later.'

'I had to act, father. Barstow would be laughing his head off now if I hadn't.'

'I'd like to wring Barstow's neck. And Hardy's. He can still betray us, you realise that?'

'It's a risk. But what he knows will soon be out of date.

341

I'll make very sure in future that he works only on projects which aren't of interest to Barstow. That we can control.'

'I leave it to you,' said Grant. 'I agree with the principles of what you've done. Just make sure it works out.'

Michael, rising, smiled uneasily. 'I'm not certain, but that sounds like a threat.'

'It isn't, Michael. From now on you'll have to guard my back as well as your own, and vice versa. All of them will be watching and waiting. Even Benjamin – especially Benjamin. He's pushed you, and now he'll expect results. When you disturb the balance of power, the aftermath is always tricky. Those who've won a prize tend to get greedy, asking when the next hand-out is coming.'

He took Michael's arm and led him towards the library door. 'I expect we'll manage,' he said, and at that moment Michael was quite sure what the future would be. It had been a delusion to believe that his father could ever become one of those chairmen who take their fees and make the right noises and in reality control nothing. By ousting Bernard he had not broken clear at all. Instead, events were pushing the two of them more closely together, making them interdependent, requiring each other's support and loyalty. And at this moment he was surprised to find that he was not deterred by the prospect of their alliance at all. The past was over, the dead must look after themselves. So long as they were equals, Michael was prepared to play, and he appreciated the interest which they had in common: survival. That would have to be enough.

In the hall, his father paused before a Manet: vivid, bursting with life, an object of controversy a century earlier. 'Some men collect for status, some as an investment. For myself, these pictures have formed a kind of mirror of what I wished I might have been.'

Michael said nothing. He was temporarily puzzled, but sensed that in a minute or two he would understand everything. 'People laugh at the way I have involved myself with actors and artists and musicians. I have not done so through a desire to be fashionable. On the contrary, I have needed their company to demonstrate continually to myself that I was of their number. I believe that to build as I have done is an act of creation too. Yet I can never be sure. I think sometimes I would rather have been a painter.'

He turned and stood face to face with his son. 'Do you wonder why I am speaking like this?'

342

'No. I think I understand.'

'I have perhaps ten years left to sound out the truth further. To prove that my kind of creativity is not simply a scabrous itch for power. If you force me to retire, I shall simply cease to exist. And I shall fight you to the death before I allow it to happen. You may share the lead with me, but don't imagine I shall ever step off the stage.'

It was a plea rather than a threat. Michael was not surprised to find that he said only: 'Of course.'

'Do you know,' his father went on, 'Bernard Shaw once said that there are two tragedies in life. One is not to get your heart's desire. The other is to get it. I believe I am just beginning to understand what he meant.'

They had reached the front door, and Grant paused before he spoke again. 'About that girl, I don't *mind* you marrying her, if that's of any importance to you.'

Michael laughed. 'It's no less or more important than it always would have been. Thanks anyway.'

'Her father was in the Foreign Service. But you'd know that.'

'Yes,' Michael lied. 'I'm glad to see you've done your home-work.'

'You'd expect that, wouldn't you?'

'In the circumstances, yes.' And even now he could not avoid the twist he gave the words. 'Apart from me, there's Prospero to be considered. As a prospective fiancé I'm an asset. As a philanderer I'd be a drag. Don't worry, father. I know the rules.'

*

David tried to take the changes at Prospect House philosophically, but there were times in every day when he sat for five minutes or so, leaving the papers in front of him untouched, suffused with a kind of resentful uncertainty. The news of Hardy's reappointment, in a more senior position, disturbed him most. He made a short unconvincing telephone call to Hardy's home, pushing congratulations and the usual phrases through his teeth. Hardy, cheerful, said he was off to America with Earl Sanger for a few days. David concluded, more firmly than ever, that tied to Westbrook he was on to a loser.

Westbrook, morose and always changing decisions, was in poor form; yet though his director's vacillations irritated him, David saw it would be in his own interests to help the man through this bad patch. Indifferent work could only rebound on the whole of Westbrook's entourage.

He felt, moreover, a sympathy with Westbrook which had never been there in the old days. Success could not be shared: his experience with Hardy had taught him that. It was private to the people who found it, and those around them were merely envious spectators of the rites attending it. Failure, like Westbrook's, had to be participated in. There was a magnetic aura about it, sucking in the bystanders, striking at their common fears.

Failure also had its symbols. For Westbrook, it was a change of office. The suite he moved into, taking David and some others with him, was as handsome as that which he left. The desks were just as good, the directorial broadloom unchanged. It was the fact of moving which was a defeat. Sanger and the department which Hardy was forming, to explore new ventures for the organisation, needed more space. And Sanger was the one who stayed put. In time, workmen would come in to change the shape and sheen of the offices which Westbrook had left so that they became part of Sanger's empire, reflecting his taste and needs in cold furniture and walls naked of everything but charts. It would seem as if Westbrook had never sat there.

The place was full of rumour. One afternoon a girl came round collecting for a farewell present for Arnold Sims, chief accountant, who had once been Armfield's creature. That was one speculation confirmed, David noted.

Other reports were less down-beat. Westbrook observed on 3 June, with a gloom which normally would not have been there, that the organisation's profits were heading for a ten per cent increase on budget in the first half-year. Someone said Bernard Grant was definitely going to get a life peerage in the Birthday Honours for service to the Arts. One grey Thursday morning the announcement of Michael Grant's forthcoming marriage to Alison Bennett appeared formally in both *The Times* and the *Daily Telegraph* and less formally in the news pages of all the papers. They had plenty of good raw material, for it coincided with an announcement of the Prospero Group's agreed purchase of Lovelace's. Michael Grant was quoted as saying that he did not intend to take up motor-racing again, but several of the columnists inferred they did not believe him.

The next day he called David to his office. After they had talked for half an hour, David came back to his desk, thought about things for ten minutes, and went in to see Westbrook who looked nervously cheerful, oddly so.

'Yes,' said Westbrook, 'I knew about it. I didn't want to influence you.'

344

'It was unexpected, I must say. I don't know what answer to give yet.'

'You must take it, David. As principal assistant to the managing director you'll be close to every decision that matters in this organisation. Is that what you *want* me to say?'

'The department's got a hell of a lot on. It wouldn't be the best of times to leave.'

Westbrook looked up wearily. 'Your loyalty is touching, dear boy. But don't be dishonest with yourself, or with me. We all find situations like this confusing. There are so many standards by which you think you should be acting. Loyalty to company, if that matters to you. Loyalty to colleagues. Loyalty to self or family. I have always had a very simple rule when faced with sets of conflicting arguments. In the end I ask what's best for me. If you ask that now, what answer do you get?'

David shifted in his chair, slightly unnerved by Westbrook's directness. 'It sounds like a very different job from the one I've been doing.'

'You can't live in an ivory tower, working out things on paper all your life. Sometime you've got to go and get your feet in the mud of the marketplace.'

'Supergear wasn't exactly hygienic,' he said.

'Not muddy enough. If you want a mentor, then look where it's got Hardy.'

Westbrook didn't even sound bitter. He was simply handing out facts.

'I'm not Hardy,' said David.

'No,' said Westbrook. 'And there's no need for you to be. But for Christ's sake face the truth of the business you're in. It's so many things. It's not simple. It's service to people. It's profit motive and loyalty and vanity and wheeling and dealing and idealism and sharp practice all mixed up together. Every man has a choice which element he gives the emphasis to. Even in your new job you'll have the option of saying no if you don't like any part of what you're asked to do.'

David thought that all this was very much the scenario of conversations he'd had with Hardy except for the last sentence. He'd never heard Westbrook speak like this before. It sounded not at all like the Westbrook of a few months ago. Failure must make men turn philosophical.

'Supergear was useful preparation,' said Westbrook. 'Minor league, yet still unpleasant. But it had to be done, hadn't it?'

'I suppose so. And I'm not a raving innocent. I know the arguments.'

'Right, then.' Westbrook picked up a paper knife and drew lines on his blotter. 'You're learning. And what you've learned should make you take Michael's job.'

'I've got the weekend to think it over.'

'Do that. But you know now what the answer will be.'

The interview was over. Westbrook stood up and began to put files into the open document-case on a side table.

'By the way,' he said. 'I was talking to my wife on the phone last night. She was asking how you were getting on. She said to give you her best wishes.'

To David it seemed a strange thing to say. He waited at the door, not knowing whether to leave, but giving the other man no further encouragement to continue. Westbrook, however, seemed to feel the need for explanation. 'She's been in America for a few weeks. But she's coming back soon.'

'I expect you'll be glad to see her,' said David, since there seemed nothing else to say.

*

The house was quiet when he got home that evening. The pram in the hall was rumpled and empty. He found Sheila with her feet up in the sitting-room, sipping a gin and tonic. She put a finger to her lips.

'He's just gone off.'

'How's he been?'

'Noisy. Frustrated with the sheer boredom of lying on his back, I expect.'

He leant over and kissed her. Nothing passionate. Just the coming-home salutation. The taste of the gin on her lips made him want one himself.

'What happened today, then?' she said, and he thought of all the wives who would be asking the same question and getting answers which came to no particular conclusion. Sheila tended to become annoyed if he didn't fill her in on detail. Sometimes he would launch an anecdote which only had relevance if she knew some piece of earlier background he had omitted to tell her. Then she would purse her lips and say that he never kept her properly in the picture. On the whole he realised he should be glad about that. Presumably women began to lose interest in the minutiae of office politics once they were engulfed by children.

'Something special,' he said. 'Let me get a drink first.'

346

'I can hardly wait,' she said; there was irony in the words. He didn't blame her. They had been talking more about Prospect House in the past fortnight than ever before: about the board shuffle and Hardy's return and David's apprehension now that Westbrook was no longer so much in favour. Occasionally they had both questioned the whole justification of his job and the future which seemed to have spun out of their control. The announcement of Alison Bennett's engagement, as well as the earlier accident, had cleared the atmosphere between them. Sheila had been very good about it.

'Gerald Fielder got the wrong man,' she said one evening, and he had made a noncommittal reply, not liking himself for it, but feeling unable to do more. Water under the bridge. He knew he would never tell her and that in the years to come it would grow to seem unimportant. He had toyed with the idea of sending Alison flowers at the hospital after the crash but somehow had never got round to it. He asked himself sometimes what he would say when they next met.

He came back into the room with his drink.

'Well?' said Sheila.

He told her about the job which Michael was offering him. A raise of a thousand a year. Lots of new responsibilities. In certain circumstances a wide range of delegated power.

'It sounds like a hatchet man's job to me,' she said.

'Could be. I suppose it's what I make it, though.'

'Have you talked to Lionel Westbrook?'

He told her about that too.

'He's a strange man,' she said. 'He's taking it better than I expected. Will you be replaced, or do you think his department's being trimmed?'

'Don't be corny. That's too obvious.'

'It happened at the agency once after we lost a couple of big accounts. Every departmental boss was asked to recommend savings. The lists had one thing in common. Nobody recommended chopping himself.'

David laughed, but there was no joy in it. 'That's the trouble with business. It's so predictable.' He poked at the lemon slice in his glass. 'What do you want me to do?'

'I don't know,' she said.

'We can't go on spending half our time wondering whether I ought to be in the bloody organisation at all.'

'Darling,' she said seriously, 'if you want to get out, then do it. I can take it.'

He looked at her gratefully. They had come through the last few weeks well. 'I wish it were that simple. I can change firms, but I don't suppose it would be much different. There are things about Prospero's I don't like. Yet if I'm honest with myself I enjoy the excitement too. Perhaps I want to prove I'm still good enough to compete with Hardy. Anyway, what else is there?'

'You could change streams. Go off and be a consultant. Start something on your own. Be a teacher. Try beachcombing. You don't have to worry about your pension yet.'

'It's not that. I can't think there's anything else I *want* especially to do. There are times when I object to the idea of ending up as a swivel-chair hero. On the other hand I don't see myself as a guerilla fighter rushing off to where the action is. Ché Guevara's not my style.'

'God help the liberals,' she said. 'Always hungering after the middle ground.'

'That's not much help.'

'I couldn't resist it,' she said. 'Listening to you now, I think you've made up your mind. You want to stay.'

'I think I should give it a go.'

'So do I. But if you do, then you must put everything you've got into it. No more questions. No more agonies. Not till you've had a year of it anyway. I'll be with you all the way, if that's what you decide, but you'll have to play the rules of the game as they are, not as you'd like them to be.'

She was right, and nothing they said in the next hour of talk, not worrying about what or when they should eat, changed the truth of it. That night they made love for only the second time since the baby had been born. It was an act efficient, pleasurable and loving, as if they were sealing a contract with themselves.

The next morning, Saturday, there was a story in *The Times* about the new Hampshire development area. It was not official, but it had the ring of truth. The designated area was named. There would be a public inquiry in due course. David, recalling his talk the previous day, pulled out a map-book and checked. It didn't look at all like the district which Michael Grant had described. David wondered for a time whether to ring him, but then dismissed the idea. Michael would have heard by now, and he knew better than to be the third or fourth bringer of the same bad news. Besides, he hadn't even said yet he'd take the job of aide, and maybe adviser, which had been offered.

It was a quiet Saturday evening, spent watching television.

They were in the middle of the old movie, John Ford and quite passable, when Gerald Fielder rang.

'Look, David, I know it's been months. I just felt the urge to call.'

David was thrown. He tried to sound noncommittal. 'About what?'

'I've been meaning to get in touch for months. It wasn't easy.'

'Yes.'

'Apologies never are. I wanted to say sorry – that's all.'

He sounded so downcast that David hadn't the heart to cut him off.

'Margaret made me ring in the end. I told her, you see. I haven't any excuse for what I said to your wife. I was under a lot of pressure at the time.'

'All right,' said David. 'I can understand.'

'You did hint about that girl Alison, though. At the club. You must have been having me on.'

'Yes. Don't worry about it, for God's sake.'

'And the other. The job. I've got over it. I'm fine now.'

There was a silence on the line, just the humming.

'Are you there?' said Fielder.

'Yes. I'm glad you're okay.'

'I couldn't understand it at the time. I always believed managers were self-perpetuating oligarchies.'

'You should have been around Prospect House recently.'

'I've heard about it. How have you been coping?'

'They haven't kicked me out yet.'

Fielder said: 'I ran into Bartram the other day. He looked very off-colour. I suppose you know they're closing down Supergear altogether?'

'No,' David lied. 'Rumours are ten a penny just now.'

'Well, *you* should know. But I must say I'm glad I'm out of it.'

'We all get that feeling sometimes. What are you doing these days?'

'Hold on a minute while I close the door, David.'

There was another silence. David wanted to get back to Sheila. It was an uneasy conversation.

'David? Margaret's a lot better. She's surprised me, really. Don't know why. We're working together, do you understand me? Perhaps it was what happened to me. It seemed to change her. I know I said terrible things about her. She's scarcely had a drink in weeks. It's because I'm around at home with her more now. That's what we missed.'

349

'Look, Gerald. You don't have to say all this. I *understand*.'

'But I *want* to say it. I don't mind. We've got our eye on a clapped-out mansion down in Devon. Done up a bit, it would make a marvellous guest house. I think we'd enjoy that.'

'If that's what you want, well, good luck.'

'I've worked it out. We're selling our house here. If we don't like the guest house idea, I can always get another job down there. Someone I know wants me to go in with him. I've got a bit of capital now.'

'That's fine.'

'Bartram and me – we went for a drink. He got a bit sloshed. I know it wasn't you who pushed me out. So I had to ring. I told Margaret – you wouldn't do the dirt on me, would you?'

David evaded the question. 'That's all in the past, Gerald. I've forgotten about it.'

'All right, then. I expect you've got things to do. I'll let you know the address when we get settled. Perhaps you'd like to come for a weekend one day.'

'Thanks.'

'*Ciao*, then. I just had to ring, you see. To say I'm sorry.'

'Don't worry about it.'

'And I thought you'd want to know that everything is going to be all right for us. I hope it is with you too.'

David hesitated only fractionally before answering. 'Yes,' he said. 'I think everything's going to be all right.'

He put down the telephone but remained standing by it. He was remembering the party and telling Diana Westbrook he was Lionel's man. And Hardy was in his mind too: Hardy saying the second job is always easier after you've done the first, Hardy believing in money for value, Hardy preaching the doctrine of survival.

Finally he walked back in to Sheila and sat beside her.

'Who was it?' she said.

'Gerald Fielder.'

'You're joking?'

'No. He thought we'd like to know he's alive and well. His wife's off the bottle, he's setting himself up in business, and he's decided life is just a bowl of cherries after all. He also thinks I'm a lovely chap. So he's sorry about what he said to you.'

'Really?' she said, picking up the irony. 'Was that all?'

Then she tucked her arm into his and they went back to the movie, sitting together silently, without further questioning, because they had no desire to work out any more answers.

Acknowledgements

My thanks are particularly due to Alfred Amery, Michael Banfield, Maxwell Boyd, Michael Brown, Janet Drummond, John Hathrell, Jeanne de Quercize, Geoffrey Rowett, Colin Simpson, Charles Stewart-Hess, John Webb and Peter Wilsher for their invaluable help in ensuring as far as possible the accuracy of the technical, commercial, managerial and medical detail in this book. If there are any errors, these should be laid at the author's door, not theirs.